All
4
Love

All 4 Love

SHARAIN HEMINGWAY

MYND
MATTERS

Books may be purchased in quantity and/or special sales by
contacting the publisher.

Published by
Mynd Matters Publishing
715 Peachtree Street NE
Suites 100 & 200
Atlanta, GA 30308
www.myndmatterspublishing.com

ISBN-13: 978-1-948145-45-9 (pbk)
e-ISBN: 978-1-948145-46-6 (ebook)

FIRST EDITION

This novel is dedicated to all of the prayers sent out on my behalf.

To my loving and supportive family
To my friends who have redefined the meaning of the word
To anyone with a red line under their name in Microsoft Word
To the women who are overlooked, underestimated, or under appreciated
To the college graduate still searching for their dream job
To my future husband who is on his way home from another bad date
To my future children who I will raise to be unapologetically unique

And to you, thank you for taking this journey with me.

Sharain

H E M I N G W A Y

"ACTIVATE YOUR INNER DESIRES"

William,
Thank you for your
love and support and for taking
this journey with me!
Love,
Sharan C.

CONTENTS

Prologue - Candice..11

My Girls - Candice...14

Memory Lane - Brooklyn 18

Trade in My Dreams for Diapers and Daycare - Candice.......................23

Balancing Medical School and Motherhood - Riley...............................28

Mason, Marley, and Clooney - Michele..34

Finding Who I Am Without You - Candice....................................39

Harper Homecoming 2.0 - Riley...42

Tyson, as in *Tyson* Tyson - Brooklyn...47

Tears Falling in Her Wine Glass - Candice....................................52

Reality Check - Brooklyn...56

Back to Atlanta - Candice 59

This is *Your* Home - Candice...65

Mrs. Candice Montgomery - Candice 68

Trying Once More - Candice...71

I Needed You and You Weren't There - Candice 74

The Answer is Preen - Riley 79

Life Gets Busy - Michele...85

Bom Día Capitão - Brooklyn 88

The Cliché Doctor - Riley 92

Finding Our Way Back - Candice...99

Mr. Diamond - Brooklyn 103

Anytime, Anyplace, Any Hour - Riley 110

Just Know I Hear You - Candice...116

Change of Plans - Michele 122

I Didn't Know How to Tell You All I Needed You - Candice...............127

Detective Montgomery - Brooklyn 131

Marjorie Diamond - Michele 136

Farmer's Daughter - Michele... 138

Sexy Spades Partner for Dessert - Brooklyn 141

Anesthesiolo-something or Another - Riley 146

Check His Ego at the Door - Brooklyn 148

Thirty-Two Hearts - Candice 155

Is There an "Us"? - Brooklyn... 159

Diamonds Don't Do Drama - Michele 163

We May Not Be Blood, but You Are My Sister - Brooklyn 171

Aunt May Don't Play - Candice 176

I Love You More Today Than Yesterday - Riley....................... 180

Relationships Are Like Flying An Airplane - Brooklyn 186

Where All the Magic Happens - Brooklyn............................... 190

Face the Consequences of My Youth - Candice 195

God is Good and Life is Good - Michele 200

5…4…3…2…1! - Brooklyn... 204

Serious Conversations - Brooklyn.. 209

Carter Montgomery - Candice 214

Sister-In-Law - Riley.. 221

New and Improved - Brooklyn.. 229

Not too Sappy - Brooklyn.. 232

Regrets - Brooklyn... 236

The Aftermath - Brooklyn.. 243

Campus Tour - Riley.. 246

Closure - Brooklyn 251

These Shoes Are *Not* Made for Running - Michele 257

Game of Fifty Questions - Candice... 259

Achilles Heel - Brooklyn 261

My Brother's Keeper - Michele 265

Apology Tour - Candice 268

Thirty-Five - Michele 272

The Only Key I Care About - Riley.....................................275

Forced Smile - Brooklyn 279

I Need Time - Brooklyn 281

Unforgivable - Michele...284

Mother's Intuition - Michele 288

Meet Your Parents - Candice 290

I Forgive You - Brooklyn 293

What's There Left to Say - Brooklyn 296

The Most Extraordinary Person - Riley................................301

Prologue

Candice

Backstage once again, my heart pounding, palms sweating. Humming my favorite pre-game song from varsity basketball days. No matter the opponent, this song could get even David super hype to fight Goliath.

We Ready! (What, What)
We Ready! (Yeah, Come On)
We Ready! (We Ready, We Ready) . . . For Y'all

Snapping back to reality, I glance from behind the curtain and awkwardly lock eyes with the young hostess on stage. With her hair nervously tucked behind her ears and a navy blazer two sizes too small, she gives me a half smile acknowledging she did in fact just witness my embarrassing solo pep talk. Struggling to walk in her heels, she carefully makes her way to one of the two chairs placed in the middle of the stage. Addressing the audience, she says, "Ladies and Gentlemen, please join me in welcoming, author of the latest bestselling novel *Life After 25*, Candice Montgomery!"

An auditorium filled with two hundred beautiful shades of female rise to their feet and applaud my entrance onto the stage. I wave and blow kisses, giving complete autonomy to my inner Michelle Obama as I work this stage like a Democratic National Convention.

"Mrs. Montgomery," she says, quickly glancing down at her index card to double check her next question.

"Please, call me Candice." My interruption causes her to recheck her double check.

"Okay Candice, you have been on the bestseller list for the past five years. What makes you so passionate about your latest book?"

Turning my attention to the crowd and feeling a rush of inspiration by the waves of smiles awaiting my next syllable, I collect a deep breath to straighten my posture, "Well, I felt we needed a book that talks about life *after* twenty-five. Pun intended."

"So often in our teens and early twenties we feel as if we know exactly where our lives will be after college. We have wine and design vision board parties and dream up goals we want and wish to accomplish. We harbor this mentality that our thirtieth birthday is still centuries away and we have all the time in the world to achieve these quixotic goals we've set for ourselves. Our plans include things like marriage before twenty-five, kids by twenty-seven, and our dream house by thirty. Somehow, we are supposed to do all of that and *then* in the years to follow, receive multiple degrees, travel the world, lose twenty pounds, and get that promotion with the corner office by thirty-five. It isn't until we hit our late twenties that we realize many of us haven't even started our life's goals and that "timeline" we spoke so highly of was just something that sounded good to say aloud. I think this book really hits on life experiences real women can relate to."

"You make a great point, Candice. What advice would you give some of the women in the audience about the impossible goals we sometimes set for ourselves?" The hostess leans in, and I can tell that question may be more for her than anything.

Placing my palm on the back of her hand, I soften my expression, "Throw that timeline out of the window because it will only drive you crazy. Thanks to social media, we live in a society where we are reminded daily of the things we don't have, instead of being grateful for the things we do. I can't tell you how many people I've spoken with who openly admitted to feeling depressed *just* by strolling on their timeline."

"The decade after twenty-five is when you see all of your friends getting married, traveling, starting their dream jobs, and baby . . ." I pause to swallow the lump in my throat and regain my composure. "Baby announcements."

"The hardest thing for anyone, *including myself,* is to be truly happy for someone without comparing their blessings to yours. It's natural for anyone to pose the question, *when is it my turn?* That's what the heart of this book is truly about— experiences and feelings women go through that they may not want to admit aloud—I decided to compose a collection of stories with a little Candice Montgomery twist to it."

"So, these stories are based on *real* women?"

Giving her a "game recognize game" lifted eyebrow I reply, "Yes inspired by women I've met, seen from a distance, and even some of my own experiences. Loosely based but inspired nonetheless."

I gesture to the group of ladies on the front row laughing at what I can only imagine is some inappropriate inside joke. Pinching the bridge of my nose, I inhale deeply and hold back the tears at the sight of my best friends.

"*Life After 25* is dedicated to my three girls in the front row: Michele Peterson, Brooklyn James, and Riley Harper. We met here in the city at Charlotte A&T University . . ."

Interrupting my response, Riley jumps up and chants, "C . . . A . . ." and rest of us follow suit as if we are at a school rep rally, " . . . T . . . U!"

Having forgotten where I am for a split second, I snap back to my demure professional self.

"They are here today to support me like we have done at every milestone in our lives. I can honestly say these three women have helped me become the author I am today. They pushed and inspired me beyond reason and for that I love you ladies dearly."

. . .

After twenty more minutes of enduring googled questions based on my biography, the hostess concludes the interview.

"This was amazing. I wish you all the success on your new book, *Life After 25,* now available in print and eBook wherever books are sold. Thank you so much for taking the time with us today."

We both stand as I give her a hug before turning to the crowd. I wave and give my farewells, serving a little Oprah stage presence this time as I make my way stage left.

My Girls

Candice

$\mathcal{L}$eaving the book signing left me filled with an array of emotions I couldn't quite place. I could, however, think of one thing that could and would certainly calm my nerves and bring laughter to my evening: dinner with my girls.

Gathering the "swag bag" left for me backstage, I begin to sort through some of the items that were strategically placed inside to promote life in Charlotte. The bag includes a guide to restaurants and attractions, a shirt that says, "I LOVE Charlotte," and a neck pillow with a large crown above the letters *C L T* on the back. My heart swells, imagining returning to the city I once loved.

With everything that has happened recently, I could use a change.

My thoughts of transgressions are interrupted when I notice Brooklyn flirting with one of the hired security guards as Michele and Riley make their way to me.

"I can see that nothing's changed much," I laugh and glance in Brooklyn's direction.

"Girl, I think she's gotten worse since she was promoted to P-I-C," Riley says, shaking her head.

"P-I-C?" I ask, puzzled but still excited to hear my dear friend was promoted.

"Pilot in Command," she clarifies. "As wild as that chick is, she can fly any plane you put her in." We all laugh and nod in unison while embracing each other for a reunion hug.

Brooklyn joins us with a half smirk, a clear telltale sign she's conquered and secured a date with the security guard.

"Hey, don't leave me out! I want to feel the love too!" She playfully pouts and we make a spot for her, turning the once triangle embrace into a lopsided square shape.

Standing arm in arm in a huddle, we all take a moment and embrace each other.

Breaking the bond, we all step back and look at one another. No doubt, examining how great time and shea butter has been to our bodies.

"I am so glad you ladies were able to make it tonight." I feel my emotions rise again.

"Of course, girl. I'm glad you called and invited us. We haven't heard from you in a while. Have you gotten too famous to interact with us common folk?" Michele teases and I give her a guilty smile.

"I know and I'm sorry. This year has been hectic with the book release. I promise to do better."

"Leave it to Michele to lay on the thick guilt. I'm starved. Let's go uptown and have dinner at Aria's," Brooklyn suggests as she splits her attention between us and the security guard walking by.

"Oh yes please. My car is parked in the back. I'll wrap up things here with my team and meet you ladies in twenty minutes."

Exiting the venue, I approach my glimmering grey BMW 7 Series, a gift I awarded myself for my latest book release. Tapping the handle to unlock the door, my inner goddess rears her head as I am reminded of the look on the salesmen face at East Atlanta BMW when I explained my reasoning behind naming my car *Christian*.

....

"Well, Mrs. Montgomery you have just selected the finest automobile we have on the showroom floor," the very young but alarmingly handsome salesman says, knowingly touching my palm to hand me the key fob. No doubt a clear attempt to see if I would acknowledge his flirting, but I ignore him and admire my new tax write off.

"I think I'll call him Christian," I look to the salesman for approval.

"Christian? That's a cool name I guess, but why Christian?" He leans in, trying to inhale my Bright Crystal by Versace just a second longer.

"Christian Grey from *50 Shades of Grey*." I walk away with a devilish grin leaving the young man to lose himself in his imagination.

...

Pulling up to the restaurant simultaneously, Michele and I present our keys to the valet.

"Girl! Is this new? You change cars more than you change underwear." She laughs, and I grab her hand as we enter Aria Tuscan Grill.

We spot Brooklyn and Riley already seated and interrupt the same playful, petty bickering they have done since freshman year in college.

"If I didn't know any better, I would think you two grew up in the same house for thirty-six years. You two bicker more than real siblings," I say playfully, taking my seat.

The waiter approaches, changing the discussion happening at the table.

"Would you ladies like to start off with a beverage? We have a vast wine selection and a fully stocked bar."

We all take a moment to glance over the drink choices. Seconds later, Michele, without even looking at the menu, orders a glass of Merlot. After nodding to acknowledge Michele's order, the waiter turns and looks over to Riley.

"Umm, I'll have a glass of your finest sparkling water," Riley jokingly says before passing the drink menu over to Brooklyn.

Brooklyn takes my menu and asks, "Could you please bring us a bottle of Chateau Haut-Brion 2002 for the table and replace it with a new one once its empty? We are celebrating my girl's bestseller novel and the reunion of the finest divas to ever grace the campus of Charlotte A&T."

Riley raises a finger to signal the waiter's attention once more.

"Well in that case you can cancel the aqua and bring me two wine glasses please!" We all laugh and give the waiter our meal selections as he removes the menus from the table and walks toward the kitchen.

"Ladies, can you believe it has been thirteen years since we've all lived in the same city?" Michele breaks the silence.

"Candice has been traveling from coast to coast with her book tours, while I'm educating and shaping America's youth—"

Brooklyn interrupts, "Riley has been switching medical programs up and down the eastern seaboard—"

"I like to refer to it as finding my niche, thank you very much! With all the men you entertain, Brooklyn, you're going to need my *medical expertise* to treat something you can't take a Plan B pill to get rid of." Michele looks at me as we both almost spit our water on the floor.

"You don't have to hate on me. I'm just a girl who loves to meet a nice Madrilenian man for a rooftop breakfast looking over the Gran Vía and then hop on a flight back to the states to enjoy dinner in NYC with a handsome Wall Street wolf. The way I see it, I deserve to have a man that matches each stamp on my passport. I am the first African American Female Pilot in Command for International Skyways, might as well make an adventure out of it."

"Wow. It *has* been a while and time has been good to us ladies," Michele says.

"Won't He Do It!" Brooklyn praises, as the waiter finishes pouring the last glass of wine. Riley raises her glass.

"I'd like to make a toast to our girl Candice. Congrats on your new book and may this be the year you and Michele *finally* decide to move your families back to Charlotte. Cheers!"

Michele pulls back her glass, causing the clinking to come to a halt.

"Well I was going to wait until tomorrow to avoid overshadowing Candice's evening but, I've just accepted A&T's offer as Dean of Students!"

Barely able to contain the excitement, we all clap and congratulate her. Before I can lift my glass to take a second sip of wine, I look up at the glares of peer pressure from all three of my friends. Taking a sip of my Chateau Haut-Brion and then ever so slowly placing the glass back down on the table, I make sure to torture them with my prolonged response.

"I'll think about it, but I guess I can write my next book anywhere!"

Memory Lane

Brooklyn

"*L*adies and Gentlemen thank you for traveling with International Skyways today. Please enjoy the duration of your stay here in Charlotte and for those who are returning, welcome back."

Standing in the doorway of the cockpit, I fulfill my duties as pilot by shaking hands and waving as the passengers exit the aircraft. Continuing to hold my "professional smile," I end my shift with a brief crew meeting on another successful flight.

I'm exhausted after the long four-day flight stretch but appreciative of the upcoming three days off to recuperate. Strolling out of the terminal and turning my phone off of airplane mode, my smart watch vibrates as missed calls and messages flood in. Checking my calendar, I hurry to my car after realizing how late I am for my meet up with Candice.

After thirty minutes of fighting traffic, I pull up to a lovely, three-car garage brick home to meet Candice and her realtor. Greeting me at the car door, she and I share a laugh as we notice we've purchased similar cars.

"Great minds think alike huh?"

Candice shrugs, nodding toward her car. "More like sexy and successful minds, but I preferred the 6-Series Convertible." I hug her and we proceed toward the house's front door.

The realtor begins going through the features of the home and gives the spiel of how this area is less than thirty minutes from the airport and uptown, nice schools, great neighbors, etc. The entrance into the house is simply breathtaking. It's comprised of a picturesque foyer that opens up to a large living area on the left and a massive dining room and full kitchen to the right. The staircase, a rich shade of mahogany, spirals up to the second floor.

Reaching the top of the stairs, I notice the master bedroom's bay window overlooking the pool out back. I walk over and am soon lost in my thoughts.

I imagine kids playing in the water on a hot summer day while my husband and I lay by the pool listening to jazz.

Candice nudges me, returning my thoughts back to reality.

"What are you thinking about?" she inquires, far more interested in what I am doing by the bay window than whatever the realtor is talking about.

Unknowingly, I give her a look that clearly does not match my response, "I'm fine."

She looks at me intently and asks the realtor to excuse herself from the room.

"What's going on, Brooklyn?" Concern fills her voice. I turn, look at her, and shrug before returning to my thoughts outside the window.

"Looking at this house makes me think about all the things I want but don't have." I sigh, still staring out of the window as my thoughts continue to get the better of me. "I'm thirty-six with no children and not even a potential husband. How did I get here? I have a refrigerator covered in wedding save-the-date magnets, and I can barely find a suitable date for any of them."

Candice sits at the foot of the staged California King bed, giving me her complete attention.

"Girl, I'm sure there's nothing I can say that you haven't already read, seen, or heard before. But what I can tell you is that you are an amazing woman. You are strong, brilliant, and the best pilot I have ever met. God is simply taking a little longer to work on your husband. We both know the man who captures your heart will have to come correct in all aspects of his life."

I exhale, acknowledging my friend's best attempt to cheer me up.

Giving her a hug, I force a nasal laugh, "Thank you Bestie. I just want what every little girl has ever dreamed of having: a house that feels like home, a yard, a family. I want a husband that takes my breath away every time he walks into a room. I want a future, and up until now I've felt like I've only dated the past."

"I may be the author, but I forgot how great you are with words," she says, wiping away a stray tear.

"I'm just trying to be like you and Calvin one day." I give a natural smile but Candice turns away and looks out of the window. With glossy eyes, she displays something I've never seen on her before—hurt and embarrassment.

"What is it?" I sit down next to her sensing her hesitation to say more.

"Would it be okay if I say that I'm fine like you did and we change the subject?" she asks, giving an awkward half smile.

"No ma'am you may not. I know I seem like the wild friend, but you can talk to me about anything. What's going on Candice?"

Inhaling all the courage she could find, she confesses.

"Calvin and I are separated and possibly filing for divorce," her voice cracks and I can tell it's hard for her to say the words aloud. I pull her into me with a tight hug as she begins to silently cry. In this moment there's no need for words, only understanding.

After a few seconds, she continues.

"We've grown apart over the years. He wants one thing and I want another."

"Have you tried counseling?" I begin internally going through the list of things you're supposed to say when someone is having marital problems.

"Yes, we are technically still in counseling, but it just uncovers even more things we've been avoiding. I love my husband, but I don't know what to do. That is why I'm strongly considering a move back to Charlotte. Maybe the discussion at dinner last night is coming at a better time than I realized," she says and quickly wipes her tears when we hear footsteps approaching the room.

The realtor steps in the doorway with an apologetic smile for disturbing our private conversation.

"Mrs. Montgomery, sorry for the interruption but our scheduled viewing time is almost over. Do you have any questions about the property or the area? We have a few other options near the lake if you're looking for a more authentic nature view."

"No thank you, Maddison. Give me a few days to consider my options." Candice gives the realtor a polite smile and we exit the house, heading toward our BMWs.

"Care to grab dinner?" I extend an invitation in case she wants to continue our talk.

"Sure, I'm craving Mediterranean," she says. Nodding, I jump into my car and trail her out of the subdivision on Lake Wiley.

Merging onto I-85 North, my mind wonders what life would be like as a mother and wife. These thoughts unwelcomely send me on a trip down memory lane to my first true heartbreak, Tyson David.

...

"Juniors, welcome to Bradford Hall," the sleep-deprived Resident Assistant says while passing out a bright green sheet of paper to all in attendance. "Please fill out this emergency contact sheet and place it in the box by my door before the end of the week. Have a wonderful Wildcat semester and remember, my door is always open."

I wait as the stack of papers makes its way toward me. Grabbing two of the sheets and turning around, my lips are met by my 6'2", six-pack abs having, All-Star quarterback boyfriend, Tyson.

"Hi Beautiful, what did I miss?" he asks, flashing his All-American boy-next-door smile.

"Nothing much, just the Do's and Don'ts of the residence hall. I grabbed you a copy of the emergency contact sheet to fill out. Turn it in by Friday." I hold the paper up to his face. Taking it out of my hand, he turns away quickly as if he's being blinded by a light.

"Dang! You think he picked bright enough paper to print on?" he teases and steals another kiss before we head toward the Student Union.

Walking through campus, Ty turns on his usual celebrity charm as he takes pictures with fans touring the University. He knowingly makes a clear attempt not to look too comfortable taking the pictures with some of the female fans. Smiling over at me while he signs autographs, I pretend not to watch and instead play with my phone.

We make our way into the dining hall and he daps all the guys within arm's reach that we pass. Getting caught up with one of his teammates about the upcoming game, I leave them to talk sports as I search for my crew. I spot Riley and Michele in the far corner sharing nachos as I walk over to join them.

"Hey, are we still going to the game tomorrow?" I try to look inquisitive but already know the answer.

"Girl, you know we will be there to help you cheer on your man!" Riley teases while stuffing another chip in her mouth.

"Where's Candice?" I scan the room hoping there's still time to signal her to bring me a slice of pizza back to the table.

"She's somewhere up under Calvin, I'm sure. No pun intended," Michele catches herself and laughs at her own inappropriate sense of humor.

...

A&T games are the place to be on Saturday afternoons during football season. You can either be there or hear about it the following week. Tailgating is especially packed today since the Wildcats are having a breakout season, thanks in no small part to my man. He was recruited as a starting Freshman quarterback and has proven his value on the field.

Making our way into the stadium, I walk down to the lower level to meet Ty for our pre-game handshake and kiss.

"You ready Baby?" I dab his hand then wiggle my fingers against his.

"I got this and I got you." He jumps up for a kiss before running onto the field. The walk back to my seat is met with a lot of *oohs and ahhs* from people in the crowd. Giving an awkward smile, I try to find where my girls are sitting without falling.

As the second quarter nears an end, it's safe to say the game is a guaranteed win for us. Ty is having a good game so far with three touchdown passes and zero interceptions. A&T isn't playing an ESPN broadcast-worthy opponent so there aren't many people who are actually at the game compared to the tailgating crowd.

I look over at my girls who are all occupied with their phones and suddenly remember Tyson's parents are coming in town next week for the Homecoming game. I pull out my phone and begin looking up places for us to eat after the game.

With my focus completely away from the field and on my phone, I hear eardrum bursting *"OHHHs"* from the crowd as everyone speedily stands up. Unable to see who was lying on the ground, I look up at the stadium monitor to see my heart, my love, my Ty, being lifted out on a stretcher with a career-ending knee injury.

Trade in My Dreams for Diapers and Daycare

Candice

Walking into the restaurant, a wave of relief rushes over me from my recent confession to Brooklyn. It was the first time I had ever spoken to someone, outside of our therapist, about my marriage. As much as I love the crew, I am not entirely okay with my marital problems becoming a roundtable discussion. However, it's reassuring to be back in the city with my friends given how difficult this year has been. I thought I could replace being open about my personal life with being busy and talking to large crowds about my book. I guess I never realized how alone I'd feel even when sitting in a room full of people.

Informing the hostess to place a setting for two, I sit and stroll through emails as I wait for Brooklyn to arrive. The first couple of messages are from my agent regarding the upcoming travel schedule for the book tour, seven cities in five days. Inhaling and exhaling deeply, I try to rid myself of the anxiety and overwhelm threatening to show itself.

I skim a few more emails forwarded from fans and make a mental note to respond to all of them later in the week. Just as I notice an email from my soon-to-be ex-husband, Brooklyn walks up to the table, startling me.

"Did you order yet?" she asks, taking her seat.

"No, I was just browsing through emails and waiting on you," rambling as if I need to explain myself. We give the waiter our food and drink orders before diving into the complimentary hummus and pita bread in the center of the table.

Giving me the "concerned friend" look, Brooklyn breaks the silence.

"So I asked you to dinner because I feel like I haven't seen your face in forever and I miss you. Plus, it sounds like you're dealing with some pretty heavy stuff and can probably use someone to talk to. I don't want to pry but I am here if you want to talk. *Reach for the stars and open your heart,* remember?"

Shocked she still remembers our corny saying from Freshmen year, I feel a tad more at ease with talking about my troubles.

"You tell me yours and I'll tell you mine," I challenge her. "When you were gazing out of the bay window waxing poetic about regrets and what ifs, what was that about?" I tilt my head.

Stuffing a large piece of pita bread in her mouth, she tries to stall. I mirror her actions, chewing dramatically slow until she gives in and swallows.

"Just thinking about my last serious relationship and the relationships to follow." She sighs as she continues, "I can't help but wonder what my life would be like if Tyson and I were still together. I imagine I'd be on my third child by now and dusting off chinaware for the holidays."

This conversation has always been a touchy subject so I tread lightly before proceeding.

"What exactly happened between you two? I had never seen two people more in love in my life. I always thought you were the couple that would go the distance."

Brooklyn looks up. For a quick second, I notice a slight strain on her face as she tries to suppress tears.

"After Ty was injured and replaced as starting quarterback, he went into a bit of depression. He went from being the star to seeing his dreams of the NFL fade away. I tried to be there for him emotionally, but at the time, I was also trying to focus on my own goals and dreams. By senior year, he had pretty much wasted four years of free education and did nothing to invest in his future. He had no experience and not one potential job offer after graduation. He had a bachelor's in general education with no plans in place of getting a graduate degree or even an internship. He started working at an athletic shoe store near campus and didn't even try to become floor manager. I kept asking him about his future plans but all he would say was, 'I don't know yet but it's cool.' As much as I loved him, I couldn't build a future on *that*. I was working as a Teaching Assistant in graduate school, barely making ends meet and helping him figure out his future."

Pausing to give in and let her tears fall, she continues.

"I guess one day I woke up and felt like I was giving more of an effort toward investing in his future than he was. He was content with this hourly shoe store job and I wanted more. That's when I decided to join the Air Force. It felt like a fresh start for me, even though it was the hardest decision in the world I had to make. I loved . . ." She stops and wipes away a few stray tears. "I *love* Tyson, even to this day, but I couldn't build my future on *I don't know but it's cool.* So, I had a choice to make; either stay with him and see how it works out or choose myself. I chose the latter."

My heart aches for my friend. I move over to the empty seat to give her a hug. This time, she's the one who could use a warm embrace.

After a few short moments, Brooklyn breaks our embrace and says, "Okay, now it's your turn."

Reluctant at the thought, I get up and return to my seat just as our food arrives. Inhaling my chicken shawarma over rice, I grab Brooklyn's hand to bless our food.

"Dear Lord, please bless the hands that have prepared this meal and the stomachs that will consume it. Lord, I also pray you keep your angels around us as we try to find peace and happiness. Amen."

Looking up from my plate, I give in to Brooklyn's glare. "Okay, fine!" I huff, rolling my eyes.

"Calvin and I have reached an impasse in our marriage. At the moment, he wants more out of me than I can give him. When I quit my corporate marketing career to pursue my dreams as an author, I had a renewed outlook on life. I wanted to travel and see the world while still making some small difference. I wished he shared my desires to travel, but he prefers to stay home. He even asked me to quit my book tours to start a family. I just can't do it Brooklyn. I can't see a future where I end up a stay-at-home mom. I haven't fulfilled all of my dreams yet and I still want to enjoy being newlyweds, but he wants to have a house full of kids like the Cosbys. Even Claire Huxtable had a respectable career as a lawyer." I inhale deeply to steady my nerves.

Brooklyn looks down, taking a minute to absorb my recent revelation. "Do you think you'll ever want to start a family, *again*?" She looks at me apologetically.

"Yes...one day...maybe. I just don't know anymore. But why do I have to trade in my dreams for diapers and daycare? He wants me to give up my career but what exactly is he sacrificing in all of this? I've already sacrificed and lost so much."

Not really expecting an answer to my rant, we both take a moment to eat our meals as I internally replay arguments and conversations Calvin and I have had in the past.

God knows I love that man with all of my heart, but I cannot just give up everything I've worked so hard to achieve. If he truly loves me, how can he keep forcing this issue?

Interrupting my thoughts with the sound of her fork connecting with the plate, Brooklyn looks up.

"May I ask you a stupid question?"

I look at her sideways and smile trying to make light of a difficult conversation.

"Better than anyone I know, of course." We both laugh and she rolls her eyes.

"Why are you buying that big house? I'm thrilled you're considering moving back to Charlotte, but it doesn't make sense. Have you already decided to go through with the divorce?"

"I don't know. I have been living in and out of hotels for the last few months, avoiding my husband and our problems. I thought I could use the book tour as a distraction from facing Calvin. To answer your question, I guess I just wanted something to feel like *home* again." I quickly look down at my plate to avoid eye contact with her.

I am only giving her half of the story, but I just can't pull myself to talk about everything that's happened. I just can't.

Still puzzled, she continues the interrogation.

"But would coming home to a big empty house in a new city really make you feel better?"

Suddenly I feel silly about my impulsive urge to, once again, spend money to fill some kind of void. I look down at the key fob to my brand-new BMW and mentally kick myself.

"Why don't you come stay with me? You can take a couple of weeks to weigh your options and sort through things without any pressure or financial burden."

I hesitate before declining, "Thanks Brook, but no. I can get a hotel."

"I wouldn't dare let you do that. I have that large penthouse with two guest rooms that never get used. I'm only there a couple days out of the week anyway, so you would have the entire house to yourself. It would be like old times, just a fancier version of a college dorm."

We both laugh at her loose attempt to downplay her penthouse in comparison to a college dorm room.

"Okay but only for a few weeks until I sort some things out back in Atlanta."

"You can stay as long as you like. Besides, I think we both could use the company. I've missed my best friend."

I can't disagree.

Balancing Medical School
and Motherhood

Riley

Charlotte-Grace Memorial Hospital has one of the highest ranked medical programs on the east coast. I was lucky to be able to transfer here and still secure a spot as a resident anesthesiologist. Coming out of a three-hour coronary bypass surgery, I make my way to the cafeteria to grab lunch and check in on Blythe.

"Hi mommy, how was surgery?" Blythe yells over loud voices of teenagers in the background.

She's clearly still at school.

"It was okay. Mr. Johnson's heart will sustain to eat another cheeseburger. How was cheerleading practice? Is your grandmother picking you up?"

"Yes, Grams is on her way now but she's in a mood as usual. She says she's not some Granny Express Shuttle Bus to be running up and down the road for free."

I hate when my mom complains to my daughter. Doesn't she know I'm in surgery?

"She'll be fine." My attitude softens as Blythe decides to use the opportunity to try her luck once more.

"If I had a *car*, you wouldn't have to deal with her fussing."

"We agreed you will get a car before you leave for college. If we keep having this conversation, we may have to wait until your sophomore year."

"Mommy, no! You promised!" Blythe's whines are ignored as I rush her off the phone to get a few moments to myself before my break is over.

"I will pick you up after the game tomorrow, okay sweetie? I love you to the moon and back."

"Yes, ma'am, I'll see you tomorrow after your shift. I love you, infinity times infinity." She hangs up and joins the laughter with her friends.

I take another bite out of my sandwich and smile at the thought of how much my baby girl has grown into such a beautiful young woman. Getting pregnant my senior year of high school was one of the toughest things I ever had to endure. Quitting as Cheer Captain was nothing compared to telling my parents their little homecoming queen was pregnant. My mind drifts back to how it went down.

...

"Riley Elizabeth Harper, how could you let this happen?" My mom continues scolding me, "Instead of opening books after class, you wanted to be grown and open your legs?"

She is furious.

I remain silent as I have used all the strength and energy I have to tell my parents my high school sweetheart and homecoming king boyfriend, Deshaun Brown, got me pregnant after the football game in the backseat of his dad's old Cadillac. All I can do now is sit here and cry.

"Riley! You answer me when I'm talking to you. We had such high hopes for you, how could you do something like that to this family?" my mom cries in her dramatic fashion. I know she is more worried about the community's perception than my actual pain and sorrow. Just the thought of it made me sob harder. I look over at my dad, trying to use my tears as a plea for his sympathy, but all he can spare me are eyes of pure disappointment.

Braxton Harper, world-renowned heart surgeon, philanthropist, and Deacon at First Baptist Church, just sits with a look of disgust. His perfect, straight A daughter has a scarlet letter on her chest. I want so badly for him to silence my mom and come over to give me a hug, but all he does is stare blankly past me toward whatever future I have now jeopardized.

Deciding whether or not to keep the baby is a no-brainer. Growing up in a Christian household, abortion is a cardinal sin. So, despite the embarrassment my mom faced at the country club and Sunday church services, I walked across the stage and gave my Valedictorian speech with a large, pregnant belly and the next month gave birth to my beautiful seven-pound ten-ounce baby girl, Blythe Alexis Harper.

With a tough road ahead of me, my parents decided to make it a little easier by agreeing to take custody of Blythe while I attended college and graduated from medical school. I wanted nothing more than to become a doctor and give my parents some validation that all they had done for me was not in vain. This was especially so after all the trouble I had caused from one mediocre night with a man who was staying in his parent's basement and welcoming his fourth child. After I found out I was pregnant, I made a promise to God that the next man I would share my body with would be my husband.

My parents never asked his family for any support and we agreed when Blythe was old enough to ask about her father, we would tell her. As medical school grew tougher and I bounced around through a few programs trying to figure out my passion, my mom and I stayed at each other's throats. I couldn't do anything outside of school and work or else I would have to hear about it.

"I see you out there just enjoying life, while I'm here raising your daughter," she would say. Each Christmas, I came home to a tree full of presents for Blythe, courtesy of my parents of course, and I had to sit and endure the constant pestering of Veronica Harper.

One day I got fed up with it and snapped, "Why did you offer to help if you're gonna throw it back in my face every chance you get?" It was the first time I argued with my mom in front of my daughter and I vowed it would be the last.

...

Seventy-two hour shifts at the hospital were no joke. I worked through three, sometimes four, surgeries a day, having just enough time to grab a bite to eat and take a shower before my next surgery. Becoming an anesthesiologist is my second greatest achievement after giving birth to Blythe. I wanted so badly to build a career to take care of me and my daughter.

As much as my mom and I bicker, I am thankful for their love and support through all of this. My daughter has never wanted for anything and she gets to see her mom working toward her dream. Hearing my daughter talk about me with pride in her voice is the greatest feeling in the world. It's the reason I wake up every morning.

Leaving the hospital, I stop by Queen City Alterations to pick up Blythe's homecoming dress. It is a gorgeous strapless, black floor-length gown with a deep sweetheart neckline and a rhinestone and pearl belt at the waist. It took us three weeks and a trip to Atlanta to find the perfect dress, but I was determined to make sure my baby got the *Best Dressed* award along with the Homecoming Queen crown next week.

I pull up to the entrance of my parent's estate and wave at Antonio, the gardener, clipping the hedges. Dr. Braxton and Veronica Harper lived in a gated community filled with Charlotte's elite. Their neighbors included judges, NBA and NFL players, past governors, and a few other celebrities that may or may not be worth mentioning.

My parents moved here shortly after Blythe was born to live closer to Charlotte A&T, so I would be able to see my daughter as much as I could between classes. I was devastated when I had to move to Durham, North Carolina, for medical school and my residency. I spent every free moment balancing school and motherhood as I traveled back and forth to Charlotte to make as many "mommy and daughter" memories as I could. After a year of exceptional performance, my mentor Janice Nelson, Head Anesthesiologist at Raleigh-Durham Medical, wrote me a top-notch recommendation letter so I could transfer to Charlotte-Grace to be closer to Blythe for her senior year in high school.

"Mom?" I step into the foyer trying to get a clue of my mother's whereabouts before I waste searching efforts.

"In here, sweetie," her pleasantries startle me.

She appears to be in a good mood today, thank heavens.

"Have a seat. Would you like to join me for some afternoon tea?" We exchange kisses on both cheeks as I enter the kitchen.

"Sure." I place Blythe's dress on the back of the barstool.

"Is that the infamous homecoming ensemble I've been hearing so much about?"

"Yes. I had a voicemail from the alteration shop that it was ready. I think her shoes are already upstairs." I pause, still trying to gauge my mother's mood. "I figured I'd come sit with you this afternoon until I have to pick Blythe up from the game."

"Well this is a pleasant surprise." She joins me at the table, carefully balancing two saucers and tea cups. "So how was work this week? Your father has been entertaining some old medical school buddies at the country club all day, so I decided to relax at the house for a bit."

"It's been a good month. I have been assigned to a lot of complicated surgeries that require giving multiple anesthetic dosages throughout the procedure. More surgeons are requesting me as their first choice, which gives me great exposure and experience," I hold my head high and look to my mother for approval.

"That's wonderful, Sweetheart. Despite our differences, I am extremely proud of you."

The sincerity in her voice warms my heart.

"How are you doing?" Feeling a lot more at ease, I let my guard down.

"I am well, Darling just trying to get everything together for this event next month. I swear I don't know what these ladies did before I joined the High Society."

Remembering the stress of *my own* Debutante Ball, I quickly change the subject, "I am thinking about taking Blythe to Empire Steak House after the homecoming game next week. Would you and Dad like to join us?"

"Yes, of course. But you and I both know we are only going if she wins. If she doesn't win, get ready for a weekend of sobs and *Gilmore Girls.*"

"I can't believe my baby is already a senior in high school, I don't know when she became such a brilliant young woman."

"Yes, she is. We just need to get her across the stage without having a repeat of *your* graduation."

I knew this little bonding experience was too good to be true.

"What does that mean?" I snap.

"Calm down Riley. It all feels a little familiar, that's all." She pauses trying to let me guess her next thought. "You, getting pregnant on Homecoming night after being crowned Queen and then walking across the stage with an oversized graduation gown."

"Mom, please, not today. Just skip to the end when you tell me how much I disappointed you and Dad and how thankful I should be for the two of you stepping in." I grow annoyed and regret not going home to wait for the game to end.

"I was not going to say any of that. I thank God for what happened because it brought us my grandbaby. Now the timing wasn't ideal, but everything happens for a reason. But please remember, she's *your child* and I won't always be around to 'step in' as you so disrespectfully put it."

I can tell I went too far this time.

"Mom, I'm sorry. It's been a long week and I'm low on sleep. I am grateful for what you and Dad did for me. There aren't enough thank-yous in the world, but I always feel like some big disappointment to you. I have tried everything in my power to become someone you can be proud of and Blythe can look up to. Regardless of what I do, I will always be that pregnant seventeen-year-old disappointing daughter that you hate."

"Is that what you think of me? Child, I need something a little stronger than this tea." She gets up and walks to the freezer. After pouring two glasses of vodka and ginger ale, she walks back to the table and places a glass in front of me.

"Sweetheart, I'm not tough on you because I hate you. I'm tough on you because I love you more than I can hold in my heart. You were an honor high school graduate with a whole future ahead of you. I don't ever want you to think you can shirk your responsibilities as a mother simply because we are here as a safety net. Blythe loves you more than anything in this world, but she needs to know where you came from and how hard you've worked to make something of yourself. I won't apologize for reminding you of that. Yes, I want better for Blythe. She deserves to be a kid a little while longer without having to worry about raising one. That's what we did for you, but I am too old and too fabulous to go through it another eighteen years."

As we both laugh and try to fight back tears, I get up from the table and give my mother a tight hug that feels long overdue.

Mason, Marley, and Clooney

Michele

"Mason and Marley Peterson, if I have to call you downstairs one more time!" I make yet another idle threat as I finish packing lunches. Placing the lunch boxes on the counter, I walk to the kitchen slide door to let our dog, Clooney, in from his morning outing.

God definitely had a great sense of humor blessing me with twins and a dog all in the same year.

My husband, Jeremiah, and I had always talked about getting a grey and snow-white Siberian Husky but could never find the right fit with breeders. Watching Clooney slop water out of his bowl and onto my kitchen floor, I smile at the memory of when we first brought him home.

...

An unusual Valentine's Day starts off with my husband leaving a sticky note on his pillow instructing me not to schedule anything for after my last lecture. Shaking my head at the thought of his past surprise attempts, I walk into the building for the Department of Business at Alabama Tech to administer the first Economics exam of the semester.

Collecting the last few exams, I notice students gathering at the window outside of my classroom. Some of the girls are yelping with "awwws" and "Omg, who is that guy? His girl must be something special." I paper clip the tests and join them at the window. Like a middle school girl in love, I scream and run outside.

Standing in a navy Armani suit, my husband holds a bouquet of red roses in one hand and the cutest puppy I have ever laid eyes on in the other. It is a two-pound Siberian Husky with red and white balloons floating from its collar. Falling to my knees, I wrap my new little bundle of joy in my arms and pet him. He has the softest snow-white fur with large grey spots of fur on his tail, paws, and over his left eye. "So, I guess this means that we can keep him?" Jeremiah joins me on the grass.

I don't know if it's the fact that my husband has given me one of the sweetest gifts ever or that he is actually kneeling in the grass in his Armani suit, but in this moment, I want nothing more than to give him all the children his heart could ask for.

Forgetting that I'm a professor at Alabama Tech and not some lovestruck student, I give my husband a kiss to not only show my gratitude, but to express how much I love him.

Gathering my composure, Jeremiah helps me up while wearing a huge grin.

"Wow woman! Is this a prelude for tonight?"

"Tonight? I've cleared my afternoon *per* my husband's request. I will see you at home in thirty minutes." I pass the dog leash to him as I pick up the roses and walk back to my classroom.

...

Three weeks later I was pregnant with twins. Jeremiah and I joke to this day that he should've bought me a dog years ago if that's all it took for me to go half on a baby.

These last nine years have been nothing short of living out my wildest dreams. Mason and Marley are the most amazing children a mother can ask for. Clooney has grown up right alongside them and has become the third male of the house. I can't think of how many times he has protected our family and our house. I can't imagine what we would do without him. Instantly regretting harboring on Clooney's old age, I snap out of daydreaming and walk upstairs.

Transforming from "sweet mom" to "stern mom" by the time I reach the top of the stairs, I burst into Mason's room to find Marley pointing at a blank United States of America map and Mason reciting the corresponding state name.

"Did you two not hear me calling you?" My sternness eases as I realize why I was being ignored.

"Mommy, we have a test today on the states and Mason asked me to help him with some last-minute studying," Marley says innocently as she looks up at me with eyes that could get her out of any kind of trouble.

"Yes mommy, I want my name on Mrs. Jordan's *Star Board* this week. Marley is always on there. Since we're twins, I want to be as smart as her." Mason looks at me in all seriousness and I try to stifle my laugh. Forgetting I was ever angry, I walk over beside Marley and begin pointing at the board.

"Well if we are going to be late, we might as well make it worth our while. Okay, now let's start from the top."

…

My first month as Dean of Students has been exciting and overwhelming. The move was almost too easy and the kids are loving their new school. Jeremiah was able to transfer to a Charlotte location with his Engineering Firm and was promoted based on his experience back in Alabama.

God definitely has had a hand in putting things in place with this new chapter for my family.

I have several ideas and ambitions for the campus. It's still surreal I've been offered my dream job just short of my thirty-fifth birthday and at Charlotte A&T of all places. My Home. My Heart. My Alma Mater. I owe this place more than I could ever repay it. On this campus I found myself, my best friends, and I found my future. A&T helped mold me into the woman I am.

I wrap up the resident hall safety meetings with the campus RAs and walk back to my office. Looking over my schedule, I make a quick call to Riley while preparing my second cup of coffee for the day. Not expecting her to answer, I wait patiently for her voicemail message.

"Hello," Riley answers, startling me.

"Hey girl, in our group text you mentioned an important surgery. I just wanted to call and wish you good luck!"

"Thank you, but it was pushed to Thursday due to some complications."

Disappointment fills her voice.

"Well at least you can say I was first to wish you good luck," I say attempting to cheer her up.

"How's the new gig at our alma mater, *Doctor* Peterson?" she inquires with a hint of sarcasm.

"It's going great Riley Harper, *MD*. I feel nostalgic being back on campus. We made so many memories here, there are only a few places I can walk to that don't bring back some story," I say, looking out the window lost in old times.

"You are right about that. I may have to come visit one day for lunch. I haven't been on campus much since I left for medical school."

"Same here, I think the last time I was here was about ten years ago when Brooklyn and I went to that alumnae homecoming party trying to act like we were still twenty-one."

"Girl, we are way too old to be trying to hang with those children on the yard. Speaking of homecoming, Blythe is running in the Homecoming Court at next week's game. I would love for all the girls to come. The game is at seven." Riley pauses and I sense a request for a favor coming.

"Could you call Candice and Brook to see if they can add it to their schedules? I'll be in surgery all afternoon and I want to make sure I tell everyone in advance before I forget or you all make plans."

Relieved that the favor is small and takes little effort on my part, I accept. "Yes of course, I am headed to pick up the twins. I'll call Candice and Brooklyn on the way."

"Thanks honey, I'll see you next week."

Heading up I-77 North, I press the hands-free button on the steering wheel.

"Call Candice Montgomery," I command.

"Hey Girlie. What's going on?" Candice answers the phone breathing heavily.

"Hey. What are you up to? You sound out of breath."

"Leaving this fancy gym in Brooklyn's building. I can see why she spends so much time here, it's full of fine men." I smile but begin to internally feel a hint of jealousy rising.

It somewhat still bothers me how much closer she and Brooklyn are compared to the rest of us. I haven't heard from Candice in months and now she's crashing with Brooklyn. What's that about? I know I have a husband and the twins, but I can't be that busy and out of touch with my friends, can I?

I suppress my inner thoughts and return to the conversation.

"Oh, so you are staying with Brook while you're in town? That's perfect! We should definitely have a girls' night soon. I will make sure to bring my workout attire the next time I visit so I can flop with you and get a glance at these men you speak of. But let me stop before both of our husbands kill us."

Candice pauses but doesn't respond. I ignore the silence and begin to deliver Riley's message about Blythe and the homecoming game.

"Aww my little niece is all grown up. I can't believe she is a senior in high school," she says, and I can almost feel her smile through the phone.

"Yes, Riley has done an amazing job raising her. The game is at seven. If you like, we can all meet at my place and ride together."

I'm growing annoyed at my multiple attempts of making suggestions for us to all hang out.

"Yes, that is perfect! I'll tell Brook."

"Sure thing. I will see you ladies next week. Love you honey."

"Love you more honey," Candice responds.

Finding Who I Am Without You

Candice

Relieved Michele didn't inquire too much about my trips to Charlotte or my pause after her husband remark, I walk out of the gym and call Brooklyn.

Her sophisticated voicemail greeting is a big change from when we used to hold our phones up to random songs on the radio to record a voicemail when we were in college. We have all come such a long way—from party girls to professionals. I leave a voicemail about the homecoming game and for her to call the management office to replace the gym key fob that is no longer working.

I ride the elevator to the penthouse floor and walk to the end of the hall to PH5. Pressing the buttons to input my unique access code Brooklyn created for me, I walk into a condo fit for a queen. Every room looks like it came straight out of a magazine or shopping catalog. I internally laugh at the idea that Brooklyn probably did, in fact, walk into a showroom and had everything that was on display shipped here.

Walking into the kitchen built for a world-class chef, I grab a bottle of water from the stainless-steel refrigerator. Standing at the kitchen island, I gaze out of the floor to ceiling windows at the panoramic view of the Charlotte skyline as the sun begins to set. I try to find some sense of peace and clarity.

Okay God, I don't know if I am making the right decision coming here instead of staying in Atlanta to try and fix my marriage so I'm going to need your help with this one. I love my husband, but I can't keep hurting him if I can't be what he's asking for. I know this sounds selfish, but I can't help how I feel. Why does self-care have to feel like I am being selfish? God please lay your hands on this situation.

My prayer is interrupted by a phone call. I look down to see Calvin's name flashing across my screen.

"Hello," I say and wait for the purpose of the call to reveal itself.

I am not sure if I sound casual or concerned.

"Hi Candice, how was your day?" Calvin's tone is so calming it disarms me.

"It was good. Your call is a pleasant surprise."

"Surprise? Baby, I am your husband. Regardless of what any court says, you will always be my first and only love. I just wish you could see that and come back home," my eyes water as the pain in his voice rings in my ears.

"Calvin, I . . ."

"I know, I didn't call to start an argument. I got your message about you staying in Charlotte for a while. Have you made a decision past the separation?"

"No, I haven't made any decisions yet. I just need some time to think things through." I force those words out as tears roll down my cheek.

"I understand you need time Candice, but why do you need to put an entire state between us to think things through? Baby, all couples have problems. How can we fix ours if you're five hours away?"

I was at a crossroads.

"Calvin, I don't have any answers right now. All I ask is that you give me some time and space to think things over and focus on my next project. I can't do that in Atlanta. I need to stay here for a few weeks and write. I get it. I have put you through a lot but this is something I need right now. I have to find who I am. Unfortunately, that means finding who I am without you." I immediately regret my last sentence as I can almost hear his heart break through the phone.

"Find yourself without *me*? So, I guess you *have* made your mind up about the divorce. I will have my attorney reach out to yours. Goodbye Candice." Without waiting for me to respond, he hangs up and I am left standing in Brooklyn's kitchen with a shirt wet from sweat and tears.

. . .

Staying with Brooklyn is actually therapeutic for me. I can enjoy plenty of alone time while she is piloting across continents and when she is home, I get to connect with my friend. It has been a long time since I had the privilege of turning off my brain and hanging out with someone. Calvin used to be that person for me, but our relationship has been so estranged lately that it's been easier for both of us to work more and avoid intimacy of any form. I knew what I was doing to him was selfish, but it was also a decision I had to make for myself.

Sitting on the bed listening to R&B while typing and getting lost in my thoughts, I hear a tap on the door.

"Are you busy?" Brooklyn asks, popping her head in.

"I was just writing a few more chapters for my new project. Join me." I gesture, and she snuggles up next to me.

"Oh, your next bestseller? Can I read it?"

"No ma'am you may not. You know I am an artist and I am sensitive about my work until it is complete."

"Yes, I know but it was worth a shot. I'm sure I've given you more than enough material over the years with my crazy life. Feel free to exploit me anytime. So, what time is this game again? I need to get a manicure and pedicure before we head over to Michele's." She leans on my shoulder trying to peek at a page.

"It's at seven. How about we go together and then we can head to Michele's from there?" I look down at my nails. "I could use a good spa day."

"Then it's a date! I should be ready after my workout. Love you honey." Brooklyn gets up and walks toward the master bedroom.

Harper Homecoming 2.0

Riley

*L*eaving the hospital at seven in the morning has its benefits. Traffic is sparse and I get the best seat in the house to watch the sunrise over the interstate.

It is truly a vision from Heaven.

I have a quick chat and prayer with God and go over the list of errands I need to do before the homecoming game later this evening. I rush home to get a few hours of sleep before my afternoon turns into *Harper Homecoming 2.0.*

Startled out of my sleep, I scramble through the covers in search of my phone.

"Hello," I say, clearing my throat to sound wide awake.

"Mommy! Are you still asleep?" Blythe yells and I sit up feeling slightly reprimanded.

"No Baby, I was just about to get dressed." I hate lying to my daughter, no matter how small.

"It's okay mommy, I know you had a long night. Jasmine goes to the same hair salon and has an appointment the same time as I do. I can ride with her so you don't have to come all the way across town to pick me up. Could you call the school and have me signed out after lunch? This way, you can get some rest and meet me at Gram's house before the game." I take a moment to think about the request.

"Okay, I will meet you at your grandmother's house at four o'clock sharp. Do you have your emergency credit card with you?"

"Yes ma'am. Could I get a manicure and pedicure please? I forgot to bring my allowance with me." I shake my head, knowing this game. I've played this trick several times with my own mother and it works like a charm.

"Oh, you forgot huh? I find that hard to believe Blythe Alexis, but I'll let you get a pass just for today. Okay hair, mani, pedi, and a tip *only*. I trust you but if I get a charge alert on anything else, we will have a tough conversation tonight young lady," I try to sound stern but Blythe is better at this game than I ever was.

"Yes ma'am. Thank you. Love you, honey," I pause, stunned at her remarks.

"When did you start saying *honey*?"

"I always hear you and my aunties say it to each other. After a while it sort of sticks."

"Well, love you more, *Honey*. Have fun and I will see you this afternoon." I hang up and call the school before getting a few more hours of sleep.

I arrive at my parents' house shortly after four o'clock and wait at the top of the driveway as Jasmine backs her car into the road. I wave and roll my window down.

"Hey Jas. It's good to see you. Good luck tonight!"

"Thank you, Ms. Harper, but we all know Blythe is going to win. It's just fun to play dress up for the evening." Unable to disagree with her statement, I wave and pull in the driveway.

Walking into the house, I notice my father sitting in the living room watching sports.

"Hi Dad, where's everyone?"

I have a pretty good idea they are all upstairs in Blythe's room.

"Hey Pumpkin, Blythe and your mother are upstairs with the makeup lady. I can never quite remember her name." Dad laughs and takes a sip of his Macallan 18.

"Her name is Gina, Dad. But you're a smart man not to remember any woman's name in this house you are not related to."

"Point well made, Pumpkin. Happy wife, happy life. Go upstairs and check on baby girl and then come back down to join me for a scotch before we leave."

"I might definitely need one of those after enduring Veronica Harper. I'll let you get back to your game." I turn and head up the stairs. At the top of the stairs, I hear '90s R&B coming from Blythe's room and I cannot help but smile.

That is definitely my daughter, I can't get dressed for a big event without blasting old school tunes.

I walk in to find Gina cleaning off her makeup brushes and my mother laying out Blythe's dress, shoes, and jewelry for tonight.

"Hey mommy! Gina just finished Jasmine's makeup as a thank you for chauffeuring me around this afternoon. I'm about to get in the chair now. You look pretty!" Blythe says and walks into the bathroom with Gina.

"Hi Mom," I say before walking up to kiss both of her cheeks. "Is this a new perfume? I might have to borrow it."

"Yes, your father bought it as an apology for something he did or an event he missed a while back." She laughs and continues to straighten out the dress on the bed.

"It looks like you two have everything under control up here. I can come back and help you get into your dress once your makeup is done." I look in Blythe's direction and she smiles and nods.

"Yes, we are all set. We just need to get her through the night without having a repeat of your homecoming." My mom repeats her condescending candor and walks toward us. Before I can open my mouth, Blythe jumps out of the chair with tears forming in her eyes and yells, "Mommy! Don't."

Stunned my daughter has 1) yelled at me and 2) yelled at me in front of people, I freeze and glare at her. Everyone in the room is frozen waiting on Blythe's next words. She whispers to Gina and nods as she walks out toward the stairs.

"Grandma, could you give us a minute?" Blythe raises her eyebrow and my mother does not protest. Once she leaves, Blythe walks behind her to close the door and turns back to me. I am still glaring at her, not saying a word.

Breaking the silence, Blythe says, "Mommy, why do you let her get under your skin like that? Her comments don't bother me and they shouldn't bother you. Grandma is the *Queen of Petty*. We all know that, but you give her power every time you show her what buttons to push to get a reaction out of you."

Still at a loss for words, I sit on the bed and try to steady my breathing.

"Mommy, you and Grams need to figure out a way to resolve this bickering because it's getting embarrassing, especially in front of company. I know you two try to keep it a secret, but I've seen you two going back and forth since before I can remember, and all because of me," Blythe's voice cracks as she begins to cry, and my chest tightens.

"I want to give you something but you have to promise that after today, you will make your peace and stop letting Grandma get to you. You promise?"

She looks right through my soul and I can only nod as tears are now flowing.

Blythe walks over to her bookbag and pulls out a notebook with a piece of paper tucked in the back. "I know how hard today is for you. I just don't know why you and Grams are making such a big deal about the past. Mommy, it happened. I'm here. I love you but I'm *not* you. You are my role model not only because of who you are today but because of who you were back then as well."

She hands me the paper with a tissue underneath and sits down beside me. I take the tissue and wipe my eyes and began to read:

Dear Mommy,
Because of who you are, I am who I am
Because I am here today, you felt you had to graduate with shame
You chose to give me life so that I can live today
And each time I take a breath, here's what I want to say
Don't be ashamed of what you did, embrace that it's the reason I'm
    here
And know that every time you cried yourself to sleep, I was inside
    sharing your tears
If you had chosen a different path, I would've always been in your heart
I would've been there to talk to you,
I would've shared your pain,
I would've encouraged you when you fell down to get up and restart.
But thank you for choosing to let me live
Thank you for choosing life
Thank you for giving me the chance of one day being someone's mother
    and wife
Thank you for being my best friend
Thank you for being my rock
Thank you for being a role model by pursuing your dreams and making
    it to the top

Because of you, I have ambition
Because of you, I have a dream
Because of you I can hold my head high and never have low self-esteem
Every day you tell me I'm beautiful
Every day you say I'm smart
Because of this, I never have to go out looking to fill some void in my
*   heart*
This household has three generations of life, hope, and love
Three generations of putting God first and holding family up above
I love you to the moon and back, more than I can ever say
I just wish you knew how grateful I am that the sacrifice you made is
*   the only reason I am here today.*
I love you Mommy!

Fighting through thousands of emotions, I hug my daughter, trying to express everything through my touch.

"Baby thank you, this is beautiful. I don't think I could have prayed for a more perfect daughter. I promise I will try to not let your grandmother get to me and I am sorry you have had to witness our squabbles over the years."

"I forgive you. I just want you to be happy and I know how much you love Grams. You two are more alike than you realize."

"Trust me, I know. Which is why it bothers me that I let her push my buttons. But I will have a talk with her, I promise. I love you to the moon and back."

"I love you, infinity times infinity." We both smile and hug once more.

Blythe walks to the doorway and yells downstairs. "Hey Gina, I think we need a hand up here. Grams, could you bring me a ginger ale with a straw, please?" Blythe looks back at me with a wink. "I think we both could use a touch up since we've cried our makeup off."

Tyson, as in *Tyson* Tyson

Brooklyn

*L*eaving the spa, Candice and I make a pit stop at the mall to waste some time before going to Michele's house.

"Remember when we used to come here just to window shop and then leave with nothing but a pretzel?" Candice asks and we both shake our heads at the thought.

"That's all we could afford back then. The struggle was real," I say, still laughing. "So how is the progress with your book coming along?"

"It's okay for the most part, but I've been suffering with a bit of writer's block these last few days. I guess I have too much going on in my *reality* to focus on writing fiction." Candice smirks and stares off, lost in her thoughts.

"I get that. Have you spoken to Calvin this week?"

I don't want her to shut down, but I'm curious with how she's dealing with things.

"Yes, we spoke and it didn't end pleasantly. He's adamant about this idea of a family and I'm completely unsure. But let's talk about it later because I don't want to start crying in this mall."

Trying to change her mood, I grab her arm. "I'm craving a pretzel. Let's get some pretzel bites and then go to Michele's."

...

Since I haven't had the best relationship with my own siblings lately, I don't get to see my nieces and nephews as much as I would like. Therefore, I love when I get to spend time with my girls' kids. Although Blythe is a handful, Mason and Marley are the sweetest children I have ever known. Both are extremely well-mannered and intelligent. During my last trip to Alabama, for the twins' birthday, I had an entire conversation with Marley about the different types of oceans and seas. She clearly pays way more attention in geography class than I ever did.

On the other hand, Mason is the reason for my guilty addiction to playing video games. The last time they came to Charlotte, I bought an Xbox—partially so he wouldn't mess up my decor—but I ended up thoroughly enjoying the basketball game so much, I played more than he did. I still buy the newest edition each year.

Michele has a modern, two-car garage home but the selling point had to be the backyard. Equipped with a fully stocked patio, fire pit, and pool, it's the perfect place for any cookout or pool party.

Walking up to the front door, we are greeted by a tall glass of sexy chocolate milk.

"Hi Jeremiah," we say in harmony.

"Hello ladies, please come in. Michele is upstairs, feel free to go on up but I think there are two little ones in the kitchen asking for you." Jeremiah points toward the island in the kitchen.

"Auntie Brooklyn and Auntie Candice!" the twins say in unison and jump down from the bar stools to run toward us.

"Hey Munchkins!" Candice cheers while we both hold our arms open.

"I missed you guys. You're getting so big," I say, as we alternate hugging each of the twins and follow them back into the kitchen.

"Auntie Brook, I've been writing poetry just like you," Marley announces.

"Is that right? I haven't written poetry in a long time. May I hear one of your poems?" I give my niece my undivided attention.

Swallowing her sip of apple juice, Marley clears her throat and proceeds, *"Roses are red, violets are blue, I love my Aunties and they love me too.* I just made that one up Auntie Brook." Her infectious smile spreads throughout the room.

"That was beautiful Marley and your Aunties *do* love you. Both of you. Go get your mom," I whisper to Mason as he takes off up the stairs.

"Mommy! Auntie Brook and Auntie Candice are here!" Mason yells when he gets to the top of the stairs.

"Alright, I'm here. Hey ladies," Michele says as she enters the kitchen. "Marley, Mason, go upstairs and change into the clothes I laid out on your beds."

"Yes ma'am!" In a flash, they both race upstairs.

"Girl, they are the cutest," Candice says as she sits at the island.

"Yes, they're cute and a full-time job. Anytime either of you want to steal them away for a weekend, let us know."

I entertain the thought for a second before saying, "Are you ladies ready for high school football night?"

"I think this is the school where Tyson coaches," Michele reveals and Candice chimes in.

"Tyson, as in *Tyson* Tyson. *Your* Tyson?" She directs her question to me not realizing how crazy she sounds.

"Yes, but he's not *my* Tyson. I saw something on social media about him still being in the area as an assistant football coach. I wish him the best."

What would I say if I ever saw him again?

"I haven't seen him in years and we didn't end on the best of terms, but I hope he's well and has everything his heart desires." I notice the unmistakable eye rolls from Michele and Candice.

"What?" I ask.

"That's real big of you to say," Michele murmurs. "But it's okay to feel something, regardless if its rage, remorse, or curiosity. He was a major part of your life at one point. That doesn't just go away. Maybe you can finally get the closure you need."

I hate that she is right.

"It really is okay if you are curious about seeing Tyson tonight," Michele says.

"Thank you. You have always been our voice of reason in the group."

Maybe when he sees me, we will both realize how foolish the breakup was. Maybe . . . No! I have to snap out of it. I buried those feelings a long time ago and for good reason. I vowed to never get hurt like that again.

. . .

A detour to get food for the twins causes us to miss the first quarter of the game. None of us are upset as we only came for the halftime crowning anyway. As we make our way up the bleachers, we spot Riley and her family. I give a hand signal that I'm going to head to the restroom.

I ease into line behind two other people and pull out my phone to avoid awkward eye contact.

Exiting out of my stall to wash my hands, I notice a tall, beautiful pregnant woman at the sink to the far left. I reach up waiting for the dryer to blow dry my hands, but nothing happens.

"Here you go," the pregnant woman says handing me a napkin as I notice her stunning two-karat diamond wedding ring with a small heart tattoo on her finger underneath. "These things are always broken so I started bringing my own napkins."

"Your hair is gorgeous and congratulations!" I smile as she looks down to softly rub her stomach.

She looks like a model for a maternity commercial.

"Thank you," she says with a smile and I turn to exit the restroom.

I hike up the bleachers to join the rest of the group, saying my hellos to the Harpers and squeezing in between Riley and Michele.

"What did I miss?"

"Nothing much. The home team is winning and I'm ready for halftime," Riley says, as everyone else nods in agreement.

Halftime finally arrives and Blythe is the belle of the ball. She is escorted by a handsome quarterback and the crowd absolutely adores her. The students from her school and even some from the visiting school stand and cheer her on as she walks across the field. Just as the announcer introduces the next candidate for Homecoming Queen, I spot him. Tyson David.

He looks exactly as I remember him, just a tad bit older. He has a salt and pepper beard and smile that still bothers me in a way that only he can. I stare at his movements, watching him work the crowd on the field as if he owned the school. I feel a sharp pinch and turn to Michele.

"You're staring, and I think salivating a little," she teases me and continues clapping for the other contestants.

As expected, our girl Blythe wins the crown *and* the crowd. We all run to the field to take pictures.

Riley did raise a beautiful little girl.

Standing on the sidelines watching the twins, someone calls my name.

"Brook? Brooklyn is that you?" I turn and come face to face with my first love.

"Tyson. Hi, how are you?" I reach out to give him a tight embrace, but he steps back, putting space between us and gives me the "church hug."

"Hey how's it going? It's been forever since I last saw you," he says with more formality than expected given our past.

"I've been good, I hope you are."

"All is well. I'm the athletic director here working my way into college sports." The confidence he exudes while talking about himself sends me on a roller coaster of emotions.

"I think I saw on social media you're a pilot. That's amazing Brookie! You always fought and worked hard for what you wanted. I'm happy for you." Hearing him call me *Brookie* beguiles me.

I looked down trying to gather my thoughts and before I could open my mouth to respond, I suddenly notice the wedding band on his finger with the same heart tattoo underneath as the pregnant woman from the bathroom.

Tears Falling in Her Wine Glass

Candice

*H*eading back to those godforsaken bleachers to endure the rest of this game, I look over and notice Brooklyn lost in her thoughts.

"Hey, what's wrong?" She glances up and shakes her head before returning to her unspoken thoughts.

Finally finding my seat, I notice she has now moved farther to the left and seems a bit isolated. I walk over and sit beside her.

"Girl what is going on? Do we need to squad up and fight someone?"

"His wife," she whispers and points to the back of a woman with long, curly hair sitting about twenty rows down.

"Whose wife?" Brook looks at me with complete annoyance and I am embarrassed for not keeping up.

"Tyson's wife, Candice." She exhales from frustration.

"I'm sorry, I had a slow moment."

I need to be more conscious of my surroundings.

Before I can get my next sentence out, our group of two turns into four as Riley and Michele make their way to our far-left corner.

"Why are you two so far from the rest of us?" Riley asks as she and Michele sit down.

I turn around and silently mouthed "Tyson's wife" as I nod toward the woman sitting at the bottom of the bleachers. Riley looks at Michele completely confused, but Michele shakes her head and rub Brooklyn's shoulders.

"I'm sorry love. I'm sure this was the last thing you wanted to find out seeing him after all these years."

Brooklyn turns at an angle, now able to face each of us and says through watery eyes, "It's worse!" She gestures as the beautiful mystery woman gets up to leave the stands, "She's pregnant!"

We all look in her direction as her toned physique turns and reveals the perfectly round baby belly and we gasp.

"I don't think I am in the mood for dinner after the game. I'll catch an Uber home. Candice, here, will you bring my car home when you get back to Michele's?" Brooklyn hands me her keys.

"No. I'll go with you. We can get your car tomorrow." *I can't imagine what Brook is going through right now. I would die if I saw Calvin with another woman.*

Brooklyn rejects my offer, "No. Tonight is about Blythe. You all go and have a good time with my niece. I am just going home to lay down. I'm feeling a little tired from traveling yesterday."

Fully aware she is giving us the half-truth, we all look at each other, waiting for someone to object to her request but eventually we give in.

"Okay but I will call you as soon as dinner ends," Riley says and we all nod.

"Okay fine. My Uber is here," she gives us a forced smile and heads down the bleachers but not before taking one last glance at what should've been her future.

Not wanting to make a scene, we watch our best friend walk towards the exit after witnessing her heart shatter for a second time over this man.

"We can't just sit here enjoying a football game while Brook is hurting like this." Guilt starts to get the best of me.

"Enjoying? I haven't *enjoyed* this game since we arrived. You all know I don't do sports. I'm just here for my niece," Michele says. "And you know Brooklyn. When she says she wants to be alone, that is exactly what she means. Let's give her a few hours and then we can check on her."

I don't agree with the game plan at all, but I also want to respect Brook's wishes.

The remainder of the game was unbearable. I kept thinking about the look on Brooklyn's face when she said "Tyson's wife" as if the words alone were enough to shatter her spirit.

I hate that my friend is in this kind of pain.

Michele is distracted with the twins and Riley is with her family, so that leaves me sitting at the game lost in my thoughts, yet again. I couldn't help but think about Calvin.

I never want to put him through that kind of pain, but he wants me to dedicate my entire life to birthing his children. I don't think I'm that kind of woman. I still have so many dreams and ambitions and I can't go through that kind of —

Riley interrupts my thoughts.

"Hey ladies, so Blythe insists she hangs with her friends tonight instead of going to dinner with us. My parents said they are tired, so I think we should go check on Brook."

I am already halfway to the car.

...

After dropping the twins off, I trail Michele and Riley in Brooklyn's car back uptown. Not wanting to feel left out, I call Michele to continue our conversation from the ride to her house.

"Girl we were just about to call you," Michele answers the car's Bluetooth and continues, "I was bringing Riley up to speed about the whole Tyson situation."

"Blythe goes to the school. Riley, how are we just finding out about this?" I interrupt trying to hold back the frustration in my voice.

"I'm always at the hospital during most of the games, and the few I've attended, I guess I never saw him," Riley admits.

Michele chimes in. "Jeremiah told me just yesterday when I mentioned the game was at North Charlotte. He said he ran into Tyson at the barbershop and they talked about his recent move to North Charlotte High School. He didn't say anything about a wife and certainly not a baby on the way. I would have definitely warned Brook." We continue talking as we pull into Brooklyn's garage.

Walking up to her door, I suddenly feel like an intruder for walking in unannounced but I proceed to put in my access pin to unlock the door. The house was dark aside from the lights of downtown Charlotte shining through the large glass panes.

"Brooklyn?" I yell out into the darkness, looking around.

"I'm right here." She turns on a lamp and we all walk over to her and sit.

"Why are you sitting in the dark?" Riley asks and lays on the floor below Brooklyn. She sits up and a pile of tissues fall to the floor.

My best friend has been here crying her eyes out while we were watching a senseless football game.

"Talk to us, Brook," Michele says while I continue to stare at the tissues covering the floor.

"I'm fine, I just needed a moment to feel sorry for myself," Brooklyn says as she walks toward the kitchen to pour another glass of wine.

"I didn't want anyone to see me out of character, so I chose to leave the game. Did it hurt seeing Tyson? Yes. But I don't have too many regrets about the decision I made . . . I don't think I do." We all remain silent to let her process her thoughts.

"I loved him with all of my heart, the best way I knew how. I left him to better myself and to hopefully give him the motivation to go out and better himself. I guess I always hoped one day he would come and find me, possibly thank me for the added push. But instead of pushing him towards greatness, I pushed him away from me. Maybe he was always meant to be great and I was coddling him. He just needed to be rid of me to be great."

Brooklyn sinks to the floor and begins sobbing, "I lost him. She's perfect and he loves her. I can tell. I couldn't stay at that game because I couldn't bear to watch the love of my life look at anyone the way he used to look at me. That was supposed to be me. I was supposed to have that two-karat flawless cut ring and the baby bump. Not her. It was supposed to be me!"

Reality Check

Brooklyn

Unable to regain control, I give complete autonomy to my tears and lay on the floor in Riley's arms crying. I am too weak to stand, and I feel as though my entire world has collapsed on my chest. In this moment, I am grateful my girls are here.

I don't think I could have made it through the night without drunk dialing or social media stalking Tyson.

Michele breaks the silence by asking, "Brooklyn, what do you need? How can we help?"

"Nothing. There is nothing you can do. Maybe I need a hug, I guess." On cue, my girls give me a group hug on my kitchen floor.

What would someone think if they were spying through the kitchen window?

The thought of this makes me laugh a little and it surprises everyone.

"What are you laughing at?" Candice asks looking confused. I chuckle again and reveal my thoughts. This was definitely the small humor I needed to pull myself together. We all get up off the floor and I make a mental note to dock Donna's, my housekeeper, tip for not thoroughly cleaning under the cabinets and refrigerator.

I take a sip of wine and calm my nerves. "Sorry for the dramatics. I guess I never really had my official meltdown over him and the breakup."

"It's okay. We completely understand. I don't know if I could have held it together as long as you if that had been me," Candice says.

For some reason I'm bothered by her response.

"Candice, may I ask you a question?" Suddenly I'm not sure I want to open this can of worms.

"Yes of course," she says, looking somewhat confused.

"What exactly is going on with you? Is my nonexistent love life not enough of a reality check? You have a husband who loves you and all he wants is to start a family." I immediately regret putting her on the spot.

Michele and Riley instantly turn their attention away from me and onto Candice. Returning the same feeling of being annoyed, Candice looks at me and shakes her head. I try to give her an *I'm sorry* look, but my betrayal has already put her in the spotlight.

"Reality check?" Michele asks, "Candice, what is she talking about?" We all wait patiently for Candice to gather her thoughts.

"Calvin and I are separated and possibly filing for divorce," she says with a reaction much different than at the restaurant.

Was there more to the story that she wasn't telling?

"Oh no!" Riley leaves my side and makes her way to Candice. "I am so sorry. I had no idea."

"I made it a point to keep it under wraps. I love you ladies to death, but I am just a private person. Don't take it personal, I have had my personal life thrown back in my face too many times."

Now I know there is something more.

"Candice, as you can see, I opted to come home alone and cry with my bottle of wine. Trust me, I completely understand being private. I guess I hoped these past few weeks has allowed you to trust us more." Candice rolls her eyes at my sentiments.

She's definitely not happy about me telling her business.

Riley chimes in, "Yes, Candice we are your girls. The good. The bad. The ugly. You have seen and prayed with me through some of my darkest times in school. Helping me to stay committed to my celibacy and talking me off the ledge anytime I thought about quitting. I owe my life to you."

The tears flowing down Michele's eyes didn't require any words to defend her love and loyalty for our group.

"Calvin and I have been trying to have a baby for the past five years. After my second miscarriage earlier this year, I gave up. He wanted to keep trying but emotionally I just couldn't," she confesses. I feel like a complete idiot.

Here I am sobbing over "what ifs" and losing a boyfriend and my best friend has suffered severe pain and loss. What's worse is that she felt she couldn't share it with us. With me.

I walk over and hug her as tight as I can, breaking the last shred of strength she had to hold back tears. Wrapping her arms around me, she too let out a cry that must have been building internally over time.

"I can't be the woman he wants. I can't give him the one thing his heart desires. He says he wants me, but I know that is not enough. This is why I can't be with him. He deserves someone who can give him children and I can't go through trying again."

"Have you two ever discussed adoption?" Michele asks, trying to give a helpful solution.

"Yes, but it's not the same as giving birth to your own child. I couldn't bear to raise someone else's child knowing I have already buried two of my own."

I grab my glass of wine and walk over to the couch. The girls follow suit by refilling their glasses to join me in the living room. We sit in silence for a second and allow Candice to continue her confession.

"This last year has been torture on our marriage. We have tried counseling, church, and it all ends the same. For about a month, he drops the subject of children but then he's ready to try again. How can I tell this man, whom I love more than life itself, that I can't be with him because I may be barren? I figure it's just easier to let him hate me and leave than for him to settle with me knowing he wants more." She stops talking and scowls at me. "Does that answer your question, Brook? Is that enough of a reality check for you?"

Back to Atlanta

Candice

*W*aking up from the sounds of vacuuming in the room next door, I make my way to the restroom to complete my morning moisturizing routine. Twisting my hair into a messy bun, I run into Donna in the hallway.

"Mrs. Candice, my apologies, did I wake you?"

"No, it's fine Donna, I needed to get up anyway."

"Well in that case, good morning. Ms. Brooklyn is having her coffee and watching the news," she informs me as if she could read my thoughts and walks toward Brooklyn's master suite to begin cleaning.

The air between Brooklyn and I has been a little awkward since the evening after the homecoming game. We have been pleasant toward each other, but it doesn't feel genuine. We need to have a heart to heart but I haven't pushed my pride aside to cave in.

"Good Morning," I say entering the kitchen. Without turning her attention from the television, Brooklyn responds, "Good Morning back. How did you sleep?"

"I slept okay. I hate that I didn't wake up early enough to get a workout in before I get on the road."

I haven't told Brooklyn I was leaving earlier than planned.

I pause and wait for her reaction.

"You're heading somewhere? Work related I hope?" *It's like she can see right through my lie.*

Without waiting for my response, she continues, "I meant what I said when I offered my place for as long as you need. I know things have been weird between us, but that doesn't change the fact that you are my girl. I may be overreacting when you say you are leaving but I just want you to know you are always welcome here."

Laughing at Brooklyn's accuracy in identifying her dramatics, I smile inside because I needed to hear her say that.

"Yes, it is *technically* work related, but I also wanted to give you some space to process as well. It sucked seeing you that broken-hearted Brook." She stares off, taking a moment to revisit that pain.

"Girl, it was awful and embarrassing but that's my cross to bear. God took me through all of that to prepare me for what's next, so I just have to *let go and let God* with this one. Candice, it was insensitive of me to discuss your situation like that and I'm sorry. I was so caught up in my own mess that I unknowingly took it out on you. You didn't deserve to be put on blast like that and I hope I didn't lose your trust in me as a result."

"I forgive you Brook. I should've told you all a while ago anyway. It was bound to come out eventually. I just didn't expect it to be such a dramatic *Brooklyn James Production.*" We both laugh.

"Girl, I don't know how you all put with me sometimes."

. . .

The drive back to Atlanta was therapeutic. I finished one of my many audiobooks about success and achieving goals and spent the remaining trip down I-85 South listening to my gospel playlist.

As I lost myself to the sounds of praise and worship, I turn the radio down and begin to sing one of my mother's favorite hymns. I remember, as a child, hearing her sing it around the house or in the car. I always noticed how she would really pour her soul into the lyrics when her heart was heavy or burdened. I could not think of a more burdensome time in my life, so it was fitting to sing a few lines of the song aloud.

"Pass me not, O gentle Savior,
Hear my humble cry;
While on others Thou art calling,
Do not pass me by.
I'm calling
Savior, Savior,
Hear my humble cry;
While on others Thou art calling,

Do not pass;

Please don't pass me by."

Repeating the lyrics over and over in my head I pray and talk to God as his presence fills the atmosphere.

God, where do I go from here? I could really use my mom's guidance through this. God, why did you take her from me? I need her now more than ever.

I silently sob down the highway as I begin to reminisce on my parents. I lost them at such a young age that it's getting harder and harder to keep their memories alive. I miss them more than I can form in a sentence. I spent my entire adulthood trying to be the kind of wife my mother was to my father, but I think at this point, I am pushing Calvin away to the point of no return. I need to forgive him, but I need to forgive myself first.

I continue to get lost in my prayers.

God, I know you don't make mistakes so please look over our babies up there. Tell them that Mommy and Daddy love them very much and there's nothing and no one in this world that can replace them in our hearts.

I mourn over my two lost babies.

God, why did you put me through all of this? Was enduring the death of both my parents not enough; I also had to have two lives ripped out of me? God why?

I turn off at the next exit and park as I mourn my mom, dad and two babies I never got the chance to meet.

...

Once I arrive in my home city, I call my agent to confirm my upcoming engagements.

"Candice! How are you my darling. Please tell me you've made it safely back to Atlanta," Trinity says, portraying a dramatic Broadway enthusiast.

I laugh before responding, "Yes, I am just arriving madam. I wanted to confirm the agenda to make sure I have enough time to sleep in tomorrow."

"The first event is an 8 a.m. breakfast reading at the Hilton and then we will head over to South University for a lunch summit. I have booked you a suite at the Hilton so *technically* you just have to ride an elevator downstairs once you are ready. Maybe that will give you a few extra minutes to sleep."

"See you get me, Trinity. With thinking like that, I might have to give you your Christmas bonus early. Please call the hotel and have me checked in. I am heading to that side of town now." I hang up with Trinity and make one more phone call.

"Good afternoon, Williamson and Associates, how may I direct your call," the perky receptionist says and waits for a response.

"Hi Amber, this is Candice Montgomery calling for Regina."

"Oh hello, Mrs. Montgomery. Mrs. Williamson is in court for the rest of the afternoon. I will leave a message for her to return your call as soon as possible," Amber says, and I can't help but mirror her energy.

"Great! Thank you so much Amber and have a wonderful rest of your day."

...

Stepping out of a much-needed shower after that long drive, I put on my robe and order room service. While ordering my usual salmon and asparagus over a bed of rice with a glass of Chardonnay, I contemplate calling Calvin to tell him I am back in town.

All of a sudden, I feel guilty and a little silly for staying in an expensive hotel when I have an entire house only a few miles away. I push the thought aside and pull out my laptop to check a few emails. After plowing through as many emails as my mental capacity could withstand, I am interrupted by a knock on the door.

The handsome concierge brings the tray into my suite and sets the dishes on the table. He moves slowly, ensuring he does not cause the dishes to make loud noises and also, if I'm reading his actions correctly, trying to steal a glance at me.

Realizing he is looking at a sliver of skin now showing through my robe, I tighten my belt and he blushes before turning his head back to finish arranging the dishes. Flattered I can still pull the attention of a young tenderoni, I playfully return lustful eyes as he exits the room. Closing the door, I scold myself for acting juvenile and begin to think of how much I miss my husband.

Just as I savor my last bite of salmon, my phone vibrates and I have to rearrange the pillows on the bed to search for it. Catching the call on the last ring, I answer "Hello."

"Candice, Regina here. How are you? My receptionist left a message to return your call," she says all in one breath.

Regina is one of the best attorneys in Atlanta. She has seen me through book deal after book deal and now she is assisting me through one of the toughest decisions of my life: divorce.

"Hi Regina. Yes, I am just getting back in the city. I figured we could schedule a meeting in person and talk through all of these email threads we have." I take a sip of my wine.

"Yes, I agree. What is your schedule this week? Are you available for a lunch meeting—my treat? Let me know which day and my receptionist will set it up and send you the address."

I accept and laugh knowing "my treat" means it's a *business expense* I will be billed for later.

...

Once my book tour resumed, it was nonstop. Trinity had a full morning planned with readings, Q&A, and book signings. It felt good to be back on my grind. The past few weeks in Charlotte were relaxing but it also left me with too much time to get lost in my thoughts.

The more I worked and grew my business brand, the less I had to think about my personal life. These book events were my escape from reality. I hand the autographed book back to the last woman in line at South University and pose for a quick photo before leaving Trinity and her team to wrap up. With a few minutes to spare, I make my way downtown to meet Regina for lunch.

The restaurant had a steady lunch crowd but was spacious, so I didn't feel claustrophobic. I inform the hostess I am here for the Williamson party and she escorts me to a table upstairs.

The ground floor must be for the general public and the upper level is only for reservations. It was quiet enough to conduct business, but the music selections made it feel less like a boardroom lunch meeting and more like a casual gathering. Looking in my direction, Regina waves and finishes typing a few last-minute thoughts before putting her phone in her briefcase.

"Candice, it has been entirely too long. How are you sweetheart?" she says, hugging me. Although Regina works for me, we have been together so long that our partnership has turned into a mutual friendship.

"I am well. How have you been? Still taking over ATL, one courtroom at a time?"

"Girl, I have to argue twice as hard to get half the cases that some of these men are freely handed but that's okay. I didn't build my business to one of Atlanta's top-grossing law firms by complaining and tucking my tail between my skirt when things are challenging."

I love seeing women, especially black women, gain success in any form.

We place our sushi orders and she jumps right into business.

"Candice, I know I have been flooding you with emails regarding you and Calvin, but I have always respected you too much to not be completely honest and transparent. As your lawyer, but more importantly as your friend, I have to ask you one more time. Are you sure you want to go through with this? No judgement either way, I only want you to take a moment to really think about what this means," she asks.

"Regina, I don't know. I feel like I can't keep dragging Calvin through this heartache." All of a sudden, I feel like putting my guard back up.

"Candice, I know this is hard. This is a *big decision* you are making but if counseling hasn't worked then I am inclined to agree that separation is a less permanent compromise. Take this time for yourself and try not to have much communication with Calvin. I am certain his lawyer has instructed him to do the same." I take a minute to think about what she is asking me to do.

"I can try but it will be difficult, considering we share the same address," I remind her.

"I know but try. It will benefit you by keeping the communication solely between his council and myself." We take the remainder of the lunch session to catch up on happier topics.

This is *Your* Home

Candice

The next morning is just as hectic as the day before. Trinity has me around town from one event to the next with only an hour in between for breaks and travel. After finishing a lunch reading and book signing with Atlanta's High Society Book Club, I am burnt out and need the rest of the day to recharge.

I say my goodbyes to Trinity and head toward my house to get a few additional items since I am still camping out in a hotel while in town. The thought of continuing this charade is starting to make me sick to my stomach. Calvin and I need to talk about everything and soon. For now, I will follow orders from my lawyer by minimizing all communication with him.

Turning into my neighborhood, I look over to the lake behind my property and briefly reminisce on the early morning jogs. Some days we would end our run by lying down at the lake to watch the sunrise. I missed doing those things with my husband. Pulling into the driveway, I suddenly feel like a guest at my own home.

Should I have called Calvin to tell him I was stopping by, so he wouldn't think someone was just snooping around the house?

Waiting for the garage door to open, I'm startled by an identical noise from the partnering garage door. As the left door rises, I see Calvin's black BMW i8 taillights in reverse. I look at the clock on the dashboard.

It is only 2 p.m., why is he home in the middle of the day?

The ten seconds that lingered for both of our garage doors to open was all it took for my thoughts to instantly play out the worst possible scenarios in my head.

Is someone else in the car? Was he meeting someone here for a lunchtime rendezvous? Has he moved on? Did he have another woman in my house? What if he gets her pregnant?

With each question, my heart breaks piece by piece falling into my lap as I grip the steering wheel waiting for the rising door to reveal the truth.

As I pull into the garage, Calvin jumps out and waits for me to park. Slowly getting out of my car, I make a point to peek into the passenger window, but it is a failed attempt as the tint is too dark.

"Hi," I say trying to gauge his facial expressions to see if he is hiding something.

"Hi back." His tone disarms me, yet again. I suddenly feel the urge to explain myself.

"I came back in town to attend a few commitments and decided to stop by the house to get a few things."

"Babe, this is *your* home. You don't ever have to explain coming here. I'm actually heading back to the office. I left some briefs on my desk that I need to prepare for my meeting tomorrow. I came to grab them and decided to have lunch here. How long will you be here? Will you be home when I get off?" I can hear the hope in his voice.

"I'm not sure. I don't think it's a good idea right now to stay. I have a hotel downtown for the rest of the week." With each word, I sense his ego being bruised.

"Very well then."

He gets back in his car and we both silently stare at each other through his windshield, wanting to say so much but choosing to say nothing at all. After a few awkward seconds, I break my gaze and walk into the house.

Taking one last glance at Calvin's car before closing the door, my nerves get the best of me and I open the refrigerator to get a bottle of water. As I examine the contents inside, I am shocked at the sight of only takeout food containers, beer, and water bottles. I look over to the trash that is almost overflowing with more takeout boxes.

My nerves continue to unwind as I now realize my husband has not had a home-cooked meal in weeks. Looking around the kitchen, I remember the love that once filled this house and it's enough to make me rethink going through with the divorce. Without a second thought, I rush to open the door to the garage, trying to stop Calvin before he leaves.

Looking out to the street expecting to see his taillights down the road, I see the car never made it out past the mailbox. Confused yet relieved, I stand, staring and frozen in the doorway as Calvin drives his car back into the garage. He ends a conversation with someone on the car's Bluetooth speaker and turns off the engine. Stepping out of the car, he opens his mouth to speak but I finally find my words and interrupt him, "Calvin, we need to talk."

"I know, I just told my secretary to cancel my afternoon meetings." I can feel my eyes begin to swell with tears. Turning to go back into the kitchen, I grab two wine glasses from the cabinet and a bottle of Cabernet.

It may be lunch time in Atlanta but it's five o'clock somewhere.

I grab one of the wine glasses and take a sip. Calvin watches me intently and removes his blazer to reveal the Audemars Piguet watch and cufflinks I bought him for Christmas last year. I return the fixed gaze and then turn to walk into the living room.

Without saying a word, he places his blazer on the bar stool and proceeds to follow me with his glass of wine. We both sit on the sofa, physically leaving a small gap between us but emotionally we are farther apart than we've ever been.

I take a moment in the silence to glance around the living room at all the memories Calvin and I have captured over the last fifteen years together. Looking over the fireplace mantle at our wedding pictures is enough to send me over the edge but I quickly turn my attention back to my husband. Struggling to keep the upper hand in the situation by remaining silent, I once again cave in to start the discussion.

"Calvin, I don't know how to fix this." I place the glass down on the coffee table.

"Fix what? *Us*?" he asks, looking somewhat confused but sincere.

"No, it's more than that," my voice cracks and I softly pinch myself to keep my emotions at bay.

"Baby talk to me. What is it? You have my undivided and unwavering attention." He clicks the silent button and places his phone and the wine glass next to mine. "Just talk to me Candice," he pleads.

I know our relationship will never be the same after what I am about to say next.

Mrs. Candice Montgomery

Candice

"Ladies and Gentlemen, please join me in congratulating our graduates," Dean Altman says, acknowledging the group.

"I hope Charlotte A&T University has equipped you all to lead bright and promising futures. Take care and God bless!" We all take our graduation caps and toss them in the air as the band plays the university's fight song.

Walking out of the coliseum, I search for the one person in the stands cheering me on. Since it was such a large graduating class, waiting on my friends would be a hassle so I figured I would run into them once we all found our families.

"Candice, I am so proud of you!" Aunt May says as she opens her arms.

Although we connected a few short years ago, her hugs always make me feel as if I have known her my whole life.

"Your mother and father would be proud of the woman you have become. I know they were looking down from heaven smiling from ear to ear as their baby girl received her college degree." She smiles through watered eyes.

Thinking of my parents brings a tear to my eye and Aunt May squeezes me a little tighter before continuing.

"I hate my sister and I weren't close when she and your father died in that car accident or else you would have never been tied up in that godforsaken foster system. The day you found me, I dropped my life in Germany and made plans to move back to the States. I made a promise to God and my sister that I would do right by you. We are the only family we have Candice. I don't have any children but from this day until my last breath, I will love you like my own."

Not wanting to go down that emotional and traumatic roller coaster at my graduation, I inhale and exhale deeply, trying to force my emotions back into their hiding place.

Welcoming the wanted distraction, I turn to see all three of my girls walking over in their caps and gowns waving and smiling. Our small corner of two quickly turns into a party of twenty as Riley, Michele, and Brooklyn's family and friends soon join us.

"Candice! We did it! We are officially alumni of Charlotte A&T," Michele says as we huddle for a hug.

"Ladies, may I cut in?" a male voice asks over our celebratory screams. Turning my attention to a familiar voice, I freeze and look down. In his graduation gown, Calvin is down on bended knee with his family standing behind him.

"Candice Ashley Smith, I have been holding onto this ring trying to keep us both focused on passing final exams and walking across the stage. Now that we are college graduates, the only thing I know for certain about my life is that I want to spend the rest of it with you. Candice, I love you so much. Will you marry me?" Calvin holds the ring with shaking hands as he gazes steadily into my eyes.

As my friends, family, and a few surrounding strangers all hold their breath and await my answer, I look down at Calvin and nod repeatedly.

"YES! Of course, I will, my Love."

Before the ring is completely on my finger, Calvin lifts me into the air as if showing the crowd his most prized possession.

...

The year following graduation is no cake walk. I love having a fiancé. I do not, however, love planning a wedding while Calvin and I are both in graduate school. Our nights consist of cheap Chinese food, wedding checklists, and working on our dissertations. Aunt May is a saving grace financially, as she insists on helping Calvin and his parents fund my half of our early August wedding. Although we may be struggling, we are hopelessly in love.

Our wedding day is nothing short of a fairy tale. We have an intimate list of fifty guests in front of the park's waterfall in North Charlotte. I am a nervous wreck, but my girls have taken care of everything to make the day go off without a hitch.

Being as close as we are, it is impossible to decide on a Maid of Honor so we agree to take turns being a maid of honor in each other's wedding. Brooklyn won the first round as Maid of Honor for the Montgomery Wedding.

"Candice are you ready?" My aunt walks in and immediately starts to tear up. "You are the most beautiful bride I have ever seen. Let me help you with your veil," she says as she walks over to the mirror.

I love my aunt and am happy someone from my biological family is able to walk me down the aisle.

"Yes, let's go make me Mrs. Candice Montgomery."

Trying Once More

Candice

"Calvin wake up." I nudge my husband and he slowly turns over.

"Good morning Babe," he says with sleepy eyes.

"Good morning, I have to tell you something but don't panic," I instruct and wait for him to respond with a nod.

"I'm pregnant," I whisper, holding my breath and waiting for his reaction. I see the mental wheels turning as he registers what I said.

"Pregnant? I'm going to be a father?" I try to match his infectious smile and obvious joy.

Working on a master's degree during a pregnancy is one of the hardest things I ever had to balance. My nights are long, trying to study and finish papers, while my days are nonstop. Calvin and I argue about my sleep schedule and not getting enough rest for the baby, but I am determined to be a mom *and* finish school. At the beginning of my second trimester, I am rushed to the hospital after fainting in class.

"Mr. Montgomery, she's awake, you can see her now." The nurse goes into the waiting room to retrieve my husband.

"Candice, thank God you're okay." Calvin kisses my hand and looks up at the nurse, "She *is* okay, right?"

The nurse's sorrowful expression says everything her mouth will not. I dig my nails into my empty stomach.

"Yes, Mr. Montgomery, she is okay," she says and pauses.

Calvin, still emotional while holding my hand looks back at the nurse.

"And the baby?" The room is silent as the nurse shakes her head. Calvin falls to his knees crying as I faint once more, unable to fight through the pain coursing through my body.

...

After losing our bundle of joy, Calvin and I both prayed about it and decided to have faith in trying again. We are both advancing professionally and beyond being financially and mentally ready with his career as a stock broker and my ever-growing marketing career.

"Husband," I kiss Calvin to wake him up before church, "I think I am ready to be a mom again."

This time, I am determined to reduce any stress that could bring harm to me or my baby. Calvin and I agree we will wait until we are clear into the second trimester to announce it to our friends and family.

At twenty-seven weeks into my pregnancy, I dance around the kitchen fixing Calvin his breakfast shake and singing to my baby as I do every morning.

"Good morning wife," Calvin walks into the kitchen and kisses me from behind while rubbing my stomach, "Good morning son."

"Your son kept me up most of the night kicking around like he was practicing karate."

"Not karate, he is warming up his legs for basketball practice."

"What time does your conference start today?" I ask, not remembering the logistics of yet another event full of suits, cigars, and stock talk.

"Everything starts rolling right before lunch. I have about a four-hour drive to Nashville today and then I will be rubbing your beautiful belly and watching ESPN with our son before you go back to sleep tomorrow."

Later that night, a pain in my lower abdomen jolts me out of my sleep. I quickly rub around my stomach to try and feel Calvin Jr's kick. Nothing. Scared and in too much pain to drive, I reach for the phone to call 9-1-1 but my cell phone is not on the nightstand. In a panic, I quickly scan the room and remember that it is downstairs.

Pulling all the strength I can manage, I slowly walk down each step, breathing through the pain. At the bottom of the steps, I am met by a pain in my spine that brings me to my knees. No longer able to walk, I crawl to the coffee table to get my phone out of my bag. I dial 9-1-1 and then I call Calvin. I wait for the beep and leave him a message that something is wrong and I am on the way to the hospital.

Sliding to open the front door to wait for the ambulance, I cry and talk to my baby.

"CJ, you have to fight. I can't feel you kicking but I know you can hear me. I promise you with all of my heart that if you fight, I will use every fiber of my being to make sure you make it out okay. I haven't even met you yet and you are the best thing to ever happen to my life so Baby Boy, I need you to fight. Mommy's got you," I plead to my son as I see emergency lights flood the street and then the driveway.

On the way to the hospital, I beg the paramedics to keep calling my husband. I yell for them to call the hotel, the company, anyone. Forced to go straight into surgery, the nurses promise they will keep trying to reach him.

I have never been so scared in my life and the one person I need is at a business conference.

The doctors rush me into the emergency room and inform me that my baby is losing oxygen by the second and I need to have an emergency C-section in order for CJ to have any chance of survival.

One last scan on the ultrasound and the room goes into a familiar silence. In a panicked rage, I scream for someone to tell me what is going on.

"Mrs. Montgomery, we can no longer find a heartbeat," the doctor informs me, and my world goes black once more.

I have never felt so alone as I do right now.

Giving birth to a stillborn ruined me. I had to push my baby boy out, never getting a chance to hear his cry, his laugh. Never getting a chance to look into his brown eyes or feel him grip my finger with his tiny hand. What's worst, I had to do it all by myself, without my husband to hold my hand and endure this pain with me.

I Needed You and You Weren't There

Candice

Unable to look Calvin in the face, I stare at the two wine glasses on the coffee table then back to the wedding pictures on the mantle. We look so happy in the frame that it causes my heart to ache thinking about the current state of our marriage.

"Calvin, the day I left the hospital I promised myself I could never go through that kind of pain, that kind of loss, that kind of heartache, again. Having to physically push our lifeless son out broke me. Unknowingly, it broke us."

I struggle to keep my tears at bay before continuing, "Lying on that bed, I could feel our son inside of me even though he was no longer there. It was like a piece of his soul was still trapped inside of me fighting and kicking to stay alive." Looking at me through distress-filled eyes, Calvin remains still and listens.

"I held his lifeless body in my arms, praying to God that he would just wiggle an inch to let me know he was still with us but Baby, he was gone. I felt alone on that operation bed. I felt useless and there was nothing and no one that could replace the emptiness, the hole that was in my heart for our son." I give in to the tears impregnating my eyes.

"I blamed myself. I blamed you. I blamed God. How could God take something so precious away from us? I did everything right. I did everything by the book! I thought I had learned from my mistakes the first time and still I had to go through that pain." I fixate on Calvin as my anger rises.

I just have to get this out. I have to live in my truth.

"I know it's not your fault and I know you tried to be there, but you weren't. I needed you and you weren't there. I had to do that by myself, crying for the doctors to find you. I used all of the prayers I had to try and save our son, but we still lost him Calvin. Why did God take my baby?

After that, I lost myself. I lost who I was and what I stood for. For a long time, I didn't know how to go on being someone's friend. I didn't know how to go on being someone's wife—so I shut down, mentally and physically. As hard as you tried to be there for me afterwards, by then it was too late. The damage was done. The one time I needed you to help bear the pain that was too heavy to carry myself, you weren't there. I blamed you. I was mad at you to the point of pushing you away. But that's what I needed in order to save you from my self-pity and anger."

On cue, Calvin dissipates the silence.

"Honey, we can fix this if you just let me back in. We can attend counseling—anything. Candice, I will move heaven and earth for you." He pauses to fight back tears. "The second I got that call, my world went dark. I did everything in my power to get to you. Driving one hundred miles an hour, I prayed like never before. I asked God to wrap his angels around you and CJ. When I finally got there, I sat and watched you sleep as I cried for you and for CJ. My son, our baby boy," he says as tears soak his white Armani shirt, revealing the tattooed cross over his right pectoral.

"He never got the chance to meet us Candice. Seeing his lifeless body in that cold room instead of safely in your arms ruined me too. I should have never gone to that conference. I should have been here with you and our little man." He reaches for me, but I pull away.

Reliving the pain of my baby again, I can't be touched right now.

"I also blamed myself. If I was home, I could have gotten you to the hospital sooner and maybe our son would still be alive," he says, the words coming out in spurts as though choking him.

"I understand you were going through something traumatic and I can't begin to imagine what that did to you. Every day I prayed that if I couldn't help to bring you peace or if I was the reason for your pain, God would move me out of the way to help you process everything. This last year has been torture but I vowed I would give you as much time as you needed. I just didn't think you resented me to the point of leaving our life together." He pauses and clears his throat, undoubtedly hurt by his own words.

As we both sit in silence, I realize it is the first time we have discussed that night. I guess we both suppressed it in order to survive and without knowing it, vowed to never mention it again. Not talking about what happened may have been the killing point of our marriage—the unspoken resentment that broke us.

"You deserve a woman who can give you the one thing I can't. As much as you want a child and a legacy, I have to accept that I may be barren. We can never try again and go through that kind of pain; it will completely destroy me. It took a long time for me to even be able to talk about it. Calvin...maybe I'm not enough for you." I exhale, grateful to reveal my truth.

Heartbroken and shocked, Calvin looks at me.

"Baby you are *more* than enough. You've always been enough. Having a kid would be like a cherry on an ice cream sundae but Candice *you are my Sunday*. Whether we are talking ice cream or the Sabbath, you are my sunshine."

He places his hand under my chin and slightly turns my face towards his before continuing, "Yes, the idea of having a child is nice but to even consider having a child with anyone besides you is *never* an option. There will be kids in our lives. We have more nieces and nephews than we can handle."

"I know you say that you don't have to have kids, but you *do* want them. I want them for you. The best thing for us to do . . ." I pause before my next thought. "The best thing for *you* to do is to let me give you this out. Please just . . ."

Calvin interrupts.

"Sweetheart, you don't give me enough credit or maybe you don't understand the magnitude of how much I love you. Losing my unborn son broke my heart but losing my son *and* my wife, destroyed my soul. As a man, the one thing I vowed to you, to God, and to our families, is to protect you from hurt, harm, and any danger. To provide you a life filled with love and as minimal pain as possible, but I couldn't do that. I wasn't there . . ."

Trying to reclaim his strength, he continues, "I lost my son. *We* lost our son. There will never be another Calvin Jr. but Baby you have to understand that God forces us to endure things to make us stronger, to bring us closer together." Falling to his knees, he props himself up between my legs, putting us eye-to-eye.

"Candice, if God felt the need to call our son home, it is because he had a plan for CJ. He knew before our son took his first breath that he needed to be in Heaven to fulfill a purpose, so we have to accept that. We have to accept that our son was so special, God felt this world didn't even deserve to meet him. It took me a long time to accept that. It took me a long time to be okay with the idea that I would have to live in this lifetime and never get the chance to meet Calvin Jr. But Baby, I need you back with me because I'm barely holding on. I'm barely keeping a straight face. I am barely breathing," he professes while gripping my thighs to hold himself up.

"*You are my rib* and I don't want to do life without you now that I know what it's like with you, Candice Montgomery. I need you to forgive me so I can forgive myself. I'm so sorry I wasn't there." His head bows slightly as tears falling melt against my jeans.

"My biggest regret is not being there for my family. I'm not that type of man. That is not how I was raised. I am a man who takes care of his family. I am a man who loves his wife beyond reasoning. I understood you needed time to heal. I am okay with that. I will give you all the time you need but I can no longer give you space because Baby, I am no longer functioning. I can no longer wake up in this house not knowing if I will have you in my arms when fall asleep later that night. I need you Candice." With his head in my lap, we both sob for our son, our marriage, and our pain.

Sitting back in the chair to regain his composure, Calvin looks up at me through clouded eyes and reaches for me once more. This time, without hesitation, I am in his arms, in his lap as we hold each other and continue to cry. This is the first time I have ever seen my husband so vulnerable, so heartbroken, so compassionate.

I am sorry and upset that I wasn't honest with myself but more importantly, honest with him about everything that was going on. I never took the time to consider he was hurting.

Grasping both of Calvin's cheeks, I lift his head and gaze into his mesmerizing light-brown eyes. I have never loved him more than I do in this moment.

I gently kiss my husband. We lock eyes and kiss again, this time trying to blend our pain. A mix of *I'm sorry, I love you,* and *I need you.*

Calvin stands, his arms still wrapped around me. Taking a few steps, he leads me over to the mantle and slowly guides me down to the floor. Beneath a ledge filled with photos of much happier times, we continue to kiss our pain away. Pulling away, he wipes the stray tears falling down my cheeks and says,

"You are all I need in this world, Mrs. Montgomery. I need you to be *mine*."

With a cloudy head, I pull his face down to mine and say, "I. Am. Yours."

For the first time in a long time, I make love to my husband.

The Answer is Preen

Riley

While reviewing the O.R. board for today's scheduled surgeries, I notice I'm the assigned anesthesiologist to assist Dr. Young with a heart valve replacement and I blush.

Out of all the men in this hospital, Dr. Young wins the award for throwing me off of my game just at the thought of him.

Just as my mind begins to wander, Beth walks up beside me.

"Hey, Riles, why are you staring and smiling at this board?" Before I can think of a lie, she finds her answer.

"Oh, I see you're working with Dr. Young again today. That's the third time this week. What did you do to get so lucky?"

"I was just reviewing the scheduled surgeries for the rest of the day, I hadn't even noticed which surgeons I am working with," I lie and walk away from the board as Beth follows.

"Cut the act Riley, I see the way you stare at him when he walks by. You look like a lovestruck schoolgirl with her first crush. Oh, I also know he's returned the same goofy look a few times. Why don't you just say something to him? Go ahead, tell him how you feel."

"*Tell him how I feel?* Why would I do something like that? That would be awkward."

"Awkward? Girl this is Dr. Jameson Young we're talking about. Thirty-one-year-old humanitarian, two-time recipient of the Newman Tucker Medical Award, and the newly appointed head of the department for Cardiothoracic Surgery. Riles, if you don't ask him out, I will do it for you,"

"Do we even know if he is single?"

"I'll see what I can dig up," Beth responds. "But a man that sexy is probably a heart surgeon by day and a heart breaker by night."

Sitting in the O.R., I complete my pre-op check. After the scrub, nurses wheel Mr. Hammond in for his heart valve replacement. I place the oxygen mask over his face and instruct him to count backwards from one hundred. Once the anesthesia is administered and Mr. Hammond is completely unconscious, I turn to one of the nurses.

"Terri, we are all set. Please let Dr. Young know we are ready to begin surgery," I say, still monitoring the patient's vitals.

"Yes Doctor," she says and pages the surgeon.

When Dr. Young walks in, I can feel his presence without ever turning to see him.

It's like my body can sense when he enters a room.

Walking up to the operating table, he goes through his routine of checking instruments and playing his favorite jazz album to set the ambience for the next couple of hours. As the surgery begins and the jazz fills the room, I imagine he and I dancing to the melody. Thankful that the mask is covering my salivating mouth, I snap out of daydreaming and continue to watch his brilliance.

"Suction please," Dr. Young holds out his hand and one of the interns responds to his request.

"Okay, part one is complete," he says, lifting the old heart valve out of the patient's open chest. Our eyes meet and he winks.

In a failed attempt to play it cool, as if I wasn't fixated on his every move, I nod back and then look over to the monitors to pretend I am checking the patient's vitals.

"*Dr. Harper,* how is our patient?" he asks, and I scramble trying to find my voice.

"All signs are good and Mr. Hammond is still sound asleep," I respond.

"Well Mr. Hammond has the best anesthesiologist looking after him so he's one lucky man."

Oh my! Is this fine man flirting with me? Stay professional Riley and pull yourself together! He's probably just being overly nice.

"Thank you but I think you literally have his heart in your hands," I coyly say back.

For a brief moment, Dr. Young stares at me intently and I can't look away. It's as if he is trying to tell me something with just his eyes. Without saying more, he retreats then continues talking through the procedure with one of the medical residents.

Once the surgery is finished and Mr. Hammond's heart function is fully restored, I walk to the courtyard to get some fresh air and stretch my legs before my next surgery. I make a quick call to check in on Blythe and then pull out one of my unfinished crossword puzzles.

Halfway engaged with my puzzle, I go through and begin to fill in all of the easy answers before a friendly voice startles me.

"Preen," he says again and I turn around.

"Excuse me Dr. Young?" I ask confused.

"Your crossword puzzle. Thirteen across is asking for a five-letter word for Fancify. The answer is *preen*," he says as he sits next to me. "Do you mind if I join you? I like to come here and get some fresh air between surgeries."

I nod and watch him as he carefully places his coffee on the arm of the bench and then pulls out his phone. Looking back at the newspaper, I pretend to be more interested in my crossword than the gorgeous man sitting beside me.

How long was he looking over my shoulder searching for an answer? Hmmm, he smells so good. He is either incredibly smooth or criminally creepy.

Looking up from his phone, he asks, "Dr. Harper, do you know of any great places to take preteen boys in Charlotte? Forgive my eavesdropping but I remember hearing you talk about your daughter during one of our surgeries."

"Call me Riley, please," I say, still trying to keep my composure. "I didn't know you had a wife and children, Dr. Young."

"If you prefer Riley, then I must insist you call me Jameson," he suggests, and I can't help but return his smile.

Oh, I guess I will take incredibly smooth for two hundred, Alex.

"No Riley, I do not have any children, nor do I have a wife. I do, however, have a handful of nieces and nephews. My sister is visiting this weekend for a wedding and asked if I could spend the day with my two nephews. I'm just struggling to figure out what kids like to do these days," he admits.

"Take them to a football game downtown or an indoor trampoline park."

"That's perfect. Thank you, Dr. Harper, I mean *Riley*." He smirks and the way he says my name almost has me undone.

"You are most welcome Jameson." I blush.

The next morning after my last scheduled surgery, I go home to get a few hours of sleep before I have to pick up Blythe for our Saturday lunch date.

Even being as tired as I am, I am determined to spend as much time as possible with my baby girl before she leaves for college next year.

Walking into the house, my watch vibrates to indicate an incoming call. I look down and see Beth's name flashing on the screen. I place my bag on the kitchen table and search for my cell phone. No luck. After about five more minutes, I suck my teeth and remember it is still charging in the car. I run back outside to retrieve my phone and my wallet, which somehow fell out of my purse and onto the passenger seat.

Geez Riley, you really need to get some sleep.

"Hey girlie," Beth says after a couple of rings.

"Hey B, please don't tell me you need me to cover your shift. Any other time I would, but I am beyond tired," I try to sound extra exhausted.

"No, seventy-two hours is enough. You definitely need a break. I'm calling regarding a certain, Mr. Heartbreak."

"Mr. Heartbreak? Is that what we're calling him now?" I laugh at her corniness.

"Girl we might be calling you *Mrs. Heartbreak* soon. Word around the hospital is he's been asking about you and your background, showing an extra special interest in your aspirations to stay at Charlotte-Grace." Beth pauses to add dramatic effect. "He asked Mike, the cardio scrub nurse, if you were single."

"Why didn't you start with that, Beth!" I protest while on the edge of my seat. "He's been asking about me?"

"Apparently, you aren't the only one walking around the hospital looking lovestruck. I'm headed into surgery, let's catch up tomorrow. Later girl," Beth says and hangs up leaving me lost in my thoughts.

He's been asking about me? I never thought about dating a younger man but what's five years? He's intelligent, successful, and seems to take an interest in kids. I've never introduced Blythe to a man, this would be something new.

I snap out of my thoughts embarrassed that I haven't even been on a date with this man and I am already worrying about how my daughter will feel toward him. As I try to grab a quick nap on the couch, my phone rings again.

"Hello."

"Hey Riley, it's Michele."

"Hey, what's going on? I haven't been in the group chat much these last few weeks because one of our anesthesiologists is out on maternity leave. My routine is pretty much eat, sleep, surgery, repeat," I jabber on while fighting my exhaustion.

"All is well on my end. Honestly, the group chat hasn't had much activity since the meltdown at Brooklyn's."

"Yes, that was pretty intense. You and I stood there looking like deer caught in someone's headlights as Brook and Candice stole the show. I hope they were able to make up. I spoke with both of them separately, but I didn't want to get in the middle. I learned my lesson in undergrad."

"That is kind of my reason for calling. I was thinking about hosting Thanksgiving dinner at my house this year. I wanted to call you and extend an invitation to your parents as well, although I know your mom likes to have a big event at the Harper Estate."

I yawn and close my eyes. "Actually, she was thinking about doing something small this year since she and Dad will be returning from Australia days before, so this may be a better option. I'll mention it to her. Thank you."

"Perfect! I'll start making the arrangements as soon as everyone confirms. Talk to you later, love you Honey," Michele says, and I hang up after almost falling asleep during the call.

...

Pulling up to my parents' house, I honk the horn before getting out and walking over to the passenger side. Blythe walks out just as I am fastening my seatbelt. I roll down the window, "Get in. Let's practice your interstate driving."

Before I can finish the sentence, Blythe is halfway to the driver's side of the car.

"Buckle up and hand me your phone," I instruct her and then we are off to lunch.

Blythe parks in front of our favorite Mexican restaurant and turns the car off.

"Mommy, may I ask you a question?" Her tone alerts my attention.

"Of course. You can ask me anything."

"I know we don't talk about my dad much, but do you ever think about him?"

I'm speechless. "Not really sweetheart, I mean I haven't had a conversation with him in years. Why do you ask?"

Where is this coming from?

Blythe pauses and begins twirling her fingers, a clear sign that she is nervous. "Blythe, what is it?" I ask fearing the worst.

"It's just that I'm going off to college next year and I don't want you to be alone. I've never seen you go on dates, so I thought maybe you were still in love with my dad." I try to stifle my laugh.

"Sweetheart no, I am not still in love with your dad. We parted ways years ago with nothing in common except bringing you into this world. I *do* go on dates; they just don't make it to the point of me wanting to introduce them to you. I never wanted a parade of men in and out of your life. We have a pretty unique living situation as it is with your grandparents. I don't want to add to the chaos."

As Blythe gets out of the car, I open the door, confused.

"So wait, that's it? You bombard me with questions about my love life and then stop talking?"

"No, I'm not done but I'm hungry. We can continue over lunch."

I shake my head and laugh as we walk arm in arm into the restaurant.

Life Gets Busy

Michele

The sisterhood sleepover at Brooklyn's a few weeks ago still has me on an emotional roller coaster. For Brooklyn, I am heartbroken she had to get life thrown in her face but Candice—I can't imagine the pain of losing one child, let alone, *children*.

Two miscarriages. I would lose my mind.

Waking up on a warm Saturday morning, I turn over and find myself watching Jeremiah sleep. I can't help but feel a newfound appreciation for God, my husband, and the life we built. I prayed to God every day to help me grow a marriage and build the kind of home that my mother did for me. I wanted it all: mom, dad, kids, dog, white picket fence, the works.

I place my head on Jeremiah's chest, waking him.

"Good morning beautiful."

"Good morning darling. How did you sleep?"

"I slept okay. But my dreams are nothing compared to my reality."

"So, you are just going to whisper sweet nothings while blowing your morning breath in my face?" I tease him and return another soft kiss.

"Till death do us part Babes, morning breath and all." He curls his lips to blow, stinging my nose hairs again.

"You know exactly what to say to make a girl smile. One of the many reasons why I love you, Jeremiah Peterson."

I sit up to look at him, unknowingly furrowing my eyebrows.

"What's on your mind?"

"What do you mean?" I ask, trying to look clueless but failing.

"Michele, I have known you for the better half of two decades. I know your facial expressions, your body language, I know your soul better than I know my own. If something is bothering you this early, then you must have gone to sleep with it on your mind. Talk to me."

I take a moment to gather my thoughts.

"It's about Brooklyn and Candice."

"Oh, was there a disagreement between them?"

"No, well, not exactly. Remember I told you that Brooklyn ran into Tyson at Blythe's homecoming game and I ended up staying over for girls' night?" He nods.

"Well there's a little more to the story. Turns out, Tyson not only has a gorgeous wife but she's pregnant. Brooklyn had a world-class melt down, but I think she's okay now. Candice, however, revealed that she and Calvin are having problems."

"Problems? Did someone cheat?" he asks, still trying to play a pointless guessing game.

"No! Well at least I don't think so, but she recently had a miscarriage and is still traumatized. He wants to keep trying to have kids, but she doesn't want to go through it again which has caused a strain on their marriage."

Jeremiah looks off into the distance, lost in thought.

"That's tough...for both ladies. I even feel for my boy. I haven't seen Calvin since our fraternity's 70th Anniversary last year. I know those girls are like sisters to you, are you okay?"

"Yes, I'm okay. I know Brooklyn will bounce back but Candice really needs us. I had not realized how much I missed having the whole gang back together."

Jeremiah laughs, "Yeah, okay. Just remember you have a husband and twins at home who take priority over your girls-gone-wild escapades."

With that, I head downstairs to let Clooney outside to take care of his doggy duties and find the twins. Hearing the television blasting in the living room, I poke my head around to see Marley and Mason sitting on the floor eating cereal and watching their Saturday morning cartoons.

Without disturbing them, I make my way into the kitchen to find a countertop covered in evidence of two nine-year-old's attempt to make cereal. Opening the kitchen door to let Clooney out, I clean up the milk stains and cereal before preparing the coffee maker.

While waiting on the machine to brew, I call Brooklyn, but I get her voicemail. After leaving a message, I try my luck with Candice.

"Hello," Candice answers.

"Hey, it's Michele"

I wonder what kind of mood she is in.

"Good Morning. How are you?"

"I am doing good. I think I am finally getting the hang of the day-to-day on campus. These kids are a lot different than we were back in the day."

"Girl, I can't imagine. What's going on?" she asks, and I decide to get straight to the point.

"First I wanted to call and check on you. How are you? Are you still in town?"

"No, I'm traveling for a few book events and actually, I am okay. These last few weeks were a lot but I'm glad I was finally able to open up about everything that's been going on. I hate it took this long." Hearing her words causes my guilt to rise.

"Candice, I honestly want to apologize for not reaching out to you. Months should have never gone by without us checking on one another. Life gets busy, but you girls are my family. It won't ever happen again."

Have I become so caught up in trying to be the perfect wife and mother that I've neglected my friends? I've always made it a priority to be there for them, how did I let so much time pass?

"I think we get so caught up in life, we replace actual conversation with social media and passive texts. We think the act of liking a post is just as effective as calling someone to tell them you're thinking about them. I have to do better too," Candice says then pauses.

Neither of us speaks for a few seconds, allowing the weight of her words to settle.

"I'm not sure of your upcoming schedule, but I am hosting Thanksgiving dinner this year and I would love for you to be here. The twins miss having their aunties all in one room."

"Okay, so you are going to try the twin guilt trick? In that case, yes, I'd love to be there. I will see you in a few weeks. Love you, Honey."

Bom Día Capitão

Brooklyn

"Welcome back, Captain James. When should we expect your return?" the airport valet asks as he opens my driver door.

"Hi Henry, how are the grandkids?"

"Growing like wildflowers, ma'am. Little Gregory is starting kindergarten next fall and Annie is two going on twenty-two."

"That's great! I'd like to see some pictures when I get back. I have the same schedule as always, but if anything changes, I will have someone from my team let you know." I reach down preparing to lift my luggage onto the curb.

"No ma'am, let me get that for you. You just focus on getting those people safe and sound to and from Madrid. I love bragging about you to my granddaughter. I hope she grows up to love aviation just like you. Have a safe trip Captain."

"Thank you, Henry."

There is something nostalgic about life at the airport. All the different faces passing through the terminals to take a journey someplace else.

After making my way through security, I stop by my favorite coffee shop.

"Captain James, it's good to see you as always. Can I get you the usual?" asks the cute barista, ignoring the older man in front of the register waiting to place his order.

"Yes, please and thank you, Terrance." I take a seat facing the main corridor.

My favorite thing to do before a flight, is to people watch. I notice different people and try to guess their backstory. *Where are they going? Where are they coming from?*

As Terrance brings over my coffee and gets shut down after yet another attempt at flirting with me, I sit and sip on my Café Mocha thinking about the last couple of weeks. Thinking about Candice, about Tyson, and my mess of a personal life.

How did I, a college educated Air Force Captain and now Pilot in Command, end up single, heartbroken, and childless at thirty-six?

Each time these questions come up, I can't help but think of Tyson. Checking the time on my watch, I feel a sudden burst of inspiration to write my thoughts out the only way I know how—through poetry.

You called it selfish
I called it self-preservation
You called it picky
I called it particular
You were looking to fill a glass,
While I was trying to build a kitchen.
I can't help what I felt, and I can't help how I see
That covering how I feel wasn't good for you or for me
I tried to be patient, tried to be the one you need
But how much of me did I cover for you to feel complete?
I know it wasn't your intention and it's sad to admit
Being honest didn't mean failure or that we just quit
It simply meant we arrived in the same airport
At the same time
In the same line...
But my flight was departing
And yours was delayed, running a little behind.
I tried to wait on your connecting flight
But it was a promise I couldn't make
And although it was hard to say goodbye,
It's a risk I was willing to take.

...

With three hours remaining until we land at Adolfo Suárez Madrid–Barajas Airport, I take my hourly walk around the plane to stretch my legs once more. I maneuver through the aisles until I reach the rear galley to chat with some of my crew members.

"Hey Janice, I hear you are hopping off in Madrid. Are you finally taking your long overdue vacation?"

I'm always excited to hear about my team seeing the world outside of the airports and hotels.

"Yes Captain. I'm catching a connecting flight from Madrid to meet my sisters in Dubai," she says unable to contain her smile.

"Oh, Dubai is absolutely gorgeous! You must visit the Burj Khalifa, it is breathtaking." I think back on my last rendezvous in the UAE.

I am overdue for another visit.

On the last trip of my four-day stretch in Madrid, I decide to turn my upcoming days off into an adventure. The only question I have to ask myself is, *where to?* I have been to almost every continent but the last place I wanted to be was back home in Charlotte, sulking in my feelings. I needed the touch of a man and the feel of shopping bags in my hand.

Scrolling through my contacts, I come across one of my old flings, Renaldo. Grateful that the Wi-Fi is still connected, I message him.

Hi, Renaldo. Charlotte is cold, so I was thinking of coming to Brazil for a little sunshine on the beach.

About ten minutes later, my watch vibrates indicating a new message.

Bom dia Capitão. I have relocated to Rio. I await your visit.

Remembering that his English is about as good as my Portuguese, I smile at his short, sweet, and to the point response. Using the International Skyways mobile app, I make my connecting flight arrangements from Madrid and start to mentally prepare for my next three days in Rio de Janeiro.

Arriving at one of my favorite hotels with panoramic balconies overlooking Leblon and Ipanema beaches and the Cagarras Islands, I over tip the taxi driver before walking into the lobby to check in. Purposefully still in my pilot uniform, I slowly remove my cap and undo my messy bun to let my long, curly hair cascade down my back.

"Bom dia. May I please have a Club Room," I ask softly, hoping the uniform will work its magic.

"Bom dia Senhora. Apologies but all of our Club Rooms are booked due to the software conference. May I interest you in an Ocean Front Room just a few floors below?" the concierge asks with a polite smile and thick

Portuguese accent.

"Yes, you may for two nights. Please and thank you." I hand him my credit card.

"You are all set Captain James, the elevator is straight through this corridor to your left. We hope you enjoy your stay here in Rio de Janeiro."

"Obrigada," I thank him and turn toward the elevator.

Pressing the up button, I make a mental note to message Renaldo once I get showered and settled.

These back-to-back flights from Charlotte to Madrid to Rio really took a toll on my body.

Just as the elevator doors open, I hear my name. "Brooklyn? Brooklyn James, or should I say *Captain James*," the foreign yet familiar voice says.

"Malcolm?" I ask as the elevator doors close behind me.

The Cliché Doctor

Riley

*B*eep! Beep! Beep!

"Crap, I'm late!" Jumping out of the bunk bed in the On-Call room, I scramble to put on my shoes and lab coat.

Beep! Beep! Beep!

The beeper continues to go off as I run to the O.R. for my next surgery. Bursting into the scrub room, I am met by one of the cardiothoracic surgeons.

"Nice of you to finally join us Dr. Harper," he says sarcastically.

"Dr. Wilson my apologies, it won't happen again," I assure him and internally scold myself for my unprofessionalism.

"Make certain it doesn't. One more minute and I would have had to report this to Chief Myers."

Thank goodness that the Head of Anesthesiology will not have to hear about this incident.

Dr. Wilson finishes his surgical scrub and continues to caution me, "You have done great work since joining Charlotte-Grace. Surgeons are fighting to have you assist in their O.R. We don't want a derogatory mark like this to tarnish your reputation Dr. Harper. Now let's go save some lives."

Leaving the operating room after another successful heart transplant, I make a quick trip to the cafeteria to get a fresh cup of coffee.

"Hey Beth, where are you headed?" I ask before almost getting run over.

"Hey Riles, let's catch up later. I'm running late," she says before disappearing around the corner.

I wonder if she was late working with Dr. Wilson today also.

I arrive to my next surgery twenty minutes early and finish my daily crossword puzzle just before the nurses bring in our triple bypass heart patient. I proceed to go through my pre-op check and coordinate with the nurses to make sure all vitals are good before putting the patient to sleep.

As soon as our patient is unconscious, I look over to the scrub room window to make sure Dr. Wilson is ready to start but, to my surprise, in walks Jameson.

"Good afternoon everyone," he says, and you can hear some of the scrub nurses giggle under their masks.

"Good afternoon Dr. Young," Kim, the youngest nurse says. "I thought Dr. Wilson was scheduled for this surgery?"

"Aww Nurse Kim, I'm hurt you would rather work with that grumpy old fart than with me."

I guess his flirting in the courtyard with me was just a warmup for his performance with the nurses.

Loving the attention, Kim continues to engage. "Of course not. I will change out his music playlist for yours."

"Thank you," he says innocently and turns to wink at me. I melt.

"Dr. Harper, you are unusually quiet this afternoon. Are you also upset about the last-minute change?"

"Oh, no Dr. Young, I am always happy to have you. I mean *work* with you— here, in the O.R., performing surgeries." My nerves are just rattled.

This man knows how to throw me off my game.

"Good, I'm happy to be here too. Charlotte A&T University requested an appearance to talk to the Freshman Pre-Medical class this afternoon and I happily volunteered Dr. Wilson. I'm camera shy and he's not, so now you have me instead of him. Shall we begin?"

Nurse Kim turns on some smooth jazz and everyone gets into position.

"You know, Dr. Young, I completed my undergrad at Charlotte A&T," I say with a hint of pride.

"Is that right? Well had I known, I would have personally attended and taken you along with me for moral support." I can feel the jealousy rise in the room.

After the surgery, I walk outside to my favorite bench in the courtyard and briefly scan the empty benches, secretly hoping Jameson is free to join me.

Snap out of it Riley. Clearly, he flirts with everyone. Not just you.

Disbanding my fantasies, I lose myself in a new crossword puzzle.

"I was hoping you were out here. May I join you?" Jameson asks, and my inner Riley is jumping up and down.

"Are you following me, Dr. Young?"

"Remember, out here it's *Jameson,* and maybe I am. You've had my attention since you joined the team Riley." My insides perform a full cartwheel.

"I am sure you've said that same line to someone other than me."

"What makes you so sure of that?" He tilts his head intently and licks his bottom lip.

Oh my. Control yourself, Riley.

"Seriously Jameson, you're young, successful, and not to mention, very attractive. I'm sure women, like Nurse Kim, throw themselves at you all day long." My insecurity begins to rear its ugly head.

"You find me attractive, huh? Yes, I suppose some women do but I am not looking for the *catch of the day*, so I don't entertain them."

"What are you looking for?"

My interest is now fully invested.

"You don't speak much about your personal life or hanging out at the bar after shifts like most of the staff. I have heard nothing but praises regarding your impeccable anesthetic work and I've even had to negotiate with my colleagues just to get you in my O.R. Aside from your brilliance and breathtaking beauty, if you don't mind me acknowledging, I'd like to learn more about this woman sitting in the courtyard always lost in her crossword puzzles," he says. I am rendered speechless.

This beautiful specimen of a man is talking about me? He's interested in me? God must be playing a joke with me.

"Jameson, I'm flattered but . . ."

He cuts me off. "Before you turn me down, could I at least thank you for the football recommendation for my nephews? They had a blast and were even able to meet some of the players afterwards. Just dinner, to show my gratitude. After that you never have to eat with me again, at least until your next good deed."

"Okay one date, I mean dinner. One dinner." My caramel cheeks are the reddest they have ever been.

God this man is too young and too smooth to be interested in a prude single mother like me.

The next night Blythe insists on playing one hundred questions.

"OMG! Mommy where are you going? Are you going on a date? With a man? Who is he? What does he do? Is he a doctor? Does he work at your hospital? What does he look like?" she blurts out all in one breath.

"Sweetie, help me zip up my dress," I say, trying to sound nonchalant. "Yes, I am going to dinner with a doctor from Charlotte-Grace."

Blythe dramatically falls onto the bed.

"Mommy! Seriously? I haven't seen you get this dressed up for 'just dinner' in a while. This is more than dinner."

She walks over and looks at me through the mirror as I apply my lipstick, "You really like this man! You can't stop smiling mommy. Oh, you have to tell me more, please!"

I give in.

"Okay, fine. He is Head of Cardio at the hospital and just as fine as he is smart. I have worked with him on a number of surgeries and he's expressed interest in getting to know me outside of work. He asked me to dinner tonight and I accepted. End of story, Blythe."

"Okay, I'll let you slide *for now*, but I want to hear all the details tomorrow. Tonight, you stay out as late as you like," she says, smiling after kissing my cheek and turning to walk out of my room, "and mommy, you look HOT!"

. . .

Arriving at Portofino's, an upscale Italian restaurant, I hand my keys to the valet and walk inside. Without saying a word, the hostess instructs me to follow her upstairs. Carefully following and watching each step to avoid falling in my heels, I watch as she opens the entrance to the rooftop dining area. Sitting at a candlelit table in the corner, overlooking Charlotte's night skyline, is Dr. Jameson *Oh So Fine* Young.

"Dr. Young, your guest has arrived," the hostess says as Jameson gets up to pull back my chair.

"Yes, she certainly has. Please have the waitress bring a bottle of Antinori Tignanello. Thank you," he says in a perfect French accent as he returns to his seat.

Oh my, he can speak French too? This man is way out of my league.

Already impressed by the rooftop view and the wine selection, I look out into the night sky and take it all in.

"You are absolutely stunning, Riley. Thank you for accompanying me this evening."

"Thank you for inviting me." I smile and stare at him.

For a moment, no words are said but the unspoken chemistry at the table continues to increase. The waitress arrives, breaking our longing gaze. After he tastes and approves the wine, she pours two glasses and takes our food order before leaving us alone again in the corner of the rooftop.

"Are you fluent in French?" I ask trying to distract the sexual tension in the air. He tilts his head in confusion, so I explain, "The wine selection, you pronounced it perfectly."

Smiling, he takes a sip of water and the moisture left on his lips causes my inner thigh to pulsate.

Control yourself Riley!

"Yes, my mother insisted we all learned at least one additional language growing up. I was a bit of an overachiever and opted for three: French, Spanish, and Yoruba."

"The first two I can deduce the reasoning but, Yoruba?" I ask.

"I did a few medical missions in West Africa. I guess I sort of just picked it up after a while."

What's the catch? This man is just way too perfect.

"Enough about me, please. Tonight is about getting to know the mysterious Dr. Riley Harper." The way he says my name causes me to shift in my seat, "So Riley, tell me more about your daughter."

"Blythe is a senior in high school and has one of the brightest young minds I have ever seen. She's my heart and my best friend."

"You light up when you speak of her, you must be very proud." Unable to control my smile, I simply nod.

"How about you, Jameson? What makes you light up?"

"Well let's see. For me, it's my nieces and nephews. I haven't had the pleasure of getting married and having children of my own, yet, so I tend to spoil them. My sisters all fuss and complain that they can't compete with the *fun uncle*. I am usually the one buying them whatever they want and then drop them off with bags of toys and gifts," he says, and that same light is radiating now in his eyes.

"Sisters? How many siblings do you have?"

My interest in Jameson Young is now on max capacity.

"I have three sisters. One older and two younger. My dad and I spent a lot of time hanging out together trying to escape being outnumbered in a house full of women." I notice his mood dampens.

"Are you close with your father?" I try to deduce what caused the shift.

"Yes, I was. He passed away a while back from heart complications. I guess that makes me the cliché doctor who became a heart surgeon to fill some void of not being able to save my father."

I reach over to hold his hand.

"That doesn't make you a cliché, Jameson, that makes you a humanitarian." Barely able to finish my sentence, Jameson softly squeezes my hand and electricity shoots through my body.

What is happening to me? No man has ever made me feel this way or has it really been that long since I've been on a real date? Have I been celibate so long that I unknowingly blocked intimacy completely out of my life?

After one of the best conversations I have ever had over dinner, it was time to end the evening. This is the first time in a long time that I am not ready to leave someone. Slowly walking back downstairs and outside, we reach the valet stand and hand them our tickets.

"Tonight was lovely," I say as I turn to face Jameson, still holding his hand.

"It was better than that, Riley. It almost felt like we have done this a thousand times before. It felt so natural. So right."

All I want in this moment is for him to kiss me.

"It is taking everything in me *not* to kiss you, but I don't want to ruin the evening by being too forward. You are far too special of a woman. I want to *earn* those lips."

He pulls my chin toward him.

Moving just inches away from my lips, he turns his head and kisses me softly on the cheek.

"Good night, beautiful," he whispers. The valet jumps out of my car and in a maladroit manner, I walk over to get in.

Finding Our Way Back

Candice

"Mrs. Montgomery, it's so nice to see you," Alice says with the sweetest smile.

She is by far my favorite out of all Calvin's past secretaries. She's always professional and I never have to question any ulterior motives (like a few of the ones before).

"Mr. Montgomery is finishing up a meeting, but I've been instructed to ask you to wait in his office." She motions in the direction, knowing I am quite familiar with the building.

"Thank you, Alice."

The office looks a lot different than the last time I visited. He replaced the wooden office desk and bookshelves with all new stainless steel and glass furniture. It is so fitting and sophisticated for Calvin. My favorite addition is the all black leather couch facing Atlanta's skyline. I could lay here all day looking at the downtown buildings and clouds while listening to music.

Continuing to wander around his office, I admire the plaques and awards on the shelf and look at all of our travel pictures from past anniversaries.

We are long overdue to capture new adventures.

Sitting behind his desk, I turn to feel the sun through the panoramic windows and close my eyes as the soft leather from the executive office chair conforms to my body.

As the door opens, I hear Alice inform Calvin of my arrival, but I don't turn around. Stepping into the office and closing the door, the sounds of the corporate conversations disappear as Calvin secures the lock.

"*Mrs. Montgomery,*" he says in a seductive manner walking over to face me while I still have my back turned.

"*Mr. Montgomery.*" I match his tone. "You look as handsome as always in a suit. When I left you this morning, you were still in your boxer briefs."

"That can be rectified." He softly bites my bottom lip.

Seductively playing along I ask, "Desk or couch?"

With eyes blazing from passion, he lifts me onto the desk and whispers, "Both."

...

Leaving Calvin's office, I decide to skip the gym and go shopping instead. Once I turn onto the interstate, I call Riley.

"Candice, how are you?" she asks.

"Riley Harper, you are in a really good mood. I'm guessing I caught you at a good time." I can't help but smile at the sound of her voice.

"I'm doing good. I took today off so I was actually able to sleep in for once."

"*You?* Taking a day off, just because? This is a first. I'm calling because I felt like I have talked to Brook and Michele in the last few weeks but not you. I knew you were busy working but you crossed my mind and you know I have to call when someone crosses my mind."

"That's sweet of you. Yes, I have been the absolute with communication the past few weeks. I have pretty much been living at the hospital and spending as much time with Blythe before she ships off to college. How are you? Last time we spoke, you said you were going back to Atlanta. How is everything?"

"Honestly Riley, things are better. Calvin and I had a long overdue talk and we were able to have multiple breakthroughs in counseling. I guess the sleepover at Brooklyn's was the reality check I needed." We both laugh.

"That Brooklyn is something else, but you have to love her. That's great Candice. I have been praying since that night, for you and for your marriage. You two are my Barack and Michelle. God will continue to help you find your way back to one another. I am certain of that."

I fight back happy tears. "It was hard but you're right. We are finding our way back every day and it feels really good."

"Just promise you will never disappear on us like that again. All this time we thought you were traveling and working, but I won't bring up the past.

Let's keep moving forward. Did you speak to Michele about her Thanksgiving extravaganza?"

Laughing at Riley's sarcasm I respond, "Yes, she called me about it and then used the twins to guilt me into saying yes."

"Not the Marley and Mason one-two combo. Hopefully it wasn't video chat. She had them call me on video to sing 'Happy Birthday' once and then slid in to ask me a large favor before hanging up. How could I say no after that? Just evil." I laugh knowing exactly how Michele uses her twins' cuteness to guilt us.

"I will be back in Charlotte just before Thanksgiving, I have a few more events until then. Let's grab lunch so you can tell me all about the reason behind this mood you are in." I pause and wait for her to think of a lie.

"What are you talking about?"

"Riley. I have known you for more than a decade, you don't *take days off just because*. I've once seen you work four days straight on zero sleep, energy drinks, and honey buns. So '*honey bun*' I know you. Something is up, and I want to know all about it."

"Is it that obvious?" she says, and I can feel her smile through the phone.

"Yes, it kind of is. You are a perfectionist. You don't take days off because you don't like to miss learning opportunities during surgeries and you normally sound tired on the weekdays. What's his name?"

"So, you really don't believe I am just having a great and well-rested day?"

"That may also be the case but there's more to this story, I can feel it. If you don't want to tell me now, that's fine. I will let you have your little secret until I see you. Love you, Honey." We hang up.

My girl is on cloud nine, it must be something major if she is waiting to give details.

Stepping inside a lingerie boutique, my phone vibrates. Ignoring it, I walk over to observe a few of the new items on display and select one of the lace options. The petite young lady behind the counter comes over to assist.

"Lovely piece you've selected. Would you like a fitting room and glass of wine?" she asks.

"Yes please," I respond as I pull out my phone to check the message. It's Calvin.

Think of three of your favorite movies. I'm cooking

I smile at the message and then get a mischievous idea. Putting on the lingerie, I send a picture and respond.

You cook dinner and I'll take care of dessert.

Mr. Diamond

Brooklyn

"What on earth are you doing here?" I ask, still trying to regain my equanimity after being spotted in a foreign country.

"I was just about to ask you the *same thing*," Malcolm says with a half-smile and lifted eyebrow. "Is Brazil part of your route? I see you have crossed over into the big league of piloting international flights since I've seen you last. How long was that—six or so years ago? Give me a hug, girl."

Placing my uniform cap on top of my luggage handle, I wrap my arms around Malcolm's broad shoulders, inhaling his cologne.

Malcolm Diamond is a former professional football player, finesser of all females, *and* Michele's older brother.

"Yes, it has been a while, it's great to see you. It looks like life has been good to you."

"I could say the same for you, Brook." He steps back and admires my uniform. "You have come a long way from that little country girl I met when I visited Michele on campus. All grown up and grown out. Time has been good to you."

"Yes, it has. That feisty girl from Wilmington is still in me but I only let her out for special occasions these days. You still haven't answered my question, Mr. Diamond. What brings you to Brazil?"

"A few years back a buddy of mine created an athletic monitoring software that tracks performance metrics and variances. When I was still playing in the league, I was one of his first investors. After retiring with my knee injury, we partnered up to leverage some of my industry contacts and started a company. This morning, we had a meeting with the South American Football Confederation to discuss the upcoming season and how we can help teams prepare for the World Cup. This software conference is just an added bonus to network and scope out any competition," he says, as I hang on to every word growing more and more impressed.

The Malcolm I remember was a playboy and immature cocky athlete, but this man looks like a business professional and a boss. I am intrigued.

"How about you, did I guess correctly that Brazil is part of your flight route?" he asks.

"No, I just came for a few days of relaxation. The weather here is a lot better than Charlotte." I attempt to remain cryptic.

"And the beaches too. Well Ms. Brooklyn, I've held you hostage in front of this elevator long enough. I'm sure you're tired from the flight, but would you like to join me later for dinner to catch up? I have a feeling I would enjoy your company far more than talking megabytes and java programming with some of these guys."

"I would love to. How does eight o'clock sound?"

"Eight is perfect. Enjoy the rest of your afternoon, Captain James and I'll see you tonight." He winks and turn to walk away as I press the elevator button once again.

...

Stepping into the lobby, I briefly take in the atmosphere and energy of all the people talking about everything and nothing at the same time. Out of habit, I stare with curiosity, exploring the types of people mingling at the hotel bar.

It is easy to differentiate the people with intentions of making an impression and the ones who are only present for the complimentary drinks.

Walking up to the bar, I order my first caipirinha of the evening, Brazil's national drink. Before I can give my card to pay, a young techie snaps his fingers at the bartender saying, "Hey Bud, put her drink on my tab."

Mistaking my half smile and nod as an open invitation, he walks over to claim the empty stool beside me.

"Hi Beautiful, I've never seen you at these conferences before. Are you an Admin or Dev?" he asks trying to sound cool, but his misplaced confidence partially annoys me.

"Excuse me?"

"Administrator or Developer. I already know most of the female developers and they aren't lookers, so a pretty thing like you must be an

Admin. Me, I'm a senior developer and future architect. It would benefit you to get to know me better."

Now I am completely annoyed.

Before I can open my mouth to go off on this rude and egotistical geek, Malcolm walks up.

"Sweetheart, sorry to have kept you," he says as he kisses me on my cheek. "Shall I close out your tab, so we can go to dinner?"

Playing along with the charade, I fix his collar and respond, "No honey, this young man put my drink on his *company sponsored* room tab." I look over at the young tech who is now sliding off of the barstool.

"Mr. Diamond? Malcolm Diamond. You were my dad's favorite professional football player growing up and one of my idols in the software industry. I have been trying to get a developer position at your company for the last year. Danny Grubbs, sir."

The young tech extends his hand for a greeting, but I grab Malcolm's hand before he can reach it.

"Honey, Danny here says it could benefit me greatly if I would get to know him better." Instantly all of that ego and cockiness dissolve from Danny's now pale face.

"Get to know him better?" Malcolm looks at Danny. "Tell me, Mr. Grubbs, what exactly would my wife, a formidable pilot, need to do to get to know *you* better?" Danny's face turns from pale to completely white.

"Mr. Diamond, I didn't mean any disrespect."

I cut him off.

"Yes, you did, you meant exactly what you said. Work on your game and learn some manners young man."

I take Malcolm's hand as I climb down from the barstool, "Now we can go, *husband*."

...

Sitting in the back of a cab reminiscing on old times, we arrive at a small and intimate restaurant near the coast of Copacabana Beach. Wanting to continue enjoying the ocean breeze, we opt to eat dinner on the outside patio.

Trying to use our phones for assistance in translating between English and Portuguese, we struggle for about ten minutes to overcome the language barrier between us, the menu, and the waiter. Eventually we give up and decide on the two items that were familiar.

"Two Caipirinhas and a large order of Feijoada to share," Malcolm says and hands the menus back to the waiter.

"I haven't had Feijoada in forever. It kind of reminds me of my grandmother's cooking back in Wilmington."

"You know South American cuisine and Soul Food are very similar. If you brought Africa and South America together, the continents would fit like a puzzle," Malcolm says, and I smile at his random trivia knowledge.

As dinner arrives, my stomach begins to growl loudly. *I hadn't realized my last meal was yesterday on the plane.*

"Someone's hungry." Malcolm smiles and hands me the spoon, "Ladies first."

The Brazilian dish is as good as I last remembered. For a few minutes, we both enjoy our meal in silence, listening to the sounds of the water crashing against the shore.

"So Brooklyn, this question has been on my mind all day. Why exactly are you in Brazil alone? I know you said you are here for relaxation, but this is a bit far for a few days of fun in the sun." He pauses and searches my eyes for an answer.

"Honestly, I had a strange couple of weeks and needed a break. I wanted to go someplace where no one knows my name, but I guess that plan failed."

"I mean I don't want to interfere with your TLC time so please let me know when you get tired of my presence. Although, not to be forward, I am really enjoying your company."

"I am really enjoying you as well. You seem different than the last time I saw you. You seem, and please don't take offense, a lot more level-headed, mature, and resolute. I kind of always saw you as the playboy, frat type—driving fast cars and chasing faster women. What's changed?"

"Wow, I guess we both are going straight in with the tough questions." He takes a sip of his drink and continues, "Okay, I'll tell you my story if you tell me yours. Deal?"

I look at him intently and feel a type of comfort with him that I haven't felt in a long time.

"Okay Mr. Diamond, you have a deal." I smile and raise my glass for him to toast. Bringing his glass down, he pauses for a moment and takes another bite of his meal, clearly trying to stall.

"A few years ago, I met this woman who ruined me, in a good way. I was at the prime of my career. I had money, endorsements, fame, women, you name it. Walking off the field at one of our away games, I noticed her. She was about five rows up from the field but still, I noticed her. Later that night, I saw her again at an afterparty and I took my shot. I tried to get her number, but she shot me down. Can you believe that? Me, Malcolm Diamond, getting embarrassed and turned down like that. Eventually our paths crossed again, and we got into a relationship. She was kind, patient, and beautiful but I was so caught up in the game of winning that I was pretty much done with her once I conquered her. It wasn't until I saw her recently that I had the reality check of my life." He pauses and I continue to listen to his every word.

"For my 38th birthday, my old teammates put together a yacht party in my honor. I was thrilled but noticed the majority of them brought their wives, fiancés, or girlfriends to the party. The few single ones were either divorced or major womanizers, like me. It was on that boat that I ran into her again. She was older but still as beautiful as I remembered, only now married to one of my teammates. I couldn't get mad because I never claimed her in public so technically, how could anyone know about our history. But it hurt me, Brooklyn. Bruised my ego for sure. We caught up for a bit and she said something that has never left me. She said if you keep living this life pretending you don't need anyone, eventually you will end up not having anyone. Getting off that boat, I decided to get my life together and frankly, grow up. So, what you see now is the product of a man putting away childish things," he says and tilts his head. "Now, a deal is a deal, your turn."

Motioning for the waiter to bring a second round of drinks, I honor my agreement.

"I'm not sure if my story is as enlightening as yours, but you are right, a deal is a deal." I finish the last bite of my meal before speaking.

"There was a guy I dated in college. Dated is probably an understatement—I was head over heels in love. He had a career-ending knee injury, like yours, and it crushed him. It crushed us. We had an abysmal breakup and I decided to join the Air Force and leave that life and hurt behind. I, too, had a recent reunion with my past that turned life as I knew it on its axis. I ran into him at my goddaughter's school of all places. His career is thriving, and he found love again *and* has a child on the way. I had not thought about this man in years but seeing him again, with this new life and an unborn child made me question if the decision to leave back then was the right one. I have been trying to wrap my mind around it. Did I throw my future away because I was too afraid of the unknown?" I look up at Malcolm as the energy between us shifts.

"So, that is why I am in Brazil. I didn't want to go back to Charlotte, back to my empty house, and even emptier bed. I wanted to get away and have fun."

"Now that we have both shared our truths, we should focus a little more on making this a fun evening. I don't think I am ready to say goodnight to you Brooklyn," Malcolm says and I do not protest.

The next morning, I wake up with nothing on my mind but Malcolm. After dinner, we walked along the beach and talked all night. Although I have known him for years, this was something different. We talked as if we had been close our whole lives. Last night he went from the arrogant big brother type, I've known him as since college, to a man I could see myself falling for. Really falling for. Grateful for my phone distracting me from overthinking one evening with a reformed womanizer, I look at the screen to see a message from Renaldo.

Crap, I forgot all about him.

Bom dia. I hope you arrived safely to Rio. Will I see you this evening? I ponder on my response.

Bom dia Renaldo. Yes, I arrived safely, thank you. My schedule has changed while I am here, let's try to catch up on my next visit. I reply and feel a little guilty.

That guilt quickly dissipates when I see Malcolm's name appear on my screen.

Good Morning Gorgeous. I was hoping to disrupt your day of relaxation again. Would you mind giving me a tour of Rio today?

I smile at the message and respond.

Good Morning. I have never seen the historic attractions. Let's be touristy together!

I look over at my suitcase and realize I don't have any sneakers for a day of walking, but my thoughts are interrupted once more by a vibration.

You've made my day Captain James! I have two meetings to finish and then I'll change and pick you up from the hotel. How does two o'clock sound?

Looking over at the clock displaying a quarter after ten, I respond and then get dressed to go do a little shopping.

...

Stepping into the lobby a little after two o'clock, I spot Malcolm standing in his fresh Polo shorts, shirt, and shoes to match.

Jesus, this man is fine.

He has the type of presence that makes me forget about anyone else in the room. The way he looks at me with those dark-brown eyes, it beguiles me. Holding two freshly carved coconuts with umbrella straws, he walks up and kisses me on the cheek.

"You look amazing Brooklyn. That V-neck tee is giving me the tease of a lifetime," he whispers and hands me a coconut. "Let's toast to an amazing afternoon, shall we?"

Walking outside, I follow Malcolm, expecting to see a cab waiting, but only a Harley-Davidson is parked in front of the hotel. A valet walks over to Malcolm with two beanie helmets and passes one to him. Taking our coconuts and discarding them, Malcolm removes my sunglasses and places the helmet atop my head.

"Please forgive me if I mess up this beautiful hair of yours but it's my job to keep you safe. I thought we could see the streets of Rio from the back of a bike instead of the backseat of a cab."

After securing my helmet, he tightens his own straps and tips the valet. I stand back and wait for him to start the bike before he reaches out his hand for me to climb on back.

Wrapping my arms tightly around Malcolm's waist, he reaches down and kisses the back of my hand before revving the engine.

I am not sure if it is the vibrations from the engine or Mr. Malcolm Diamond himself, but once again, electricity shoots up my legs and through my entire body as we ride off through the streets of Rio De Janeiro.

Anytime, Anyplace, Any Hour

Riley

"Another job well done, team," Jameson says as he removes his surgical goggles. "Nurse Kim, please have the post-op blood work expedited as soon as we get the patient settled into ICU."

I complete my post operation check and then prepare to leave the room. Walking into the hallway I feel a slight tug on my hand.

"Follow me," Jameson whispers and quickly exits into a supply closet.

"Riley I…"

Before he can finish, I wrap my arms around his neck and kiss him, passionately.

"Jameson, we have been dating for weeks and it has been the best time of my life. I admire you wanting to *earn* my lips and take it slow, so I need you to hear me when I say this, you have earned my lips ten times over."

"Woman, you continue to surprise me," he says and we go back to making out.

"What was the original reason for you pulling me into this closet?"

Jameson straightens my lab coat and then repositions his.

"After tasting those lips, does it really matter?" His charming smile makes my legs quiver.

"It does if it was important, although I didn't mean to attack you like that. It has been difficult to see you at work and not be in your arms."

I almost don't recognize my own voice. He has me completely under his spell.

"Riley, feel free to attack me like that anytime, anyplace, any hour." He grabs my chin and softly kisses my bottom lip before whispering, "These are your lips now."

With that, we are up against the door with our lips intertwined once more.

The time I have spent with Jameson has been amazing. I have never had a man care for me, every part of me, the way Jameson does. In such a short time, I have certainly fallen for him.

But can I tell him that? How soon is too soon? He has not even met my daughter yet. Is it too soon to introduce him to Blythe? She's almost an adult but she's also my best friend. I need her input, her acceptance.

Waiting in the parking lot to pick up Blythe from practice, my phone vibrates against the car's seat.

"Hello," I answer without looking at the screen.

"Hey, beautiful, have you left yet? One of my surgeries was pushed due to complications so we have to monitor the patient overnight. Since we have been ships passing in the night these last two days, would you like to have dinner?" Jameson asks.

"Hi handsome, I am actually picking up Blythe. We made dinner plans. Would you like to join us?"

Oh crap! What did I just do?

He pauses and instantly I wish I could take it back.

"Wow, really? I would love to. I've been anxious to meet Blythe, but I wanted it to be on your terms. I know how much she means to you." His sincerity calms my nerves.

"Yes, in a short time you have become very important to me."

"Riley, you don't know what it means to hear you say that. May I pick you two ladies up around eight?"

"Eight o'clock is great, I can't wait to see you."

Just as Blythe walks up to the car, I hang up trying to figure out how I will break the news to her. I have no doubt she will be thrilled but I am not sure if I am ready.

Once she meets him, it becomes real. Am I ready for that? To have a man completely in my life, in our lives.

"Hi, mommy," she says as she throws her bags in the back seat.

"Hi sweetie, how was practice?"

"It was okay. Football season is coming to an end, so we are mostly preparing basketball cheers for next semester. Coach cancelled practice tomorrow because a lot of us have a French *and* Calculus exam on Friday."

"Do you feel prepared, should we cancel dinner tonight?" I ask, trying to find any excuse to prolong the inevitable.

"No ma'am. I am more worried about retaking the SAT after the holidays. My first score was *okay,* but I think I can do better a second time."

My little Blythe is an overachiever like me.

...

Getting out of the shower, I yell out into the hallway, "Blythe, when you get dressed come here."

Still in my robe, I walk back in front of my bathroom mirror and begin to apply makeup.

"Mom, I thought we were going somewhere casual for dinner. Why are you putting on a whole face of makeup? I just have on ripped jeans and a shirt." Blythe raises her eyebrow and looks at me through the mirror. Unable to contain my smile, I turn to face her.

"Before I say this, I need you to wait before bombarding me with questions, deal?" Even more suspicious, she silently nods.

"Jameson is joining us for dinner." I pause to see if she will remain inaudible and then continue, "We are getting pretty serious and I think it's time for the most important people in my life to finally meet."

Blythe remains silent but with eyes wide and eyebrows lifted, she holds her hand over her mouth waiting for me to finish as promised.

"Now, you may drop your hands and let it out."

"MOMMY! Are you serious? You're actually going to introduce us, he must be someone *very* special!" she shouts, jumping to hug me. Unable to contain my calmness against her excitement, I smile so hard my eyes begin to water.

"Yes sweetie, he is wonderful, and I think I may be falling in love."

"Love? My mom, Riley Elizabeth Harper, is in love! Today is the best day ever! Mommy I am so happy for you!"

"Yes, but please get it all out now before he picks us up. I am not sure if I am ready to tell him the love part yet, so I need you to keep that between us. I do, however, want you to be yourself tonight and feel free to ask him anything you wish. If he's going to be a part of my life, that means he will also be a part of yours."

"I mean, yes, he'll be in my life in a *stepdad* sort of manner, but I'm going off to college next year. You are pretty much done raising me, Mom. I think I have turned out pretty good, so it's time for you to live your life and be happy. I can't wait to meet Mister Doctor Jameson! Now if you'll excuse me, I need to go change for *our* date with your future husband."

…

"Mom, he's here," Blythe sings as the doorbell rings.

Opening the door, we share a smile at the sight of Jameson standing in the doorway with a bouquet of roses in each hand.

"Good evening, ladies," he says, lifting the roses in his right hand. "Red roses for my heart." He passes me the roses and kisses my cheek.

"And a colorful assortment of roses for the lovely Ms. Blythe." He reaches and kisses the back of Blythe's left hand before extending her the bouquet of roses. Without making any sounds, Blythe looks at me and mouths, "O-M-G."

"Thank you, these are beautiful." I blush and look over to Blythe admiring her roses as well.

"Yes, thank you Mr. Jameson," she says and reaches for my flowers. "We can do a formal introduction at the restaurant, let me place these in vases in the kitchen and then we can leave."

Waiting for Blythe to disappear into the kitchen, Jameson grabs my waist and pulls me closer to him, unexpectedly feeling all of his manhood.

God, help me. This man gets finer each time I see him.

"I've missed you these last two days, thank you for inviting me," he says before softly kissing me.

"I've missed you too. I see you are quite the charmer. Those roses gained you some cool points."

"Tonight is important to me because Blythe is important to *you*. I am ready for whatever she throws at me. I am in this for the long haul, Riley."

Before I can respond, Blythe returns into the living room smiling at the sight of Jameson and I standing so close.

"I'm ready when you two are." Blythe winks and picks up her jacket from the back of the couch.

After some light conversation in the car, we arrive at a sushi restaurant uptown. Jameson walks around and opens both of our car doors.

"Ladies," he says as we both step out.

The restaurant has a decent crowd and the music is a mix between Pop and R&B. Once we are seated and place our drink and appetizer orders, Blythe jumps right in.

"So, Mr. Jameson, it's a pleasure to finally meet you."

"The pleasure is all mine," Jameson responds and squeezes my hand under the table.

"I've heard a few things about you from my mom, but I'd like to know a little more. Where are you from?"

"Of course, and I would like to get to know you as well, if you'll let me. Well first, I'm from Connecticut, the majority of my family is still there except for my youngest sister, who is studying abroad in Europe."

Instantly piquing Blythe's interest, she sits up.

"Studying abroad? I've seen colleges mention it in brochures but I'm not sure if I could do that."

"It's actually not as scary as you think. You essentially spend an entire semester in a country learning the cultures and languages. It's a great way to start traveling and seeing the world. I studied abroad my junior year in Africa to learn about unique medical cases," he says and seeing them discuss travel and education eases my worry and doubt.

I am in love with this man.

"Wow, I never thought about it like that. Maybe I was too quick to dismiss the idea. Let's table that discussion for another time. Now for the two-million-dollar questions."

"Are you my mom's boss?" she asks and Jameson and I both laugh with relief.

"No, I am not your mom's boss. We work together. I technically have a Chief position over Cardiac surgeries, but we are in two completely separate departments. We are more team members, in a sense"

"Good, I've seen too many hospital TV dramas with that type of situation and it doesn't usually end well. Okay, my last question." She sits up and crosses her arms on the table.

"Are you serious about my mom?"

Without an ounce of hesitation, Jameson grabs my hand and faces me,

"Yes, I am crazy about your mom, Blythe. I have never met such an amazing woman in my life. She's smart, talented, a loving mother, and the most beautiful sight I have ever laid my eyes on. I hope when you two talk about me tonight, you give her your stamp of approval because I want to be around for a long, long time."

Grabbing Jameson's face, I softly kiss him and whisper, "I love you."

Just Know I Hear You

Candice

After finishing my facial moisturizing routine, I pull out my flexi rods and silk bonnet. Looking at myself in the mirror, I roll my eyes and let out an annoyed sigh. I hate the nightly hassle with my hair, but I know the consequences if I refuse to curl it, so I push through.

Once I roll a flexi rod on the last section of straight hair, I put on my bonnet and one of Calvin's old college shirts before walking downstairs.

"Babe, would you like something from the kitchen?"

I walk by Calvin who is lost in his tablet, probably looking over stock trends.

"I'll take a beer, and do we have any more pretzels?"

Placing the pretzel bag on the table and the drinks on coasters, I snuggle up next to him on the couch. Kissing me on the forehead he says, "Thank you honey."

"Who's winning?" I motion to the football game on the television screen.

"I have no idea. I have been looking at this tablet since I came downstairs. The TV is just on to fill the silence."

"Is everything okay? You seem preoccupied." I turn the audio from the game down and face Calvin.

"Things are fine. I'm actually moving some chess pieces around so I can be more available to you. In counseling you mentioned several times that you want to travel more, is that still the case?"

"Yes, I still want *us* to travel. Before my parents died, we had a bunch of family vacation plans to see the world. My mom would talk about Paris like it was the most magical and romantic place on earth. I want to see that magic one day, but I want you to be there with me."

"Just know I hear you. I think I was so focused on building a future for us that I forgot to live in the present with you. All of those hours I spent at the office, I should have been here with you processing everything that has happened. I know that now. We can see as much of the world or as much of this couch as you like."

"You are the man of my dreams. I am truly sorry for my part in all of this."

"We both have to forgive each other, love. It'll take some time, but I feel closer to you now than ever before, so I know counseling is doing something right," he admits and reaches for the remote to turn the volume back up on the game.

Before he can press the button, I grab his hand.

"I want you to know I also hear you, Calvin. I have battled with this for a while, but I think I am open to talk about adoption. Maybe this was God's plan all along, for us to give an abandoned child a life and home to call their own. I can be a great mother and I have no doubt you'll be an amazing father. This kid will be showered with unconditional love."

A tear falls down my cheek. Calvin grabs my shoulders to turn me around.

"Are you serious?" He looks at me intently.

"Yes, I want us to adopt a child." Before I can finish the sentence, I am in my husband's arms.

"Candice, you are the woman of my dreams and you've just made me the happiest man on earth. I love you," he says and kisses my bonnet, my forehead, and my nose before making his way to my lips.

…

"Good morning Mrs. Montgomery," Amber says with a wide and bright-eyed smile, "Mrs. Williamson is in her office and expecting you." She motions toward the direction of Regina's office and I proceed down the hall.

As I enter, Regina gestures to the phone at her ear and points toward the meeting table facing downtown Atlanta. I notice the two salad boxes and smoothies on the table and walk over to have a seat.

Hanging up the phone, Regina walks over and sits in front of the other salad, placing three large manila envelopes between us.

"Apologies for the phone call, I was getting some updates on a pro bono case," she says, "I thought we could have a lunch meeting. I hope you like seared tuna." I nod and open the box to five pieces of tuna perfectly placed atop a Caesar salad.

"This looks delicious, thank you."

"Would you like Regina, your friend, or Mrs. Williamson, your lawyer first?"

"Let's talk business first."

"I received a letter from Calvin's lawyer to withdraw the petition for divorce. It *appears* both parties have found their way back to each other during the separation," she says failing to hide her smile.

Passing me the first envelope and a pen she continues, "I will just need a few signatures stating both parties have mutually agreed to stay married and regain control of all joint assets." I read over the forms and sign each page under Calvin's signature with pride as Candice Smith Montgomery.

Looking up at Regina I say, "Okay, I think I need my friend now." We both stand and hug for a brief moment.

"I am proud of you Candice. I know this wasn't easy. Sometimes it takes a hard decision to force people to realize how much they mean to each other. I'm glad you both chose to fight for your marriage. To fight for each other."

"Okay back to business, I see you have two more envelopes," I say wiping stray tears and motioning at the table.

"Yes, Mrs. Montgomery." Back to formalities. "Trinity reached out to me regarding interest in turning *Life After 25* into a motion picture." Regina tries to maintain a calm demeanor delivering the news, but I can barely contain myself.

"A movie! *My book?* Are you serious?"

"Yes, Hollywood wants your book on the big screen! I have to do a little more digging to make sure we have you covered on all ends, but things are looking good so far. And for the last item on the agenda . . ."

She picks up the remaining envelope. "I have the draft you sent me of your recent book with some notes. I imagine you have been doing a lot of writing these past few months. I am always here as an extra pair of eyes." She hands me the two envelopes and we finish eating our salads while catching up.

...

Leaving the airport from an event in Nashville, I call Brooklyn.

"Candice, hey. How are you? How was your return back to Atlanta?" she says happily.

"I am doing well. I have a few positive updates for you. Are you back in the States?"

"Yes, but I am leaving out tomorrow. What's going on?"

"I'm coming in town next weekend and staying until Michele's Thanksgiving extravaganza. You're planning to attend, right? We need the whole gang back together for this one."

"Yes, I will be there. My sisters and I are still not on good terms, so I doubt I will be going to Wilmington. I would rather be with friends I enjoy than family who resent me," she says. I try to steer the conversation back to a happier mood but make a mental note to talk with her about this later.

"Yes, I'm sure there will be fun, laughter, and more wine than you can stand. I hear Mrs. Harper is coming, so you know the expensive bottles will be served. This is my courtesy call that you will have a seven-day roommate. Also, are you free the weekend before Thanksgiving?" I ramble on trying to get everything said before I forget.

"I'm not sure which statement to address first. First, you are always welcome here but thank you for the heads up and second, yes I am off the weekend before Thanksgiving until the weekend after."

"Great! I wanted to grab dinner with everyone to catch up before the holidays."

...

Stepping into the kitchen entrance from the garage, I place my luggage down by the door and filter through the mail on the counter.

"Honey," I call out without looking up. No response. "Calvin?" I say once more and walk into the living room.

The television is on the sports network but still no Calvin. I notice the patio door is open, so I walk toward it, still in search of my husband. As I get closer to the door, my nostrils are filled with the aroma of mesquite barbeque and burning charcoal.

Stepping onto the patio, I pause at the sight of Calvin singing our wedding song and flipping ribs on the grill. "Calvin," I say but he doesn't turn around. Walking behind him, I wrap my arms around his waist. Startled, he removes his headphones and turns around.

"Oh, hey baby, I didn't hear you come in. These noise-cancelling headphones are serious," he says, closing the grill.

"Yes, they are. I called you a few times but you were caught up in your own little concert. I still love that song."

Bending down and picking me up to give me a bear hug he says, "I still love you. Welcome back."

"I was wondering when you were going to light up the grill before the weather became too cold." I walk over to the patio bar to pour us both a glass of wine.

"Yes, I called Gerald earlier about coming to cover the pool and thought it would be a good idea for us to have dinner by the fire pit. I hope you have a taste for ribs and salad. That's about as far as the dinner menu extends this evening."

"Fine with me, honey. I am just happy to be home. I don't know how Brooklyn can live in and out of airports. It's exhausting."

After filling our second wine glass, I set the table as Calvin places the ribs and salad bowl in front of us. "Bon appétit," he says, and we say grace before digging in. After two minutes of eating in silence, Calvin looks at me and starts laughing.

"What?" I ask, confused.

"My classy wife, licking her fingers while eating barbeque ribs is quite the sight to see."

"Be quiet. No matter how many houses and luxury cars we may buy, I will still use my hands to eat ribs."

"Yet another reason why you're my ride or die chick." He winks and smears a dab of barbeque sauce on my nose.

"Calvin, I want to talk to you about something." I begin wiping the excess sauce off of my hands.

"What's that?"

"It's about Thanksgiving. I know it's a big deal with your family, so I won't ask you to miss it, but Michele invited all the girls to her house this year and I think I should go." I wait to see if I should respond using defense or offense.

"We've never missed the big holidays together, Candice."

Okay, let me prepare my defense.

"Baby I know, but with everything that's happened this year, I don't think I can take the pity looks from your family and then your mom and sisters judging me regarding the separation. I'm not ready to face it. Soon we can take a trip there, but I don't want to deal with that during Thanksgiving." I pause and wait for Calvin to think about the point I'm trying to make.

"Okay Candice. I don't like it, but I understand. My family can be a little intense and Thanksgiving would multiply that times a thousand."

"Yes, your mom and sisters love their baby boy Calvin."

Looking at me with a fake pout, Calvin asks, "I thought that love extended to you also?"

Taking the rib out of his hand and kissing his barbeque flavored lips, I whisper, "Oh it most certainly does, Mr. Montgomery. Let me show you."

Change of Plans

Michele

"Have a good evening Dr. Peterson," my secretary says as I pass her desk.

"You have a better one Joyce. Enjoy your vacation next week." I smile and then turn to walk out of the administration office. The holiday break cannot come soon enough. As much as I love my students, I am overdue for a break from the chronicles of campus life.

Getting into the car and throwing my briefcase on the passenger seat, I sit for a minute and look through my daily list of tasks on my phone. After reviewing the remaining items, I pull out of the parking lot and call Jeremiah.

"Hey baby," he says.

"Hi babe. How was your flight from New York?"

"The usual, hotel, construction site, airport, back home. I will be glad when the project is done. We are behind schedule and it's causing me to push start dates back for future projects. But enough of my day, how are my babies? I hate I came home to an empty house."

"Marley is still a daddy's girl and Mason wants to talk to you about PEE WEE football. I am on my way to pick them up now and take them to this sleepover weekend for the McConnell son's birthday. I already packed their overnight backs. Can you grab them and bring them downstairs?"

"Yes ma'am. Now that I know how my twins are doing, how is my wife?" he says seductively.

"Missing her husband like crazy."

"The sooner you can drop the kids off and get back home, the sooner I can show you how much I've missed you."

. . .

Pulling up to the studio, I make a phone call while I wait for the twins to finish their piano lessons.

"Hey Michele," Brooklyn says.

"Hey, are you stateside?"

"Yes, I am stateside for a whole ten days. I hope I don't have withdrawal from the sky life."

"Yes, well I am here if you feel a relapse coming. So, what's the agenda for tomorrow? I am trying to plan my day accordingly."

"Girl I am not sure. This is all Candice's idea. She should be here soon; I can tell her to call you. The extent of what I know is that she has some news to share. I can only assume it is about Calvin. I pray it's good news." Brooklyn sighs.

"Yes, God knows I have been praying for the two of them. I still can't believe she went through all of that without telling us."

"Yes, but it couldn't have been easy to talk about a second miscarriage, Michele. You remember the first one and how much she struggled through it and everyone kept talking about it or mentioning it when they saw her? I honestly can't blame her for wanting to avoid reliving the pain over and over again when someone brings it up."

"Yes, I guess I didn't think about it like that. We all need to do a better job of checking up on each other."

"I won't disagree with that point," Brooklyn says as I see my twins running to the car and wave to their instructor standing at the door.

"Well I'll let you go. I will see you tomorrow, Brook. Love you Honey."

Opening the trunk, I meet the twins at the back of my Yukon to load their bookbags before helping them buckle into their booster seats. While passing them their tablets, Marley says, "Mommy, we were learning Beethoven today."

"Yes, Mrs. Tucker says we need to practice every day at home before the upcoming recital," Mason informs me as if I don't already know.

"Okay, so that means less TV time and more practice on the weeknights. Do y'all agree?"

"Yes ma'am," they both say and nod in unison.

Turning onto the interstate towards home, I break the silent concentration my kids are giving their devices.

"Are you both ready for a sleepover weekend?"

"Yes!" Mason says with excitement, but Marley nods with a hesitant smile. Looking in the rearview mirror I lock eyes with my daughter.

"What is it sweetie? Do you not want to go?"

"No ma'am, I want to go it's just . . ." she pauses and turns to look at Mason. I can tell she doesn't want to sound like a baby in front of her brother.

"How about this, go to the sleepover and if at any time either of you want to come home, you call me. No matter the time of day or night. Deal?" I ask, looking at them both through the mirror for confirmation and I can see the worry leave Marley's face.

"Deal!" She smiles and returns her attention back to the tablet.

Pulling into the driveway, Jeremiah opens the front door holding two overnight bags.

"Daddy!" they both yell in unison.

"Wait in the car you two," I instruct as I open the trunk and swap the twins' bookbags for the duffel bags.

"Hi baby." I kiss my husband softly.

"Ewww gross," Mason says from the backseat. Walking over to Marley's side, Jeremiah opens the back door of the car.

"Hey baby girl. How's daddy's little princess?" Reaching as far as the seatbelt will allow, Marley stretches her arms to wrap around her dad's neck.

"Hey daddy! How was your trip? Did you bring us back anything?"

"It was good and yes I did. You can get it when you get back from your sleepover. Little man! Have you been practicing our handshake?" Redirecting his attention to Mason. "Let me see it." He stretches his hand over to Mason's side to perform their secret boy's handshake.

"I always forget the last part." Mason pouts and then promises, "I'll keep practicing."

"That's my boy. You two have fun. I will see you tomorrow. I love you."

"Love you too dad," they both yell and wave as he closes the door.

"And I love you too mommy. Hurry back," he says, playfully patting my backside as I get into the driver's seat.

...

Meet at Riley's at seven o'clock, use your key is the text message I receive while getting dressed to meet the girls for dinner. I decide not to question the secrecy or short notice.

Pulling up to Riley's, I notice neither Candice nor Brooklyn's car is in the driveway. Using my key as instructed, I walk inside Riley's house and wait in the living room. I always admired Riley's taste of decoration and her love for the safari theme. Turning the TV on to wait for the group's arrival, I call to check on the twins.

Just as I end the call, I hear the front door open.

"Hey Michele."

"Hey Riley."

"Change of plans, one of my surgeries ran over so I told Candice that we could do the dinner here. Feel free to kick your heels off and grab a pair of socks out of my top drawer."

I would have worn sweats if I had known we were staying in for dinner.

"Thank you," I say trying to sound nonchalant, but I secretly hate not being included when plans change.

"Let me go freshen up and then I'll join you. Brook and Candice should be here shortly, they stopped to pick up wine and dinner." She disappears to her bathroom.

Taking off my shoes and jacket, I go into Riley's room to get a pair of socks to protect my feet from her cold hardwood floor.

I guess everyone decided to have a full conversation about the evening without me. Ever since I had the twins, I've always felt like the lone wolf in the group. Brooklyn and Candice are joined at the hip and Riley is just off doing her own thing. It's like everyone assumes I'm too preoccupied to be included anymore.

Rolling my eyes at my childish jealousy, I grab the first pair of socks I can find from Riley's dresser and walk back into the living room.

Twenty minutes of strolling through emails on my phone, I hear the front door open once again.

"Hello," Brooklyn says walking in carrying two take out bags. Candice is right behind her.

"Hi beauties," I greet them walking over to help place the food and drinks on the counter. We begin embracing each other and searching Riley's cabinets for wine glasses and plates.

"I'm so happy we are all together," Candice says

"So, are you going to give us this much anticipated update?" I blurt out.

"Yes, but I am not the only one with an update."

Just as our interest piques, Riley walks into the room. "Hey ladies, something smells good."

"I was craving Chinese so I'm forcing it on you all for dinner." Brooklyn shrugs her shoulders as she takes a sip of wine.

As we all fix our plates and sit around the coffee table in the living room, Riley, Brooklyn, and myself all look at each other and then fervently look to Candice. Looking up from her plate, she smiles, "Okay fine. I'll start."

I Didn't Know How to Tell You All
I Needed You

Candice

Taking a sip of wine, I gather my thoughts as my girls sit patiently waiting for me to speak.

"First off, God places people in your life that afford you the option to choose *not* to carry some burdens alone. I didn't realize that at the time, so I chose to carry this burden on my own until it completely broke me down. As a result, I broke away from my family, my husband, and my friends. I started buying materialistic things that didn't matter. Cars, clothes, jewelry, and almost another house here in Charlotte—anything to try and fill the void. I went to such a dark place that I had lost myself and I blamed everyone and everything for the hurt I was feeling."

"I did not intentionally keep things from you all, but I also didn't know how to say it aloud to anyone. Once I talked about it, it would become real and I wasn't ready to face that reality . . . not then." I take a sip of wine, trying to steady my nerves.

This will be the last time I talk about my miscarriages, so I want to make sure I get it all out now. I will always love my baby boy, but the pain is too much to keep reliving.

"You guys, we have a . . ." I clear my throat to keep from choking on the words, "*had* a son, Calvin Sylvester Montgomery Jr. At the beginning of my third trimester, I had complications that resulted in me having to give birth to my stillborn son. We hadn't told anyone, outside of immediate family, that I was even pregnant because of the miscarriage with the first baby. I couldn't bring myself to tell anyone I had lost our son because it was just too painful to bear. It had gotten so bad that I was willing to push my husband away because of my fear of being infertile."

Before I can finish the sentence, Brook, Michele, and Riley all make their way next to me. As my voice cracks, I continue, "I didn't know how to tell you all I needed you, but I did need you."

Sobbing for a second, I look up to see my girls all sitting silently waiting for me to clear my head, my heart, and my conscious. "Once my book tour started, I used that as an excuse to isolate myself from personal problems and to focus on work. I talked to thousands of women about life experiences and cherishing people over possessions, not realizing I was preaching to myself but couldn't accept my own advice. I was completely losing who I was, that is until Brooklyn's favorite person came in town and checked me."

Smiling as she wipes a tear away, she asks, "Aunt May?"

"Yes, Aunt May. After avoiding her calls for months, she took matters into her own hands and made a trip from Germany to one of my events. That night we talked everything out. How I had lost my way and how I was trying to find meaning in the world again. When I lost CJ, I felt that same pain as when my parents died: alone and abandoned."

"She explained to me how I can't change what's going on around me until I change what's going on within me. I couldn't figure out what that meant until I invited you girls to my event here in Charlotte. I had been alone for so long, I forgot what it means to have sisters. You ladies are my family and I was missing my family," concluding my uninterrupted rant, I pause and allow my friends to smother me with hugs.

"Candice, we love you. I am so sorry you had to suffer through all of that," Riley says while Brooklyn and Michele nod in unison.

"My nephew is in a better place. I just thank God his mommy was able to find her strength again," Brooklyn says and places her head on my shoulder.

"It was tough Brook, real tough."

Wiping my tears, I take a deep breath to settle my nerves and try to change the mood.

"So, fast-forwarding to today. I am in a better place mentally and physically. Calvin and I are in counseling with breakthroughs that have brought us closer together than ever. The divorce is off, the marriage is still on, I have my girls back in my life and . . ." I pause for dramatic effect, "I just signed a contract to turn *Life After 25* into a motion picture!"

On cue, everyone screams.

"Candice! This is exciting. I'm so happy for you," Michele says, clapping with joy.

"Girl! So, we're going to Hollywood?" Brooklyn stands and starts dancing.

"Yes, we are going to Hollywood!"

As the excitement settles, I look down at the table with plates still full of cold Chinese food. "Would y'all like to move to the kitchen to warm our food up?"

"Yes, let's try to do this dinner thing again." Michele laughs.

As we place our food in the microwave and sit to the kitchen table, I look over at Riley smiling at her phone. "Brook and Michele, remember when I said I'm not the only one with an update?"

Before I could finish my question, they both turn to Riley as she looks up from her phone.

"What?" she says innocently.

"You know exactly what Dr. Harper, spill the tea!"

With a lifted eyebrow, we all take a sip of our wine and look at Riley.

"Okay fine. I met a guy. We went on a date. I'm in love. End of story," she says nonchalantly, and I almost spit my wine out.

"You're in love? No ma'am we need details. Start at the beginning and don't leave a single word out," Brooklyn says as we all scoot our chairs in closer.

"You guys, he is amazing. His name is Jameson, Dr. Jameson Young. He's the Chief of Cardiothoracic at the hospital," she pauses knowing we need time to relish in this bit of information.

"So, did he just sweep you off of your feet before or after a surgery?" Michele asks teasingly.

"No, it wasn't like that, at first. He was really persistent and patient. He let me fall for him on my own terms and he never forced anything. The night I introduced him to Blythe, I told him, "I love you." It didn't matter if he said it back. I knew how I felt and I knew I couldn't hold it in any longer."

"This man has met my goddaughter *and* you told him that you love him? Riley!" Brooklyn can no longer contain herself.

"Yes, I love him and he's crazy about me. I struggled trying to downplay how I felt because it has been only a short time but when you know, you just know I guess."

"Sweetie, I am so happy for you. You deserve all the happiness in the world. This Dr. Young must be an amazing man because you are just glowing! I can't wait to meet the man that has Riley Harper sprung," I tease and sip some more wine.

"Well feel free to invite him to Thanksgiving dinner," Michele says, and Riley shakes her head.

"Thank you but he has not met my parents yet and we don't want that to be the first time he meets Dr. Braxton and Veronica Harper."

"Oh no! You have to prep him thoroughly before meeting your parents." We all laugh and reminisce on Riley's old boyfriends her parents chewed up in the past.

"Well he'll definitely get brownie points for being a surgeon, and a heart surgeon at that," I add.

"Could Mr. Heart Surgeon be the one to taste the forbidden fruit?" Brooklyn says playfully.

"It's always about sex with you isn't it?" Riley rolls her eyes.

"What? Everyone else was thinking it!"

"I mean since Brooklyn brought it up, inquiring minds would like to know. Are you keeping your pledge of celibacy until marriage?" Michele adds.

"I would be lying if I said the thought hasn't crossed my mind. In seventeen years, I've never met a man who makes me feel the way Jameson does, so it scares me to think about what happens if he decides he doesn't want to wait," she says, and I can tell this is a delicate subject.

"I'm sorry Riley. I didn't bring it up to make you feel bad. I'm just excited for the day someone loves you *and* makes love to you the way you deserve," Brooklyn says trying to lighten the mood.

"I know. I just have a bad habit of getting in my head sometimes. But anyway, that's my news—would anyone else like to share an update?"

Riley and I look at Michele and Brooklyn. Michele shakes her head and shrugs and Brooklyn shakes her head but looks off to the side.

A clear sign that she is lying but I chose not to call her out on it, at least not yet.

Detective Montgomery

Brooklyn

"Happy Thanksgiving," Candice says walking into the kitchen.

"Happy Thanksgiving to you. Jamaican Blue or Columbian?"

"Always Jamaican," she says as I hold two coffee cans up, "You may want to add a splash of bourbon or cognac to help us get through this dinner."

She may be on to something with that idea.

"How is Calvin handling you missing your first Thanksgiving together in over a decade?" I ask aware of the extent of my question.

"He says he doesn't like it, but he understands. I'm not quite ready to deal with his family. He and I are really good now, but you know once he told his mom and sisters about the separation, I became the *Evil Queen*. This is a prime example why you shouldn't discuss problems in your home because you may forgive them, but your family will bring it up every chance they get."

"Girl that's the truth!" I place the mug and agave sweetener in front of her. "Well I, for one, am glad you're here. I didn't feel like dealing with my family this year so I'm happy to have the gang back together."

Taking a sip of her coffee, Candice tilts her head.

"Do you want to talk about it? That's the second time you've brought it up."

"Not really, it's the same old tale. I get hit up for money. I say no. I'm the bad guy. This year I decided not to go home to avoid the guilt trip that would ultimately end with me giving in to the request. I'd leave Wilmington hundreds, sometimes thousands, of dollars broker than I came just to stop hearing the complaints," I say and shrug. "They are still my family and I love them but I'm no one's punching bag or personal ATM."

Raising her coffee mug in the air she says, "I'll toast to that. What time did Michele ask us to arrive?"

"I think three o'clock. We are tasked to bring ice and sodas. She clearly knows neither of us are trying to cook a dish. I'm going to the gym for a workout before I eat my weight in fried turkey and banana pudding." I finish my cup and walk to my master suite.

On my way to the gym, I call my mom.

"Happy Thanksgiving Brooklyn. Hold on. Jakayla put that down and get out of my kitchen before you make my cake fall. Go outside and play with your cousins," she reprimands my niece then softens her voice again. "Are you already at Michele's house? Tell everyone I said hello and Happy Thanksgiving."

"No, we don't have to be there for a couple of hours. Candice and I are still at my house," I say and begin to feel a little guilty for letting pettiness stop me from going home for the holidays.

"Well good. You know you'll be missed here. Everyone keeps asking what time you are coming in town and I just have to break their hearts by telling them you aren't coming."

My mom loves to be overdramatic with everything. I guess I can thank her for my over-the-top behavior.

"I doubt *everyone* will miss me." I reference my sisters.

"Even Wanda and Tracy. Y'all need to stop all of that bickering or at least put it on hold for the holidays. Don't let them or any amount of drama keep you from ever coming back home Brooklyn. We are still your family." My guilt rises even more.

"I know mom but they know how to get under my skin. I didn't tell them to have all of those kids."

I hate how petty and ugly I sound right now.

"Now you stop that Brooklyn Antoinette James. Today is about family and thankfulness. I will not stand for any of *that*. Not today!" she scolds.

"Yes ma'am. I love you and tell everyone I said hi." I hang up before saying anything else I can't take back.

· · ·

Walking out of the convenience store, I place the bags of ice and sodas in the trunk and open the driver's door to get in. Candice hops in the passenger's seat and tosses me a bag of potato chips saying, "You already know dinner isn't done yet, this should hold us."

"Good idea and Michele hates it when you try to sample food before dinner is served."

As I pull onto the highway, Candice turns the music down. "Brooklyn, I have a question."

"Well it must be serious if you have to turn the music down. I really like that song. Please, ask away." I look over to try and gauge her expression.

"The other night at Riley's when she asked if anyone else had an update, you shook your head but looked away. You are a terrible liar best friend. My question is, was that look about your family or something else?"

How in the heck does she remember a slight glance? How does she still know me so well even after all of these years?

"Okay fine. Yes, I am a terrible liar. You, however, are too observant," I tease.

"True but that doesn't answer my question. I have laid every single one of my burdens down by the riverside, what are you hiding Brooklyn James?"

"Okay Detective Montgomery," I say sarcastically, "Shortly after you went back to Atlanta, I took a trip to Brazil. When I was there, I ran into Malcolm." With a confused look on her face, she doesn't say a word.

"Malcolm Diamond," I add.

"You're lying! Malcolm, Michele's brother? I haven't seen him in years. What is he up to and what . . ." She pauses as her mind tries to connect invisible dots and then screams.

"Brooklyn! You didn't? Was it good? Wait, you would've told me if it was just a fling. Was there something more? You have to tell me before we get to the house. Is he going to be there today? Is this the real reason you are staying in Charlotte for the holidays? Why is your life more eventful than any book I can think to write?" She rants nonstop and I just continue to drive and smile.

"Are you done?" I turn and laugh at Candice slowly shaking her head in disbelief. "*Now,* do you see why I opted not to say anything at Riley's?"

"Yes I'm done, the floor is all yours."

"I will tell you but you have to promise this discussion does not leave my car. Especially today!" I look over for confirmation as she nods.

"When I was in Brazil, Malcolm and I ran into each other and ended up spending my entire trip together. I'm not sure what it is, Candice, but there is something different about him. For the entire trip, I was on cloud nine. We visited the favelas, Christ the Redeemer, and kissed at the top of Sugar Loaf Mountain at sunset." I pause realizing how crazy I sound.

"That sounds good and all, but I feel like there's more. What's the *more* that you are not telling?" She asks.

Why doesn't she just leave well enough alone?

"I honestly don't know. In Brazil I felt something but once I returned stateside, we talked a few times but nothing of substance which leads me to believe it might be more like a fling to him. He is known for being quite the womanizer," I admit.

"We made love on beaches in Brazil and opened up to each other. I felt a spark that I had forgot even existed. If he feels something more then he will have to tell me because I refuse to overthink this and end up looking stupid,"

I hate I am coming off sounding so bitter and hurt.

"Well, it sounds like you came back from South America with good memories, nonetheless. Do you know if he will be here today?" she asks once more.

I'm now annoyed talking about this.

"I'm not sure. I think I mentioned it, but we shall find out in a few."

As we walk up Michele's driveway, I look around in search of Malcolm.

You have no idea what kind of car this man drives.

"Happy Thanksgiving ladies," Jeremiah greets us as he opens the door.

"Hi Jeremiah," we say in a playful tone like young schoolgirls.

"The ladies are in the kitchen. Let me take those bags," he says as he takes the two bags of ice from each of our hands.

Stepping into the kitchen, everyone is in aprons cutting, stirring, or peeling something. Already knowing the routine, Candice and I grab aprons and begin chopping and mixing as well.

"I will leave you ladies to it," Jeremiah says before kissing Michele on the cheek.

"Bye Jeremiah," Riley, Candice, and I say in the playful tone again before bursting out laughing.

"Y'all are going to stop embarrassing my man like that." Michele laughs as Mrs. Harper walks over to give us a hug.

"Hello daughters. How have you been? It has been too long since I've seen you."

"I am well Mrs. Harper, blessed and highly favored as one would say." I smile and I walk over to stir the collard greens.

"Amen to that, sugar. Would you ladies like a glass of wine?" We both look at her with a tilted head. "I'll take that as a yes."

Wanting to make one final attempt to search for Malcolm I say, "Where are my nieces and nephew?"

Wiping flour on her apron, Riley says, "Blythe is in the den with the guys watching football but most likely on her phone and I think the twins are upstairs."

Walking into the living room I greet everyone and chat a little with Blythe but still no Malcolm. Giving up on the failed mission, I walk upstairs to play with the twins.

"Auntie Brook!" they both sing in unison.

"Hey my babies. How are auntie's twins doing?"

"We are good Auntie Brook. I'm beating Mason at his racing game," Marley brags.

"Auntie Brook, Marley's cheating, she keeps running me off the road when the race begins," Mason pouts. "I'm going to get her back."

"Let me try to beat her." I squeeze between the two of them on the floor and he hands me the Xbox controller.

"No Auntie Brook, I'm going to beat you," Marley says as we start the race.

Marjorie Diamond

Michele

After I finish spreading butter cream icing on the twins' favorite red velvet cake, I call to check on my parents. "Hey Chele Bear. We will be there in less than thirty minutes. We had some car trouble and had to call Malcolm to pick us up," my mom says without waiting for me to greet her back.

"Is everything okay? Are y'all okay?" I begin to feel guilty knowing I was calling to fuss about her tardiness.

"Yes Suga, we are fine. Your father insisted on driving that old Chevy to Charlotte. I told him that old bucket of metal needs to be sold for parts, but he swears up and down that it's a classic and it needs to see the open road every now and again. We had to drive all the way from Alabama with no air condition and an old eight-track stereo that only played two tracks."

I explicitly remember how miserable family road trips were in that busted old car.

"Okay well I will see you soon. Remind Malcolm not to forget to stop and buy two packs of playing cards. Jeremiah's dad spilled bourbon on the ones we had." I hang up and begin icing my husband's favorite carrot cake.

"Was that your mother Dear? Are your parents coming?" Mrs. Harper asks already knowing the answer from eavesdropping.

"Yes, they were having car trouble. Malcolm picked them up and they are on the way."

"Excellent. I haven't seen Marjorie Diamond in years. It will be so lovely to catch up with her."

...

As we begin prepping the table with food, a beep from the security system informs me the front door is open.

"Hello. Anybody home?" a male voice says.

"Malcolm, what's going on my man," Jeremiah walks to greet them at the front door.

"Just living my brother."

"Where is my handsome son-in-law," my mother says walking in behind Malcolm.

"Hey Momma," Jeremiah says kissing her on the cheek.

"Hey Baby. You and Malcolm go out there and help Clyde get my sweet potato pies out of the backseat."

"Hey Mom," I say walking over to get the bags out of her hands.

She always insists on bringing her entire kitchen when she has to travel for the holidays.

"Hey my Chele Bear. Where are my grandbabies?"

"They're upstairs, I'll go get them. Mrs. Harper, Riley, and Candice are in the kitchen getting dishes prepared to serve. I'll be back down in a second." I run upstairs realizing I haven't heard the twins in quite a while.

I wonder what is keeping them so quiet and occupied?

Opening the door to Mason's room, I discover my babies and my friend with their eyes glued to the television.

"What is going on in here?"

"Hey Mommy. We are taking turns trying to beat Auntie Brook in a race. She is still undefeated," Mason says, and I roll my eyes.

"You two go wash up for dinner." I wait for the twins to run off and help Brooklyn to her feet. "I can't believe you are in here playing this game like some big kid or is this just your way of avoiding helping to cook dinner?"

"What can I say? I'm just a girl who loves her video games." Brooklyn smiles.

"Everyone is here so we are about to eat."

Once we reach the bottom on the stairs, I see Jeremiah and Malcolm walk in behind my dad. "Hey baby sis," he says hugging me with pies in both hands.

Staring past me, I turn to see what he is looking at. "Oh Malcolm, you remember my friend Brooklyn from college, right?"

Farmer's Daughter

Michele

"Mom how much longer do we have to stay here?" I ask for the tenth time.

"Hush up child. Sit down on that crate and finish reading. I'll quiz you on it later," my mom says as she continues to help customers choose from a selection of vegetables from our home farm.

Every Saturday morning it was the same thing: waking up before the sun just to help my mom and dad set up this table to sell our picking of produce. Each week I would say a small prayer no one from school would walk by and spot me selling vegetables.

Fitting in in high school was already tough enough without being labeled a farmer's daughter.

Malcolm was the football star at our school and had practice on the weekend, so he always had the perfect excuse to sleep in. Since the only sport I was good at was running my mouth on the debate team, I was the chosen child to accompany my parents for a fun day at the Farmer's Market.

"Hey Marjorie," an older lady says as she walks up to the table.

"Hey Denise, I have some fresh okra just for you," my mother says with enthusiasm.

"You are always looking out for me. Those supermarkets try to charge you an arm and a leg for a little ole bag." I hold the book up to my face, in hopes that no one will recognize me.

Loading the truck to leave, I happily slam the tailgate and hop into the cabin of the old pickup truck. Sliding in the middle seat between my parents, my dad hops in and places his raggedy straw hat on my head and says, "Let's ride ladies."

"How far did you get in your book?" my mom says after five minutes down the long dirt road home.

"I finished it," I say and discreetly roll my eyes.

"Let me see the book." She holds her hand out for the worn paperback copy of *Their Eyes Were Watching God* by Zora Neale Hurston.

"Who's the person Janie is telling the story of her life to?" She begins flipping through pages.

"What?"

"I told you that I was going to quiz you when you finished."

Oh, she's serious.

She looks up and lifts a stern eyebrow. "*To whom* is Janie telling the story of her life? If you get any wrong, you're cooking the family dinner tonight."

"Pheoby. She's telling her life's story to Pheoby Watson."

"Okay good. Now for a tougher one, what is the direct cause of Tea Cake's death?"

Overly confident I smile and say, "A bite from a rabid dog."

As we pull up to the house, my dad yanks the gear shift into park. Passing me the book back, my mom unbuckles her seat belt and hops out.

"Nope. That is incorrect," she turns to help my father unload the truck, "Grab this box of beans and potatoes. I think your father wanted country fried steak and mash potatoes for dinner. Ain't that right Clyde?"

"That sounds darn good," my dad says. "I'll unload the truck. Get to it baby girl."

As my inner overachiever grows annoyed that I failed the pop quiz, I follow my mom into the house.

"What do you mean?" I refute but mindful not to raise my voice, "Tea Cake *did* get bit by a dog and died from rabies."

"Yes, he did have rabies but that was not my question. I ask you what the direct cause of his death was. He didn't immediately die from rabies; his direct cause of death was a rifle shot from Janie. Now come on, I'll help you wash and snap the ends off of the green beans for you to cook."

. . .

Growing up in a small town in Alabama and an even smaller house on the farm, there are three things my family cherished over everything else, God, family, and football. Every evening we were required to be home for dinner and every Sunday we had to be front and center at church. The only night they made an exception was Malcolm's Friday night football games. I, for one, hated going to any sporting event but my mom instilled in us at a very young age that *family supports family.*

"I'll see you tomorrow, Ms. Edwards." I smile at the librarian as I check out a few more books to get me through the daily ride home from school.

Malcolm transferred here his freshmen year to improve his chances of getting recognized by a college football scout. The school was on the more affluent side of the city and was a seventy-minute round trip each day, so my dad allowed him to drive the family car since football practices ran so late.

As a school teacher in a small rural town, my mom was a big advocate for any advantages when it came to education so when I was told I could skip the eighth grade and go straight to high school, she insisted I attend school with my big brother.

"Hey Pie Face," Malcolm teases as I approach him beside our dad's old Chevrolet.

"Hey Big Head, sorry I'm late. I got caught up in my homework and lost track of the time."

"It's cool, I know you hate waiting every afternoon for me to get out of practice." He throws my bookbag in the back seat, "Marjorie Diamond is going to kill us for being late to dinner though. Let's go."

Sexy Spades Partner for Dessert

Brooklyn

rozen dead in my tracks, I stare at Malcolm as he asks Michele to take the pies into the kitchen.

"Captain James."

Still unable to move, he steps closer and wraps his arms around me, causing his cologne to give me flashbacks of Brazil.

"It's so good to see you again Brooklyn," he whispers before discreetly nibbling on my left ear lobe. My entire body tingle, and I realize I have yet to say a word.

What is this man doing to me? Say something Brooklyn.

"It's good to be seen." I give myself an invisible hi-five for the witty comeback.

"Mmmm. Yes. It. Is," he says in a low moan licking his bottom lip and my legs almost fail me.

Walking into the dining room to join the group, I look over at Candice who is wide eyed and almost melting in her seat from the sight of Malcolm and I walking into the room together.

Rolling my eyes, I walk over and sit next to her as I am sure I will need her to help me get through dinner.

Before I can completely sit down, she squeezes my hand tightly, trying to use her eyes to ask a million and one questions. I simply pat the back of her hand twice and pull away.

"Control yourself. Please," I whisper and turn to my left to make small talk with Blythe.

"Are you having fun yet?" I tease Blythe.

"Not at all Auntie Brook." She rolls her eyes, "Could you help me with convincing mommy to let me meet my friends at the bowling alley after dinner? Please godmommy?"

"Will there be boys meeting you and *these friends* you speak of? Don't lie. I can't help you if you lie."

"Yes, but it will be a group of us. I am honestly going to meet Ashely and Jasmine, I can't necessarily control if Brandon and his friends will be there."

"And that is how we will sell it to your mother." I wink before joining hands to bless the food.

Just as I begin to bow my head to pray, I look over at Malcolm Diamond's beautifully chiseled body. He winks at me and before I know it, I squeeze Candice's hand. She looks up and then across the table as I whisper, "Lord help me, this man is finer than I remember."

...

As dinner progresses, we all have an above average helping of food until we can no longer chew.

Unable to take Malcolm out of my peripheral, Blythe nudges me, "Are you ready for *Operation Bail Blythe out of Boredom*?"

"You are something else. Wait thirty seconds and then follow me," I instruct Blythe as I tap Riley to follow me into the kitchen. Standing up from my chair, I can feel Malcolm's eyes on my every movement.

"What's going on?" Riley asks completely oblivious of tonight's events.

"Your daughter is going to walk in here in twenty seconds to help me ask your permission for her to go bowling with friends. Let her go. This dinner is boring for someone who is too old to play with the twins and too young to listen to adult conversation. If she is not back by curfew, I will personally help you drag her out of the bowling alley. Scouts honor," I say placing two fingers over my heart.

As instructed, Blythe walks in innocently and Riley rolls her eyes at me before turning around.

"Mommy, could I please go to the bowling alley with my friends?" Blythe looks at me and I wink.

"Yes Blythe, but how are you getting there?"

"Ashley and Jasmine said they can pick me up and I will be back before curfew I promise. Thank you, thank you, thank you mommy," she hugs Riley while giving me a secret hi-five behind her back.

"Go and say goodbye to everyone before you leave."

"Yes ma'am." Blythe runs excitedly out of the kitchen.

"You brought me in here because you knew I would say no to her at the table?" Riley turns and glares at me.

Shrugging my shoulders, I playfully kiss Riley on the cheeks, "It was a 50/50 chance."

Returning back to the table, Candice nudges me.

"Girl, he has not stopped looking toward the kitchen entrance since you left." I tap her on the thigh to silence her and pretend to have an interest in the group conversation going on at the table.

"What did I miss?" I ask aloud, not really caring if anyone responds.

"We're not talking about anything important. I am more interested to get on this card game. Any takers?" Michele's dad, Clyde Diamond, says.

"I'll be your partner," I say to him before glancing over at Malcolm.

"Oh yes. I get a good dinner *and* a sexy spades partner for dessert."

"You better watch it, Clyde," Mrs. Diamond says, "Don't get zapped in front of all these people."

"I think I'm going to catch the game with Nelson," Mr. Harper says as he joins Jeremiah's dad in the living room.

"Malcolm, let's go set the tables up on the patio and whoop these chumps," Jeremiah says.

"I'm with that brother-in-law." Malcolm winks at me. Once again, my legs get a little weak.

"That's a good idea Babe," Michele says, "Bring both of the tables from the garage and we can have a Mothers versus Daughters game."

"You know Riley and Candice can't play spades," I say jokingly.

"My baby sure can't." Mrs. Harper joins us, laughing, "But that's okay, Marjorie and I won't beat on them too bad."

"If y'all are talking about spades, I'll sit this one out and just enjoy listening to the trash talking," Candice says returning from the kitchen with Riley.

She looks at me then over in Malcolm's direction.

I knew I shouldn't have said anything to her.

"Sit near me, maybe you can learn a few things," I whisper to her and we both laugh, knowing exactly what my true intentions were. Getting next to Malcolm.

Sitting at the card table across from Clyde, I glance to the other table at Michele and Riley fussing over a lost game. Laughing to myself, I focus my attention back on the game in front of me.

"It's our turn to bid partner. This is the last hand and they need four books to win," Clyde says, "How many books do you have?"

Rearranging the order of my cards, I silently curse the hand I was dealt.

"I have one and a possible," I say with little assurance looking down at the only two face cards in my hand, a queen of clubs and an ace of spades.

Malcolm bends down to pick up a napkin the wind blew off of the table. On his way back up, he runs his finger up the back of my calf lifting my sundress. My body stiffens a little as I bite my lip to muffle an escaping moan.

"Let's go ten!" Clyde says confidently, destroying my unexpected high.

"Wait what? That's not how this works!"

"Are you sure?" Jeremiah and Malcolm look at each other stunned.

"I guess Pops has the good hand," Malcolm laughs.

"Yes, I'm sure. Just trust your partner. I got you," Clyde says, and I give a worried smile.

I hate losing but I always enjoy a wild and crazy round of spades.

"Okay partner. It's all on you. You win the hand and I'll collect the books." I throw my hands up to surrender control but not before giving Malcolm a side eye to acknowledge his mischievous actions under the table.

"One more book and we win," Malcolm says, smiling at me.

"Yes, y'all need to get the rest of these books or that's game for us," Jeremiah chimes in.

"Just play your hand Sucka," Clyde is unfazed.

I, however, have just been a pawn in whatever strategy Clyde is executing on this card table. He has somehow managed to win seven books to their three, with no help at all from my one and a possible bid. With three cards remaining in our hands and no spades left on the table, Malcolm plays a five of hearts. I freely place down an eight of heart, Jeremiah a four, and Clyde wins the round with a queen of hearts.

We need two books to win.

Clyde plays a ten of diamond, Malcolm plays a three of hearts, and I play a nine of clubs. We all look to Jeremiah.

"This game is way too intense." Candice scoots her chair in.

"I cannot believe this!" Jeremiah yells. He throws down a six of hearts.

"What!" Malcolm says shocked, "Partner, I figured you had something to win that book." I look at Clyde, who is still unfazed by the intensity of the game.

At this point, I am on the edge of my seat from the suspense.

"Last card," I say, now completely invested in the unfolding of events.

"You ready for this partner?" Clyde asks smiling at me.

I simply nod with anticipation, not really sure what is about to happen next. Clyde plays a five of clubs. I look down at the card in my hand, and then look back up at Clyde who is smiling.

How in the world did he do this?

"Your turn son," he says to Malcolm as he takes a sip of his bourbon.

Malcolm places down a seven of diamonds and I nonchalantly throw down my Queen of clubs. We all look back to Jeremiah who is lost for words.

"Man, I quit!" he says and throws his card across the table. Jack of clubs.

"That's game!" Clyde says and stands to give me a hi-five.

"O-M-G! That was the most intense game of spades I have ever seen!" Candice says and claps as my partner and I taunt the losing team.

"Now, that's how the old heads play spades. You youngsters are so caught up in those Jokers and wild cards, you forget to count the suits. I told you I had you partner." He gives me another hi-five.

"Who's next!" I yell and walk into the house.

Anesthesiolo-something or Another

Riley

"What is going on over there?" I ask as Candice pulls her chair up next to mine.

"Girl, Brooklyn and Mr. Clyde just ran a Boston on the guys when they thought they had the game won. Jeremiah is mad. You might have to go check on your husband."

"He doesn't like losing." Michele shakes her head and takes a sip of wine.

"Candice how are you darling?" my mother asks, "Riley tells me your book is going to Hollywood. I bet that is exciting. I am proud of you."

"Thank you," Candice says modestly.

"What? Hollywood? That's big-time baby girl!" Mrs. Diamond says, "I'll be sure to tell the girls at the church we need to plan a movie night soon. We've already read all of your books." We both smile and look over to Michele shaking her head at her mom's extra-ness.

I always enjoy Mrs. Diamond's supportive spirit. Every chance she got to leave the farm to cheer on her "Chele Bear" at school, she was right there. The loudest one, but she was always there. I also loved the homecooked meals and cakes she'd bring from the farm to campus when we returned from holiday breaks.

Heck I would trade mothers with her in a heartbeat.

"You ladies have all become something any mother would be proud of," Mrs. Diamond says. "My Chele Bear is a dean at her alma mater, Candice is an author, Riley here is an Anesthesiolo-something or another, and Brooklyn an international pilot. You ladies are truly what it means to be Phenomenal Black Women."

"I will definitely toast to that." My mother holds her wine glass in the air.

Returning our attention back to the card game, Mason runs up from playing in the yard with his sister and Clooney. "Mommy, can we go next door to play with Hendrix and Brandy?"

Michele takes a napkin to wipe the icing off of his face, "Yes, but ask your father to walk you over there so he can make sure it's okay with their mother, Yolanda. Oh, and take Clooney into the house." Mason runs over to Marley and their beloved dog and they all run inside.

My thoughts drift to Jameson.

What would our son look like? Do I want to have another child? I still need to have a talk with him about my celibacy. What's the right time to bring up that kind of conversation? Gosh, I miss him. Why is Connecticut so far?

"Riley, your turn," my mom says, snapping me back to reality. I throw down a card without paying attention to what has already been played.

"How is that baby of yours Riley?" Mrs. Diamond asks, "She ran out of here before I could get her to sing for me."

I smile, knowing how much Blythe hates to sing on command. "She's a great kid and growing up faster than I'm ready to admit. She'll be a freshman in college this time next year."

"Wait. Little Blythe is about to graduate already? Has she decided which school she will attend in the Fall?"

"Not yet, she's applying to a few schools."

"Charlotte A&T included," my mother adds proudly, looking at me and then to Michele and Candice.

"Yes, Charlotte A&T is on the list, but I want her to choose a school for her, not for me."

"Regardless, I am sure she will make you proud," Mrs. Diamond says as she slams her card down. "Game! We win again chumps."

Check His Ego at the Door

Brooklyn

*R*eturning into the house after an epic and unexpected victory in spades, I twist the knob to discover someone is already occupying the downstairs bathroom. Walking back into the living room, I glance over at the men watching the football game and then proceed to make my way upstairs. Just as I reach the twin's bathroom at the end of the hall, I turn around to see Malcolm holding two suitcases in his hands.

"What are you doing up here?"

"I was bringing my parent's luggage into the guest room. Why are you up here?" He places the luggage down and slowly glides toward me.

"I was . . ." Before I can finish my thought, he pins me against the wall and kisses me. Hard.

Holding both of my wrists above my head, I can feel Michele's family pictures on the wall shift as our hands and lips dance with each other.

Pulling away from me breathless he says, "I have wanted to do that since I saw you standing at the bottom of the stairs."

Feeling heady, I look up trying to piece together what just happened. Still unable to find my words or my equilibrium, I remain on my tip toes, holding onto Malcolm's broad shoulders.

"Brooklyn, I have not been able to stop thinking about you since Brazil. You know how to leave quite the impression on a man." He grazes my collarbone with his lips. My insides throb.

"Malcolm, I haven't stopped thinking about you either," I admit as I finally find my footing and let go of his shoulders. Still holding my waist, he pulls me closer and plants back to back kisses.

He walks back downstairs first and then I follow a few minutes later to avoid suspicion. Upon my return, we lock eyes. He's sitting with Jeremiah and all of the men discussing football. Blushing from the thought of him touching me, I turn to walk into the kitchen.

"Girl where have you been?" Candice whispers as she looks at the table where Mrs. Harper, Michele, and Riley are sitting.

"I was using the upstairs restroom." I prance innocently towards the pan of banana pudding.

"Brooklyn," Mrs. Harper says, "Come and join us. I want to hear about some of those exciting countries you've visited."

Just as I begin to dig into a few travel stories, Michele's mom walks in. "Hey Sugas, what did I miss?"

"I asked Brooklyn to tell me about some of these fabulous countries she has visited over the years," Mrs. Harper responds.

"Oh yes, I'm sure you have stories for days and men to match the destinations." We all laugh.

My friends laugh especially hard because they know there is some truth to her statement.

"Good girls never kiss and tell," I tease and place a scoop of pudding in my mouth.

"I know that's right Suga," Mrs. Diamond says as she holds up a fork full of pie. "To the places we've seen and the men who've seen us."

"I like you Brooklyn. You're successful, beautiful, *and* smart," she says and we all stare trying to figure out what she is about to say next. "I wish my Malcolm would bring someone like you home." I laugh nervously and look over at Candice who is about to slide off of her barstool.

"Well thank you Mrs. Diamond, I'm flattered."

"Mom, you know Malcolm isn't trying to settle down. He thinks he is twenty-five and still in the league, chasing women," Michele says and a little piece of me dies on the inside.

I need to change the subject. I don't want to hear about this.

"That may be the case now but it just means he hasn't met his match. When a man meets a woman that forces him to check his ego at the door, that's the woman he will move heaven and earth to build a home for," she says. Talking to Mrs. Diamond and Mrs. Harper makes me miss my own mother.

"You said a mouthful there Marjorie," Mrs. Harper says and looks at Riley but decides not to say anything. I can almost see the tension release from Riley's shoulders when she eyes her mom to back down.

"Well ladies, it is getting late and we really must get going. Michele, thank you for inviting us to your lovely home. This has been a Thanksgiving to remember. Marjorie, we mustn't wait so long to see each other again. Let me go and round up my husband," Mrs. Harper says.

"Yes, I think we are about to head out as well Michele," I say looking around for Candice who is nowhere in sight.

"I can stay and help if you need," Riley adds. "Blythe ditched me to go with her friends this evening."

"No that's okay, you go ahead. I will help Chele clean up. It'll give us some time to bond and for me to show her how to repurpose the collard green juice," Mrs. Diamond says.

"Yes ma'am. Well in that case, I will get going also."

Walking over to Michele, we extend our hugs, kisses, and goodbyes. "Thank you for dinner. Everything was amazing." I leave her and Riley in the kitchen to search for Candice.

Stepping outside, I find Candice leaning against the car ending a conversation. Once she hangs up, I walk closer.

"Is everything okay?"

"Yes, I had a missed call from Calvin. I called back but it went to voicemail. He probably wanted to check on me since this is our first Thanksgiving apart since we met."

"I know. I expected him to pop up after we blessed the food in a dramatic Calvin Montgomery fashion." I attempt cheer her up.

"Girl, that is definitely something my husband would do. Is everyone leaving?"

Just as I part my lips to answer, the front door opens. Turning around, I find Malcolm walking toward my car.

"Wow Captain James. Is this your ride? I like it. It's so fitting." His smile causes my cheeks to rouge. "Are you leaving as well? May I join you?"

I look at Candice, trying to weigh my options.

I really want to see him, but I can't just ditch my girl. She seems a little sad after that phone call. But I really need to see what his intentions are after the recent conversation his mom and Michele had.

Before I can respond, Candice makes the call.

"Hey, I'll take the car to Riley's and see you tomorrow, okay?" She winks at me and holds her hand out for the keys.

"Okay. I'll see you tomorrow." I place the key fob in her hand and silently mouth *thank you.*

"Umm hmm," she mumbles sarcastically and returns to the house.

Turning around to this fine pillar of sexy behind me, I bite my lip seductively and whisper, "Malcolm would you mind giving me a ride?"

Without a second thought, he guides me to the passenger side of his carbon black Aston Martin and holds open the door.

"After you, madam."

I slide into the plush leather seats and eye the front door, praying no one walks outside and spots us.

Pulling onto the main highway, Malcolm reaches over to grab my hand. I attentively watch as he raises it to his lips and tenderly kisses the back.

"Brooklyn how is it that you are more beautiful than the last time I saw you? How've you been?"

"I've been well. Working and traveling for the most part."

"Isn't that one in the same?" His smile causes me to shift in the seat to distract my inner goddess.

"Fair point. When I left you in Brazil, you had a follow up meeting with the South American Football Federation, were you and your partner able to secure a contract?" I ask not really caring but wanting him to know I remembered.

"Yes, we did. Thank you for asking. We signed a two-year contract for all football teams in South America."

"That's amazing Malcolm, congratulations!" I lean over to kiss his cheek. The stubble from his beard connects with my lips, and I salivate.

"Thank you but enough about work, let's go do something fun. Are you down?" he asks and I nod with excitement.

Turning off the interstate, we arrive at *Jake's*, a bar with a banner on the window that says *Karaoke, Wings, and Beer.* Giving his best boyish grin, Malcolm asks, "Do you like karaoke?"

"I am not much of a singer."

"Perfect, neither am I."

The building looks small on the outside but the inside is quite spacious and filled with billiard tables, bar games, and a small stage for karaoke.

"Find us a pool table and I'll get some drinks," Malcolm says leaning into my ear so I can hear him over the noise.

Searching for an available table, I catch the eye of a few men staring. Normally, I would have given them a flirty smile, but I was with Malcolm Diamond. I was so into him that no one else was even worthy of a glance. Sitting next to an empty table, I place two pool sticks on top as a sign of occupancy.

Using my phone to avoid awkward eye contact while I wait, I look up and lock eyes with Malcolm walking from the bar. He is holding two bottles of beer in one hand and a rack of billiard balls in the other. I put my phone in my purse to give him my full attention.

The short distance from the bar to the table is all it takes to electrify the spark between us. For a second, we just stare at each other as if no one else is in the room but the two of us.

Placing the bottles down on the table behind me he says, "I am going to apologize in advance if you catch me staring too hard." I blush a little and begin to rack the table for a round of 8-ball.

Lining the balls up to my liking, I remove the rack and pass a pool stick to him. "Since I racked them, you can break," I say seductively.

"Yes ma'am." As he reaches for the stick, he makes sure to touch my hand in the process. "Let's make this interesting. If I make a shot, I get to ask you a question. If you make a shot, the floor is yours."

I nod and take a sip of the beer, frowning at the aftertaste.

I am not a fan of beer, but it didn't matter, I am on cloud nine at the thought of spending time with my Brazilian rendezvous.

Malcolm positions himself behind the cue ball, trying to measure the strength of his shot. I notice the muscles on his arm flex as I squirm in my seat. My eyes are fixated on the thin sweater hugging his rock-hard abs and I bite down on my bottom lip just thinking about touching him.

"Brook. You're turn."

"Huh. Oh, yes." I try to play it cool as if I was staring at something behind him.

"I have high balls *and* I have two questions."

"Ask away." I say as I make sure to brush up against him while I analyze my next shot.

"Careful Captain James, if you keep that up, we may leave this bar sooner than planned." My insides jump.

Fine by me.

"Your question Mr. Diamond," I say and slowly bend down in front of him to take my next shot. This shot choice did not give me the best chance of getting a ball in the pocket, but it will definitely increase my shot of keeping Malcolm's attention.

"Do you prefer the mountains or the ocean, and why?"

"That's technically two questions, but I will give you a pass just this once." I reach for the beer, intentionally brushing my hand against his arm.

"I'll have to think of a way to show my gratitude," he says as I walk back over to the table and quickly make my shot.

"Ocean. I love the sound of the water, the miles of blue waves when looking out of an airplane window, and the fact that there is still so much of it that we have yet to explore."

Why must I sound so nerdy at times?

"Good answer Captain James."

Walking behind me, he kisses the nape of my neck. I press my hips backwards into him, tightening my grip on the pool stick for balance.

"I have a shot right here, but I am enjoying the view far too much to ask you to move," he whispers while nibbling my ear. I move back to the barstool and take another sip of beer to slow my breathing.

Malcolm does something to me.

"Next question. List three things you find attractive in a man."

Taking a moment to think about my answer, I gaze once again at Malcolm's chiseled body in that sweater and jeans and lose my nerve.

"His mind, his heart . . . and his body." I bite my lip a little to distract other parts of my body.

"You're going to have to stop biting your lip Brooklyn. I can't focus."

"Okay, my turn," I say, "What is your greatest accomplishment?"

Looking attentively, he pauses before answering. "I haven't accomplished it yet, but it would be to have a family."

"I get that. You want children for your legacy."

"No, I said a *family*. I want the whole package. Wife, kids, house on the lake, minivan at the soccer games."

"Like your sister," I mumble and examine the table for a high percentage shot.

"Yes, I've outgrown the *playboy* lifestyle and ultimately, I want what my sister has and what my parents have."

"I don't think I could drive a minivan." I laugh trying to lighten the mood.

"So, you're already seeing yourself as part of my accomplishment?" He tugs my arm forcing me into his space.

"No, I was just saying . . ." My words are silenced with a kiss.

I look down at the table and notice that there are a lot more of my balls still standing than Malcolm's. Finishing the last swig of beer, I say seductively, "It appears you've won, any more questions?"

"Yes, just one. Your place or mine?"

Thirty-Two Hearts

Candice

Walking back into the house, I make my rounds into the kitchen and living room to say goodbye to everyone. I grab Riley's arm as she walks toward the door.

"I'll walk out with you."

She looks at me confused, "Okay. I think Brooklyn is outside waiting for you. She just said her goodbyes. Did you not see her?"

Without saying a word, I continue walking out of the house until we close the front door.

"Brooklyn already left," I inform her. "I will follow you and crash at your place tonight. I'll tell you all about it once we get there."

"Y'all are always leaving me out of the good stuff!" She rolls her eyes and walks to her car.

...

"Okay, spill it," she commands before I can even take a second step into the house.

"But I need some jammies."

"You'll get some *jammies* when I know what the heck is going on."

"Okay. Fine. Brooklyn and Malcolm's paths kind of crossed once or twice before today. She wanted to spend the evening with him at her place, so I decided to come and hang with you," I say innocently and walk over to the couch.

"Wait, what?!" Riley throws a couch pillow at me. "You mean to tell me the entire evening those two secret lovers pretended they hadn't seen each other in years? How did I miss this?"

I throw the pillow back at her as she sits down. "Girl I don't know. It took everything in me to keep a straight face."

"Is it just a fling or more than that?" she asks, and I choose to keep Brook's trust by deflecting.

"I don't know. You will have to ask her that for yourself. I just didn't want to walk out of her guest room and see something that can't be unseen so that's why I'm here."

...

Stepping out of the shower, I call my husband to end our epic game of phone tag.

"Hey Love. Let me step into this room so I can hear you," he says as the noises in the background go silent.

"Hi, Honey, I miss you."

I really mean it. Seeing Brooklyn and Malcolm lust after each other makes me want to go home to my husband.

"I miss you more Baby. You have no idea. Next year I don't care where we spend Thanksgiving—here, Michele's place, or in the middle of the Atlantic Ocean, I want us to be together."

"I agree. This is the first and last, I promise. How are your mother and sisters doing?"

"They are good. My Mom says she was sad not being able to see you, but I told her we would make a trip back soon, so she's good. My sisters and everyone else say hello. I will say, I can understand why you opted not to come. It's been a bit much, even for me. I am tired of accepting condolences for my loss from everyone that walks into the house," he says and then goes silent.

"Calvin it's not easy but we will manage. People love and care about us, so they think that *giving their condolences* for the miscarriage helps even though it just pours salt on an open wound. I had a good day here though. Michele's mom is still as wild as ever, but I love her. Everyone says hi."

I try to change the mood.

After thirty more minutes on the phone listening to Calvin talk about old buddies he ran into from high school, I end the conversation.

"Honey, I'll let you go enjoy your family. Tell everyone I love them, and

I love you with all my heart," I say blowing kisses through the phone.

"Love you more Babe."

Walking out of the guest room, I hear Riley at the end of the hall in her room. Stepping into the room, I find her also ending a call similar to mine.

"Goodnight darling, I love you too," she says and blushes when she discovers me eavesdropping.

"Oh. My. Goodness. Riley Harper is in love!"

"Yes, yes I am."

"Tell me more. You gave us the watered-down version the other night. Where is he from? What is he like? Can I see a picture? I bet he is fine!" I bombard her with questions as I snuggle up next to her.

With each question, she turns a darker shade of red. Pulling out her phone, she opens his social media page.

"Riley! Girl he is *fuuhhh-ine*! Where did you find him?"

I am thoroughly impressed my girl snagged her a young, fine, heart surgeon.

"In the operating room I guess. I know he is a little younger than me but Candice, he is the man of my dreams. I don't think I have ever felt this way about any man. When I am around him, nothing else in the room matters and when I'm not, I think about the next time I can be with him."

"Oh wow! The other night you said you told him you love him. Did he say it back?" I ask trying to make sure my friend is still protecting her heart.

"Not at that exact moment, so you know I went home trying to wrap my brain around every little detail. Replaying the entire evening over and over in my head. I even tried to decode his good morning text message," she says. I almost want to throw my invisible red flag, but I choose to remain quiet and listen.

"The next day, during one of our surgeries together, he was cool, calm, and collected while I was slowly dying with each passing moment. After battling my emotions for the entire three hours of surgery, I walked out of the O.R. and convinced myself I was a fool and had been played. Just as I was about to go sit in my car and cry my eyes out, one of the nurses stopped me and handed me an envelope with my name across the front."

Riley gets up from the bed to get a red photo album off of her dresser. She hands it to me and smiles.

Opening the first page of the album, there are eight blank boxes drawn together in the middle resembling a crossword puzzle. Just above the puzzle, in bold font are the words, "32 Reasons Why . . ."

Still a little confused, I read the title twice more and then look at the empty crossword puzzle boxes trying to solve the riddle. Looking up at Riley I confess.

"I don't get it, but I want to so bad."

She smiles and turn the page to the words *I LOVE YOU* written in large bold letters.

"Riley! He made this? What is it?" I say flipping through the pages of medical words and pictures of different hearts as my eyes begin to water.

"He told me that the night after dinner with Blythe and I, he went home and kicked himself for not saying it back even though he had no doubt in his mind that he loves me. He decided to make me a book of all the surgeries we've worked together, a grand gesture to apologize. A book of the thirty-two hearts he had to repair for me to fall in love with him," she explains.

Although I am still as confused as ever, the look on her face tells me all I need to know.

They are in love.

"I know its nerdy, but it meant something for him to take the time to make it, so I love it."

"Listen sweetie, if whatever is in this notebook put that kind of smile on your face then I am all the way here for it. Just send me a wedding invitation." I lay my head on her shoulder as she explains the complex medical pictures.

Is There an "Us"?

Brooklyn

The next morning, I turn over to find Malcolm still in my California King bed.

"Good morning," I say as I kiss his lips.

Opening his eyes and looking around trying to recall his location, he sits up and smiles.

"You mean great morning Brooklyn," he says as he pulls me into his arms and kisses me. The longer we kiss, the more I melt against his chest.

This man almost made me say "I love you" last night. It wouldn't have mattered if I meant it, I just felt like there was nothing else to say after the way he made love to me.

My head on his chest, I play with the small hairs around his abs. "Aren't you supposed to be having family breakfast at Michele's? I know how she gets when family is in town. She insists on making sure everyone breaks bread together for the first meal of the day."

"Yes, I am surprised my phone hasn't been blowing up this morning. I should probably get going."

Not really wanting him to leave me, I send up a small prayer.

God if this man is for me, please give me a sign.

Without thinking I blurt, "Are you going to tell Michele about us?" I immediately want to take my question back.

"Do you want me to tell Michele about us? Is there an *us* Brooklyn?" His question stuns me.

Is there an "Us"? Do I want there to be an "Us"?

"I'm not certain what this is but I know I enjoy spending time with you and I don't want it to end. So yes, I would like to work toward an *us*."

He pulls my chin towards him. "I want to see you tonight. I have a flight out of Charlotte first thing in the morning. Would you mind making time for *us*?"

How could I resist this man?

I stare into his eyes, trying to talk myself out of falling for him but I fail.

"Okay. I'll see you tonight," I say and lose myself once again in his lips.

…

"Is it safe to come in?" Candice steps into my master suite.

"Yes, you can come in. I wouldn't have texted you if he was still here."

"Touché. Well good morning sunshine. Birds are chirping, and thots are twerking," she teases.

Why is my best friend so corny at times?

"I cannot with you."

Draping on my robe, I step into my closet built for a queen. On the left side, I have ten wall-to-wall shelves built to hold every shoe a girl could dream of and on the right side, a color-coordinated assortment of outfits and accessories separated by season.

Following me inside, Candice takes a seat on the suede bench in the center and begins grilling me about last night.

"Are you going to come out and tell me or do I have to ask question after question?"

I begin browsing through my fall collection before answering. "Ask away and if I feel the need to elaborate, I will."

"Fine. Have it your way. Are you two an item or is this a fling?"

Keeping my focus on the blazers in front of me, I fail at hiding my smile.

"I honestly don't know yet since we are still trying to figure it out ourselves, but things are heading in the *something more* direction. We've made plans for tonight." I use my fingers to make air quotes around the word *plans*.

"Oh. This storyline is getting more interesting by the second. Continue please." Candice sits back and crosses her legs.

"I thought we agreed you would ask questions? Honestly Candice, I don't really know what I am doing here. I like spending time with him and I want to keep seeing him. A relationship would be nice, but I can't shake the idea of the old Malcolm that we have known since college. He has not given me any reason to doubt that he has changed but I still have to keep my guard up."

Candice grabs one of my Chanel handbags and examines it.

"This will go great with my outfit. But I get that Brook. Guard your heart but don't close it off to the point that no man can get to it. A closed heart can't receive love. I also remember the Malcolm from college but we all did crazy and stupid things. He's almost forty. We have to believe that people change and for the better. Stop over thinking it and just enjoy the ride." She looks at me sarcastically and we both laugh at the inappropriate joke, "Now my real question is—what will Michele have to say about all of this?"

...

Piecing together an outfit to my liking for my date with Malcolm, I hang it on the back of the closet door and put on my jogging shoes. Tying the laces, I ponder Candice's comment.

I don't think it's really any of Michele's business, but I guess I could have a conversation with her. He is her brother after all, and I really don't want to stir up any family drama. Maybe I'll catch her next week to meet up and talk about it. I honestly don't even know how serious Malcolm and I are yet so having a conversation may be premature.

Still fixated with my thoughts, I decide to skip the gym.

"Hey, I'm going for a run. Would you like to join me?" I pop my head into the guest bedroom.

"I'm surprise you have energy this morning. Thank you but no. I am going to get on the road a day early. Since everyone has things going on, I think I'll say my goodbyes and get back to Atlanta."

Feeling a little guilty, I sit on the bed and frown. "Oh no, I thought we had one more day together."

"Girl you have your date with Malcolm, Michele is with her family, and I'm sure Riley is booed up with her heart surgeon. Y'all don't need me so I am going home to my husband."

"Yet another reason why you should move to Charlotte. Just be sure you bring Calvin next time." Candice shoots me a glare.

"Too soon?" I ask apologetically.

"Yes, way too soon," she winces.

"I'm sorry. If you accept my apology, I'll let you keep the Chanel handbag."

After helping Candice load her car and say our goodbyes, I start my five-mile run through downtown Charlotte. I need to clear my head and think through some things. I make a mental note to call and check on my mom once I get back.

I wonder how she would feel about Malcolm? She would probably love him; he is quite the charmer.

Twenty minutes into my run, my watch vibrates indicating a received text message. *I can't wait to see you tonight Brooklyn.* I smile at my watch as I press the command button for speak-to-text.

"I can't wait to see you too Baby," I say without thinking and as commanded, my watch sends the message.

Shoot! I didn't mean to add the "baby" at the end.

My watch vibrates once more, and I quickly grab my phone this time. *Baby? Hmmm I think I like that. See you tonight…Baby.* Looking at the words on the screen, I blush.

Diamonds Don't Do Drama

Michele

"Dad, could you pass me the jelly?" I ask as I hear the front door open. "Good Morning everyone," Malcolm announces, still wearing yesterday's clothes.

"Well good morning to you too son. Join us." My mom begins pouring orange juice for the twins. Sitting down on my side, with Marley between us, I lean back so she cannot hear the conversation.

"Long night?" I tease.

"Yes, I guess it was."

Clearing the empty dishes from the table, I walk into the kitchen to begin loading the dishwasher. Watching Clooney standing next to the tray hoping to catch scraps of food that fall on the floor, I softly scratch behind his ears.

"I guess you want bacon instead of what's in your doggie bowl."

"Here are the last of them," Malcolm says, placing some cups on the counter.

"So where were you last night?"

"I was out. Why are you worried about it?" he laughs and opens the refrigerator, placing the orange juice carton in the door.

"I saw you outside talking to Brooklyn before everyone left. Please tell me you didn't?"

I am confident I already know the answer. I can always count on these two to just "live in the moment," regardless of the consequences.

Slowly closing the refrigerator door, he looks at me and says, "It's not what you think. It was more than a hookup Chele."

I knew I was right about them.

"I find that hard to believe Malcolm. I know the both of you and you don't have the best track record when it comes to dating my friends. I don't think it will end well."

"Then I guess it's a good thing I don't live my life seeking *your* approval. We are all grown baby sis." He exits the kitchen.

Slamming the dishwasher shut, I press the wash cycle button and begin wiping off the counter.

"Did that dishwasher make you upset?" Mom asks jokingly. "I'm from the old school where we still get our hands wet and dirty in the sink to clean dishes."

"I'm fine. Are you and the kids ready to go? I want to stop by the mall and check a few things off of my Christmas list while they are on sale," I attempt to change the subject.

"Give me thirty minutes. I'll check on your father and the twins." She exits the kitchen and I am thankful she didn't harbor on my attitude.

I can't believe Brooklyn would do this and then to not have the decency to tell me. I really thought we were closer than that.

...

Sitting in the food court, I clean the ice cream off of Mason's hands and face. "Mommy, can we go play in the arcade?" Mason taps Marley.

"Yes mommy, please?" she chimes in on cue.

"'Okay, but stay within my eyesight," I command and hand each of them five dollars.

"Yes, ma'am. Thank you!" they yell in unison before running off.

"Now, do you want to tell me what's on your mind? You have been in a funk since Malcolm showed up at breakfast. What is going on with the two of you?" Mom inquires.

Marjorie Diamond knows me better than anyone on this planet.

"It's nothing Mom. Anyway, you haven't told me what you wanted for Christmas this year." I attempt to change the subject again.

"Michele Diamond Peterson, you are *too old* for me to resolve disputes between you and your brother, but I will not have it ruin this family weekend. We will get to my Christmas wish list later, but right now what is going on?"

Slowly taking a scoop of my melted ice cream and letting the flavor savor in my mouth, I try to stall as long as I can.

Now that I have to admit why I have an attitude, I feel a little childish for trying to get in the middle of two consenting adults.

"I saw Malcolm and Brooklyn talking outside after dinner and I am certain that is where he slept last night," I say.

"Are you upset because you think Malcolm seduced her or the other way around?"

"Mom! That's nasty." I glance over to make sure I can still see the twins.

"If it's nasty then why are you concerning yourself with what happens between your friend's sheets?"

Her bluntness is comical.

"That's just it. She's not just my friend, she's my sister and Malcolm *is* my brother. Neither one of them have had a successful adult relationship and I don't see this ending well, but Malcolm says it's none of my business," I say and eat another scoop of melted ice cream.

"Technically sweetheart, it's not any of your business. This could in fact just be a fling, but you have to let them decide. What I can say is that Brooklyn may be the challenge your brother needs. She's beautiful, successful, and not afraid to speak her mind. She's already like family and we love her. Plus, I could use some of those family discount flights. Don't be so quick to assume it won't end well and focus on having a conversation with your friend. They knew the risks from the beginning so if it doesn't work out, that's not on you. In the meantime, talk to your brother and clear the air. *Diamonds don't do drama.*" She smiles as she walks into the arcade to play with the twins.

She's right. I love how good my mom is at putting things into perspective for me. But Malcolm can have any other woman in Charlotte, why does he have to bed my best friend?

Suddenly I begin to reminisce on the last time I lived this nightmare and how I lost my childhood best friend as a result.

...

"Hey Chele. Do you have your notes from calculus? The exam study guide doesn't reflect anything I learned this year. I'm convinced Mr. Hayes is out to fail us all," Robyn jokes as we enter homeroom.

"I'm just glad this is the last exam before graduation and then we are off to college."

"Girl, I can't wait. I hate you're going all the way to Charlotte A&T and leaving me at Alabama Tech all by myself."

"We can talk and write every week I promise. You'll always be my girl, nothing is going to change that. If I could stay, you know it would." I reassure her.

"Michele don't be crazy. Momma Marjorie was not about to let you give up a full academic scholarship. You're my girl. I want you to go off and be great."

Robyn and I have been inseparable for as long as I can remember. Our families go to the same church, so it was destined that the two energetic girls in the youth choir would become best friends. From cutting bangs to getting our first secret tattoo, we don't do anything without the other. Robyn was my best friend for life.

When I had to change high schools due to Malcolm's football career, we schemed and plotted for a whole year to convince our parents to let Robyn transfer. Now that we are about to graduate and part ways for college, I plan to spend the entire summer making memories with my homegirl.

"There's a party at University Village tonight. Do you want to go?" Robyn asks as I open the front door.

"Shhh. My mom is in the kitchen." I place a finger over my mouth and motion for her to follow me to my room.

"You're almost eighteen and about to go to college. Your mom still tripping about you going out?" She teases.

"I'd rather just avoid the conversation all together. Before Malcolm left for school, he was out all night every weekend, but she treats me like I'm some fragile china doll. I'll ask if I can stay with you and go to the party from there."

"Hmmm speaking of forbidden. How is your fine brother doing? If we get married then you and I will be real sisters?" Robyn says and begins looking through my closet.

"Eww. That's my brother. Stop being nasty."

"I'm just saying. Anyway, what are you wearing to the party because all of your clothes look like you are going on a church mission trip to Africa?"

...

The party is packed. Everyone from school is there and even a few people from the neighborhood who returned home for the summer.

"Girl I don't want my braids smelling like smoke. Let's go in the backyard and get some air," Robyn says, referring to all the smoke clouding the three-bedroom townhouse. Once we are outside, we walk toward a group of girls from school.

"Hey Robyn. Ya'll just got here?" Melissa, Robyn's older cousin, inquires.

"No, we've been here a minute. What's the next move?" Robyn asks as a familiar voice peeps up from behind.

"Baby sis. I didn't know you were here," Malcolm says and all the girls blush.

"Hey Malcolm. When did you get home?" Melissa eyes my brother like a vulture.

"Earlier. I'm just chilling out until summer workouts begin. What's up?" I roll my eyes at the sight of my friends fawning over him.

"I'm about to bounce. Do you need a ride home?" He directs his attention back to me.

"No, we're good. I'm staying at Robyn's."

"Actually, I was kind of hungry. You mind stopping to get some food then dropping us off at my place," Robyn suggests. I can tell she's loving the attention in front of our friends.

"Cool let's roll."

Once we leave the party and stop at the local diner, Robyn takes a special interest in my brother and his football stories.

I feel like a third wheel at this table.

"So, Malcolm do you think you guys have a shot at the championship this year?" Robyn asks as the food arrives.

"I hope so. The loss last year was tough but I think it made us stronger."

I excuse myself from the table.

This is too annoying to watch.

Once we get back to Robyn's, it seems like she only has one thing on her mind—Malcolm.

"Girl. Can we talk about something, anything else other than my brother please," I beg as I wash off my makeup.

"Okay. But he kind of asked me out tomorrow night. But only if you are cool with it," she says.

"Seriously? I mean my brother is a playboy. You should aim higher."

"It's just a date Michele. It's not like we are getting married."

"Fine. Go. But don't say I didn't warn you."

Little did I know, this would be the end of our friendship.

. . .

Walking into the house, I place the bags at the top of the coat closet and make a mental note to wrap them for Christmas.

"Hey Dad, where is everyone?"

"Jeremiah's sister came to pick up Nelson and the guys went hooping," Dad says, "You know your old man would've gone and showed those young boys a thing or two, but my basketball days are over."

"When did those basketball days ever start, Clyde?" My mom blurts out walking into the living room.

"I'm going to put some dinner together, sweetie. Check on the twins and take that nap you keep mentioning," she says.

Once I get upstairs, I peek my head into Mason's room.

"Mommy, could we play with the scooters you got from the mall today?" Marley asks, pausing their game console.

I thought I was being discreet when I bought those.

"I'm not sure what you are talking about, so I guess the answer is no," I lie and turn to walk out.

"But mommy . . ." they both yell as I close the door and walk to my room. I contemplate calling Brooklyn to clear my head and my heart, but I think I need to talk to my brother first.

It's a clear betrayal. Why would they have to sneak behind my back if it wasn't? How long has this been going on? It's hard to believe that yesterday was the first time they've seen each other.

"Baby, clear your evening, I have plans for us," Jeremiah kisses my bottom lip to wake me.

"What?" I ask softly still half asleep.

"Your favorite Neo Soul band is in town for one night and I got us tickets"

"Soul 4 Life is in Charlotte? Oh, I love them!"

"Yes, I know. Your mother agreed to watch the twins this evening, so it will be just you, me, and S4L dancing the night away," he says, and I can't help but smile from ear to ear.

I love surprises from my husband, no matter how big or small.

"What time does the concert start?" I look at the clock trying to calculate how much time I have to get ready.

"It starts at 8. You have two hours to get dressed." He smiles knowing exactly what I was thinking.

"Okay Baby."

Walking into the living room, I find Malcolm and my dad playing chess. "Who's winning?" I ask not really caring or knowing anything about chess.

"Malcolm is giving me a run for my money," my dad sulks.

"Do you mind if I steal my brother away?" Malcolm looks up at me confused.

"Sure, I think I'm going to get another slice of your mother's sweet potato pie," dad says and walks into the kitchen. Motioning for Malcolm to follow me outside, we walk to the patio and sit down.

"What's up, baby sis," he says, and I can't tell if he is being sarcastic or sincere.

"Malcolm, I didn't like the way we ended the discussion after breakfast. I probably could have addressed the issue in a more tasteful manner, but I was coming from a place of hurt. This is one of my best friends and you are my brother. I am protective of you both and love you both dearly. Why did you feel you had to keep it a secret?" My attempt at trying not to sound melodramatic fails.

"Chele, honestly I didn't think it was that big of a deal until you mentioned it earlier. Of course, I would have told you when things got serious but right now we are just trying to figure out how we feel."

Maybe this is more than a one-night stand.

"How long have you two been seeing each other?" I ask, careful not to upset him and force him to shut down.

"We rekindled a few weeks ago when I ran into her in Brazil. We caught up that night at dinner and ended up spending a few days together. I enjoy spending time with Brooklyn," he admits.

When was Brooklyn in Brazil? How long is a few weeks ago? We just had dinner at Riley's last week and Brooklyn didn't say anything. What was that about? Why couldn't she tell me then instead of sneaking around at my house during Thanksgiving dinner?

"This isn't just some fling?" I ask aloud.

"No, it isn't just some fling. I like her and she likes me. We're figuring out if any additional feelings exist on top of that. I'm sorry for how I reacted earlier, that wasn't cool. I should have been more considerate of your feelings. I do think you need to have a conversation with your girl. I don't want to come in the middle of your friendship." I can tell his words are sincere.

"Thank you for that and I'll talk to her. I love you Big Head," I tease before hugging him.

"I love you more Pie Face."

We May Not Be Blood,
but You Are My Sister

Brooklyn

Finishing the last touches of makeup, I apply my *Voluptuous Velvet* lip stick on to complement my little black dress. I have no idea where Malcolm is taking me tonight, but I figured this dress would be perfect for any occasion. Just as I begin transferring a few items to one of my velvet clutch bags, the security monitor on the wall in my closet informs me I have a guest at the front door. Pressing the talk button, I look at Malcolm's tall image on the screen.

"Hi handsome. I'll buzz you in. Fix us a drink and I will be there shortly," I instruct and examine my dresser for a perfume selection as my thoughts drift to what life would be as Mrs. Brooklyn Diamond.

This is definitely a man I could love, but am I ready for that? Am I completely ready to be someone's one and only?

I push the thoughts to the back of my mind and walk to the living room to meet my handsome date for the evening.

"Wow," Malcolm stands from the bar holding two drinks, "You look absolutely stunning Brooklyn."

"Thank you. You clean up nice yourself," I say, and he blushes.

Hmm, I guess I can have the same effect on him as well.

"Thank you, Madam. Here you go."

As he hands me the drink, I inhale the familiar aroma in the glass.

"Scotch? My Dad always said if a man offers me scotch, he either has something serious to say or something to celebrate. Which is the case here?" I hold my glass of Macallan 25 up to toast his.

"Your father sounds like a wise man. I hope to meet him one day." His words cause butterflies to sprout into my stomach.

"My father *was* a wise man. He didn't know all things, but he definitely knew a little about everything." I try to hide the pain in my voice and fight back a tear.

I miss my dad every day.

Pulling my chin toward him, Malcolm kisses the remaining scotch on my bottom lip.

"You said *was*," he whispers softly and looks at me intently.

"He passed away the summer of my sophomore year in college."

"I'm so sorry." The sincerity in his voice makes me want him even more.

"Thank you. Maybe that's why I am so passionate about working out and traveling. My father died from diabetes at age fifty-five and never got the chance to see any of the world outside of North Carolina."

I force another swig of Macallan down to calm my nerves.

"That's young. I hate that I'll never get to thank him for having a hand in raising such a beautiful daughter," he says and sits back at the bar to let me process my thoughts.

Grabbing a napkin from the counter to wipe the lone tear in the corner of my eye, I walk over to kiss Malcolm. I am not sure why I did so but, I just wanted his arms around me.

"So, does my father's theory still holds true? Do you have something serious to say or are we celebrating something?" I ask with my arms wrapped around his shoulders as he holds my waist.

"It's the former, I'm afraid."

"What's going on?"

Is this why we haven't left for our date yet?

"I had a conversation with Michele today about us. I think you two should talk," he confesses.

"Yes, I know. It's been on my mind since you left. I will talk to her this week."

"How about tonight?"

Quickly pivoting to turn around from checking my make up in the mirror I ask, "What does that mean?'

Smiling his brightest smile, he walks over and kisses me before I can question his intentions.

"Jeremiah and I bought tickets to the Soul 4 Life show. So, tonight is kind of a double date. Definitely not my idea but it would be good for all of us to clear the air. I promise I will make up for it later."

"Okay. I will talk to her tonight," I say softly.

"You're amazing." He stands to inhale my perfume before kissing my collarbone. My knees betray me, and I have to hold his shoulders to keep my balance.

"You don't play fair Mr. Diamond."

Looking at me through heated eyes he says, "Feel free to pay me back anytime Captain James. Let's go."

...

Riding to Maxwell's Lounge, Malcolm looks over as I sing off key to the radio.

"I guess you like this song, huh," he teases.

"Yes, the lyrics are beautiful. I dream of having that kind of love one day."

"What kind of love is that exactly?"

"I ain't looking over fences trying to find a better view. My search for all that ended when I first laid eyes on you," I recite the lyrics and return his smile.

"And the grass is always greener 'cause the sun shines when you smile. And when I'm holding you the world makes sense, on my side of the fence," Malcolm sings the rest of the lyrics and my heart melts.

He can sing! What can't this man do?

I blush as I hold his hand, happy that the night skies can hide my red cheeks.

"I didn't realize you were a fan of country music."

"Yes, I love multiple genres, but country music speaks to the soul," he admits and kisses my hand before focusing back on the highway.

Pulling up to Maxwell's, I look at the small building. There have definitely been some upgrades done to the lounge since the last time I visited. Once Malcolm scans the tickets at the door, I motion that I am going to the ladies room.

Walking to the back of the lounge, I glance around at all of the couples sitting and jamming to the sounds of soul coming from the band. I used to love coming to see Soul 4 Life when the girls came to town. Walking into the restroom, I see Michele waiting in line.

"Hi Darling," I say.

"Hi Brook," she says a little confused.

"Malcolm and Jeremiah set us up on a double date," I begin filling her in, "He thought it would be a good chance to clear the air."

"I knew there was something up with this random concert surprise. Want to hash it out after we both potty?"

I laugh. "You have been around your twins for far too long but yes, let's talk after we *potty*."

Walking out of the restroom, Michele and I both spot our men. "Hi Jeremiah," I say, trying to act surprised and nonchalant.

"Hi Brooklyn," he says and smiles at Michele who is glaring at him for participating in this scheme.

Bending down to Malcolm's ear away from our guests I whisper, "May I hold your car key? I have to talk to my friend." As he reaches in his pocket, I lick his ear and moan.

"I see you didn't waste much time to pay me back." He runs his hand up my thigh.

"Oh, you haven't seen anything yet Mr. Diamond," I tease and stand to face Michele. "Care to follow me outside?"

Walking to the car, I hit the unlock button on the key fob and Malcolm's Aston Martin lights up. Getting in on the driver's side, I slide into the leather seat and grip the steering wheel. The leather was still warm from the ride over. Michele gets in on the passenger side and looks around.

"I don't think I've been in this car. He usually drives the Range Rover when he comes to town," she says and then looks at me. "You two look really good together Brooklyn."

"Michele, I'm sorry for not talking to you sooner. I honestly wanted to know if it was anything worth telling before I announced it," I attempt to sound as apologetic as possible.

Taking a moment to gather her thoughts, I patiently wait.

"Brooklyn, if my brother makes you happy, then I'm happy. What hurt me was the fact that you felt you needed to hide or sneak around behind my back. We may not be blood, but you are my sister. You can talk to me about anything."

"I know and it's so unexpected. Honestly Brazil was supposed to be a fling but somewhere we both started to feel something."

"Girl, that's the Diamond charm. When were you in Brazil? That wasn't part of your flight schedule."

I guess I might as well be transparent about everything now.

"I was in a weird place after seeing Tyson at the homecoming game and then the whole ordeal with Candice. I needed to get away to process things. I had a friend in Brazil and decided to pay him a visit since I had a few days off," I say and pause.

"Him? Brooklyn you went to Brazil to see a man?" I can hear all of the judgement in her voice.

"I went to Brazil for me and *just so happened* to know a friend that lived there. I never even got to see him because Malcolm and I spent the entire trip together from the time he stopped me in the lobby." I smile at the memory.

"You don't have to tell me the details right now. I can see you're happy Brooklyn. I want you both to be careful. Don't rush into anything and take time to get to know one another. I'm glad you both see this as more than a fling. If this makes you happy, you have my blessing," she says, and I sigh.

"Thank you Chele. Yes, I am happy."

Aunt May Don't Play

Candice

"These are your last three events of the book tour. How do you feel?" Trinity asks as she passes me the schedule for next week.

"It's bittersweet. I am happy to get off the road, but it means I now have a lot more pressure to finish my next book," I admit and take a sip of my strawberry ginger smoothie.

"Don't put too much pressure on yourself girl. Your greatest books have been the ones you took your time with and lived a little before writing. Don't let this project be any different. Your fans love your stories because they are real and relatable. You have to go through some things to tap into those kinds of emotions. Stop worrying about typing the words and just let life write the book for you." Trinity looks at me and I am speechless.

"When did you get so wise?" I tease.

"Who knows. I guess all of your Q&A sessions are starting to sink in." She laughs. "Do you have any plans for the holidays? I am sure you are tired of traveling."

"Yes, I am tired of traveling. I think we will just relax through Christmas. My husband and I are contemplating hosting a New Year's Eve party this year, but we shall see," I fabricate a little.

I really am thinking about hosting one, but Calvin has no idea. I will have to do some convincing to get him on board with the party. I figured it would be good to stay home and have people come to us for once.

"That sounds fun. Well, if you decide to host a party, let me know. I will definitely make some arrangements to attend," she says and we both get up to leave the bistro.

"What time is our flight?"

"At four o'clock. We should probably make our way to the airport. I checked our luggage with the concierge this morning, I'll go get them and call us a cab."

Sitting back down in the hotel lobby, I call my husband.

"Hey Love, how's Houston treating you?" Calvin asks.

"It's okay. I'm ready to get back home. It's been a long week and I miss you," I say, feeling a random tear swell.

My emotions have been all over the place lately.

"I miss you more Love. I have a surprise waiting when you get home tonight."

"Oh, I like surprises. Could you give me a hint?"

"No hints. Just get home. I love you and have a safe flight," he says and moves the phone away to speak to a distraction in his office.

"I love you more Honey. I'll let you get back to work. See you tonight." I hang up.

Pulling into my driveway, I check the group chat from the girls. I decided against the internet option on the plane and chose to get some much-needed rest instead. Skimming through the messages, I see that Brooklyn has admitted to dating Malcolm and Riley is still head over heels in love.

I send a summary message of my response to all the discussions and close the garage door before going inside. Placing my luggage down at the kitchen door for Calvin to take upstairs later, I hear my favorite Bob Marley album playing.

Stepping into the living room, I am frozen at the sight of my 6'3, chiseled body husband wearing nothing but Jamaican striped swimming shorts. Looking around my living room, I realize Calvin has turned it into his own personal island.

He has moved the furniture so two beach chairs and a small table covered with a beach towel is sitting in the middle of our living room. Atop of the table are two plates of curry chicken, rice, and cabbage.

Walking up to me, he places two colorful leis around my neck and hands me a bottle of Red Stripe.

"What is all of this?" I ask unable to break my smile and amazement.

In his best attempt at a Jamaican accent he replies, "Me want to take me queen to de islands. Me want to take her to Jamaica." Breaking character, Calvin laughs at his terrible accent. "To commemorate the end of your book tour, I booked us a trip to Jamaica after your last event in Miami. I already spoke to Trinity; you will sign autographs, take pictures, and before the sun sets, you and I will be lying on a beach in Montego Bay drinking cocktails." He takes the beer out of my hand to hold my waist.

"Calvin, thank you. I can't think of a more perfect way to say, welcome home. I love you." I kiss my husband passionately.

"Welcome home Baby," he whispers and carries me upstairs to help me out of my travel clothes.

...

Walking into the study, I find Calvin on the treadmill talking stocks to one of his associates. Sitting down to admire the view, I grab one of the many books from our home library and browse through the pages.

It's difficult to read and focus on other books when I am writing one of my own so there are still a few novels that we have added to the collection that I need to read.

Hanging up the call, Calvin removes his noise canceling headphones and stops the treadmill.

"Good morning Love. You were sleeping so peacefully, I didn't want to wake you," he says, wiping the sweat dripping from his beard.

"I was actually thinking about going for a run around the lake, but I see you've already completed your morning workout," I tease and grab the towel to wipe the sweat off of his chest and lower abdomen.

"I still have about five miles left in these old legs. If you are asking, then I would love to join you." He mischievously pulls me closer to his chest causing my silk tank top and pajama shorts to absorb some of his sweat. "Oh no, I guess we'll both need to get out of these sweaty clothes before we leave."

It is a beautiful day in Atlanta. A cool December morning where most of the neighbors are out tending to their gardens while others have landscapers to care for their lawns. I am the latter. Calvin and I agreed if we can afford to live in the neighborhood, we can afford a professional landscaper. Locking the front door, we turn left out of our driveway to start the four-mile jog to the lake and back.

"Is Aunt May coming in town for the holidays this year?" Calvin asks, breaking my train of thought.

"I am not sure, I will have to call her and confirm. If so, she'll probably meet us in Fayetteville with your family for Christmas. You know she hates sitting in a car for long periods of time." We both slow down to control our laughing.

"Oh, trust me Babe, I remember. Our last trip to Germany was definitely one for the books. What was supposed to be a two-hour family trip from Leipzig to tour the Berlin Wall turned into four hours of road rage and road closures from construction. Aunt May don't play."

"She is something else, but I do miss her. Maybe I can convince her to stay through New Year's." I pause and decide to use this opportunity to suggest my plan. "What do you think about hosting a New Year's Eve party this year?" I ask, trying to sound as if the idea just popped into my head.

Resuming our pace, he asks sarcastically, "Yes, I like that idea. Did you want to do something small or prefer to have a *Candice Montgomery Production*?"

"Definitely small." I roll my eyes, "The girls and their significant others, Aunt May, and whoever else your heart desires."

Turning to look at me as we reach the lake he smiles, "My heart only desires you, but I'll add a few people to the list. I think twenty or less will be more than enough people in our house. You said significant *others*. Plural. Jeremiah and I go way back but Brook and Riley landed a man?"

I stop at our favorite bench on the lake and take a few slices of bread out of my running pack to feed the ducks. Sitting down, I pass a slice to Calvin saying, "Oh Baby, you have no idea. This will be a New Year's Eve to remember."

I Love You More Today Than Yesterday

Riley

"Blythe, have you seen my navy clutch?" I ask, already knowing the answer to the question.

"Yes ma'am, it's in my closet. I'll go get it for you," she replies as if I was asking her permission to use it.

"Thank you and my diamond studs please, since you are gathering my belongings." I finish pinning half of my hair up.

"Mom, you look beautiful." Blythe steps into my bathroom, "Where is Mr. Jameson taking you this afternoon?" I finish applying my plum lipstick and blow an air kiss in her direction.

"We are going to a winery."

"Oh. That sounds nice. Hopefully you won't be outside too much, it's chilly today."

"I hope so too Baby," I say as we both turn at the sound of the doorbell, "I'll get it. Straighten my bathroom counter for me please."

I place the lipstick and a few items into the navy clutch before stepping into the hallway.

"Wow. You look amazing Riley," Jameson says when I open the door.

No matter how many times he says those words, I blush as if it's the first.

Looking down at my paisley shift dress and navy point toe heels, I do a quick twirl for my man.

"Thank you. Just one last touch." I place the bag on the coffee table before putting on my diamond stud earrings and jacket, "Okay. Now I'm ready."

Arriving at the winery, Jameson steps out of his silver ice metallic Camaro and walks over to open the passenger door. I grab his hand and adjust my body, so my legs are hanging out the side of the car. I casually glance at Jameson from head to toe, admiring his ensemble. He is wearing denim jeans with a navy V-neck shirt underneath a light grey Armani Exchange cardigan.

I rarely get to see him dressed down outside of the hospital, but it is always a treat.

"Riley, those legs are beseeching me to touch them," he whispers as I stand and find my footing. Grabbing the small of my back, he pulls me closer and kisses me as I hear the car door close and lock.

"Your lips are mine and my legs are all yours." I wink as I graze my thumb across his bottom lip and softly kiss his cheek.

We have not had sex yet, but it is getting harder and harder to resist this man. I swore to myself that I would wait until my wedding night, but Jameson is the only man that is making me question that decision. He has been nothing but patient and caring with me and all of my awkwardness. There's no doubt that I love him, maybe we are ready to take that next step.

Continuing to weigh the decision back and forth in my head, Jameson reaches for my hand as we walk into the winery. Everything is laid out so beautifully as a couple walks up to greet us.

"Good afternoon Dr. Young, it's always good to see you," the older man says.

"Thank you, Harvey," Jameson says and looks over to me. "Harvey and Donna this is my girlfriend, Dr. Riley Harper." I blush from his formalities.

"Riley" would have been just fine but my heart flutters at the look of pride he has introducing me.

"What a pleasure it is to have you Dr. Harper, my husband and I started this winery over fifty years ago and this young man helped us save our business. We owe everything to him so when he called and asked us to clear the place for an afternoon with a special lady, that is exactly what we intended to do," Donna says, and I blush once more.

He requested to close a winery just for me?

"Please have a seat. We have some of the best reds and whites your taste buds have ever experienced," Harvey says as he pulls out my chair. I sit down.

He pours us both a glass of Chambourcin and I stare at the deep red wine as it funnels out of the bottle and into our glass.

"This is made from a French-American hybrid grape that thrives exceptionally in North Carolina. It pairs really well with steak or dark chocolate," Harvey says, and I turn to Jameson who hasn't taken his eyes off of me.

"Oh, I love chocolate," I attempt to make small talk.

"So. Do. I.," Jameson says through heated eyes and my entire body quivers.

I am not sure if I can hold out too much longer. This old man is talking about some dusty grapes and candy, and somehow Jameson found a way to make it sexy. He has me completely beguiled.

"I will let you two enjoy the selection," Harvey says as he walks away to give us some privacy.

I wonder if he noticed my sudden blushing from Jameson's comment.

"This place is beautiful. How did you help save their business?" I ask trying to suppress my current thoughts.

"I brought my mom here on one of the anniversaries of my father's passing some years back. That particular year, she decided not to spend the day in Connecticut and wanted to visit me here in Charlotte. Usually it's a sad and somber time for her but that day, seeing her out in the vineyard laughing and talking with Donna was the happiest I'd seen her in a long time."

"After that, she never made another trip to Charlotte without stopping by this winery and taking home some new blend to show her church ladies. When I found out that Harvey and Donna was getting pressed to sell their land for some superstore being built, I just couldn't sit by and do nothing. A few of my buddies and I grouped together and became silent investors to help them out and I take the profits to invest in other local businesses," he says, and I am speechless.

"So, you own a portion of *this* business?" I ask not really familiar with the logistics of investing.

I could definitely learn a few things from him.

"Technically yes," he says, "But it wasn't about the money. I would have given anything to keep that smile on my mother's face and since this place means something to me, I wanted to share it with you."

I finish the remaining wine in my glass and motion for Jameson to sit beside me instead of across the table.

"Yes ma'am," he says, and he switches seats.

As soon as we are eye level, I softly hold his face in my hands, rubbing the top of his beard with my thumbs.

"I love you Jameson. I am not sure what I did to deserve you, but I thank God for thinking of me when he made you."

"I love you more Riley. More today than yesterday but not half as much as I will love you tomorrow," he says and kisses a lone tear as it falls down my cheek.

Leaving dinner, I look over at Jameson who is singing along to a classic Stevie Wonder album.

"I don't think I am ready to go home. Could we go somewhere?" I ask.

"Of course, Gorgeous. Where would you like to go? It's getting too cold to be outside," he says and looks at me.

"Let's go to your place."

"Okay. My place it is," he says and turns off of the exit towards downtown.

Pulling into the parking deck, I continue to weigh my options on whether or not I should give in to temptation.

Jameson could have any girl he wants. I'm sure women throw themselves at him all day long. What if I tell him that I want to wait until marriage and he loses interest? I don't think I can handle that kind of rejection.

"Riley," he says breaking my internal deliberation, "Where are you? Physically you are here but mentally you seem to be elsewhere."

Looking over to him I shake my head and give a half smile. "I'm okay. It's late so I will probably stay over. I'll text Blythe and tell her to lock up the house."

"Okay Babe, I sleep better with you in my arms anyway." He bends over to kiss my cheek before exiting and walking over to open my door.

Walking into his condo, Jameson takes off my jacket and hangs it in the coat closet.

"Since you are staying, would you like to change into something more comfortable while I pour us some drinks?" he asks. I pause.

"Yes please," I say as my body temperature is continuing to rise.

"You know where my bedroom is. Feel free to change into anything you consider comfortable. I'll get some popcorn and a movie started up."

I have stayed over Jameson's place several times and he's always been a complete gentleman. This was the first time that I cannot shake the idea of being intimate. Stepping into his master bedroom, I look at the large California King bed facing downtown Charlotte.

The lights from the cars and building are so beautiful and calming at night.

Walking over to his dresser, I look through the drawers to find a t-shirt. After two failed attempts, I get to the third drawer and find an array of cotton shirts. I settle on a grey Charlotte-Grace Medical shirt that is long enough to cover my unmentionables, but not much else. Removing my shoes and dress, I put on the t-shirt and walk over to the floor mirror, admiring how my body is still in top shape after thirty-six years.

"Oh, those legs Dr. Harper," Jameson says breaking my attention.

Turning around I walk over and place my arms around his shoulders. "Dr. Young, you startled me," I say seductively.

"You are radiant Riley. That shirt has never looked this good on me. How did I get so lucky?" He bends down and intertwines our lips.

"Jameson, I . . ." I say, breaking our kiss and stepping back from him.

"What is it?"

"I have to tell you something," I force myself to say and walk over to sit on the bed.

"Baby what is it? You know we don't have any secrets." His tone is a lot more serious as he sits beside me.

Facing him, I exhale deeply and speak my truth.

"Shortly after Blythe was born, I vowed I would save myself until marriage. For seventeen years I was committed and disciplined to keep that promise but lately you are making me feel things in places I never knew existed. This is why I was so silent in the car tonight. I was contemplating on whether or not I am ready for us to become intimate," I admit and look up at him.

"Are you sure that's what you want Riley? Are you sure you're ready?" he asks.

"I'm not sure. I think I am, but isn't that what you want also? I know women have been throwing themselves at you your entire life. I am sure you have desires and needs Jameson. Can you truly say you can wait until marriage to be intimate with someone?" I feel my chest begin to tighten.

I am now completely exposed. If he says no, then this will pretty much end our relationship.

Staring at him, I try my hardest to fight back the tears awaiting his response. Grabbing my hand, he pulls me onto his lap.

"Is that what you have been worrying yourself with all day? Thinking that we need to have sex to sustain our relationship? Baby listen, from the first time I walked into that operating room and saw your light brown eyes lost inside of a crossword puzzle, I knew you were a woman worth moving mountains for. It took me a long time to build up the nerve to ask you out on a date and even more effort to get you to say yes. If you are willing to open up your heart and love me then I am willing to wait for you as long as you need. I meant it when I said I am here for the long term. I don't need sex Riley, I need you."

Relationships Are Like
Flying An Airplane

Brooklyn

Turning over, I watch the sunrise over downtown Charlotte. I really did love this view from my penthouse, even if I was hardly ever home. I reach for my phone on the nightstand, expecting to see my *Good Morning* text message from Malcolm and smile.

His daily routine consists of a 5 a.m. workout and a 6 a.m. text message. We both agreed I will never be up that early unless I am flying a plane, but he insists he wants his name to be the first thing I see when I wake up.

This man, this man.

I reply to his message and smile, once more, as I press the send button.

These last few weeks have been amazing. I still have my guard up about his past but each day, I feel those walls collapsing brick by brick. I am afraid to admit aloud that I am falling for him but I am. I'm just not sure if he feels the same. His actions make me believe he does, but we have not had the official conversation. I continue to bounce around my thoughts and fears.

Is it too early in our relationship to have this conversation? Would having this conversation make things awkward? Maybe I should just let it play out. I need to talk to Candice. I need my human sounding board.

I send a quick text message instructing her to call me when she wakes up and roll back over to try and get another hour of sleep.

Two minutes later, my phone rings.

"Unless you are crossing the Atlantic Ocean, something must be troubling you to be up this early," she says without waiting for me to greet her.

"You know me so well. Yes, my thoughts are troubled. It sounds like you are in a car, where are you headed?" I ask trying to delay discussing my feelings.

"I am on my way to the airport for my last events of the tour, Orlando, Tampa, and then Miami."

"Girl, you travel about as much as I do. May the force be with you and your luggage. When is the Miami event? I may be able to attend your last appearance and celebrate on South Beach for the weekend," I say.

"On Thursday and I would love for you to come but Calvin is whisking me away to Jamaica this weekend." I can feel her smile through the phone.

"Oh my. Y'all are relationship goals for real. I am happy to hear you two are in a much better place. Well in that case, let me just say how proud I am of you and that I will be there in spirit. I will stay in Charlotte and let you enjoy your *husband*," I tease.

"You are something else, but thank you, love. So, are you ready to talk?"

I stay silent on the phone listening to the background noises of car horns on the receiving end of the call.

"Is it family, work, or Malcolm?" she asks, breaking the silence.

"Am I that predictable? This sounds like déjà vu or at least a movie title. *Family, work, or a man: the complexities of Brooklyn James*," I say.

"Unfortunately, my dear friend, it's the story of most of our lives. So, tell me what's on your mind." Her response reassures me.

"It's about Malcolm." I pause.

"What about Malcolm? Did something happen?" she asks, and I can tell she is ignoring my dramatics and trying to get straight to the point.

"No, he's actually great. These last few weeks have been unbelievably refreshing and that scares the crap out of me," I finally admit. "I can feel myself falling for him, but I am having trouble deciphering if this is the old Malcolm trying to run game or a sincere and mature man. I guess I have been playing the shallow end of relationships for so long I am not sure what it feels like to be completely submerged in feelings for someone."

Taking a moment to absorb my confession she asks, "Are you afraid that if you admit your feelings for him, you'll get hurt, or are you afraid that he's falling for you too?"

"I guess both," I reply and continue to ponder her questions. "I really like him and want to see where things could go but I can't shake the idea of the Malcolm we've always known. He hasn't officially claimed me or asked to be exclusive. How do I know that I'm the only one? Am I about to mess everything up by overthinking?"

"Your concerns and feelings are valid, but it's not fair to make assumptions without talking to him Brooklyn. I don't think you are giving yourself enough credit. You could very well be the woman to tame the one and only Malcolm Diamond. A man like that can say more with his actions than he ever could using his words. What do his actions say?" she probes.

"His actions display sincere intentions. We talk daily, and he makes the effort to spend time with me. The conversations are beyond stimulating and the sex is out of this world. What scares me is that I don't know if I am falling for him or the idea of having a husband," I admit as my thoughts run wild.

Am I so afraid of being alone that I am projecting ideas onto Malcolm that may or may not exist? We have only been on a couple of dates, and this could still just be something casual in his mind. What if he is seeing other women also? What if I am not the only 6a.m. "Good Morning" text message that is sent after his workouts?

My thoughts quickly run to the worst-case scenarios and my chest tightens.

"Brook, stop thinking the worst," she says as if she's in my head. "The two of you saw something that drew you to one another. Don't think too far beyond that. Have an honest conversation with him about your feelings, even if they seem hard. If you want to be exclusive, tell him and if you don't, tell him that too. Stop focusing so much on his past and your future that you end up ruining the present relationship. Trust me, I know this firsthand. Relationships are like flying an airplane," she says, and I sit up.

"What?" I ask confused but intrigued with the metaphor.

"It is. Think about it. I've been sitting in this airport parking lot watching planes and it takes a lot of work and factors for a successful takeoff. Maybe this can help you relate, so hear me out." She pauses and I want to laugh but refrain.

"Aircrafts and relationships both require a preliminary check, much like introductory questions about a person's name, family, credit score, an all-around system check before taking off. Getting a relationship off the ground takes a lot of time, commitment, and complete honesty about your feelings.

I imagine in order to get a massive plane airborne, you need a great deal of throttle and speed. Not enough speed or thrust, and the nose of the plane may lift a little but eventually goes back down. And you have to do all of this at full capacity before you reach the end of the runway or best case, you have to turn around and try again. I won't mention the worst case, as I am about to board a small plane to Orlando," she says and we both laugh.

"Fair point and I like the comparison. It's technically and theoretically incorrect but metaphorically, spot on. Thanks for the early morning chat. I will have a conversation with him and try to express myself. I promise."

"Good. If he likes you, he'll listen, and if he cares, he'll accommodate. I am excited for the update but let me get off this phone before I miss my flight."

I walk into my closet before ending the call, "Okay, have a safe flight and a productive week. Love you, Honey."

Changing out the worn clothes in my carry-on luggage for some fresh outfits, I call Malcolm on speaker.

"Good morning beautiful. I was just thinking about you," he says and my heart flutters.

"Good morning to you too. Are you in meetings all day?"

"No, a few phone conferences but nothing requiring my physical presence. How about you? I thought you would be in the sky by now."

"Not yet. I have a few hours before *my* physical presence is required," I tease.

"Oh, how I just love your wit Captain James. It's a shame I am not in Charlotte, I could put some good use to those extra hours before liftoff. When is your shift over? It's been too long since I've seen you."

"Yes, *it is* too bad you live all the way in Atlanta, but I return Thursday morning from Madrid and then I am on a break."

"Duly noted. Make plans to spend your break with me."

"Okay, done. My break is all yours, Babe."

Where All the Magic Happens

Brooklyn

" *L*adies and Gentlemen, thank you for choosing International Skyways Flight 454 nonstop to Madrid, Spain. This is Captain James speaking. We have just reached a cruising altitude of 37,000 feet. We're looking at clear skies so I will turn off the seatbelt sign. We have a flight time of eight hours and five minutes before we reach Adolfo Suárez Madrid–Barajas Airport so please sit back, relax, and enjoy your flight," I finish my scripted welcome speech and complete a control check with my co-pilot.

"Mark, how was Matty's graduation? I feel like he's all grown up now, I hope he hasn't gotten too big to be called Matty?" I ask.

"I think Matty is limited to family and close friends. Now a days, he just goes by *Matt*. The graduation was great. He's moving to New York after the holidays to start an internship with Durant & Associates and then off to law school in the Fall," he says. I can see the pride in his eyes.

"You must be extremely proud. That's great to hear." I settle in my seat for the long flight ahead.

...

A tap at the cockpit door draws our attention as one of the flight attendants walks in.

"Captain James, one of our passengers in first class has requested a brief tour of the cockpit. They mentioned they're an old friend of yours," Janice says, and I turn to look at her puzzled.

Not wanting to cause alarm before finding out who it is, I play along and agree to the tour.

"Sure, I think we can spare a few minutes, please invite them in." I remove my aviation headset and put on my pilot cap. "Mark would you mind taking over while I *entertain?*"

"Sure Captain." He nods and continues focusing on the controls.

Standing as the door reopens, my jaw drops, and my inner thigh immediately begins pulsating.

"Captain James, this is Mr. Malcolm Diamond," Janice introduces him and then turns to exit the cockpit.

"Hello Captain James," Malcolm says, and I cannot move my feet. My back remains turned to Mark and he reaches out his hand to greet Malcolm.

"Good evening Mr. Diamond, I am Co-Pilot Mark Humphries. Thank you for flying with International Skyways," he says before returning his attention to the controls.

"Thank you for having me," Malcolm says. "And what a pleasure it is to see you again, Captain James." He opens his arms to hug me and I quickly grab his hand to shake it, trying to remain professional.

"Mark, Malcolm here is an old friend from college and what a complete surprise seeing you on this flight to Madrid," I say and lift my eyebrow.

What is this man up to? This is my job. I wouldn't just pop up at his office without notice.

Removing my cap, I smooth the stray hairs from my messy bun and place it back in the garment closet.

"Well this is it. This is the infamous flight deck, where all the magic happens." I blush from my corniness.

The way Malcolm just stares makes me uneasy, in a good way. Breaking his focus, he looks around to admire the control center.

"Wow there are so many buttons, knobs, and switches."

"Yes. I think the majority of the buttons are just here for show. We want passengers to think we have a lot going on in here," Mark chimes in and we all laugh.

"Yes, a fair amount of the dials are set when the plane is first placed in service and their settings rarely change. The most used are the control wheel, throttle levers, and rudder/brake pedals. They are used to add speed and stir the bird," I explain, and Malcolm looks at me impressed.

Feeling a lot more relaxed and confident talking about my job, I gesture to him.

"Feel free to step up to get a closer look. By law you can't go past this line." I point to the thick white line behind the piloting seats.

"I'll stand back here with you and give you a quick tour of the panel," I say leaning on the back of my seat so Malcolm could get a better view of the Captain's side. Standing a little behind me, he checks his feet to make sure he is safely behind the white line. With Mark facing forward observing the controls, I begin to point at the monitors on the control panel.

"This is the primary flight display and that over there is the altitude indicator," I say completely in my element as I lean on my tippy toes to point, "the radar display . . ."

Turning completely red, I pause and quickly look over to observe if Mark can see Malcolm's hand slowly wandering up my leg and lifting my skirt.

"Wow. This looks extremely complex," Malcolm says unfazed.

Thankful that Mark is still preoccupied with the controls, I slowly slide back down to find my footing. My body temperature is soaring, but I resist my headiness and try to remain professional.

"Mark, I am going to step out and catch up with Malcolm for a few minutes. If you need anything, I will be right outside the door," I assure him and direct Malcolm out of the cockpit.

Closing the door, I quickly think of an excuse to send one of the flight attendants to go to the back station while I have a private conversation up front.

"Marcy, would you mind checking on the crew in the back?" I ask.

"Yes Captain," she says and gives a polite smile to Malcolm. Walking behind her, I close the curtain to block the view from the first-class cabin. Turning around, Malcolm continues to stare with vehement eyes.

Unable to control myself, I push him against the beverage cart and release all of my built-up tension through a kiss. Careful of our volume, we begin making out as if we need each other's oxygen to survive. Running his fingers through my hair, he tugs at my bun causing my curls to fall down my uniform.

"What . . ." I ask, pulling away to catch my breath, "What are you doing here?" He licks his lips and pulls me closer, still holding my backside.

"I asked you to clear your break for me," he says mischievously. "Did you?"

Inhaling a few times to steady my breathing I reply, "I did."

Still smiling he kisses the back of my hand, "Well, you're piloting to Madrid and I've never been to Madrid. I thought this would be a good way to spend your break."

Stepping back in case someone interrupted us, I say, "Wow, you are just full of surprises Mr. Diamond."

"I know. So, is this okay? Are you mad?" He looks at me apologetically and all I want to do is wrap my arms and legs around him.

"No, I'm not mad. *Surprised*, yes, but not mad," I say and smile to reassure him.

"Good. Well, I'll be in first-class if you get bored and need to come back out of the cockpit to continue *this* discussion. Otherwise, I'll go and take a nap in anticipation for our next three days in Madrid." He kisses me and opens the curtain to return to his seat.

Completely baffled, I stand there for a moment and try to piece together the events that have just transpired. Tying my hair back up as best as I can to its original state, I return to the cockpit and slide into my pilot seat.

Lost in his own space I am thankful that, like most men, Mark doesn't notice my change in demeanor.

"All good?" he asks, never looking up from a book.

"Everything's cool," I respond and reach for my phone to connect it to the internet. Suddenly remembering we have one of our team pilots overnighting in Madrid, I quickly send him a message.

Hey Jack, if you are still in Madrid I may need to cash in a favor. I send the message and wait for a response, brainstorming a backup plan if he declines my request. I am still expected to pilot the return flight, so I have to find a way to stay in Madrid with Malcolm once we land.

Twenty minutes of racking my brain with a backup plan, my phone vibrates.

Hey Brook. Yes, I spent my break here, headed back to the States tomorrow. What's up?

Reading the message, I almost jump out of my seat with joy.

This plan will work!

I quickly type my request.

Hey, would you mind taking my shift for the return flight tomorrow from

Madrid to Charlotte. I will owe you two shifts!

I press send and anxiously await his response. A few moments later my phone vibrates.

Sure, it's no problem. Meet you in the lounge to complete the paperwork. I send a quick thank you and mentally prepare for three days of bliss in Spain.

Face the Consequences of My Youth

Candice

"Babe, you told me to wake you up at ten," Calvin says rubbing my side. "It's 9:55."

Adjusting my vision to the sunlight I roll over, "9:55 isn't ten o'clock. I still have five minutes." I try to pull the covers back over my head, but he tugs at them exposing my entire body.

"We have a lot to do today, *per your checklist*. We might as well start now. Aunt May is in the kitchen and from the smell, she is making eggs and burnt bacon." He laughs and pats my backside, "I'll go make sure she doesn't start a kitchen fire. Get dressed."

Walking into the bathroom to begin my morning routine, I hear my phone ringing. "Hello," I answer without looking at the screen.

"Hey, I have Riley and Michele on three-way," Brooklyn says.

"Happy New Year's Eve," Michele and Riley both say in unison.

"I figured it was easier to quickly chat over the phone than to discuss this via messaging," Brooklyn adds, "Do you need us to help with anything? We are all getting on the road around three o'clock."

"No, I think we are good. Calvin is going to pick up the food and beverages while Aunt May and I coordinate with decorations. The other two guest rooms are awaiting your arrival. Brooklyn were you coming here with Chele and Riley or going to *Malcolm's*?" I ask teasingly.

"No. I will be the awkward fifth wheel coming from Charlotte. Thank goodness Michele's truck has an extra row so I don't have to be stuck between Dr. and Mrs. Lovebirds in the backseat. I'll probably get dressed at your place and leave with Malcolm afterwards." We all laugh together.

"Stop with the dramatics. You're only a fifth wheel because Malcolm lives in Atlanta," Riley says. "I am excited for you all to meet Jameson though."

"We are too," Michele says. "But if he made it through Veronica Harper during Christmas, he's already a winner in our book." We all laugh.

"You can say that again. Mrs. Harper is cold-blooded with her interrogations," I say before ending the call. "Let me get dressed and out of this house. Drive safe and I will see you all tonight. Love you!"

"Good morning family." I smile as I walk into the kitchen.

"Guten morgen, wie geht's?" Aunt May asks and takes a sip of her coffee.

"I am doing well. Thank you," I respond to the only German sentence I completely understand.

"That is good to hear my darling niece. Your beloved spouse insists on preparing breakfast since we had a disagreement on my preference of crispy bacon," she says, and Calvin turns from the stove and gives me a side eye.

"Auntie, crispy and burnt are not the same thing." I laugh reaching for a coffee mug in the cupboard. "I've accepted the fact that culinary skills just aren't in our genes and I thank God for sending me a husband who loves to cook." Walking over to kiss Calvin's cheek, I grab a fresh piece of bacon from one of the pans.

"Yes, well that is a great fortune dear. I will just continue to enjoy a life of fine dining and having others prepare my meals." Aunt May says and retrieves her own piece of bacon.

"If you two keep this up, there won't be any bacon left to eat with the pancakes." Calvin shakes his head. "Love, could you put out three place settings at the bar? Breakfast is almost ready."

...

"Let's take Calvin's car since he'll need the bigger trunk for food and drinks," I say as we walk through the kitchen and into the garage.

"Oh, the i8. This is my second favorite of our models," Aunt May says as she lifts the passenger door. Adjusting the driver's seat, I reach up to lower my door.

"Second?" I ask as I press the garage button, "Which model is your first? You've pretty much had every model and color during your long career with BMW."

Throwing her Birkin bag in the backseat, she shrugs. "Why work for a car manufacturer and not drive the product? I notice I've converted you and Calvin over to the *German way of living* as well."

"Yes, you have and Brooklyn too. She has the 6 Series convertible. Same color as mine."

"Now *that* is my all-time favorite model. I knew Brooklyn was my favorite of your girlfriends for a reason. It's timeless and a treat to drive. The i8 is sporty and fast but the butterfly doors are a bit of a hassle and not very practical." I tend to agree.

We had to pay extra to build a larger garage, so his doors could open and close with ease, but I'd do anything to make that man happy.

"Calvin loves this car. I keep asking if he wants a truck so he doesn't have to continue stuffing his golf clubs in the passenger seat, but he declines. Boys and their toys." I laugh and turn onto the interstate.

"I imagine he'll change his mind about upgrading the car soon. Have you two discussed adoption any further?" her question catches me completely off guard.

"Yes, we have our final evaluation interview in a few weeks to assess whether we are suitable parents." I make a failed attempt to hide my nervousness.

Patting my leg, she says, "You're ready Sweetheart. You'll be a great mother."

Motherhood isn't what scares me, what if the child doesn't like me? What if the child grows up wanting to leave us for their biological parents?

Looking at Aunt May, I begin to openly discuss some of the worries bouncing around in my head.

"Did you ever consider adoption?" I ask and try to look apologetic in case my question sounded inconsiderate.

"I did for a while. But at the beginning, I was so focused on advancing in my career that I pushed away the idea of children and any man who made me choose between the two. When I was finally ready to entertain the idea, I had to face the consequences of my youth."

"What do you mean by consequences?"

"When I was in my early twenties, I was dating this guy, Benjamin Watson. He was unlike any boy I had ever dated back then or like any man I have dated since. I was young and in love. We had our whole future planned out. He was going to take over his father's auto repair shop and I was working at the BMW Plant in Greenville, making a name for myself. I had a comfortable life with a boy who loved me enough to make plans to marry me and start a family."

"A few years into my career, I came up with an idea to improve the communication between plants and shortly after I was offered a promotion at our headquarters in Germany. I was just a young girl from South Carolina, so this was the biggest opportunity of my life and there was no way I could turn it down. I thought he would want to move with me to Germany or even try long distance, but it turned out to be the breaking point of our relationship. He gave me an ultimatum, a life in Greenville with him or a life apart in Germany. I chose the latter." She pauses.

"Two months after I arrived in Germany, I discovered that I was pregnant. I had made such a mess of my life back in the States that I couldn't return home and there was no way I could raise a baby alone in a foreign country." She wipes a tear as it falls down her cheek and I hold my breath in anticipation.

"I aborted my first and only child by the first and only man I truly ever loved," she confesses.

"Aunt May, I am so sorry. I never knew. Did you ever tell him about the child?" I ask trying my hardest not to cry with her.

"No, he went on with his life and married a beautiful woman who gave him a family after I uprooted my life to Germany and never looked back." Her eyes fill with sorrow. "By the time I decided I was ready to have children, I was too old and had no prospects in sight. That's when I thought about adoption," she says and adjusts the climate temperature on her side.

"The adoption process in Germany is a little different than the one here in the States and since I wasn't a full citizen, it was pretty much impossible. I cried and prayed at the thought that I had ruined my chance at happiness. I thought I would be alone for the rest of my life until the day a feisty young college freshman called me," she says.

Pulling into the superstore parking lot, I turn off the engine and face Aunt May.

"I feel like I am getting to know you for the first time all over again. How did I not know these things? Mom rarely talked about you when I was growing up. I only knew she had a sister from the photo albums she kept. You two looked like best friends when you were younger. What happened? Why didn't you at least reconnect after I was born?" I bombard her with questions, trying to piece together my childhood memories.

"I was so focused on my career, I rarely came to visit. I thought sending money home back to the States could somehow replace my absence, but it never did. I was gone and disconnected for so long there was no way to contact me as your last living relative. You got lost in the foster system because of me," she says putting her hand over her mouth to stifle a cry.

We need to get out of this car to get some fresh air.

"Candice I am so sorry for all you had to go through. I am sorry I was not there for you when you needed me most. I accept I have to live with the guilt of losing my sister, but I made a promise to God that I would do right by you. So no, I never adopted or had any children of my own and technically you are my niece by blood. But the one thing I know for sure is that you are my daughter in every sense of the word. I will never try to replace your mother but know that until I take my last breath on this earth, I will do everything in my power to make up for lost time."

"I love you Auntie and I forgive you. You have to forgive yourself also. It may be your fault for losing contact with us, but it is not your fault that my parents were killed in that car accident. I may not have found you when I wanted to, but I eventually found you when I needed you most. I couldn't have made it through the last few years without you. We're family and I love you," I say, opening the car door and stepping out.

"I love you more, niece. You have grown into an amazing woman. Your mother would be so proud," she says as we hug in an empty parking space, "Now let's go shopping for this party of yours."

God is Good and Life is Good

Michele

"*H*un, Candice's house is just past the lake and to the right."

"I am glad you remember," Riley says, "I haven't been here in so long, everything looks so different."

We all awkwardly chuckle.

"None of us have," Brooklyn says, and I look out the window to process an unwelcome guilt.

"We've agreed to do better." Jeremiah reaches over to grab my hand.

"You have a big heart Babe. Stop beating yourself up," he whispers and then projects his voice, "We are about to have a New Year's Eve to remember. You have your girls and we get to welcome Jameson to the gang. God is good, and life is good."

"You can say that again." Riley smiles and bends over to kiss Jameson.

"Get a room you two," Brooklyn teases as we pull into the driveway.

"What kind of car is that?" Riley asks, pointing at the black BMW in the garage, "It looks like a spaceship."

Jameson and Jeremiah both look at each other and laugh. "That's the i8, it's one of the newer models. I was looking at getting one for myself at some point," Jameson says as the guys walk to the back of the truck to unload the luggage.

"Yes, enjoy it for the both of us young blood." Jeremiah laughs, "You have to give up those kinds of toys once you have kids. There's nowhere to put a car seat."

"Fair point." Jameson winks at Riley causing her to blush.

My girl is head over heels in love. Talking with him during the car ride he seems to be a great guy, I just hope they make the distance. Riley deserves this kind of happiness everyday of her life.

Walking to the front porch, the door opens as Candice stands there waving.

"Hey lovelies," she says with a huge smile. Walking into the foyer we stop and admire the pictures on the wall and the beautiful array of flowers.

"You've redecorated. This looks beautiful Candice," I say.

"Thank you. Come in and make yourselves at home. Calvin is finishing up the hors d'oeuvres in the kitchen and Aunt May is probably upstairs putting her party face on."

"Oh Aunt May! I can't wait to catch up with her. Did she bring some Grasovka from Germany? You know chocolate and vodka are my two favorite things together." Brooklyn sounds like a kid on Christmas.

"Yes, she did and wouldn't let me have any until you got here," Candice says and rolls her eyes, "I swear she loves you more than me."

"I won't disagree with you there. May I change in your room? I'll search for Auntie once she's dressed." Brooklyn walks up the stairs without waiting for an answer.

"That girl is something else." Candice laughs. "So, where are your guys?" she smirks, looking at Riley. "Specifically, where is Dr. Heartthrob?"

"How many nicknames do you all have for him?" she blushes. "He's outside with Jeremiah getting the luggage."

Right on cue, the guys walk up to the front porch.

"Candice. What's going on my sister," Jeremiah says, placing the luggage down to give her a hug.

"Nothing. Just living my brother."

Jameson places the remainder of the luggage down and stands beside Riley.

"Candice, this is my boyfriend Jameson. Jameson, this is one of my best friends, Candice," Riley says proudly and steps back.

"I've heard so much about you. It's a pleasure to finally meet you," Candice says, hugging Jameson.

"The pleasure is all mine. Riley speaks so highly of you ladies. I knew meeting you all was my last rite of passage with Riley," he says bluntly, making everyone laugh.

"What can I say? We love our girl."

"And so do I," Jameson adds.

"Okay Loverboy. Let's take the luggage upstairs and catch up with Calvin," Jeremiah interrupts.

"He's in the kitchen finishing the chicken dip. Ladies, shall we grab a drink and then intrude on Brooklyn trying to get sexy for Malcolm?" Candice suggests, and we walk over to the bar.

Grabbing Brooklyn's drink with my spare hand, I slowly walk up the stairs, careful not to spill any martini on Candice's plush white carpet lining the steps. Once we reach the top, Aunt May approaches us in the hallway.

"I thought I heard voices downstairs. How are you ladies? It's so good to see you again," Aunt May says as she kisses each of us one by one on the cheek. "Someone is missing." She looks around still fluffing the curls on her wig.

"Your darling Brooklyn is in my room getting dressed." Candice rolls her eyes.

"Since she's indisposed, I'll take her martini."

"Yes ma'am," I say as I hand her the glass and we enter Candice's enormous master bedroom.

As everyone gets comfortable on the couch at the foot of the bed, I opt to squat on the large suede ottoman.

"Brooklyn, your favorite Aunt is here," Candice teases and gestures a kiss to Aunt May.

"Coming." Brooklyn slips into her dress. "Auntie May! I've missed you," she says as her bare feet glide across the soft carpet. "I hope you've been well."

"My goodness Brook. You are even more luminous than the last time we embraced," Aunt May says as Riley and I look over at Candice who is green with jealousy.

Laughing, I nudge her and whisper, "Stop pouting. You know you have a special place in Aunt May's heart. Brooklyn just likes the attention."

"I know." Candice rolls her eyes and then turns her attention away from us, "Brooklyn tell Aunt May about your new boo."

"A new suitor? Oh, tell me more," Aunt May begs and sits back on the couch awaiting the details.

"Yes." Brooklyn exhales and rolls her eyes at Candice's jealousy.

These two ladies act just like siblings. Fighting for attention and throwing one another under the bus.

I shake my head at the thought and then listen in as Brooklyn begins to blush talking about my big brother.

"His name is Malcolm. He's a retired athlete and owns a software company. He's sexy, sweet, and a man I could see myself going the distance with," she says and then looks at me. "He's also Michele's older brother."

The room goes silent waiting for Aunt May's response. She looks around the group and then smiles.

"Well from the look on your face, I don't think there is much else to say. If he makes you this happy then I am ecstatic. Michele, why didn't you tell me you had a sexy older brother? I would've put my bid in long before Brooklyn sank her teeth into him," she teases, and everyone erupts with laughter.

Aunt May knows how to work a room.

"Well, you'll get to meet him tonight," I say. "Try not to give Brooklyn too much of a run for her money."

Aunt May points in Brooklyn's direction as she finishes applying her makeup, "If my dear Brooklyn is wearing *that* dress with *those* legs then I've lost the war before the battle has even begun. Any man would be a fool not to claim that prize."

"You can say that again," Candice says as she raises her glass. "A toast to a wonderful evening, ladies."

5...4...3...2...1!

Brooklyn

*A*s the evening picks up, I find myself searching for Malcolm. Every time the front door opens, my heart jumps into my throat as I await his familiar face. I haven't seen him since Madrid a few weeks ago but we've talked a few times.

I am still uncertain about where we stand. The two conversations we've had about our feelings weren't exactly productive as they ended with both of us tangled between the sheets. I would begin to talk about my feelings and he would compliment me in a way that makes me lose my focus. Next thing you know, we are going half on a baby and nothing gets accomplished. I know how I feel I just haven't heard him say the words. Are we even too old for him to ask me to be his girlfriend? Is that childish?

I continue getting lost in my thoughts as Candice makes her way to me.

"Hey Brooklyn. You remember Regina, my attorney?" She asks and hands me a drink as she eyes my watered-down mojito. "This is her husband, Jeff. He's a pilot also. I don't know the logistics, so I'll let him tell you the details. I told him you were a PIC for International Skyways."

"Yes, it's nice to see you again Regina and a pleasure to meet you Jeff," I say, trying to put on my corporate smile. "How long have you been in the sky?"

I nod as Jeff talks about aviation, but all of my attention is fixed on the front door.

Not listening to a word Jeff is saying, I smile and say, "Wow. That's awesome. I started my tenure in the Air Force and then made my way to commercial flights. How are the logistics in and out of Hartsfield?" I ask another random question, not caring about the response.

Tuning in on Jeff's last sentence I respond, "Yes, I've considered flying privately but the hours are so crazy. We must catch up later this evening. It was a pleasure seeing you both, but if you excuse me, I am going to find a powder room." I attempt to get out of the conversation without being too rude.

"*Pressed olives . . .*" Candice whispers, startling me as I try to sneak past the crowd to walk outside. This was our code word we used when we need to have an honest discussion. Standing next to her with our drinks, we put on fake smiles and begin talking.

Over the years we have mastered this charade. From a distance it looks like we are just smiling and chatting it up but most of the time we were having serious conversations we didn't want to draw attention to.

"You have been staring and pining at the front door all evening," she says. "I am not saying you should talk to other men because that would just be disrespectful, but you should at least try to engage with the crowd. You are beginning to look anti-social."

Putting on my fakest smile and taking a sip of my fresh mojito I say, "Girl, my emotions are in a whirlwind and this rum is kicking in. I'm trying."

"Umm hmm," she nods toward the door, "There's your man. Hopefully you'll be back to normal now that you've seen him. Don't walk over there looking all desperate. Let him come to you." She walks over and puts her hand on Calvin's shoulder where he is laughing with some of his colleagues.

Approaching Riley, I decide to try and make small talk until Malcolm notices me.

"Are you enjoying the party?" I ask with my back toward the front door.

"It's okay. I don't know half of these people but it's nice to be out and about for a change," she says and smiles with a lifted eyebrow. "Your man is walking over here so you no longer have to pretend like you didn't see him arrive."

Dang, am I that obvious? I should really get a grip. Brooklyn James does not pine over a man. This is so not me.

"Thanks for being a good wingman," I say apologetically.

"Umm hmm." Riley acknowledges my man, "Hey Malcolm, it's nice to see you again." She extends her arms to hug him.

"Dr. Harper. It's always a pleasure," he says looking down to my Louboutins, then up my legs to the hem of my Chanel black dress, slowly examining my body until our pulsating pupils meet.

I feel as if he is undressing me with his eyes and it's making the space between my legs heat up.

I bite the inside of my lip hard, trying to distract my hormones from overwhelming me.

"I'll leave you two alone," Riley says and walks away.

"Brooklyn you know how to take a man's breath away. You look amazing." He pulls me in close for a hug.

Wrapping my arms around him, we share a short embrace, but the chemistry is enough to erupt a volcano.

"You look very handsome yourself. I'm glad you could make it."

"Knowing that I am promised a kiss from you at midnight was all the motivation I needed to show up." He winks and my legs quiver.

"Malcolm, how's it going my man?" Jeremiah interrupts our longing stare.

"Bro, my sister finally talked you into visiting Atlanta. Now you have no excuse not to come by the crib," he teases and they both share a manly embrace.

"All work and no play man. Your sister and a set of twins take up all of my time, but the drive wasn't bad. We may be able to work something out," Jeremiah says and points at Jameson.

"Jameson this is Malcolm, Michele's older brother. Malcolm, this is Jameson," he says, and he and Malcolm share a smirk.

"Cool. Do you live here in Atlanta?" Malcolm asks taking the bait.

"No, I live in Charlotte, I'm Riley's boyfriend," Jameson says proudly.

"Wow. Little Riley has a man? In that case let's quit all the formalities, you are family. I have some Montecristos in the car. We'll light them up later tonight. Excuse us gentlemen," he says, then grabs my hand to pull me down the hallway to the last door.

"Is this a bedroom?" He opens the door.

"No, it's the study," I whisper as he quickly guides me in, careful not to be spotted.

"Even better." He locks the door, "I wouldn't want to defile any room someone has to sleep in tonight."

Trying to find my equilibrium, I walk backward until I am leaning up against Calvin's desk. I place my hands on the edge, careful not to knock anything over.

"Malcolm, I . . ." before I can finish the sentence, he lifts my entire body onto the desk and wraps my legs around his waist, knocking the lamp and mini globe onto the floor.

"Shhhh or someone will hear you," he whispers seductively and slowly kisses my bottom lip, then my collarbone, as he continues to make his journey down my entire body.

...

Walking out of the study, I decide to go up to Candice's room to regain my composure.

"I'll be back down in a second. I am going upstairs to the powder room," I say to Malcolm as he nods and kisses me on the cheek before walking back into the party.

Stepping into the master bathroom, I glance in the mirror at my sex hair and smirk.

Yes, it was definitely a good idea to come upstairs and freshen up. The girls would never let me live this down if they saw me.

Rejoining the party downstairs, I spot Riley and Michele sharing a laugh.

"Girl, I was looking for you. Where have you been?" Riley says, and Michele rolls her eyes after looking in Malcolm's direction.

Were we that obvious?

"What did I miss?" I attempt to change the subject.

"Not much. We have thirty minutes before the New Year countdown," Riley says and turns her attention across the room, "It looks like the boys have hit it off and started a bromance."

Candice and Aunt May walks over.

"Brooklyn, where is this sexy scoop of man you are dating? I have not had my proper introduction yet," Aunt May says and we all laugh. I gesture to Malcolm who has not taken his eyes off of me, then watch as he walks over to the lioness's den.

"Hello Ladies. I believe I already know everyone except this elegant beauty here." He kisses the back of Aunt May's hand and she blushes harder than I ever have.

"Malcolm, this is Candice's aunt, Maylene Bell. Aunt May, this is Malcolm Diamond." I make the introduction and wait for Aunt May to steal the show.

"It's a pleasure to meet you Ms. Maylene." He smiles showing his perfectly white teeth.

"Oh, the pleasure is all mine and call me Aunt May. I hear you and Ms. Brooklyn are a bit of an item." My heart jumps into my throat.

"Brooklyn is a lovely woman and I am enjoying getting to know her," he says and softly kisses my cheek.

"Yes, she is one of a kind. You'd be wise to remember that. Well it was lovely to have met you Mr. Malcolm," she says and leaves with the rest of the ladies following to give us some privacy.

Grabbing the glass of champagne from Malcolm's hand, I softly kiss his cheek and whisper, "Are you ready, Baby?"

He grabs the small of my back and pulls me closer as the countdown begins.

" 5…4…3…2…1! Happy New Year!"

Serious Conversations

Brooklyn

*W*alking back into the kitchen, I begin preparing a cup of chamomile tea. Since my thoughts are all over the place this morning, I need something to help me calm my nerves.

Grabbing my favorite *Cranky When NOT Flying* coffee mug, I drop in the tea bag and close my eyes to inhale the aroma as I fill the cup with hot water.

Jumping up on the kitchen island, I slowly sip the hot beverage while staring at the skyline from my panoramic windows. With all the cars and people carrying on with their daily routine to work, I am thankful my penthouse is soundproof from outside noise.

As I sit continuing to enjoy the effects of the tea, I get lost in my thoughts once more and begin to think about Malcolm. I can't wait to see him tonight. The New Year's Eve party feels like forever ago and we haven't had much time to spend together. I have been airborne nonstop since the beginning of the year as January is one of the busiest times for the industry. We have only been able to chat via text message and the occasional phone call. I am already in the doghouse for canceling three consecutive dates due to work.

Maybe I should cook something tonight for him, but what?

Unsure of what to prepare for dinner, I decide to call my mom and pluck a recipe from her brain but also to try and talk my feelings out. She is known for having some advice or wise anecdote to help me out of a funk.

"Brooklyn, Darling," my mom cheers. "I was just thinking about you. You remember Nancy from around the corner? Well her son just sold his mobile phone app to some large company in California. It's an app that translates instant messages once they appear on your phone or something like that." I roll my eyes at my mom's obvious attempt to try and hook me up with the neighborhood's prodigy.

"Yes, I remember him. Brandon, right?" I try to pretend this is the first time she's tried to set us up.

"Yes, Brandon. He was two grades ahead of you in school and boy has he made a name for himself. Nancy said that he paid off the mortgage and bought her a new car! He'll be in town for a few weeks. You should come home, I'm sure you two have a lot to catch up on," she insists, and I completely ignore her tactics.

"Mom how are you doing?" I try to change the subject.

"I'm good Baby. Your sisters have me here babysitting for the day."

As much as my mom loves kids, she shouldn't have to babysit every other day.

"Now how is my baby girl?" I don't get to see you as much as I like."

"I'm good mommy," I say, and I feel my chest tighten.

"What's wrong Baby? You only call me "mommy" when something is troubling you. Do I need to come to Charlotte?" she says in a way only a mother could.

"No ma'am. It's nothing like that."

"Okay then, tell *mommy* all about it," she says.

Taking a deep breath, I jump off of the kitchen island and begin to pace around my living room. This is a habit of mine when I need to have a *serious* conversation on the phone.

"There's this guy. We have been seeing each other for a couple of months and things are moving along great but . . ." I pause. "Mommy I think I am falling for him."

I walk back into the kitchen and take another sip of tea as I battle with the tears threatening to form.

"Well that's a good thing, Brook. Why do you sound so sad about it?" she asks and waits for me to respond.

"I guess I am afraid if I tell him how I feel, he may not feel the same way," I admit.

"Well sweetie, your worrying is warranted but life is about taking chances. Sometimes you just have to leap and hope the other person catches you. If they don't, it's okay that you fell and got hurt. The important thing is that you remain open to love and the next time you find it, you'll know that you need to run faster and jump harder to stick the landing," she says and that was the quote I needed.

Most of the time her random sayings don't mean much in the literal sense, but the metaphors somehow always work.

"I want what you and Dad had. You two just always seemed so in sync. I wish I could meet a man like that," I say and begin to miss my father.

"Child. You put your father so high up on this pedestal that you make it impossible for any man to reach. Your father was an amazing and loving man, God rest his soul, but he was still only a man. He had flaws and he worked my last nerve, but I loved him with every fiber of my being. We had our tough times, but we got through them by talking and being honest with one another. Once you can be completely honest about your feelings to yourself then you'll be able to open up to your guy," she says.

"Thanks Mom. You always know what to say to make things seem less scary." I wipe the tears as they continue to fall.

I really did miss my mom.

"You are welcome Baby. I do miss having you around. I will try not to play matchmaker if you promise to come home more," she teases, and I laugh before ending the call.

...

"Hi Beautiful," Malcolm says, standing in the doorway.

"Hi Back," I try to sound nonchalant but fail. "Come in."

Walking into my living room, he places his briefcase and bespoke suit jacket on the couch.

"How was your flight?" I ask, walking into the kitchen to pour us both a glass of wine.

"It was okay. My negotiations could've gone better, but I'll wait and see what their counteroffer looks like." He removes his tie and loosens the top two buttons on his shirt.

Too caught up in my own thoughts to comprehend what he is talking about, I respond, "Hmmm. Well I hope it works in your favor. Dinner will be ready shortly. I'll prepare the plates if you take the wine glasses and bread over to the table."

"Yes ma'am," he says and purposely brushes against my backside as he walks around the kitchen island while I remove the lasagna from the oven to cool.

Sitting down at the table, I place a large serving of lasagna and salad in front of him.

"Babe, this looks great. Thank you," he says.

"It was my pleasure. I figure every once in a while, I need to feed you outside of the bedroom." I bite my lip seductively but mainly to try and focus.

"I hope you didn't waste time making dessert, I already know what I am having after dinner," he says through heated eyes causing butterflies to invade my stomach.

Oh, this man.

After saying grace, we begin to enjoy dinner. I push a few of my lasagna noodles around trying to work up the nerve to say something.

"May I ask you a question?" I say and suddenly feel timid.

"Sure, what's on your mind." Malcolm continues to stuff his mouth with lasagna.

"How do you feel about me? About us?"

"What do you mean?" he asks, still savoring every morsel of food.

Taking a sip of wine to regain my courage I confess, "I have a bad habit of overthinking things and misreading situations so I need your help to shut off my brain."

Malcolm places his fork down and takes a sip of his wine. "So how exactly are you reading *this* situation Brooklyn?" he asks, his question throwing me a little.

"These last few months have been amazing and I love spending time with you. Your actions say you feel the same way, but I would be a fool to assume something until I hear it from you," I say modestly.

"Fair. I'm not great with words, I am more of an action man but if you need to hear me say it then okay. Brooklyn, I am crazy about you. I don't want to get caught up in labels, but you are special to me. You have been in my life all along but at the same time, it's like you came out of nowhere. You know all about my childish past and yet you still gave me a chance to be in your present. I have never met a woman who gets me the way you do," he says and my heart jumps into my throat.

He's crazy about me!

"Wow. Seriously?" I try to process Malcolm's revelation.

"You are really going to soak this up, huh," he teases. "We play video games like teenagers, and you're actually good at it. You don't mind my travel schedule because yours is just as crazy. You're a southern belle who knows her way around the kitchen. Your bedroom appetite far exceeds mine and did I mention, I'm dating a pilot! Aunt May was right when she said you are one of a kind!"

Pushing back from the table, he stands and softly cups the back of my neck, forcing me out of my seat. Standing eye level, we briefly scan each other's pupils wanting to say so much but unable to find the words.

"Does that clear any misinterpretations you were worried about?" he asks as he bites my lip.

"Yes," I moan through lasagna-flavored kisses and wrap my arms around him as he lifts me onto the kitchen island, the same spot I was once so worried how he felt about me.

Carter Montgomery

Candice

"Good Morning Mr. and Mrs. Montgomery, may I get you a water, coffee, or tea?" the receptionist asks as she directs us to the conference room.

"A cup of tea and a water please," I respond, and Calvin squeezes my hand.

He knows I only drink tea when I am nervous or stressed.

"Honey. This is no different than any of the other interviews we've had with the agency. We've got this," he whispers and kisses my cheek.

He was right, but something felt different this time. Our other interviews have been at our house, in our own environment. The fact that we are asked to be here in person means either we have been denied as suitable adoptive parents or they have actually matched us with a child.

The thought of either outcome sends my nerves into a spiral. Sitting in the conference room, I begin to feel nauseous and light-headed.

What is going on with me and why am I so nervous?

"Excuse me," I say to Calvin and expeditiously walk to the restroom before my breakfast redecorates the office floor. Looking at myself in the mirror, I slow my breathing in an effort to calm my nerves.

Candice Smith Montgomery, you are fierce, phenomenal, and a force to be reckoned with. You have so much in life to be thankful for and so much love to give to this child. You can do this, just like you've done everything else you set your heart on. College Graduate, Wife, Author, and now a Mother…God's got you through everything else and he'll get you through this.

I finish the pep talk to myself and then gargle some water to get rid of the upchuck aftertaste. Popping a mint into my mouth, I exit the lavatory and return to the conference room to sit beside my husband who is already speaking with our agent.

"Mrs. Montgomery, what a pleasure it is to see you again," Pamela says as I try to decipher if her facial expression is preparing us for good or bad news.

"Likewise. I hope you have been well since our last meeting." I unknowingly squeeze Calvin's hand tightly.

"Thank you both for meeting me here today on such short notice. I can tell you are very anxious, so I won't stall any longer. You were added to the suitable adoptive parent register a few days ago and before we could inform you, we found a match!" she exclaims and my heart leaps into my throat.

"You mean. You found us a baby?" Calvin asks as his eyes begin to swell with tears.

"Yes, a beautiful baby boy." She slides a large portrait in front of us, "His name is Carter."

Holding the picture, Calvin and I both give way to a silent cry.

"A son? We have a son?" Calvin asks, staring at the picture in awe.

Carter is a beautiful two-year old with black curly hair, light-brown eyes, and a smile that will overwhelm your heart to the brink of explosion. I fell in love with him at first sight.

"He's beautiful," I say, continuing to cry as I held the picture. "Our son, Carter."

Patiently waiting for us to regain our composure Pamela says, "I will give you two a moment. Excuse me." She gets up to place a box of tissues on the table and gives us a polite smile before exiting the conference room.

Turning and looking at Calvin, who is still shaking his head in disbelief, I place the picture down to hug my husband.

"Baby, I have never been so happy in my life," he says squeezing me tight.

"I know Babe. We have a beautiful and healthy baby boy. God has blessed us with a child to raise and love unconditionally." I cry and let my emotions get the best of me.

I don't know if it is the joy of becoming a mother or feeling the wetness of my husband's tears run down my back but in this moment, I am an emotional wreck.

"Yes, He did. I have been praying long and hard for this. We've been through so much to get to this moment," Calvin says, and I begin to cry even harder.

"Babe we can't go there right now or else I'll never stop crying in this office," I plead.

"Yes, let's pull ourselves together before they think we are unfit and too emotional."

"You make a good point." I chuckle and pass him a tissue. Even with swollen, teary eyes, Calvin still makes my heart flutter.

I whisper, "I love you Calvin."

...

"Good Morning," Brooklyn says, more chipper than usual.

"Good morning to you too," I whisper as I slide out of bed trying not to wake Calvin.

Walking downstairs and into the kitchen, I increase my volume, "You sound energetic this morning. What's the occasion?"

Brooklyn moves the phone away from her mouth and orders two large café mochas with soy and no whip crème.

"I am down the road. Get dressed," she commands.

"Down the road? When did you come to Atlanta?" I question but she ignores.

"Get dressed. I'll be there in twenty minutes. Love you, mean it." she hangs up.

Ending the call, I begin to feel annoyed and excited with Brooklyn's unexpected visit.

She knows how to shake things up, that's for sure. How did she find time to make a trip to Atlanta with all the work travels? I guess Malcolm has really done a number on her.

I walk into the bedroom and glance over at Calvin who is still sound asleep.

He's going to hate going to the farmer's market by himself today.

Jumping into the shower, I close my eyes as the water splashes on my face and I begin to pray.

Thank you, God for this overwhelming abundance of joy. You have made my husband the happiest man on Earth. I pray that you wrap your arms around this family as we begin this new chapter of parenthood and allow Baby Carter to embrace us with his little open baby arms. Amen.

I finish my silent prayer and allow the water from the shower to wash away my tears beginning to fall.

Stepping out of the shower, Calvin passes me a towel. I had been so lost in my thoughts that I hadn't noticed him enter the master bathroom.

"You could've joined me, husband," I tease and stand in front of my side of the vanity.

"I considered it, but you looked like you needed the moment for yourself." He begins brushing his teeth as I do the same.

"I did. Thanks for noticing. Brooklyn is on her way," I say after wiping excess toothpaste from my mouth.

"I didn't know she was in town," Calvin says after spitting and continuing to brush.

"Neither did I. I'm sure Malcolm has something to do with it, but it will be a pleasant surprise to see her. Will you be terribly mad if I ditched our Saturday visit to the farmer's market?" I look at him with my puppy pouting eyes and he rinses his mouth before kissing me with wet lips.

"Go hang with your girl," he says as he takes his shirt and boxers off and turns toward the shower.

Dang why can't Brooklyn be an hour away, I wouldn't mind taking another shower.

I continue to weigh my options as I examine the muscles flexing on Calvin's back through the mirror.

Turning around he teases, "You can join me if you like. I will gladly take the blame for the increase in the water bill this month." I walk over to kiss him.

"No, I don't want to start something and not finish it. Besides, I need to talk to Brooklyn about everything that's happened."

"Take all the time you need today, Love. This will change our lives forever. I'll survive at the farmer's market," he says and pats my backside before hopping into the shower.

"I pulled up ten minutes ago, but I decided to call my mom and give you a little more time," Brooklyn says as I open the front door.

"You are ever so kind, thank you." I reach out to hug my best friend.

"How is Mama James doing? Please tell her I said hi the next time you talk to her."

I grab one of the coffees out of Brooklyn's hand before walking into the kitchen.

"She is doing good. My sisters have her playing nanny dearest, as usual. One day I will buy a large house and move her onto the east wing, so she can sit down and relax. But I honestly think she likes being needed," Brooklyn says as she follows me to the kitchen.

"You might be right. I'm sure all the running around with the kids keeps her feeling young. To what do I owe the pleasure of this visit?"

"Can't a girl just visit her best friend without any ulterior motives? she says innocently, and I roll my eyes.

"Yes, a *girl* can but not you."

"Maybe I was in the area and missed your face. Did you ever think about that?"

She insists on prolonging her true intentions.

"Girl cut the act. You live five hours away, but your *boyfriend* is less than thirty minutes from here. Are you spending the weekend with Malcolm?"

"Yes, I came in town Thursday and am going back tonight. He had meetings all morning, so I figured I would come and visit my bestie."

"I'm flattered. It's nice to know you've been here since Thursday and I get to see you hours before you depart," I say and internally kick myself for sounding petty.

"Don't be like that," she says, "I knew you were busy during the week, so I planned to hit you up today. Do you and Calvin still visit the farmer's market on Saturdays? Please give him my apologies if I ruined your weekend routine."

"Yes, but I wanted to talk with you anyway so seeing you in person will make this a little easier," I confess and steady my nerves.

"What's going on?" she asks just as Calvin enters the kitchen.

"Good Morning Ladies. Brooklyn it's good to see you again." He walks over and kisses me before grabbing my coffee and taking a sip.

"Hey Bro. I was just apologizing to Candice for disrupting your Saturday trip to the farmer's market," Brooklyn says.

"It's all good. I am going to head out before all of the good buys are gone. Babe, I'm blocked in, so I'll take your car. Love you. See you later Brooklyn." He kisses me once more and walks out with my coffee still in hand.

"We love you too," Brooklyn yells and we all laugh.

Waiting until the garage door through the kitchen closes, Brooklyn gets up and walks into the living room as I follow.

"So, what's going on?" she asks giving me her undivided attention when we both sit on the couch.

Standing up, I walk over to the mantel to retrieve a framed picture of my latest admiration. Passing the picture to Brooklyn without saying a word, she looks at it puzzled.

"Who is this adorable baby? Do you have a godson I don't know about?"

"No," I say, as tears fill my eyes, "but you do. This is Carter Montgomery, your godson."

On cue Brooklyn's eyes overflow with tears as she begins to put together the riddle in her head. "You've decided to . . . I have a . . ." still unable to complete her sentences. "This is *my* godson?"

"Yes. We are adopting him and will bring him home in a few weeks. I would like for you to be his godmother, Brooklyn," I say as my hormones and emotions get the best of me.

"Of course, I will. It will be an honor. Thank you, Candice, this means the world to me." Neither of us can control our emotions now.

"You mean the world to us, to me. If anything ever happened to me or Calvin, I'd want you to be the one to show our son the world and raise him to strive to achieve for greatness," I say and mean every word of it.

"Best friend, you don't have to leave us for me to help raise and show him the world. Auntie Brooklyn will be right here every step of the way, even if I have to hop on an Atlanta flight every other week." She reaches over to hug me. "I am so happy for the two of you!"

"Thank you, Bestie. This was a big step for me after everything that's happened, but Calvin is over-the-moon happy, so I feel like it's the right decision," I say, and a slight feeling of nausea returns.

"I'm sure he is but how do you feel Candice? This impacts you just as much as it does him."

"I guess I am still a little nervous about the idea. I know I will be a great mother, but it just all became real too fast. I thought I had more time to mentally prepare for bringing a child into our home, into our world," I admit and feel my nerves begin to calm themselves.

"I totally get that. Well you are not in this alone. I know last time you felt…" Brooklyn begins to choke on her own words but shakes it off. "Just know you'll never have to feel alone again."

Nodding to assure her I know what she is trying to say, I reach over to hug her.

Wiping the tears from our eyes we both sit back and admire the picture of Carter once more.

"He really is the cutest kid I've ever seen. He's going to grow up and break a lot of hearts." Brooklyn smiles and wipes one last tear away.

"Yes, and I haven't done a thing to the guest room to prepare for his arrival." I force myself back to reality.

"That's an easy fix. We can go shopping now if you like."

"Thank you Brook but no, this is something I want to do with Calvin. He's so excited about a son. But enough about me, how are you and Malcolm coming along? I take from the extended stays in Atlanta that things are good?"

Smiling like a Cheshire cat, she confesses, "Things are great actually. He's slowly forcing me to break down walls I forgot I ever built."

"That's good Brooklyn! Seeing you light up when he walked into the New Year's Eve party was confirmation enough for me. If you are truly happy then that's all that matters. Also, I am selfishly glad that I will get to see you more in Atlanta now," I say.

"Yes, I do love the idea that my best friend and boyfriend are in the same city, but I really am happy Candice. He just gets me. The good, the bad, and the crazy. He gets me."

"Wow! Is Captain Brooklyn James falling in love? Say it isn't so!"

Sister-In-Law

Riley

"*I* will pick you up on Sunday once we land."

"Mom, you do know I am old enough to stay home for the weekend, right?" Blythe asks sarcastically as she opens the passenger door after I park in my parents' driveway.

"Yes, I know but you don't have a car and I don't want you on the other side of town stranded. I'll feel better knowing you are safe with your Grams and Pops." I grab her duffel bag from the back seat and feel somewhat guilty.

"Again, this could all be avoided if I had a car," she whispers.

"Not today Blythe Alexis. I love you. Call me if you need anything," I say before giving her a hug and kiss.

"Love you more mommy. Tell Mr. Jameson I said congrats."

Sitting in the driveway until she walks into the house, I honk the horn at my dad walking out of the garage. Putting my car in reverse, he waves me down to disrupt my quick drive by drop-off attempt.

"Hey baby girl, where you headed in such a rush," he says, slowly strutting to the driver's side of my sedan.

"Hey Dad, I am late to meet Jameson and go to the airport," I lie trying to avoid a long-winded conversation. "His award banquet in Connecticut is tomorrow so Blythe is staying with you all for the weekend."

"Oh yes, I remember now, he's receiving the Hartley Humanitarian Award. That's a major accomplishment for a young African American surgeon. Please extend my congratulations to him."

My father sounds prouder of Jameson than he ever was of me.

"I will Dad. I have to go, I'm running late. Love you. Bye," I say and roll my eyes while rolling up the window.

I guess this means that my father approves.

...

"Good evening Dr. Young and welcome back," the young flight attendant says as we settle into our first-class seats, "May I get you and your guest a beverage while we complete the boarding process?"

"Nice to see you again Kristina. Yes, I would like a Jack and coke and get this lovely woman a glass of Chardonnay," Jameson says before sending a wink my way.

"Wow, I thought Brooklyn was a professional traveler, but you fit right in with this lifestyle," I tease as the flight attendant passes me a glass of wine.

"I take this flight often when I go home to visit my family. Coincidentally the same crew members are frequently scheduled to work the evening Charlotte to Hartford flights," he says, and I can tell he is trying to overexplain the young and attractive *Kristina* being so friendly. Looking out the window and smiling, I take of sip of wine and send up a small prayer.

God please let his family love me as much as I love this man. Amen.

Disrupting my thoughts, Jameson grabs my free hand and kisses it softly.

"Is everything okay? I lost you for a second. Where did you go?" he asks.

"I'm just a little nervous about meeting your family, that's all."

"They will love you. Maybe even more than I do considering you will be the first woman that I'm bringing home," he says.

"Seriously? Well that doesn't lessen my anxiety at all." I sigh and consume my entire glass of wine.

"Try not to let that scare you too much instead, wear it as a badge of honor. You're the only woman who is, without a doubt, beyond worthy of meeting my family. I have never loved anyone more than I love you Riley." He pulls my chin up to his for a kiss.

God, what did I do to deserve this man and what can I do to never mess this up?

...

"Are you ready Babe?" Jameson asks as he places our luggage down to open the front door of his mother's house.

"Yes, I'm ready." I smile and exhale deeply. Turning the key and opening the front door, three kids run full speed to the doorway.

"Uncle Jamie!" they all scream at once.

"Hey kiddos," he scoops them all up with both arms. "I've missed you guys."

"Uncle Jaime, I lost two teeth and got five dollars from the tooth fairy. See," one of the little girls says as she opens her mouth for Jameson to examine.

"Whoa Gabby, make sure you add it to your piggy bank. You have another one that is loose here in the front." He puts them down as the other two insist on giving him an update on their little exciting lives.

Clearly forgetting my existence for a moment, I stand back and smile as he kneels in front of the kids and actively listens to each of their updates.

"Kids let your uncle get past the front door," a gentle older voice from the kitchen says and I wait patiently for the person to appear in the foyer.

This is more nerve-wracking than waiting for exam scores in medical school.

Standing at a mere five feet, four inches, a silver-haired woman walks out wearing a floor length kimono and a warm smile. She is a light caramel complexion with dark mocha freckles under both of her eyes. Stunned by her beauty, I stand smiling, waiting for Jameson to make an introduction.

"Kids go upstairs and play, I'll bring you some snacks in a bit," she says, and they all turn to run up the stairs.

"Thanks Mom, that could've gone on for hours." Jameson laughs and brushes off his pant legs while standing and leaning over to kiss his mother's cheek.

This is his mother? My goodness she is beautiful!

Still standing awkwardly with a smile frozen on my face, I look at Jameson with a lifted eyebrow.

"Yes, of course," he says as if he can read my mind, "Mom, I would like for you to meet my girlfriend, Dr. Riley Harper. Riley this is my lovely mother, Deborah Young."

Blushing once again from Jameson's formal introduction of me, I extend my hand toward her.

"Mrs. Young, it's a pleasure to finally meet you." I awkwardly wait for her to shake my hand.

"Baby, we are a hugging family. Come here," she says smiling as I bend down to hug her. Her hug felt so warm it was hard for me to let go.

"Jameson, she is absolutely stunning. Why have you been hiding her for so long?" she asks, stepping back to examine me.

"I wasn't hiding her; I just didn't want to overwhelm her. The ladies of this house are a lot for anyone to take on all at once," he admits and kisses me on the cheek.

"Well take that luggage upstairs while Riley and I grab a cup of tea. Your sisters went to the airport to pick up Mandy."

"Why didn't she just ride from the airport with us?" Jameson asks walking toward the stairs.

"She flew into New Haven. She has a new love interest at Harvard and will probably stay there after your banquet tomorrow."

She interlocks with my arm and guides me into the kitchen.

"Mrs. Young, you have a beautiful home," I say as I sit at the bar while she prepares tea.

"Sweetheart, the way my son speaks so highly of you please, call me Deborah Jean . . . or *Mom*." She winks, and I immediately turn red.

Mom? What has he told her about me? Has he discussed marriage with her?

Suppressing my thoughts, I smile. "I'll go with Deborah Jean until further notice."

"Fair enough." She places two saucers in front of me, "Riley, I have been *so* looking forward to meeting you. Tell me a little more about yourself. Jameson says your father is a surgeon and you have a brilliant daughter named Blythe. I would love to hear more."

Stunned that Jameson has clearly done way more than talk me up, I clear my throat and take a sip of tea.

"Wow, Jameson has been quite chatty," I say and she laughs.

"My son is *infatuated* with you. You and medicine are all he talks about." I blush once more.

"Well, I am originally from a small beach town called Nags Head, North Carolina," I say and prepare to give my spiel of comparing it to a more familiar town in the Carolinas like Wilmington.

"Is that near Roanoke Island?" Deborah Jean asks.

"Yes, it is. I'm impressed. I had to pull out a map for Jameson when I first told him."

"My baby is great with hearts but not so much when it comes to geography."

"So, I was born there, attended Charlotte A&T University for undergrad, and then Duke Medical School shortly after. I just recently moved back to Charlotte to finish out my residency and to be closer to my daughter," I say trying not to reveal too much too soon.

"Yes, the lovely Ms. Blythe. Jameson tells me she's off to college in the fall, you must be so proud."

Jameson has probably already told her my entire life's story. As displeased as that makes me, I still love that man.

"Yes ma'am, I am extremely proud. She is still deciding between her top three schools, but I'm thoroughly pleased regardless of where she decides to go," I say, and I can feel my chest inflate with pride.

"That is just marvelous. I look forward to meeting her one day." She smiles and I shake my head at my uncontrolled blushes. Suddenly the front door opens, and the laughs of women fill the silence.

"Jameson, where is our sister-in-law?" one of the voices yells to the top of the stairs.

"Hi ladies," I hear Jameson say as footsteps approach the kitchen. I stand to endure another embarrassing introduction and Deborah Jean grabs my hand before I can move toward Jameson.

"Girls, this is Riley. Riley, this is my eldest daughter Lisa, then Vanessa, and my youngest, Amanda," she says pointing to each by name and then winking at me. "No need for another torturous and overly formal introduction from my son. You're one of *my* girls now." This time Jameson's cheeks turn a light shade of red.

"Well then, come on in and give us a hug," Vanessa says as they all stretch their arms out for me to join. Uncomfortable with all of the affection, I muster up a fake smile and allow them to smother me with hugs.

"Okay ladies. Don't scare her off with all the love and affection," Jameson says and rescues me.

"I told you they were a lot. I'm sorry." He looks at me in apology.

"Oh no, it's fine. I'm happy to finally meet you all. I've heard so much about you." I nod at Jameson with approval.

...

Walking into the banquet, I feel a little like Cinderella going to the ball. Michele and Brooklyn have styled me in a stunning navy, strapless mermaid gown to complement Jameson's charcoal Brioni tailored suit and navy bow tie.

Positioned comfortably on his arm, we work the room and socialize with some prominent names in medicine and philanthropy.

"Ladies and gentlemen, please find your seats," the emcee announces from the podium.

Making our way to the front of the room, I feel an array of eyes glued to us as we glide to the table with a sign marked *Reserved for Humanitarian Recipient & Guests*.

Pulling out my chair, Jameson kisses the nape of my neck and says, "Riley, you sure know how to make an entrance. If you weren't already mine, I would have been fighting my way through the crowd the moment you walked in for your attention." Blushing, I raise my hand to cup his cheek and lower his head for a kiss.

"I am all yours for as long as you'll have me," I whisper, and he walks over to pull out the chair for his mother and Mandy.

"Okay, you two. Save that for the celebratory nightcap." Lisa smiles as both her and Vanessa's husband pull out their chairs to sit.

"Welcome to a night filled with Medicine, Miracles, and Martinis," the emcee says and the crowd chuckles. "Tonight, we have the privilege of honoring some of the most talented and selfless individuals in medicine."

As the evening progresses, I feel myself falling more and more in love with Jameson. Many of the younger doctors who are receiving awards personally thank him for his support and mentorship over the years. Watching him stand on stage and shake the hands of twenty-five first-year medical school students receiving a scholarship in his father's name almost brings me to tears.

This man is phenomenal.

As he stands on the podium speaking to the young futures of medicine, I glance around the table at his family. Stunned that they are all staring at me in awe instead of Jameson, I turn to Deborah Jean and give her a confused look.

"Riley you really do love my son, don't you," she asks and the cracking in her voice almost unravels me.

"Yes ma'am. Very much so." I nod confidently as she grabs my hand and squeezes it.

Jameson walks back to his seat just as the lights dim for a short video. Looking up at the screen, my eyes widen in awe at the sight of a young Jameson in Africa treating ill children, examining difficult medical cases, and testimonials from past patients and other surgeons who have worked with him. When a clip of his father comes on the screen, he squeezes my hand and turns to his family who have all lowered their heads with sorrow.

Once the video ends, an older, yet distinguished man walks up to the podium. "Ladies and Gentlemen, I have had the privilege of mentoring this extraordinary young man over the years and have even learned a thing or two myself from him. Please join me in welcoming two-time recipient of the Newman Tucker Medical Award, Co-founder of the James Young Memorial Scholarship, and this year's Hartley Humanitarian, Dr. Jameson A. Young."

A sea of applause fills the room with mine being the loudest. Standing to my feet, I clap like a proud parent at graduation as Jameson buttons his blazer and walks on stage.

"Thank you everyone," he says modestly. Looking out into the crowd as the cheers settle, he looks down at me and smiles.

"I think my speech to the scholarship recipients may have been longer than this one, but I would like to say a few additional words. My father wasn't a rich man, but he was a man rich with love. He loved his family until the day he took his last breath. I became a heart surgeon because I never again wanted to be in a position where I couldn't help someone with a heart as loving as my father's. For some reason I always felt like a cliché in that aspect until someone very special told me that it doesn't make me a cliché, it makes me a humanitarian," he says and winks at me.

On cue, I blush and wipe another stray tear from my eye.

"So, this award goes to all of you young and brilliant minds out there who, at times, feel like a cliché for your reasons of getting into medicine. Know that it's okay to be a cliché, just be a phenomenal and selfless one. Thank you all," he says as we stand to our feet once more to applaud and celebrate him.

Returning to his seat and resting his hand on my thigh I whisper, "You are amazing Dr. Young. If you weren't already mine, I'd move a mountain to get to you."

Turning and smiling from ear to ear he whispers, "I am all yours for as long as you'll have me Dr. Harper."

New and Improved

Brooklyn

*S*orry *Babe, I have to extend my trip in South America. I'll make it up to you. I promise.* I read the message from yet another canceled opportunity to spend time with Malcolm.

Something has to give, I am starting to feel like we are more or less pen pals than a couple. Or whatever we are.

Responding, I roll my eyes with annoyance. The last few weeks, I have wanted nothing more than to be cuddled up with my man and it is starting to make me feel vexed. I miss him. I decide to go for a run to blow off some steam.

...

Turning onto Mint Street, I take the scenic route past the Panther's stadium, and end my run at my favorite coffee shop across from my building.

Waiting in line to order my coffee, I use this time to check my phone. I purposely put my phone on silent, so it does not disrupt my run. Pulling my phone out of the arm holster, I check to see if I have any missed messages, *specifically from Malcolm.* Nothing.

Oblivious of my surroundings, I keep my head down in my phone as I slowly move with the line of people waiting to place their orders.

"Brookie?" I hear a familiar voice say and look up to see Tyson David standing tall in an all-black suit and tie.

Gosh, he looks even better than the last time I saw him.

"Hey Ty . . . I mean Tyson. How are you," I sound more shocked than I intended to.

"I'm doing well. What are the odds of running into you here?"

"Very likely, considering I live in the building across the street," I say sarcastically and we both laugh.

"Wow, so you really have moved on up to the East side."

"I guess so but from the looks of that suit, life seems to be treating you just as well." I step up to the counter to place my order.

"Good morning, may I have a grande café mocha with soy and no whip," I say, and Tyson quickly hands the barista his debit card before I can reach for mine.

"Please let me," he insists. "I see nothing has changed after all of these years when it comes to your coffee of choice."

"Yes, I'm still the same girl deep down inside, always running late on account of a coffee detour."

"May I join you to catch up?" he asks as we search for an empty table in the busy bistro.

"Sure," I say even though I had all intentions of going back home to shower and call my man.

There is something about his demeanor that intrigues me. I want to know more about this new and improved Tyson David.

"So, what brings you uptown?" I ask when we find a seat at a small table in the back corner.

"I was actually accepting a job offer as offensive line coordinator for Charlotte A&T." His face illuminates with pride.

"Really? That's amazing. Congratulations!"

"Yes, I had been trying to get my foot in the college sporting community for a long time now. I just hate that I will have to leave my boys back at North Charlotte. Those kids have really changed my life over the years," he says, and I notice the same spark in his eyes he used to have when he played football.

Wow, we both have come a really long way since we said goodbye.

"So how is everyone?" Tyson asks, changing the subject, "Every time I see Blythe on campus, all I see is a mini Riley from back in the day."

"Everyone is good. Riley is preparing Blythe for college in the Fall, Michele and Jeremiah have the perfect set of twins, and Candice and Calvin are still our Michelle and Barack," I say with sarcasm.

"That's good, and how about you? Are you seeing anyone? Is it serious?" He takes a sip of his coffee.

Looking down at my phone at the disappointing screen of zero messages or missed calls yet again, I smile at Tyson.

"Yes, I am and yes, it is pretty serious." I attempt to oversell it with false confidence.

"That's awesome Brookie. I'm so happy for you," he says and reaches over to touch my hand. Looking down at the wedding band on the hand touching me, I slide my hand back and grasp my coffee cup.

"And how about you? That's a lovely wedding ring," I gesture my head toward the table.

Sliding his hand back, he examines the ring and smiles, "Yes, I got married about two years ago. We both worked at North Charlotte High. It's one of the classic love stories of two faculty members falling for each other. We're expecting our first child this summer," he says trying to overexplain his wife in an effort to encourage me to discuss Malcolm, but I choose not to.

"That's great. I'm happy that you found someone who makes you happy," I lie. "It was great seeing you Tyson, but I have some errands to run before the day gets away from me."

Standing up, he innocently grabs my hand causing me to stop dead in my tracks.

"It was really great seeing you again Brooklyn. Take care of yourself." He opens his arms for a hug.

Reluctantly, I return the gesture and prepare for the awkward "church hug" again. Even with the respectable space between us, his hugs still somehow make me weak and heady.

I have to get out of here. Now!

Giving him a half smile, I turn and walk out of the coffee shop and force myself not to glance back at him.

Not too Sappy

Brooklyn

"Captain James welcome back. As you know, this is only a forty-five-minute flight to Atlanta but would you like a beverage or snack before we take off?" the flight attendant asks as she directs passengers boarding the plane.

"No thank you, Carol." I begin fiddling with my phone.

This has quickly become a routine of jumping on the Charlotte to Atlanta flights once I land from Madrid. Getting a chance to see Candice and spending time with Malcolm was something I started looking forward to each trip.

Walking out of the airport, I smile as Malcolm's Aston Martin smoothly glides up to the curb.

"Good morning beautiful," he says as the trunk slowly opens awaiting to store my luggage.

"Hi handsome," I softly kiss my man as he stands holding the passenger door for me to sit.

Closing the trunk and jumping into the driver's seat he says, "I have missed you Captain James. You have no idea."

"I've missed you more. I don't want to see airports until Saturday. Let's get out of here." He drives the car toward the terminal exit.

"I have a surprise for you waiting at the house," he says as he lifts my hand to kiss the back.

"Oh, I like surprises. I have one for you as well. It's in a little pink bag in my suitcase."

"Hmm, I think we will enjoy your surprise first," he smiles and floors the gas pedal, forcing my head to hit the back of the seat.

...

Walking into Malcolm's five-star bachelor's condo, I notice a large black box on the floor with a red ribbon. Overwhelmed with joy, I turn and look at him.

"What is that?" I ask jumping like a kid on Christmas.

"Open it and see." He takes my jacket off to hang in the coat closet.

Kneeling down at the box, I slowly unravel the tie and turn back to glance at Malcolm as I grasp the lid with both hands.

"Open it," he says smiling.

Removing the lid, I look down in the box and my jaw completely drops.

"Malcolm, when did you find the time to get all of these?" I ask still stunned at what I was looking at.

"I told you that I would make up big time for canceling our dates. This is my grand gesture to you," he kneels down in front of the box with me. "A complete collection of your favorite classic movies. I have everything in there from *Casablanca* to *Citizen Kane* to *The Graduate* and all in authentic film reel."

He stands and presses a button on his media control panel commanding a projection screen to descend from the ceiling.

"I even had a cinema film projector installed," he says and reaches out to help me stand. "Since you always tease me for not seeing any of these, I figure we could spend the next few days and watch them together."

Still in complete shock, I stare at Malcolm without saying a word.

"Do you like it or is it too much?" he asks patiently waiting for me to take it all in.

"Malcolm, this is the sweetest thing anyone has ever done for me. I love it! Thank you!" I leap into his arms.

"Good. You had me worried for a second. I hope it's not *too sappy* and you revoke my man card for this," he teases, and lifts me on the back of his black leather sectional.

"No Mr. Diamond, it is just sappy enough. Your man card is still active, and I will continue to keep your sensitive side a secret. Scouts honor," I tease and place two fingers over my heart.

"Thank you. Now that you have seen my surprise, are you going to change into yours?" The atmosphere quickly shifts in the room.

"I'm already wearing it," I whisper just before biting the edge of his ear lobe.

Raising my arms, I patiently wait as he reaches down and pulls my dress over my head, letting it slide off of the couch and onto the floor.

"I am in complete awe of you," he steps back and admires me wearing nothing but my birthday suit and red Louboutin heels. I reach down to remove my heels and he grabs my hand and scoops me into his arms.

"No ma'am. Keep those on," he says as he slowly kisses me on our short walk to the bedroom.

...

Waking up, I roll over to discover that Malcolm is no longer in bed.

"Babe?" I yell, and I can hear him in the distance talking to someone. Grabbing his shirt, I fasten a few buttons, just enough to cover my unmentionables. Walking into the kitchen, I see Malcolm in a heated discussion on the phone.

"That was not the original agreement. When I left, I thought everything was secure and the contracts would be signed this morning. Why do I even pay you if I have to do everything myself?" he continues to yell on the phone completely oblivious of my presence. "You're fired, I'll take care of it myself!" He slams the phone down on the counter and is startled when he looks up to see my face.

"Babe, I'm sorry. Did I wake you?" his tone and demeanor soften.

"No, I rolled over to lay on your chest and you weren't there," I say meekly.

"I'm sorry. One of my associates completely dropped the ball, *pun intended*, on this deal with the Football Association in South America. I have to get on a flight today to clean up his mess," he says. I try to stifle my disappointment.

"What about our weekend together? Malcolm, we haven't spent time in weeks."

I hate that I sound like a needy girlfriend.

"Babe, I know but this deal could completely dominate our share in the market. I know you don't understand but this is huge," he says.

"Can't you send your partner instead?" I mentally prepare to lose this battle.

"No, Brooklyn I can't send my partner. This is my deal. I am closing this," he says and then suddenly realizes how harsh he sounds. "Babe. I'm sorry. I should be back by Sunday and I promise to make it up to you. Why don't you stay here and spend the weekend with your girl until I return?"

"I didn't come to see Candice, I came here to spend time with you. But go ahead to South America and close your deal Malcolm. It's clearly more important to you," I snap and storm off to the master bedroom to get my things.

…

Stepping into my penthouse, I drop my luggage at the door and begin to sob. I have an overwhelming mixture of anger, sadness, and disappointment that I can no longer contain.

Lying on my couch, I wrap myself in a throw blanket and cry until I have emptied out my emotions. Once my eyes are sore and dry, I silently make a promise to myself that this will be the first and last time I cry over Malcolm.

I just can't believe he doesn't see how this deal is hurting our relationship. I could very well be in love with him, but I can't keep playing second to his career. There will always be some new deal that he needs to close, am I really ready to compete against his success and ambition?

Feeling my phone vibrate in my back pocket, I look at Malcolm's name on the screen and press the decline button. Suddenly my phone pings indicating a received text message.

Babe, did you make it home? I really am sorry.

I read the message and contemplate whether or not I should respond. I send *yes* and then throw my phone on the floor before pulling the blanket over my head and continue to cry until I fall asleep.

Regrets

Brooklyn

Getting cozy in my pilot's chair for another long flight to Madrid, I consider texting Malcolm. Since my dramatic exit from his place, we haven't spoken much. I imagine he wants to give me some space to cool down, but I honestly just want him to get in the boxing ring and fight for me. Fight for us.

I stormed out of his place, hoping he would change his mind about leaving but he didn't. Then a little piece of me wished he would've shown up Sunday once he returned but no. Not even so much as a phone call. I pull out one of my novels and begin reading, hoping a little piece of fiction could help me forget about my reality.

After an hour of reading, I hear my phone vibrate. Excited to finally get a chance to talk to my man, I look at the screen displaying a message from an unknown number. Disappointed, I unlock my phone and stare at the message.

Hi Brook, it's Tyson. I am not sure if you still have the same number, but I figured I'd give it a try. I was leaving campus today and I saw that your favorite open mic club was closing down. Just thought I'd let you know. I remember how you used to love reciting new pieces there when we were in undergrad. I hope you are well.

Rereading the message several times, I try to figure out what I should say, if anything. Even though Tyson's message is completely random, it is a kind gesture to inform me about Backyard Bluez closing. I have some great memories of that place, so I decide to be cordial in my response.

Thanks for letting me know. It saddens me to think that I can never get back on that stage and express myself.

I press send and continue reading my book just before my phone vibrates once more.

If you are in town, they are having a one night only amateur showcase tomorrow night. I could stop by after I leave campus to support an old friend's last hurrah on stage.

I put my book down and stare at the message. Contemplating to myself, I begin to weigh the consequences of my options.

It's just platonically catching up with an old friend who's happily married, and it would be nice to get up on stage again. I haven't recited a poem in years, this might be just what I need to sort all of these emotions I am dealing with.

Grabbing my phone, I respond

Why not. I could use a little nostalgia. I'll be there around 9pm.

I press send and start to think about which piece I will recite tomorrow.

...

Pulling up to Backyard Bluez I look around at the parking lot which hasn't had much maintenance or upkeep over the years. There are a few cars filling the lot but nowhere near the crowd this place was accustomed to holding.

I used to love walking here after classes and pouring my heart out on stage. Sitting in my car for a moment more, I press my hands-free command to call Malcolm.

"You've reached the voicemail of Malcolm Diamond. Leave a message."

My heart aches a little not being able to talk to him but I wait patiently for the beep and leave a message, "Hi Babe. I was thinking about you. Call me when you get this message." I hang up and proceed to the front door of my blast from the past.

Stepping through the entrance, my ears are instantly filled with the sounds of smooth jazz. Glancing around, I search for Tyson and then look down at my watch. Nine-thirty.

Girl that man probably went home to his pregnant wife

I walk to the bar to get a drink. The lack of cars in the parking lot is a false representation of the crowd. Backyard Bluez was packed with a balanced mixture of eighties and ninety babies. Finding a seat at the bar with a great view of the stage, I wave my hand at the bartender to order a drink.

"May I have a Moscow Mule please," I say and hear a familiar voice.

"Make that two mules with Tito's please," Tyson says as he pulls a barstool closer to get an equally great view of the stage.

"You made it," I say, sounding far more excited then I intended.

"Yes ma'am. I am a man of my word. I hope you will keep yours by actually going on stage."

"I actually wrote a new piece just for tonight," I tease and take a sip of my freshly made mule.

"Well a toast to your new piece." He lifts his copper mug as I mirror his actions.

As the night progresses, we continue to drink and reminisce on old times as the emcee calls poets to the stage. We laugh about the time we forgot our wallets and had to hustle another couple out of fifty dollars playing a game of pool to pay our tab and then about the time Candice and Calvin both brought dates here to make the other jealous and their dates ended up leaving together.

"Man, I didn't realize how much time we spent in this place," Tyson says as he orders another round of drinks.

"Yes, I wonder if our *Dollar of Love* is still jammed underneath the pool table," I stumble off of the barstool towards the billiards section.

"I forgot all about that thing," Tyson says holding my shoulders as I try to find my footing in my heels.

Holding on to the side of the table, Tyson reaches under the cue ball slot and pulls out a small folded dollar. My heart jumps into my throat.

"I can't believe it's here after all this time," I say as I read my side of the vow, "To my Tyson, I will love you until eagles forget how to fly and it's twenty below in July."

Passing the dollar to Tyson, he turns it over and reads, "To my Brookie, when violets turn red and roses turn blue, I'll be still in love with you."

Continuing to hold onto the table to keep my balance, I stare down at the dollar and say nothing.

"We used to come here anytime we had a really big argument and read these vows to each other," Tyson says, "I used to mean every word I wrote on this dollar."

"Tyson…"

I start to speak just as the emcee on the microphone calls the next poet, "Please welcome to the stage, Brooklyn."

I look at Tyson confused, "Did you…"

"Yes, when you went to the restroom. I didn't want you to lose your nerve, so I signed you up. Go, let's hear this new poem you wrote." He begins to applaud so that I cannot back down from going up on stage.

Walking through the crowd, I quickly realize how tipsy I actually am. Once I finally make it on stage, I pull out a piece of paper from my back pocket. A poem I entitled "My Favorite Diamond." It was my love letter to Malcolm.

Standing up on stage, I look out at all the faces in the crowd waiting for me to speak and I begin to feel nervous.

Just as I decide to walk off stage, Tyson sits down in the front row and smile, "You got this Brookie."

Putting the piece of paper back in my pocket, I decide to recite something else from the heart, "Hi everyone, this piece is called *Regrets*."

You called it Selfish
I called it Self-Preservation
You called it Picky
I called it Particular
You were looking to fill a glass,
While I was trying to build a kitchen.
I can't help what I felt, and I can't help how I see
That hiding how I feel wasn't good for you or for me
I tried to be patient, tried to be the one you need
But how much of me did I cover for you to feel complete?
I know it wasn't your intention and it's sad to admit
But being honest didn't mean failure or that we just quit
It simply meant we arrived at the same airport
At the same time
In the same line…
But my flight was departing
And yours was delayed, running a little behind.
I tried to wait on your connecting flight
But it was a promise I couldn't make
And although it was hard to say goodbye,
It's a risk I was willing to take.

Ignoring all of the claps and finger snapping, I stare at Tyson who is still sitting on the front row with his eyebrows furrowed. Walking off of the stage, I scurry through the crowd trying to get back to the bar.

I really need a drink to calm my nerves.

Raising my hand to the bartender, he nods and prepares my beverage of choice.

"Brooklyn," Tyson walks up behind me, "*What, was that?*" His question throws me off guard. I don't really know what reaction I was hoping for but that wasn't it.

"I don't know. I just had to get it off of my chest," I confess and take a large sip of my drink.

"Was that the new poem you wrote? You wrote a poem about me to perform here tonight?" he continues to bombard me with questions, but I ignore him.

What the heck were you thinking girl? This man is married, and you are with Malcolm.

"I'm sorry Tyson. I don't know what I was thinking. I originally wrote a poem about the guy I'm dating but once I got on stage my mind went blank. All I saw was you looking up at me and the alcohol took it from there I guess." I try my hardest to explain but I just feel so embarrassed.

I finish my drink before placing a fifty-dollar bill on the bar and attempt to stand.

"Goodbye Tyson," I say and hurriedly stumble out of the bar towards my car.

Gosh, I didn't realize that I had drank so much. Maybe I should call an Uber.

"Brooklyn!" My thoughts are interrupted as I turn to see Tyson approaching my car, "You're intoxicated. I can't let you drive like this. Give me your keys." He walks me to the passenger side and reaches his hands out for the key.

"It's a push start. Just get in, the key fob is in my pocket," I say and sink down into the passenger seat.

I have definitely made this night very awkward.

Pulling out of the parking lot, we both sit in complete silence as I stare out of the window continuing to mentally kick myself for what just happened.

"Where is your car?" I ask trying to break the awkward silence.

"It's still on campus in the faculty lot. I'll take an Uber home and get it tomorrow. Are you ready to talk about what just happened?" He turns and looks at me as I sink even lower into the chair.

"It was stupid and inconsiderate of me. I'm sorry," I say and mean every word, "I think I had one too many Moscow Mules."

Looking over at me with a lifted eyebrow he says, "My mom always says the truth comes out when the liquor is being poured."

Pulling up to the coffee shop that I can probably never visit again, he stops, "Which building is yours?"

"This one," I say passing him the access card to enter the parking garage. "Park on the third floor."

Pulling into a spot near the elevator he turns off the car and we both sit in silence.

"When did you write that poem?" he asks turning to look at me.

"Shortly after the homecoming game."

"Is that really how you felt Brooklyn? Like you had to reduce who you were to make me feel complete?" he asks, and I'm baffled that he remembered a line from the poem.

"Tyson, please just accept my apology and let's pretend this night never happened. You can go on with your life and I will do the same. No harm no foul." I open the car to begin walking toward the elevator.

"No, I won't accept your apology."

I quickly turn around and glare at him. "What?" I ask as he closes the driver side door and walks closer to me.

"I said I won't accept your apology. Not until you accept mine," he says now standing directly in front of me. "Brooklyn, from the bottom of my heart, I am sorry for ever hurting you. I was lost after my knee injury and all I cared about was feeling sorry for myself. You deserved a man who was trying to build a future with you and all I wanted to do was complain and push blame on everyone but myself. You were right to leave me. I didn't deserve you."

I stare at him, not realizing the tears that are now clouding my vision.

"Why didn't you come back to me once you figured life out?" I ask now feeling my legs lose their strength.

"Brooklyn, you left *me*. You went on with your life and became this amazing woman and phenomenal pilot. You had your whole life ahead of you and I was no longer a part of that. I mourned over you and our relationship for years. I was completely in love with you. I still do love you...I just can't have you," he confesses and without thinking I throw my arms around him and press my lips to his.

Pushing me away, he stares at me as we both try to steady our breathing. As he stands holding my waist, I use his shoulders to keep my balance while the alcohol continues to tamper with my equilibrium.

Still sharing a breathless silence, the elevator door opens, and he quickly picks me up and pins me against the back of the elevator kissing me, hard.

"Which floor is yours?" he asks without separating our lips.

"PH," I say as I wrap my legs around his waist for stability.

Reaching behind and pressing the button, he continues to devour my lips.

Once the elevator reaches my floor, we both step off and look at each other, contemplating our next actions.

I pause, giving him a chance to get back on the elevator and go home but he just stands there with heated eyes. Walking down the hall to PH5, I put in my access code and allow my first love to assist me in a decision that we can never take back.

The Aftermath

Brooklyn

*R*ing, Ring, Ring. Beep. Ring, Ring, Ring.

Waking up from an unfamiliar sound. I look down to see an arm wrapped around me. Not really remembering what happened last night, I turn over as my vision adjusts to the sunlight piercing through my bedroom window. Gasping all the air I can fill in my lungs, I realize the arm belongs to Tyson. He jumps up out of his sleep, startled.

"Tyson, No! We, we didn't," I say as he leaps out of bed. Grabbing his pants off of the floor, he pulls his phone out of the back pocket.

"My wife has been calling me all morning. I have to go," he says and hurriedly begins to get dressed.

"Do you need a ride?" I ask without thinking and he looks at me puzzled.

"Shoot! My car is back on campus. No, I'll call an Uber," he yells in panic.

Still sitting up in bed I watch him, mortified, as he scrambles to retrieve all of his belongings.

I cannot believe I just slept with my ex, a married man. I was raised better than this. I am so ashamed of myself. How could I have let this happen?

I begin to let my thoughts run rampant as Tyson monitors his phone for the arrival of his Uber.

"Brooklyn, we have to talk about this but not now. I have to go home and do damage control," he says and my heart jumps into my throat.

"Are you going to tell your wife about this?" Horror immediately fills my face.

"I don't know Brooklyn. Maybe," he says exasperated, "Are you going to tell your guy?" His question sends my thoughts up the emotional roller coaster.

Oh my goodness, Malcolm! This kind of betrayal would kill him and destroy any future for us. There is no way I can tell him. I can't bear to hurt him like that.

"No! This was a mistake," I blurt out and Tyson stops and looks at me.

"Brooklyn, my ride is here I have to go." He turns to walk out without a second glance or goodbye.

This was a mistake, wasn't it? Why didn't he agree? Does he not feel that way? Brooklyn, what have you done?

I throw my head into the pillow and scream. Inhaling to let out another cry, my nostrils are consumed by the scent of Tyson.

I have to throw these bedsheets away.

Stripping my bed to cleanse my room of the aftermath of infidelity, I hear a thud from the sound of something hitting the floor. Reaching down to pick up my phone, I noticed a missed call and voicemail from Malcolm. Dropping the sheets on the floor, I listen to the voicemail.

"Hey Brook. Sorry I missed your call; I was on a plane coming back to the States. I decided to stay in South America a few extra days to make sure that when I got back home, I would be completely and readily available to you. I saw how disappointed you were when I left, and I took some time to reflect and check myself. Brooklyn, you're a priority to me. I will do better at managing my business affairs so that you don't ever have to feel like you're competing for my attention. Baby I'm sorry. I am back in Atlanta when you're ready to see me. I miss you too."

Listening to the voicemail, I sink to the floor as my legs go numb.

I can never tell Malcolm about this. He would never forgive me. God, what have I done?

Hopping out of the shower, I decide to return Malcolm's call. My heart is so heavy with guilt, I am not sure if I will be able to face him.

"Hi Babe," he says somewhat out of breath.

"Hey sweetie, how's your morning coming along?" I try to sound nonchalant.

"My morning would've been a lot better if I was able to wake up next to you," he teases, and I begin to feel a lump in my throat.

"I wish that too Baby," I pause trying to suppress my thoughts from running me wild.

"Brooklyn. I'm sorry about how I handled the situation," Malcolm says, taking my silence as a sign that I may still be upset, "This last week has been tough not having you in my arms."

"Malcolm I . . ." I begin to speak but he cuts me off.

"Before you say anything just know that I'm all-in, Brooklyn. I know that there's a world around me and there will always be some business deal to close but what's in front of me is more important. *You* are more important." The sincerity in his voice unlocks the floodgate to my tears.

Campus Tour

Riley

"Are you sure you don't want me to tag along?" I ask Blythe as she unfastens her seatbelt.

"Mommy, we talked about this. I want to fall in love with Charlotte A&T University on my own terms. Persuading me to tour your alma mater is pressure enough, I need to do this campus tour alone," Blythe says and kisses my cheek. "Go. Visit Aunt Michele and I'll call you when I'm done. I love you." She jumps out of the car to join the group of eager high school seniors.

Pausing to admire how beautiful and mature Blythe has turned out, I send up a small prayer before driving off.

"Lord, thank you for helping me to be a good role model for my daughter. Despite all the sacrifices I had to make, you always made sure that Blythe knew she was loved beyond measures. Please look over my baby regardless of what college she chooses. Also, if it'll help God, could you make this experience far better than the other campus tours? Amen."

Walking up the stairs of the admissions office, I begin to reminisce on all of the campus memories that made me fall in love with Charlotte A&T.

Blythe would absolutely love it here. She's far more social and active in extracurriculars than I ever was. I am not ready to let go of my baby just yet, especially to some college halfway across the country.

I continue to push my thoughts around as I make my way to Michele's office.

"Good Morning, I am here to see Dean Peterson." I smile at the young secretary and wait for her to look up from her cellular phone.

She's clearly a recent graduate who has not yet mastered the proper etiquette of acknowledging someone when they walk into an office.

"Good Morning is Dean Peterson expecting you?" she asks confused and looks at her computer screen, I imagine she's pulling up Michele's schedule.

"Yes," I lie, "Please inform her that *Dr.* Riley Harper is here for her 11 a.m." Startled by the shift in my tone of voice, the secretary smiles and recovers.

"Yes, of course. My apologies, Dr. Harper. Please have a seat and I will inform Dean Peterson of your arrival. She is just wrapping up a meeting," she says and quickly picks up the phone.

Sitting down to wait, I feel my phone vibrate indicating a received message. Looking at my screen I chuckle at the message from Blythe.

Please do not sneak around campus with Aunt Michele to spy on me. I'm a big girl. Love you Honey. Laughing at the message, I reply with a smiley face emoji.

Still waiting for Michele to finish her meeting, I type a text message to Brooklyn to see if she is in town. I press send and look up just as Michele's office door opens.

"Dr. Harper, please come in," she says in a serious and professional tone. I get up and try to stifle my laugh as I walk past her secretary's desk.

Closing the door, we both start laughing as we sit on the couch. "Dr. Harper, really?" Michele asks still laughing.

"I didn't have a meeting scheduled and I figured the title would help my chances." I shrug innocently, "Please don't fire your secretary. I think I frightened her enough."

Michele shakes her head and we both laugh again.

"She's still young and learning. I will definitely have to check her, but I'll let it slide just this once. So, what brings you to campus?" she begins looking at an email on her tablet.

"Blythe has her campus tour today. Did I interrupt anything or are you free for lunch?"

"My goodness is her tour *today*? I completely forgot," she says tapping on her tablet, "Yes, I would love to. Let me push my 11:30 meeting until this afternoon and then we can go."

...

Pulling up to a diner across from campus, I look around confused. "Is this place new or has it always been here?" I ask examining all of the collegiate paraphernalia on the wall.

"This used to be *Alley Cats*," Michele responds and laughs.

"I knew it seemed familiar! They turned a night club into a diner? Wow!" I continue to look around amazed at the changes.

"The bar area still gets pretty wild in the evenings but yes, it is primarily a restaurant now and the food is really good too."

"I texted Brooklyn to see if she was in town to join us, but I haven't heard from her," I say as the waiter places the menus down and walks away.

"Girl, Brooklyn stays on the go. She's usually either in Madrid or in Atlanta when I talk to her," she says.

"So, she and Malcolm are still going strong? That's good. I need to catch up with her and Candice soon. It's just been so much going on." My guilt begins to rise.

"Don't feel bad, we all have things going on, it's life. But yes, as far as I know, they are still good. They looked extremely happy at the New Year's Eve party."

Placing our orders with the waiter, we catch up on the last couple of weeks.

"So how are Jeremiah and the twins?" I ask trying to keep the conversation going.

"Jeremiah is just finishing a project in New York and starting a new one next month here in Charlotte. It's been tough with him traveling so often so the kids and I are elated that we get to have Daddy back home every night. The twins are great. Marley is a mini Momma Michele with a hint of Grandma Marjorie in every way and Mason is just trying to get from under her shadow and be his own little man," she says and smiles.

"Those two are by far the cutest little beings I've ever met. You've done a beautiful job raising them."

"Thanks, Riley, but you have a soon-to-be distinguished honor High School graduate. Blythe is living proof that all the sacrifices you've made were for good reason. You've raised an extraordinary young woman. You should be even more proud of yourself. I know I am."

"Thanks Love. That means a lot to hear. These next few months will be tough to get through, but Blythe is eager and excited about college."

"Isn't that a good thing?" she asks. "Why do you seem so sad?" Taking the napkin from the table, I dab the corner of my eye to wipe the tear threatening to fall.

"I'm just an emotional wreck nowadays when it comes to Blythe. I guess I'm not ready for my baby to leave home. I wish I could've been there or done more when she was growing up. I just . . ." I pause my confession.

"Aww sweetie, I get it. You've fought every obstacle after you got pregnant and chose to live the kind of life that your daughter could grow up to admire. You didn't let your parents or Blythe's father, or anyone stop you from getting your degree and then going on to graduate from med school. When Blythe introduces you to her friends, she can proudly say that is my mom, *Dr.* Riley Harper. There is not an ounce of doubt in anyone's mind that Blythe doesn't know how much you love her, I assure you," Michele says as her own tears join the party.

"Yes, but selfishly a little piece of me wants her to go to school at A&T so that she will still be close because her other two choices are a plane ride away. I'm just trying to mentally prepare myself for whatever she decides."

"I can imagine that's tough. I know how close you two are. I will be a bucket of tears when my babies graduate." Michele reaches to soothe my hand.

"She's my best friend. I gave birth to my best friend."

The waiter comes to the table and places our food down. "Dean Peterson, can I get you ladies anything else?" he asks.

"No thank you. Everything looks great," Michele says as I quickly wipe my eyes.

Taking a bite of her salad she says, "One thing I do know is that no matter where Blythe goes to school, she will thrive and do well because she'll always have a support system back home. She will always have you, her grandparents, us, and now Jameson. Speaking of, how is my *soon to be* brother-in-law?"

Blushing at the thought of Jameson, I take a bite of my club sandwich. "He's amazing Michele. I honestly can't thank God enough for bringing him into my life when he did. My parents love him and Blythe adores him. She told him that leaving for college will be a little less painful knowing that he'll be here to take care of me."

"That is very true. We are all grateful you won't be home alone.

Everybody needs someone. And he *is* still taking care of you, right? Do you feel like the relationship is progressing in the right direction?" she asks. I can sense the sincerity in her voice.

"Yes. We talk about pretty much everything, I have even opened up to him about my celibacy," I whisper and look around as if someone can overhear us.

"Wow, that's great Riley. How did he respond?"

"Honestly, I couldn't have prayed for a better reaction from a man. He essentially said he would wait and take it as slow as I wanted because he loves me." I blink back a tear. "He's patient with me, he loves me, and when he looks at me, it's like the entire room is irrelevant except for the two of us. I've never experienced anything like this."

"Riley you are quite smitten, and I absolutely love seeing you like this. How did the banquet in Connecticut go? I saw pictures of you slaying that dress we picked out," she asks.

"It was beautiful. Of course, I was nervous to meet his mom and sisters, but they welcomed me with open arms."

"Of course they did. Any man would be lucky to have you on his arm and all mothers are praying for their sons to bring home a woman like you. You're a catch sweetie," she says and winks, "So have you guys discussed the future or are you still just enjoying the now?"

I take a sip of water and look up with all smiles. "I am head over heels in love with that man. He's the one. He's the husband I have been praying for."

Closure

Brooklyn

Glancing at Riley's text message, I decide to ignore her invitation to join she and Michele for lunch. I don't really want to be around people, at least not until I figure out the situation with Tyson. The guilt has been eating away at me for days. The more I talk to Malcolm, the more my heart breaks thinking about what I've done to him. What I've done to us.

Still holding the phone in my hand, I send a text message to Tyson.

We need to talk.

While staring at the bubbles on the screen indicating that he is typing a response, my phone startles me when an incoming call appears.

"Hey Babe, are you home?" Malcolm asks not waiting for me to say hello.

"Hey. Yes, I am home. I am about to head out for my morning run," I say feeling the need to over explain myself.

"Okay good. I am walking into a meeting, but I just wanted to hear your voice before my day got started. My flight gets into Charlotte this evening, I can't wait to see you."

"Hurry and finish talking business, so I can have you all to myself. I miss you, handsome," I say and mean every word.

"I miss you more Doll. Have a great workout. Text me when you can."

...

Jumping out of the shower, I continue to deep condition and scrunch my curls. I rarely wear my natural curls because I prefer to have my hair straightened but today, I think I will let them run wild.

Throwing on some Victoria Secret navy tights and matching tank top, I walk into the kitchen to make an omelet.

Opening the refrigerator to grab two eggs, I hear my phone ping from a received text message. Carefully placing the eggs on the kitchen island, I pick up my phone to read the message.

Hey. Yes, we do need to talk. Could you meet at two o'clock? Same coffee shop?

I stare at my phone for a brief second trying to contemplate my response.

Two o'clock is cutting it kind of close with Malcolm coming in town but I really need to clear my conscience before I see my man. I am not sure if I can face him with this guilt still lingering over my head.

Malcolm said that he will be here this evening, so I can meet with Tyson and then be back home in time to prepare for his arrival. Still filtering through my thoughts, I finally convince myself to have my closure with Tyson.

...

Walking into the coffee shop, my stomach begins to coil itself into a painful knot. Everything about this just feels so wrong.

I wish I had never gone to that homecoming game and saw him, none of this would have ever happened. How could I have been so stupid?

Walking through the crowd of college students and young professionals, I begin to search for Tyson. When I get to the back of the room and still have not seen him, I decide to sit at a corner table and wait. After two minutes of almost losing my nerve and deciding to walk back home, I see them. Tyson and *his wife*.

He brought his wife! Is this some kind of ambush?

My hands began sweating as the knot in my stomach continues to pull tighter and tighter. Frozen in my seat with my eyes glued on the pregnant goddess, I watch as Tyson pulls her chair out and then slowly slides into his seat.

After what feels like an eternity of awkward silence, his wife finally speaks.

"I've seen her before," she says and looks up at Tyson.

"Yes, the homecoming game," I say softly and glare at Tyson for him to speak up and explain this awkward reunion.

Does she already know what happened? Did he bring her here to tell her?

What the heck is going on?

Unable to withstand the silence any longer, I confess, "I'm not exactly sure what to say."

Looking over at Tyson once more who is still twirling his wedding band, his wife says, "I'll start since it appears my husband has suddenly lost his voice. I wanted to meet the woman that my husband was willing to risk losing his marriage and family over." She inhales deeply and straightens her posture so that she is completely facing me.

"Tyson told me everything. He told me about your history, about your breakup, and the infidelity," she says. I cannot move. "Before I say what's on my mind, did you know that he was married?"

Finding the backbone to endure what I can predict is about to happen, I sit up to answer, "Yes, I knew he was married."

"Was that the only time?" her question completely throws me, and I look to Tyson, but she puts her hand up.

"I've already talked with my husband and I don't currently trust a word out of his mouth, so I'm asking you. Have you seen or slept with my husband other than that one night?" I can sense her anger rising.

"No," I say quietly.

I feel like the scum of the earth right now. I am a grown woman sitting in a coffee shop getting berated by a pregnant wife for sleeping with her husband. It doesn't get much lower than this.

"So, let me get this straight. You ran into your ex, whom you knew was married *and* expecting a baby, have some nostalgic night, and then decide to just casually commit adultery?" she asks as a tear falls and lands on her perfect baby bump. "Do you realize how much time and effort it takes to fully commit your life to someone else?" she asks rhetorically and continues, "It is hard enough to maintain a healthy and successful marriage without women like you infiltrating our bedroom? How do you sleep at night knowing you've done this to another woman, to another *black woman?*"

"I'm sorry," I confess and genuinely mean it. "I never meant for any of this to happen. I didn't seek out or seduce Tyson. It just happened, and I know both of us are completely ashamed by our actions. I know that right now my words mean nothing to you because I'm just the woman who slept with your husband but please accept my apology."

"Tyson are you still in love with this woman?" she ignores me as her emotions begin taking a toll.

"No," Tyson says without even looking me in the eye.

"I'm leaving but you two stay and get whatever closure that you need," she spats and then turns to me. "I don't know if I will forgive my husband, but I want you to remember that he is *my husband*. Find your own and stay out of our lives."

Leaning down, she whispers something in Tyson's ear that causes his entire demeanor to shift. By the look on his face, I knew that she was not to be played with.

This man is in love and if I ever thought for a second that we had a chance, I know otherwise now.

She glares at me with disgust as if she could see my darkest secrets and then storms out of the coffee shop.

As my embarrassment dissipates into anger, I glare at Tyson. "What was that! You bring your wife here to chastise me and then you just sit there like I was the only one wrong in this situation?"

I have to get out of here before my anger causes me to make a scene.

Finally finding his voice, Tyson exhales, "Brooklyn, I am doing everything in my power to save my marriage. How would I look defending you to her? She has every right to be that upset."

"When I got home that next morning, I was sick to my core. I have never lied to her in our entire relationship, so I just came clean. She cursed me out until she was blue in the face, giving me a lecture about being irresponsible and asked me what kind of example was I setting for my unborn child? Her question struck me like a dagger to my heart Brooklyn," he says.

"She was right. What kind of example *am* I setting? What we did was wrong on so many levels despite how right it may have felt in that moment," he clears his throat. "That night was a mistake and I've jeopardized my marriage and my family."

Exhausted with this entire encounter I stand to leave, "Tyson, I agree. The other night should have never happened. I was confused and a little intoxicated but it's crystal clear for me now. I am in love with someone and you are *married*. We got caught up in the nostalgia and didn't think about the consequences of our actions," I say to him and slowly begin to feel my guilt and regret lessen a bit.

"Brooklyn, I am truly sorry for breaking your heart all those years ago. You deserved better than me and you deserved better from me. I'm not necessarily asking for your friendship, but I hope that we can still be cordial going forward," he says.

"I can't take back that we had sex, but I will leave with what little dignity I have left. I forgive you, but this is goodbye Tyson," I say and the sight I turn around to immediately causes that painful knot to return to the pit of my stomach.

"Malcolm!" I gasp.

Standing behind me, Malcolm calmly places the bouquet of roses and two coffee cups on the table.

"I saw you standing here and walked over. *What the hell did you just say?*" his voice is so stern that it frightens me.

Without waiting for a response, he turns and walks into the street toward my parking garage.

"Malcolm!" I yell after him as he walks into traffic, ignoring the crosswalk signal. Waiting until a metro bus passes by, I run full speed across the street into the garage.

"Malcolm, please Baby. Just wait a second," I yell once I see him reaching for the door handle.

Running up to his car, I grab for his hand, but he forcefully pulls away.

"*How* are you going to explain what I just heard Brooklyn?" the cracking in his voice breaks my heart in half.

"Baby, please just listen," I plead as tears began to alter my vision.

"No, you listen. I have done *everything* you've asked of me in this relationship. Today, I skipped out on meetings to come here early and surprise you. I walk over to order your favorite coffee and I find you talking to some man about having sex. Do you play me for some kind of fool, Brooklyn?" he says, as his anger soars.

"Baby no! Please just let me explain," I beg.

"Fine Brooklyn, TALK!" He steps back to increase the distance between us.

"What you heard was nothing. It was just a misunderstanding," I cry out.

"Who was that?"

"That was Tyson," I confess, and he remains silent, "My ex."

"Your ex?" he asks and steps back once more to gather his thoughts. "The story you told me in Brazil about the guy that broke your heart, is that the *Ex-Boyfriend* you're talking about?"

Putting my hands over my mouth to steady my breathing I slowly nod, answering his question.

"Your first true love? How do I compete with that? How do I compete with "what if," Brooklyn? Did you sleep with him?" he continues to throw out questions and each time they pierce my heart like a dagger.

"Baby, please…" I beg but he cuts me off.

"Have you had sex with him since we've been together?" he yells and steps back once more. Dropping to my knees, I can hear my bones connecting with the concrete. As much as my legs were hurting, it was nothing compared to what I've just done to Malcolm.

"Malcolm I am so sorry. It happened once. I made a mistake. That's it, nothing more. Baby please believe me. I don't want him; it was a mistake. I want you, only you. I love you Malcolm," I continue to sob next to the driver's door of his Aston Martin.

"You *love* me?" Malcolm whispers stepping toward his car.

"Yes Malcolm, I love *you*. I want to be with you and only you," I say wiping my face as I stand to my feet.

"Brooklyn step away from my car," he says coldly.

Confused and hurt, I take two steps back as he opens his car door before pausing to look me in the eye.

"You knew what you were doing, and you knew it would hurt me, but you did it anyway. I hope it was worth it Brooklyn. We're done." He slams his door before speeding off.

These Shoes Are *Not* Made for Running

Michele

*W*alking through the student union, I glance at my watch to check the time. I have less than ten minutes to get all the way across campus. I look down at my feet and roll my eyes at my choice of Jimmy Choo heels today.

Speeding down the sidewalk, I spot one of the coaches riding a University-issued golf cart. Waving my hands to flag them down, I pick up my pace to meet him at the corner.

"Hi Michele. I mean, Dean Peterson," Tyson says, "Is everything okay?"

Sitting down on the passenger side of the golf cart, I try to catch my breath, "Yes and No. Could you give me a ride to Smith Hall? I have a meeting that I am about to be late for and these shoes are *not* made for running."

Laughing he turns the golf cart around, "Yes ma'am, I'll take you."

Searching for my phone in my briefcase, I look at the screen to see a missed call from both Candice and Riley. I make a mental note to call them before I leave campus today.

Unlocking my phone, I open the camera app and flip to the front-facing lens to use as a mirror.

Touching up my hair and make-up I turn to Tyson, "So how are you adjusting to A&T?"

"Things are great. It kind of feels like I'm back home in a way."

"Yes, I felt the same way when I accepted the position," I admit, "Who would've thought we'd be back on the campus working as the faculty members we used to tease and make fun of?" Laughing for a brief moment Tyson turns to me as his mood changes.

"How is Brooklyn doing?" His question throws me off guard.

"What do you mean? She's fine. Why wouldn't she be?" I say, and I can hear the attitude in my response. Looking at me with guilt-ridden eyebrows, Tyson stops the golf cart in front of Smith Hall.

"Thank you for the ride," I say and straighten my skirt as I stand. Reaching for my briefcase, Tyson looks away as if he is afraid to look me in the eye. "Is there something you want to tell me?" I ask.

"I don't know if it's my place to say," he admits, "When you get a chance just call to see if she's okay and tell her that I am so sorry. Now go, or else you'll be late for your meeting *Dean Peterson*." He gives me a half smile before driving off.

Walking out of my last meeting for the day, I call Brooklyn. No answer. Waiting for the beep, I walk into an empty office to leave a message.

"Brooklyn, it's Michele. I ran into Tyson on campus and he told me to check on you and to tell you that he's sorry. What the heck is going on? Please call me when you get this message."

Getting back to my desk I decide to call Candice. "Hey girl. What are you up to?" I ask casually.

"Girl where have you been? We've been calling you? I just landed in Charlotte about to meet Riley at Brooklyn's house," Candice says and my heart drops.

"What happened?" I scream and suddenly regret waiting so long to return everyone's calls.

"Brooklyn and Malcolm broke up," Candice says and pauses, "I don't know the full story, but Brooklyn called me crying her eyes out a few hours ago."

Hesitant to reveal my brief discussion with Tyson to Candice, I decide to wait until I spoke with Brooklyn. "Let me call the babysitter to pick up the kids. I am on the way," I say and quickly end the phone call.

Scrolling down my contacts list, I press Malcolm's name. No answer.

"Hi this is your sis. Call me back when you get this. Love you," I say. Hanging up the phone, I begin to prepare myself for what I had already foreseen would happen.

Game of Fifty Questions

Candice

*T*urning into the parking garage, I hear my phone ring.

"Hello."

"Hey. I just parked. Where are you?" Riley asks.

"I am pulling in now. Michele says she's coming once she leaves campus," I respond just as I instruct the Uber driver to pull into the spot next to Riley's silver Acura.

Hanging up, I get out of the car and follow Riley to the elevator.

"Girl I'm not sure what to expect when it comes to Brook but I'm prepared for the worst." Riley shrugs.

"I don't know either. I was headed to lunch with Calvin when she called. I answered on the car's Bluetooth and she didn't sound like herself. She sounded so sad. It bothered me so much that I just couldn't focus on anything once we got off the phone. Calvin insisted on dropping me off at the airport, instead of driving, since I have more airline miles than I care to admit."

"His exact words were, 'Brooklyn can be overly dramatic, but this sounds serious.' So here I am. No clothes, or shoes, or nothing, Jesus." I smirk and we both look at each other and take a deep breath before I enter the access code to PH5.

Entering Brooklyn's place, we walk around in search of our girl.

"Everything looks so clean and in place. I'm always scared to touch anything," Riley whispers.

"You know Brooklyn's penthouse is straight out of a magazine. White carpet, expensive decor, and glass tables; I don't know how she plans to have kids running through here," I whisper as we walk towards her master bedroom.

Tapping on the door, I slowly push it open and pop my head in. "Brook are you sleep?" Not waiting for a response, Riley and I barge in.

"No," she says with her back turned toward us. Taking our shoes off, we both climb into bed on both sides of her as she sits up.

"Talk to us. What's going on?" Riley says as Brooklyn lowers her head onto her lap.

"Yes. What happened?" I add as I begin softly playing in her curls. Taking a deep breath, Brooklyn lets out a soft sob.

"Guys, I really messed up," she says in a hushed tone.

Riley looks up and turns toward me with her eyebrows arched.

Taking a deep breath, I continue to play this game of fifty questions with Brooklyn. "How did you mess up? What happened with you and Malcolm?" My patience begins to dissipate.

I love my girl, but she can be excessively dramatic at times. I am hoping this isn't one of those times.

"I…" Brooklyn's confession is interrupted by the doorbell.

"That must be Michele," I say, and Brooklyn reaches over to her bedside control panel. As soon as she touches the screen, Michele's face appears.

"We're in the bedroom," Brooklyn says before entering a code to remotely unlock the front door.

Sitting in silence as Michele makes her way to the master bedroom, I quickly send a text message to my husband.

Babe, I made it safely to Brooklyn's. I'll call you once things settle.

Before I can lock the screen on my phone, he messages me back

Okay Babe. I hope everything works out. I love you.

Tossing the phone down, I look up as Michele walks into the room.

"I'm here. What did I miss?" Michele says as she throws her briefcase in the chair and steps out of her heels to join us on the bed.

"We just got here," Riley says and then looks down, "Okay Brooklyn. What happened?"

Achilles Heel

Brooklyn

With my head still resting on Riley's lap, I attempt to control my emotions enough to clearly articulate my confession. I have been lying in bed for two days trying to piece together everything that has happened. Malcolm refuses to return my phone calls and Tyson insists on leaving messages to check on me. I'm just not ready to talk to anyone until I hear from Malcolm.

I guilt-called Candice earlier after another failed attempt to contact Malcolm. Now, I regret that I made them go out of their way to check on their dramatic friend, once again.

How do I always get myself caught up in drama? I am too old for this.

Sitting up between Riley and Candice, I lean my back against my leather California King headboard. Michele is laid across the foot of the bed eyeing me like a hawk.

I wonder if she's already spoken to Malcolm. I can feel the judgment just from the look on her face. I can't believe I hurt her brother like this.

"Brooklyn. We're waiting Honey," Michele says impatiently.

Yup, she's definitely spoken to her brother already.

"Okay. Sorry," I take a deep breath, "Before I start, I need you all to listen to the full story before passing judgment. You promise?"

Michele rolls her eyes and nods. Riley and Candice both say "umm hmm" in a low tone.

"Malcolm and I have been arguing about the lack of time we were spending together. My last trip to Atlanta, I left his house upset that he was leaving me once again to go back to South America after not seeing him for weeks. I was feeling alone and hurt. I just wanted him to make me a priority," I say and pause. All of my girls remain quiet and expressionless. "I ran into Tyson at the coffee shop across the street a couple of days after I left Atlanta, but it was harmless. I was stopping in after a workout and he was leaving his new coaching job at A&T." Michele cuts me off.

"Brooklyn! You didn't!" she sits up on high alert.

"Please let me finish, Michele," I beg as tears swell in my eyes, "It was literally a 'Hi and Bye.' While Malcolm and I were still on the rocks, Tyson texted me saying how nice it was to see me and that Backyard Bluez was closing down." I try to continue but I begin to choke on my words.

"You girls have to believe me when I say, I never intended for any of this to happen," I plead but no one reaches out to console me.

"We're listening Honey, finish your story," Candice says with a straight face.

Looking at the disappointment on everyone's faces I begin to internally scold myself for my stupidity.

"Malcolm was still in South America and I still hadn't heard from him, so I decided to get out of the house and go to Backyard Bluez for their last night in business. My intentions were to recite one last poem since that place meant so much to me. I had even written a poem about my feelings for Malcolm to recite. Tyson joked that he would stop by to support me and honestly, I just wanted some kind of closure after running into him at that homecoming game. As the night progresses, we were both drinking and reminiscing on old times and he ended up having to drive me home because I had too much to drink," I say, and Riley tilts her head at me.

"So, he *had* to drive you home. You couldn't have left your car and taken an Uber?" she questions suspiciously.

"I guess I could've but at the time I was intoxicated and not thinking straight," I admit before continuing, "He drove me home and we had a heated argument about the past and he apologized for hurting me. After that, the night becomes a blur, but we had sex and woke up the next morning full of regret," I say not able to go into full details about my betrayal.

"Brooklyn, how could you?" Michele says, "I knew this would happen. Tyson has always been your Achilles heel."

"Yes, Brook. You're smarter than this," Riley says.

"I know. Don't y'all think I know that? I made a mistake. I got caught up in talking and laughing with him about our past. I was hurt and confused about my feelings for Malcolm and I had a lot to drink. I was stupid, but it happened, and I can't take it back. I know that. I just have to woman up and admit my wrongs. This is why I asked for you not to judge me. I've already judged myself. I always let my emotions cloud my judgement. After all these years, I thought that I needed some apology or closure to get over Tyson, but it turns out all I really needed was Malcolm." My words cut my throat like a knife, "You guys, he won't even talk to me."

"So, I'm still confused. Did you and Malcolm break up before it happened, or did you tell him about it and *then* you broke up?" Candice asks passing me a tissue.

"Y'all, he found out in the absolute worst way. Tyson and I met to clear the air and agree that what happened that night was a complete mistake," I say and then proceed to recap the coffee shop experience.

"HIS WIFE!" they all scream.

"Wait his wife showed up with him?" Candice blurts out before I can finish the story.

"Yes, pregnant and pissed off. She went off on me and then stormed out."

"Tyson and I were saying goodbye and Malcolm walked up and overheard the conversation. Specifically, he heard us discussing having sex days before. Next thing I know I am running out of the coffee shop chasing behind him trying to explain," I say, stepping off of the bed.

"So, he just *happens* to walk up while you and Tyson were discussing your infidelity?" Michele asks, and I know she is pretty much done with me and my story.

"I don't know Michele. I was honestly getting up to say goodbye. There's just no way to explain that to Malcolm."

"Did he actually say it was over or you two just haven't spoken since then," Riley asks with a hint of hope in her voice.

"No, it's over. I ran behind him just as he was about to leave, and he asked me point blank if Tyson and I ever slept together. I couldn't lie so I told him the truth. Then I told him that I love him."

"YOU WHAT?" they all say in unison and hop off of the bed at once.

"This is a lot to take in Brooklyn," Candice confesses.

"Do you *really* love him or are you guilty that you got caught?" Michele asks.

"I do feel guilty but it's not just that. Michele, I know that's your brother and you have no idea how sorry I am for what I did but I do love him. I knew I loved him before I ever even met up with Tyson, I was just hesitant to admit it out of fear that he didn't feel the same way. After seeing the hurt in his eyes when he drove off, I am pretty sure I've lost him for good," I admit and as the last word comes out of my mouth I sink to the floor. "You guys, I'm in love with him. How could I have been so stupid? He'll never forgive this kind of betrayal. Never!

My Brother's Keeper

Michele

After leaving Brooklyn's, the only person I want to talk to is my brother. Calling Malcolm's cell, I patiently wait as the numbing ringing ends before hanging up.

Brooklyn is notoriously known for this kind of behavior. I warned Malcolm of this, but he didn't listen. I warned them both. I'm sure he doesn't want this thrown back in his face, but he should've listened to me. I know them both too well. This was bound to happen, either he would break her heart, or she would do something careless like this.

Turning into my neighborhood, I call Malcolm once more.

"Hey Sis," he says in a low tone.

"Malcolm. Where are you?" I make sure not to initially overwhelm him with questions.

"I take it you spoke to Brooklyn," he pauses.

"Yes. Are you still in town?"

"Yeah. I thought about going back but decided to make good use of the trip and schedule a meeting with some Charlotte sport teams. What's up?" he says nonchalantly.

What's up? These Diamond men are terrible when it comes to expressing their feelings.

"I just wanted to check on you. That's all," I say still sitting in the driveway.

"It's whatever. She showed her true colors and I bounced. Her loss, not mine."

"When are you going back to Atlanta? Let's meet and talk," I say still not wanting to discuss his feelings over the phone that may force him to shut me out. I've learned in the past that Malcolm responds better in person.

"My flight is late tomorrow afternoon. I have plans for this evening, but we can do lunch tomorrow and you can drop me off at the airport, if you don't mind," he says. "See you tomorrow Sis."

"Okay. I'll see you tomorrow, Love you."

"Love you too."

Opening the car door to get out, I send up a small prayer.

Lord, please help these two to work this situation out. If they end up getting back together that is awesome but if not, please let the split be amicable for all our sakes. Amen.

Opening the entrance to the foyer from the garage, I can hear my twins upstairs playing.

"Hi mommy," Jeremiah says kissing my cheek and reaching for my briefcase. "Everything okay with your girl?" he asks, giving me a warm and enticing hug.

Sighing heavily as I inhale my husband's scent I say, "Honestly babe, I don't know and it's too much to talk about right now. I'll tell you tomorrow after I have lunch with Malcolm."

"Fair enough. Settle in and I'll run us a bath while you say goodnight to the kids," he says, and my mood instantly lifts.

"Thank you, baby," I muster some energy to go upstairs to greet my adorable yet hyper nine-year-olds.

...

Sitting at the entrance of the hotel, I watch Malcolm make his way through the lobby and smile once he sees me.

"Hi baby sis," he says placing his luggage on the back seat and then jumping into the passenger side.

"Hi Big Bro," I say playfully.

"I'm starved. What did you have in mind for lunch," he asks, and his cheerful demeanor throws me.

"There's a few places near the airport. How about seafood near the lake?"

"That's perfect," he nods and takes out his phone.

Turning onto the freeway, I look over at Malcolm and he exhales deeply. "You want to talk now or wait until I've had a few bites of my lunch?" he asks sarcastically.

"I really just wanted to check on you," I lie. "Are you okay?"

"You're a terrible liar, Chele. The truth is I cared for your homegirl deeply and she showed me that she can't be trusted." I glance over to gauge his facial expression.

His response just seemed so cold, but I am hesitant to pry.

"You know I talked to her and she explained the entire situation," I pause.

"Honestly Chele, I don't care to hear it right now and I really don't want you to get in the middle of it," he says cutting me off. "I said what I needed to say to Brooklyn and if I feel I need to say more, I will when I'm ready." He turns and give me the same look our father uses when he's fed up and I know that the conversation is over.

Apology Tour

Candice

"Good Morning Beautiful," Calvin says, and I can't help but smile.

"Good Morning Baby. How did you sleep?" I ask, still snuggled up in Brooklyn's silk guest bedsheets.

"Never as good as when you're here with me. You've been gone more days than you promised. It's time for my wife to come home," he sighs.

God, thank you for restoring my marriage before things got out of hand. I would die if I ever found Calvin with another woman. God you are so good. Thank you. Amen.

Walking into the kitchen, I turn on the news while preparing a cup of coffee. Sitting down at the kitchen table, I filter through emails and check into my return flight to Atlanta.

"Good Morning," Brooklyn says walking in with a towel around her neck.

"Good Morning Sunshine. I thought you were still sleep."

"No, I couldn't sleep much after the sun came up and decided to go for a swim." She joins me at the table.

"You should really wear your curls out more. They are gorgeous," I say.

"And high maintenance."

"Did the swim help clear your head?" I ask trying to keep the conversation going.

"Not really but it was a good workout. I've worked too hard for this body to *stress eat* my abs away." She smiles, and I can tell she is trying to use humor to cope.

"Care to chat before my flight?" She nods and joins me at the table. "Have you heard from Malcolm?"

"No. Still radio silence. You didn't see his face when he walked out of that coffee shop. I've never seen anyone look so hurt," she says as she fights to hold back a sob.

"What the heck was he doing in the coffee shop anyway?" I try to lighten the mood.

"Girl, I knew my addiction for coffee would come and haunt me one of these days. Malcolm was stopping by to surprise me with a café mocha and flowers before coming up to my place. He was picking up the order when he spotted Tyson and I saying goodbye. To be honest, I can't blame him for the way he reacted, I would have walked away too."

"Yes, that does sound bad," I say and Brooklyn sighs.

"I just hate how things have unfolded with him and especially with Michele. She won't even talk to me."

"Honestly Brook, you can't blame her. As a wife, we both see this situation differently." I pause to gather my thoughts.

"What I am about to say I want you to know that I mean it completely out of love, but you have to stop playing the victim. I know you feel bad, but you were wrong Brooklyn," I say as my own emotions begin to get the best of me. Staring at me shocked, Brooklyn blinks but doesn't speak.

"I understand that Tyson hurt you all those years ago but that is *still* a married man. Marriage is hard enough without having to worry about betrayal from your husband. Could you imagine what that kind of betrayal would do to his pregnant wife? She's at home carrying his child and taking care of his home while he was out with you. That kind of stress could do real damage to a body carrying a fetus," I say.

"No, I guess I didn't think…" Brooklyn pauses.

"No, you didn't think. I love you to death, best friend, but you have to start taking responsibility for your actions. This isn't just about losing Malcolm. You could've just destroyed a family and you'll have to live with that." I grab Brooklyn's hand.

"I am so sorry if this hurts to hear but I owe it to you as a woman and as your friend. It's time for you to own it, learn from this, and grow up. It's okay to live a fun and carefree life but when you start to bring harm to others, it may be time to reevaluate the person you are aspiring to be. You have a brilliant mind and beautiful soul and yet somehow, you keep putting yourself in these difficult situations. You deserve all the happiness in the world, but until you start making better decisions these unfortunate circumstances will continue to happen." I feel a wave of guilt rush over me.

I hate coming down so hard on her, but I think it's something she needs to hear. It's something we all need to hear every once in a while.

Sitting in silence and on edge waiting for Brooklyn's reaction, I take a long sip of coffee as an attempt to try and occupy my shaking hands.

"You're absolutely right," she whispers looking out of the window, "I caused this. I caused all of this. I didn't think about how this would affect others in that moment. I have a bad habit of letting my emotions make decisions before I use logic to justify them. I am so sorry."

She begins to cry, "I would never want someone to do to any of you what I've just done to that family."

Standing from the table, I walk over to console my friend. Sitting beside Brooklyn, I let her rest her head on my chest as she continues crying.

"I know none of this was your intention sweetie, it's just a hard reality you have to face. You'll get through this and I'll be right here to help you."

"Yes, I know. I just don't know what else to do. I've tried calling and messaging a thousand times, but he wants nothing to do with me. Candice, I really do love him."

"Can I be frank?"

"You mean you can be even *more* honest than you've already been?" she asks sarcastically and we both welcome the much-needed humor to lighten the mood.

"You may very well love Malcolm but it's hard for him, or for anyone, to believe and accept your apology with this cloud of betrayal lingering over everyone's head. Unfortunately, this is on you Brooklyn. You are about to go on the apology tour of a lifetime. If you love him then fight for him."

"Trust me, no matter how far you push a man, if he loves you or even has strong feelings, there's still a chance to make it right. If you can't fight for him then at least keep finding ways to tell him how sorry you are. No one deserves to be cheated on." I continue rocking side to side with Brooklyn lying on my chest.

"I was hurt by Tyson all those years ago, I was angry at Malcolm, and I was frustrated at myself for my confused feelings. I messed up big time. I want him back," she says and takes her cup to the sink.

Smiling I look over at my friend with an awkward sense of pride from hearing her express having feelings for someone. I walk over to the sink and hug her, "Then fight for your man."

"Malcolm hates me, and Michele is upset with me. This is all bad. I tried calling her to see what she has planned for her birthday, but she was extremely short and rushed me off of the phone."

I put my cup in the sink and open the refrigerator. Placing a bowl of green grapes on the counter, I grab two and toss them in my mouth, contemplating on what I should say next.

"Jeremiah is hosting a surprise dinner for her birthday. He asked me to tell you about the dinner as he didn't want to get in the middle of you and her. Michele is protecting her brother. She's not trying to hear how sorry you are right now. All she heard was that you cheated on her brother with Tyson. You can't blame her for choosing to stick by her family. You know how close the Diamond family is," I half smile and continue nibbling from the bowl of grapes.

"Then I guess you are right. This will take a lot of apologies before things are good again." She sighs.

Passing a vine of grapes to Brooklyn, I smile and say, "Yup. The apology tour of a lifetime."

Thirty-Five

Michele

"Happy birthday mommy!" the twins yell as they jump on Jeremiah's side of the bed.

"Thank you, babies," I smile and kiss both of them. Clooney is standing beside the bed wagging his tail with excitement.

"I guess you wanted to come in and wish me a happy birthday too, Clooney." I smile and reach down to pet my beloved Husky.

"Mommy! Daddy sent us up here to tell you to come downstairs for a surprise," Marley informs me while Mason continues to jump up and down.

"Yes mommy, hurry!" he says as he flops down on the bed.

"Okay, okay. Go tell your father that I will be there shortly." I jump out of bed to brush my teeth and remove my bonnet.

"Yes Ma'am," they smile and race downstairs with Clooney.

"Happy birthday, mommy," Jeremiah says as he meets me at the kitchen island and hands me a glass of mimosa.

"Thank you, daddy," I grasp the back of his head as I softly kiss his bottom lip.

"Eww. Gross," Mason says running back into the living room. Smiling, I turn around to join Marley at the kitchen table.

"Breakfast is almost ready my ladies. Marley run into my office and bring the two boxes on my desk back with your brother please," Jeremiah places a breakfast casserole on the dining table.

"This smells really good." I bend down to inhale the sweet aroma coming from the dish.

"Anything for my queen, especially on her thirty-fifth birthday. Baby you look as fine as the first day I laid eyes on you in the library on campus. Do you remember?" he asks and grabs my hand to stand and slow dance with him.

"How could I forget. You purposely took the last three Psychology 500 textbooks off the shelf and held them hostage until I agreed to go on a date with you."

Jeremiah smiles and continues to whisk me around the kitchen. "You have to admit that was a really slick move for a young, suave brother like myself."

"Yes, it was really smooth until you handed me the book and asked if I would help you study," I say.

"I mean I wanted a date with you, but I still had my priorities straight. I figured it was a good opportunity to learn *and* spend extra time with the finest girl on A&T's campus. I was a lucky man then and even luckier husband now Michele Peterson," he says before passionately intertwining our lips. "I love you. Happy Birthday."

"Here you go Daddy," Marley says running into the kitchen, "Mason wants to finish his gift for mommy before coming down. Here's my gift mommy." My sweet baby girl passes me an envelope with the words "Happy Birthday" scribbled in multicolored crayons.

"Thank you, Marley," I say as I begin to open the card.

"No, you have to open it when you get Mason's card. Please open Daddy's gifts first." Marley jumps with excitement.

"Okay. Fine, boss lady." I laugh at how much my child and I have in common.

Placing two small identical boxes in front of me, Jeremiah removes his apron and says, "One box is a gift for you and the other is a gift for me."

Looking at him puzzled, I slowly glance over the two boxes as if I was selecting a briefcase full of money. Reaching for the one on the left, Marley jumps out of her seat in excitement.

"Oh mommy, that's a great choice. Open it!" she says holding her hands over her mouth in anticipation.

Slowly removing the white bow on the small navy box, I lift the lid and look up at my husband.

"For tonight?" I ask holding up a Ritz-Carlton hotel key card with a lifted eyebrow.

"For the entire weekend," he smirks as Mason join us in the kitchen.

"What did I miss?" he asks.

"Daddy just gave mommy a credit card I think," Marley shrugs confused, "Okay now the other one."

Pulling the white bow off of the other small box my imagination begins to run wild at the possibilities of what's under gift box number two. Removing the lid, I jump out of my seat and into my husband's arms.

"Baby! You didn't?" I kiss him uncontrollably.

"What is it?" Mason asks and without answering, I sprint outside. Sitting in my driveway I find a much larger white bow wrapped around a brand-new Audi Q7.

The Only Key I Care About

Riley

$\mathcal{L}$ ooking up into the observation gallery as we wrap up another successful Endarterectomy, I see Jameson walk in and begin having a conversation with a fellow surgeon. Quickly, I look away and turn my attention toward the heart monitor, trying to pretend as if I am checking the patient's vitals.

It always makes me uneasy when he's watching me during a surgery.

Glancing back up to the gallery, I try to secretly catch a glimpse of him. Instantly he turns mid-conversation and locks eyes with me. Without missing a beat, he gives me a half smile and wink before returning back to his tête-à-tête.

Thankful that my mask is covering my face, I immediately blush and feel a rage of heat shooting up my leg.

Walking out of the operation room, I secretly linger in the hall waiting for Jameson to find me. On cue, he walks out of the gallery and kisses me softly.

"You were amazing, yet again, Dr. Riley. I am one lucky man." He smiles. Blushing once more, I walk toward his office.

"Do you have any more meetings before going home?" I ask as he opens the door to his office waiting for me to enter.

"No, I am all yours for the evening. What time do we have to be at Michele's dinner?"

"It's not until eight o'clock," I say and twirl in his office chair still wearing my scrubs.

Locking the door, Jameson walks over and bend downs while stopping the chair, leaving minimal space between our lips.

"I missed you last night. My late surgeries and studying and your early surgeries are interfering with my *Riley* time," he kisses me.

Standing mid-kiss, I wrap my arms around his broad shoulders and use my imagination to spell out *I love you* as our tongues dance.

"I've missed you more. I'm so used to being wrapped in your arms at night, that it's hard to sleep when you're not there," I say and sit back down in the swivel chair.

"I know Baby. The feeling is completely mutual. Since dinner isn't until eight, how about we spend some quality time together? I have a suit here in the office, so I can go to your house and get dressed."

Yes please. I would like that," I say and silently jab myself for responding like a lustful teenager.

Driving back to my house, I look in the rearview mirror at Jameson's glimmering Camaro. His car always looks so clean and new. Looking around at all of the clutter in my car, I make a mental note to sweet talk him into taking my car to get detailed.

Looking back at his beautiful face through the mirror, I notice that he is laughing on the phone with someone. Curious about who it may be, I shake away the thought and decide to call Candice.

"Hello," Candice says sounding out of breath.

"Hey. What are you up to?"

"Hey Riley. Nothing much just getting back from grocery shopping. I was craving some salt and vinegar chips and butter pecan ice cream," she says laughing.

"Chips and ice cream, together? That's an odd combination. Girl, you sure you aren't pregnant? I hate going to the grocery store, thank goodness Blythe is old enough to cook for herself. Sadly, I think she's a better cook than me." I laugh as I turn into my neighborhood.

"Riley, you know you can't boil water. Blythe must've learned to cook from her grandmother," she says and we both laugh, "You remember in undergrad when you had the entire hall smoked up from letting the water dry out of your noodles? We had to stand outside in the snow until the fire department arrived and aired out the building."

"Girl, yes the entire building hated me that night and the halls smelled like burnt noodles for weeks." I laugh.

"Yes, it did. I don't think I've eaten Ramen noodles since then."

"Sadly, that's a top-selling meal in the medical world. It's tasty and doesn't require much effort. But that's not why I called. I called to check on you, Brooklyn said that you aren't coming to Michele's birthday dinner tonight." I sit in the driveway a little longer once I notice that Jameson is no longer behind me.

Where has he strayed away to?

"Yes. I haven't been feeling too well," Candice says. "I think all of this traveling is starting to take a toll on my body. I am not the spring chicken I once claimed to be."

Laughing I look in the mirror at my beautiful but aged reflection. "None of us are Darling, I am right there with you. Let's not forget I have a grown child about to go to college."

"Yes, I can't imagine what that feels like." Candice takes a long pause and then continues, "You ladies have fun this evening and send my love to everyone. I spoke to Michele earlier; she has no clue about the surprise. You would never think she's a year younger than us the way she bosses the group around. I love my girl though. Please take lots of pictures and videos, thirty-five is a big deal."

"I will, I promise. I'll talk to you later, love you Honey."

Stepping out of the car, I notice Jameson still hasn't pulled up into the driveway. Assuming he went to pick up a light snack, I chuckle at the idea of how well this man knows me. I never buy groceries during my seventy-two-hour shifts, especially when Blythe is with her grandparents. Walking into the dining room, I look at all of the boxes stacked and waiting to be packed with Blythe's belongings.

I can't believe my little girl is going off to college in a few months. There are no books or tv shows that can prepare a mother for this. Any parent would be lying if they said that it was easy to drop their kids off to college and carry on with their day to day as usual.

Just as my thoughts take me to a place of sadness, my doorbell rings. Happy for the distraction, I shake away the thoughts and walk toward the door.

"I picked up a fruit and cheese tray for us to snack on before dinner," Jameson says as the door opens. Smiling at the gesture, I stretch on my tippy toes and kiss his cheeks.

"Thank you, Baby, and the wine is a nice touch as well."

Grabbing two wine glasses from the cabinet, I sit at the table and wait for Jameson to open the bottle.

"Harvey and Donna sent this over from the winery. She insists that we try it with an array of cheeses," he says and smirks, "You make quite the first impression on people, myself included."

"I guess I do." I smile and then blurt out before thinking, "Would you like to have a key?"

Pulling the cork out of the bottle, Jameson slowly places the wine opener on the counter and walks toward me.

"I haven't really thought about it. Would you like to give me a key to your house, Riley?" he responds.

"I don't know," I say honestly, "I wouldn't mind it. It's just, no man has ever had a key but then again no man has ever loved me the way you do."

Smiling as my compliment strokes his ego, Jameson says, "Well if you're offering, I would love that. But if you are still unsure, then I don't want you to overthink something so miniscule. I love you and the only key I really care about is the key to your heart. When I build our dream home, we will *both* have the keys to that."

Forced Smile

Brooklyn

"Here you go ma'am," the valet says as he takes my keys and hands me a ticket.

"Thank you," I turn to walk into the restaurant.

I really hate that Candice isn't able to make it to the dinner. It would have been nice to have a buffer at the table to help during awkward conversations.

Pushing my thoughts aside, I follow the hostess as she guides me to a private dinner room.

"Hey Brook," Riley says as I thank the hostess.

"Hey. You look lovely as always." We embrace for a hug.

"Thank you. I am still loving the curly hair. It's been a while since you've worn your natural curls this long. Could this be the *new and improved* Brooklyn James?" Riley teases.

"Maybe. I just wanted to switch it up a bit. Where are you sitting?" I follow Riley to the table.

The room is spacious but still has an intimate feeling. There is an extra-large dinner table in the center of the room that can accommodate about twenty people. I exchange pleasantries with a few of Michele's colleagues from work and some other coupled friends that she and Jeremiah have met over the years.

"Hi Everyone," I say as I settle in my seat beside Riley, glancing around the table in search of Malcolm.

"He's not here," Riley bends over and whispers.

"Who's not . . ." I try to lie before she gives me a stern side eye.

"Okay. You caught me," I confess. Leaning in front of Riley, as her man takes a seat I say, "Hi Jameson. It's nice to see you again."

"Likewise, Brooklyn. You look lovely this evening," he smiles and then kisses Riley hand.

As more people arrive and the table begins to fill with family and friends, my heart begins to ache at the thought of never seeing Malcolm again.

It's been weeks since he's sped off and completely shut me out of his life. I wish he would just take my call, so we could talk. I miss him. I miss us.

Attempting to keep my emotions at bay, Riley stands and announces, "Everyone, Jeremiah says they are outside. When the curtain opens, be sure to yell, *Surprise.*"

As everyone takes their seats, I put on my brightest and most forced smile awaiting Michele's arrival.

"*SURPRISE! Happy Birthday Michele!*" everyone yells as she walks in.

I Need Time

Brooklyn

As the waiters set out plates for guests to enjoy the assortment of desserts and birthday cake, everyone gets up and moves around to converse. Taking advantage of the spare seat beside Michele, I walk over and sit down as she finishes a conversation with one of her sorority sisters.

"You look gorgeous Michele. Happy Birthday." I give her a hug before passing her an envelope.

"Thank you Brook. I can't believe Jeremiah put all of this together without me knowing. Everyone looks so beautiful," she says, and I can't tell whether or not she is still upset with me.

"Of course, you only turn thirty-five once. You deserve a special day all about you." I smile.

"Yes, today has been overwhelming and thank you for coming," she says and without thinking I try my chances to clear the air.

"I wouldn't miss today for the world. I know we haven't been on great terms but you're my girl. I love you Michele and I'm sorry for—" I say but Michele cuts me off.

"Brook. You're my girl and I love you, but I can't go there. Not right now. We'll talk soon. Thank you for my card," she says before standing and walking over to another group of friends.

Feeling hurt and a little embarrassed I stand, pick my pride up off of the floor and walk to the restroom.

Standing in the bathroom stall, I practice breathing exercises to calm my nerves.

I have to get out of here. I've endured the dinner long enough, and Michele clearly doesn't care whether or not I stay.

After washing my hands at the sink, I send a quick text to Riley letting her know that I am leaving. There's no sense in going back to the party to make a scene with premature goodbyes.

Walking through the restaurant toward the exit, I reach into my clutch to retrieve my valet ticket and some cash. Once I get outside, I notice the valet booth is empty as they are all out parking and retrieving cars. Pulling out my phone while I wait, I send a text message to Candice.

The birthday dinner was lovely. Leaving early to rest up before traveling.

I press send and roll my eyes at the half-truth message I just sent. I could've stayed at the dinner longer I just don't want to, especially since there's no chance of seeing Malcolm.

Annoyed that valet still hasn't shown up, I walk back into the restaurant and decide to have a drink at the bar before leaving. Sitting at the far end of the bar so no one would spot me, I order a glass of wine to calm my nerves. Taking a sip of the deep red Merlot, I hear the faint buzz of my cell phone. It's Candice.

Why are you leaving early? Did you get to talk to Malcolm?

I reread the message her message as I contemplate my response. Choosing to wait until I get home to talk, I place my phone back in my clutch.

"Hi," I hear a familiar voice say behind me.

Turning around as butterflies escape the pit of my stomach, I am once again face to face with the man who has my heart.

"Malcolm. What are you doing here?" I ask and then feel silly for asking such a rudimentary question.

"It is my sister's birthday after all." He smirks.

Feeling a little embarrassed I try to recover, "I know but the party is almost over, so I thought . . .I guess I assumed you wouldn't be here."

"Yes, I traveled back to the States today. I told Jeremiah I would probably miss the surprise, but I'd be here. So here I am. You look beautiful as always," he says nonchalantly. Wanting nothing more than to jump in his arms and cry, I resist the urge and take another sip of wine.

"I was hoping to see you tonight so that we could talk," I whisper and blink a few times to fight back tears.

"I got all of your messages Brooklyn. What more is there to say?" his words come out coldly, and I regret not leaving the party sooner to avoid this exchange.

"Malcolm please. Just let me explain," I beg one last time.

Inhaling deeply, he orders a scotch from the bartender and then turn to me, "Okay Brooklyn, explain."

Caught off guard, I regroup and try to regain my composure.

"I know there aren't enough apologies in the world to make up for what I've done but I want to tell you that I am truly sorry for what I did and for hurting you. You have no reason in the world to forgive me but know that I will do everything I can to try and regain your trust and make this right. Malcolm, I have fallen in love with you." I pause as my eyes can no longer hold the mountain of tears piling in the corner.

Taking a napkin from the bar, I wipe my eyes, careful not to mess up my makeup.

Consuming a long sip of scotch, Malcolm looks over to me, "Brooklyn I'm not one to care easily, but I did care about you. You did something that few women have ever achieved in my life, you made me picture a future with you. How am I supposed to trust you again? How do I know that every time you feel hurt or neglected that you won't go running back to him? Looking at you now, all I can see is betrayal. Do you have any idea what that does to a man like me, a man who doesn't easily care?"

His words cut me like a surgical blade. Reaching for his hand, he quickly snatches it away and stands.

"I can't do this now. I need time." He places two twenty-dollar bills on the bar before walking toward the private dinner party.

Unforgivable

Michele

"How are the twins?" Jeremiah asks as he opens the door for room service.

"Two American Breakfast platters with egg whites and mixed fruit," the concierge says as he wheels a food tray next to the bed, "Enjoy."

"My babies are fine. Mom instructed to stop calling and just enjoy the break."

"I tend to agree with Mama Marjorie. The kids are in excellent hands." Rolling my eyes, I pull my husband onto the bed and lay on his chest.

"Thank you for an amazing weekend. I don't know how you pulled it off, but everything was perfect and a complete surprise. From the party, to my parents coming in town, to this amazing uptown weekend escape, you've really outdone yourself. I love you."

"You're welcome, wife. You're always doing for others, I figured you deserved a few days that are catered for you. I love you so much more, Happy Birthday." He pulls me on top of him as he decides to have his dessert before we eat breakfast.

...

Pulling into the driveway in my new birthday present, I notice Malcolm's car.

"I guess your brother decided to stay in town," Jeremiah says turning off the ignition.

"It appears so."

Staring at Malcolm's car, I get lost in my thoughts and begin to think about Brooklyn.

I still need to talk to her. I just didn't want to do it at my birthday party. I deserve at least one day to be about me.

"Mommy," the twins yell in unison as I step into the foyer.

"Hi, mommy's babies." I kiss them both. "Grammy is making cookies and she's letting us decorate them with icing," Mason informs me as they both run back into the kitchen.

"Hey, Mom."

I walk into the kitchen to discover that my beautiful marble island top is covered in cookie dough and flour.

"Hi Chele Bear. I'll have this cleaned up before you get back downstairs," she says already reading my mind, "Your brother is in the office on a conference call."

Not quite ready to mentally return from my mini vacation, I decide to let my mom wrestle with the twins a little longer while I unwind upstairs.

...

Rolling over, I glance out of the bedroom window to see the moonlight reflecting off of the pool water.

It appears I've slept the entire day away.

Walking towards the stairs, I notice that my house is unusually quiet. I look at the clock on the wall. It is almost midnight.

Peeking my head into Marley's bedroom, I hear sounds of the ocean on her tablet. Turning the volume down, I softly kiss my baby girl and then walk across the hall to Mason's room.

As I reach the bottom of the stairs, I can hear the rest of my family somewhere playing cards. Stepping into the kitchen to a now spotless clean marble island top, I walk over to join the adults at the table.

"Welcome back." Jeremiah smiles as I pull up a chair.

"Yes. My child was worn out. The twins left you some cookies on the counter. We put them to bed hours ago," my mom says before slamming down a card, "Y'all are set, that's game! Clyde, I told you these boys can't beat us."

"I'm out. I have work in the morning," Jeremiah stands from the table. "Babe, you're off tomorrow, why don't you and Malcolm try to beat these old timers."

My husband really did hate losing in spades.

Malcolm and I shake our heads as we know how bad our parents cheat when they play together.

"Okay baby. Goodnight," I pour a glass of wine before sitting down. "Mom, y'all have to let my husband win every once in a while, in his own house." I laugh as I shuffle the cards.

"Yeah Dad, you know he can't easily catch you cheating like Chele and I can," Malcolm adds and we all laugh.

"Why would I *let* him win? It builds character," mom teases as she cuts the cards I've shuffled, "And as far as these cheating accusations, I have no idea what you're talking about. Ain't that right Clyde?"

"That's right Buttercup," my dad says and I begin dealing the cards.

"What's the score?" my mom asks halfway through the fourth dealt hand.

Malcolm looks down at the paper and smirks, "A lot to a little bit, we're winning."

I throw down the next suit to begin the round.

"Okay Mr. Smarty, I have a better question. Have the two of you forgiven that girl yet?" We all pause.

Looking at Malcolm as he takes a sip of scotch out of frustration, I ask, "What are you talking about?"

Placing her cards face down, she gets up from the table to pour another glass of wine.

"Chele, you are too smart to play dumb. *Brooklyn*. I'm talking about Brooklyn. I know why Malcolm is still upset with her and I'll get to him in a second but just what is your stake in all of this?"

Still too stunned to speak she proceeds, "You and Brooklyn have been friends since college and her and your brother are two adults living their lives and making mistakes. You have three beautiful and successful friends and I have one handsome, yet stubborn son. Two out of the three of your girlfriends are single, you had to know that at some point the chances were high their paths were destined to cross. It's just life."

"I know Mom but what she did was unforgivable." I look over to Malcolm for reinforcement, but he's too smart to go toe to toe with Marjorie Diamond.

"Your brother told me what happened, in his own way. Now it is *definitely* unfortunate but is it really unforgivable? Malcolm . . ." she directs her attention to him.

How did I end up in the hot seat?

Annoyed at my mother's normal attempt to meddle in our business, I sit back and let Malcolm have his turn for scolding.

"Malcolm," she says, "How many women have you wronged over the years?" My father scoots away from the table and takes that as a cue to leave the conversation.

Taking an even larger gulp of scotch this time, Malcolm huffs, "What are you trying to say Mom?"

"You don't have to answer it aloud, it's just a question worth asking," she says. "I am simply saying that before you go casting stones at someone just remember that you weren't always a pillar of the community, son."

Annoyed but conscious not to disrespect our mother, he stands, "I *really* don't want to talk about this anymore."

"Then don't talk but sit," she orders, "and listen for once."

Looking over to me for help, Malcolm furrows his eyebrows, but I ignore him and continue sipping my wine giving our mom the floor to do what only Marjorie Diamond does.

Mother's Intuition

Michele

Still sitting at the now interrupted card game, I place a bottle of scotch and a fresh bottle of wine on the table while Malcolm and I painfully endure a reprimanding from our mother as we have done since childhood.

"Now call it a mother's intuition or just plain prying into my children's lives but this thing is affecting the both of you. Malcolm, son, I love you but you're almost forty and I want some more grandbabies," my mom says, and I almost spit out my wine.

"Really Mom? That's all you care about. Grandbabies..." Malcolm chuckles and pours himself a double shot of scotch.

"No, that's not *all* I care about, but it is the truth," she continues, "I've seen you parade women in and out of your life for as long as I can remember. I think, this is just karma catching up to you. I'm not saying that it is right what she did, I am simply stating a fact."

My mother struck a nerve with that comment.

As nosey and loud as she is, she always knew just how to deliver a message, regardless of how we may receive it.

"Mom. I got it. I'll talk to her. Leave this one alone," Malcolm snaps and I can see the anger rise in his eyes.

"Malcolm Diamond you don't scare me. When I'm done saying what I have to say, feel free to excuse yourself from the table. I am *still* your mother," she says and we both know that she's serious. Exasperated, Malcolm exhales deeply but remains silent.

"Now, I am not entirely sure when you and Ms. Brooklyn starting dating, but I noticed shortly thereafter that you started calling me more. One day you called me *just because* and I heard something resembling joy in your tone. I didn't know the reason behind it at the time, but I was just happy that you were happy."

"Then a while back, you called fussing about some deal in South America and I thought to myself, *never in forty years has my son called me to complain about work*. Again, I didn't think anything of it, so I didn't question why," she says, and Malcolm's anger has noticeably softened.

"And then you called a few weeks ago after Michele dropped you off at the airport and told me what happened, in so many words. You said that you were dating her friend, she did you wrong, and now you're done with her," my mom pauses and reaches for Malcolm's hand. "Now son, I don't care to know the details of what happened but what I do know is that for you to call me and talk about how she hurt you, she must have been something special to you. That fact alone, is reason enough to have a conversation with her about how you feel. If she's already apologized, let her apologize again but this time let her tell her *whole truth* and put it all on the table. Once everything has been said, you need to either forgive her or put you both out of your misery."

Without waiting for Malcolm to respond, my mom turns her attention back to me. "And Chele," she says. "Let your girlfriend apologize, tell her how it made you feel, and then forgive her. It's rare to find a sisterhood like the one you ladies have. From what I've gathered from the situation, she didn't cheat on *you*. Don't make your friendship with Brooklyn a factor that your brother has to consider while he decides whether or not to be with her. Now, I'm going to bed. I love you both, goodnight." Standing up from the table she waves her hand in the air and walks off in her Marjorie Diamond fashion.

Looking over at Malcolm we both chuckle and shake our heads.

"Momma's boy much?" I tilt my head and tease.

"Be quiet."

"In her own annoying way, she's right you know," I get up to clear the kitchen table.

"Yeah, I know." Malcolm sighs and then begins to walk out of the kitchen.

Forcing him to pause I say, "I'll talk it out with Brooklyn, and I'll support whatever decision you make."

Meet Your Parents

Candice

"Are you going to tell him? When are you going to tell him?" Aunt May continues to interrogate me.

"Yes, soon," I say and rush her off of the phone, "I have to go. I love you, bye."

Hanging up the phone, I wave as Calvin walks out of his office building and toward my car. "Hey Babe, you ready," he asks as he kisses my cheek and close the passenger side door.

"Yes, I'm ready." I put the car in gear as we prepare to start the next chapter in our lives.

...

Pulling up to the hospital, I turn the engine off and begin to tightly grip the steering wheel.

"What's wrong?" Calvin asks as he reaches for my sweaty palms.

Turning to face him, my expression revels my anxiety before I do, "Tell me I'll be a great mother."

Calvin reaches up and cups both of my cheeks in his hands.

"Candice Smith Montgomery. You are the love of my life. I couldn't imagine doing life with any other person on this planet and I don't know a single soul who is more fitting to help me raise *our* child. You will be extraordinary as Carter's mother just as you have excelled in every other aspect of your life. You over came all of your childhood obstacles, you quit your corporate job to follow your dreams and now you are a best-selling author. You are brilliant, and on top of all of that, you will now direct a movie based on a book you wrote. Candice, everything you ever wanted in life, you've achieved it. This is just another chapter that will reveal how truly amazing you are. They say that children are the lucky ones when they get adopted but I think it's *us* who are receiving a special gift from God today," he says and we both close our eyes and say a small prayer.

"Okay, now I'm ready," I lean over to kiss his cheek.

"Baby, you were born ready."

Walking into the hospital, we get on the elevator and press the number three.

Holding hands as the elevator door opens to the pediatric floor, we walk to the nurse's station before we are directed to wait in a conference room down the hall. Sitting in silence, we wait for our adoption agent to enter the room. Just as the door opens, I squeeze Calvin's hand.

"Mr. and Mrs. Montgomery, today is a big day for us all. Little Carter has been given all of his shots and has received a clean bill of health. I just need a few signatures from the both of you and then I can take you to meet your beautiful baby boy." Pamela, our adoption agent, smiles and passes us two sets of envelopes. One set to sign and the other with helpful tips on adjusting to adoption.

Slowly reading through the papers, we both shakenly sign our names as we declare full parental rights to a new member of our family.

Passing the signed papers back, she looks over them and then smiles, "Okay. Everything looks good. Please follow me."

Walking slowly past each hospital room and seeing all of the sick children, my hormones get the best of me and I begin to almost lose my nerve.

As Calvin squeezes my hand, we walk up to a playroom filled with kids running and playing with toys. Standing at the window, I glance at all of the kids playing and laughing. Some were in wheelchairs and some were running around but they all were smiling and having a good time.

Suddenly I feel Calvin squeeze my hand. I turn to see him pointing at the glass.

"There he is," he says.

Turning back towards the playroom, we both stand in anticipation as Pamela walks towards us holding our beautiful son, Carter Franklin Montgomery.

"Carter, I'd like for you to meet your parents," she says as Carter looks at me and reaches out his arms, "I will give you all some privacy. Feel free to call me if you need anything. Good Luck."

Not realizing that my hands have been lifted up since she carried Carter out of the playroom, I grab my son and hold him close to my chest, nodding as she walks away.

"Hi Carter, I'm your mom." I try my hardest not to break down crying. Looking up at me and smiling, Carter takes his little hand and touches my cheek. It's almost enough to unravel me. Realizing that I am barely keeping it together, Calvin picks up Carter and begins making his introductions to his son.

Looking up at all the nurses behind the desk who are now crying with me as they've realized what just transpired, they all nod as my husband and I walk toward the elevator to take our son home for the very first time.

Walking out of the hospital, I feel a ray of sun hit my face that can only be described as God giving me a kiss on the cheek.

As we each hold one of Carter's hands walking towards the car, Calvin looks over at me and says, "I can't think of anything that would make this day more perfect."

Just as we open the back door of my BMW and place Carter in his brand-new child safety seat, I place a picture of my sonogram in Calvin's hand and whisper, "We're pregnant."

I Forgive You

Brooklyn

"How was your trip, Captain James?" Henry says as he opens my trunk and places my luggage inside.

"Another successful flight."

"That's what I like to hear. Take some time for yourself during this break. You look like you could use a little fun." He winks before opening my door.

"Yes sir," I say as I hand him a twenty-dollar bill and drive out of the airport terminal.

I haven't had much to smile about lately in my personal life. Outside of work, my days consists of exercising and reading books. It's been a while since I've taken time for myself. Just as my mind wonders off with thoughts of Malcolm, my car's Bluetooth rings and displays a call from Michele Peterson on the screen.

I calm my nerves and prepare for a long-awaited conversation.

"Hi Michele," I say nonchalantly.

"Hey Brook," she says, and I can't gauge her mood.

Waiting for her to set the tone of the conversation, I sit patiently at the red light waiting to turn onto the interstate.

"So, I was going through all of my birthday gifts and I just read your card," she begins to laugh.

I guess she's in a good mood, maybe the conversation won't be so difficult after all.

"I screamed and laughed so hard at your message that my secretary thought something was wrong with me," she says, and I laugh along recalling the message I wrote along with a spa gift card.

"I forgot all about that epic fall in the café!" she bursts out laughing again. "That was the most embarrassing thing to ever happen. I had a tray full of pizza, french fries, and nachos and then slipped on spilled ice cream and almost did a backflip before hitting the ground. There was nacho cheese and french fries everywhere, including in my fresh box braids. All I could hear was a sea of laughs and screams."

Smiling at the memory, I turn onto the interstate as my nerves begin to settle. "Yes, that fall was legendary."

"It was traumatizing sitting there watching people point and laugh. I was just about to run and cry when I turn to see you purposely walk behind me and fall on the same puddle of ice cream to take the spotlight off of me." She pauses. "I know you fell on purpose to help make me feel less embarrassed. We both just laid on the café floor laughing with each other and ignoring everyone else."

In an attempt to act clueless, I say, "I don't know what you're talking about. There was ice cream everywhere. That floor was extra slippery."

"Yes, I'm sure it was. You've always been there for me Brook, even when you don't have to be."

"You're my girl Michele. Even when—" I speak but she cuts me off.

"Brook. I know these last few weeks have been difficult and I'm not sure I helped to make them any easier."

"Michele, I truly am sorry if I hurt you in any way. I had some serious reality checks these last few weeks, and I know my actions were thoughtless and immature. I knew better than to sleep with a married man, regardless of our history, and the last thing I ever wanted to do was hurt your brother or lose your respect. I am so sorry."

Pausing to regain my composure, I grip the steering wheel and count backwards from ten.

"I forgive you Brook. You could never lose my respect, but I was disappointed. I was disappointed that you would put yourself in that kind of drama. You deserve to be happy in life, whether that is with my brother or not." A sharp pain strikes through my heart.

What does she mean with him or not? Has she spoken with him? Is he completely done with me? I really do miss him. I just hate the way he keeps leaving things.

"I just want what you and Jeremiah have one day. You have a beautiful family."

"Thank you. Marriage is hard but if you commit to working and growing together, it is one of the most beautiful things you'll ever experience. I hope you get to feel that kind of presence from God one day."

"I pray that I do too. My biggest regret in all of this is that I hurt Malcolm. I really did fall for him but he wants nothing to do with me, so I'll just have to accept that," I say with hopes that she can reveal any indication that I still have a chance.

"Yes, I believe you Brook. Respectfully, I'm choosing to stay out of it, but I really do hope everything works out for the best." Her words are the confirmation that I was dreading to hear.

It's really over.

What's There Left to Say

Brooklyn

$\mathcal{A}$s I lay stretched out across my California King Bed—that hasn't felt the same since that unforgivable night with Tyson, listening to a love song by India.Arie, my mind drifts in and out of focus on Malcolm.

What is he doing? Why do I miss him so much? Get it together Brook, it's time to move on.

For the first time I am noticing a common theme about my life, my big penthouse, and my relationships. They are all over the top but empty.

How did I end up like this? Is it my fault that I required so much from him? I did like the way that he…

My thoughts are interrupted as my stomach grips and growls from hunger.

When was the last time that I ate? The emptiness in my love life has now moved into my stomach. I guess it's true what they say, "the way to someone's heart is through their stomach."

Peeling myself out of bed, I step over the litter of clothes sprawled across my room. Ashamed at how dependent I've become on having a housekeeper, I make a mental note to schedule a cleaning session with Donna. I gave her the last week off to avoid her pity as I wallowed around the house in my misery.

Walking toward the kitchen, I check my phone with a faint hope to see a missed call from a certain someone. Nothing. Opening the refrigerator, I decide that an avocado and egg on toast is the only thing I have a taste for.

Placing the bread in the toaster, I begin cutting an avocado in half as my phone rings. Without looking at the screen, I answer it and put the phone to my ear assuming that it's just one of my girlfriends or my mom checking on me.

"Hello," I say with little enthusiasm.

"Hi," Malcolm says, and I drop half of the avocado on the floor.

"Hi," my voice is timid. "How are you?" Pausing for his response my heart jumps into my throat as I begin to smell toast burning.

"I'm doing . . . okay. I will be in Charlotte tomorrow evening. Do you mind if I stop by to talk?"

Confused and excited at the same time, I stare down at the avocado on the floor. "Yes. I would like that," I say trying not to give too much away.

"Okay. I will see you tomorrow Brooklyn. Goodnight," he hangs up.

Backing into my refrigerator, I sink to the floor still holding the phone and a freshly burnt piece of toast.

What does this mean? Is he coming to work it out or to completely break it off with me? I couldn't tell from his tone whether or not this would be a happy visit or just another session to crush my spirit.

. . .

As the doorbell rings, my control panel lights up with a video of Malcolm at the door. Deciding to open it myself, I put my glass of wine on the coffee table and turn the tv off.

Slowly opening the door, I say, "Hi. Come in." Malcolm walks in holding a leather duffel bag.

Was he planning to stay over? Maybe this was a friendly visit after all.

"Would you like for me to take your bag?" I ask.

"Yes, these are your things that were left at my house. I wanted to make sure that I returned them." A small pin like pain punctures my heart.

I guess this isn't a friendly visit after all.

"Thank you," I say dejectedly, "I'll go empty it out and return your bag."

Standing to walk toward my room, Malcolm grabs my arm. "Brooklyn. You know I don't care about that bag," he says still holding my arm and causing me to sit back down. His touch sends a rush of electricity up my leg and I have to steady my breathing to slow the racing of my heart.

"Then why exactly are you here Malcolm? You made it pretty clear from your lack of communication that you wanted nothing else to do with me." I try to fight back tears to get through this conversation.

"I'm here because I've been replaying all of this in my head and nothing makes sense. I'm here because I want to know why? Why him? Out of all the men in Charlotte, in the world, why did you have to sleep with *him*? I think that's the part that hurts. I think I could've dealt with you sleeping with some random dude but . . ." he pauses and walks over to my bar to pour a glass of scotch.

Staring at him through moist eyes, I watch as he chugs the first shot and then pours a double before returning to the sofa. Still silent, I wait and continue to let my thoughts consume me.

How can I tell him that it meant nothing with Tyson? I didn't plan to sleep with him but that was, in a twisted way, the closure that I needed. I just didn't mean to hurt him in doing so.

"That's really all I'm here for Brooklyn. I want to know why?" The coldness in his tone send chills up my body.

"Malcolm, I was hurt and confused. Things were moving along nicely between the two of us and then all of a sudden you just became too busy for me. For us. Since our first nights in Brazil, you set an expectation that you had time for me or at least made an attempt for time and then you blew me off." I pause.

"I didn't *blow* you off Brooklyn. I'm a businessman. You knew this when you met me. Did you forget that Brazil was a business trip for me?"

"No. I know that in order to be with a powerful and successful man, then you have to be okay with him always being busy but even in Brazil you made time to spend with me. The weeks you became unavailable, you left me feeling unwanted and all I could think was maybe this was just a fling to him. Maybe this is just the old Malcolm dressed in a different suit," I say and regret my last sentence.

Sighing Malcolm takes another sip of scotch and then say, "I can't apologize for my past, but I at least thought I could have the benefit of the doubt. Did I ever give you cause to think that I was up to my old ways? I may have left too many unknowns on the emotional side, but I at least thought my actions showed you that I cared. Brooklyn when I wasn't with you, I was working. But none of these answers my *why*? Why him?"

"Malcolm, when I left Atlanta, I wanted you to stop me or at least come after me the days to follow but you didn't. You didn't even call," I say, and a tear falls on my sofa. "You are the same man who showed up on a flight to

Madrid to surprise me but disappeared when things became difficult between us. What was I supposed to think?"

I stare into his eyes, trying to find some kind of clue as to what he was thinking.

"Running into Tyson that week was a complete mistake and a regret that I will have to deal with the rest of my life. Our paths crossed, and I ended up going to a poetry lounge one night and he was there. It was completely innocent. As the night progressed, we ended up having a heated argument about our past and how we ended things. He apologized and then the unthinkable happened. You have to believe me when I say if I could take it back I would. I not only hurt you, but I also jeopardized his marriage with his wife and unborn child," I confess.

"He's married?" Malcolm huffs from disgust.

"I've already beaten myself up about it, so I don't need your judgment," I say and wipe away tears, "it happened and I'm not proud of it, but I am truly sorry for how you found out."

"Thank you for telling me." He stands.

"So, I guess that's it," I say as I can physically feel my chest tighten and my heart begin to break.

Oh God, this can't be it. I love him!

"What's there left to say Brooklyn?" he sighs as the corner of his eye fills with tears. As he turns to walk toward the door, I grab his arm, this time the electricity travels through my entire body.

"Say that I'm worth a second chance. That you're not willing to throw away what we had, and you have a desire to see what it could grow into," I cry out and let my emotions take over.

This is it. My final plea to get my man back.

"I will continue to apologize a million times for the mistake that I've made but at some point, you have to admit that we have undeniable chemistry. What I did was hurtful, childish, and stupid, but I was simply seeking the affection that I was so desperately asking from you. I am not saying that it's an excuse for what I've done but it's my truth. I know that trusting me again will be hard but you being here today tells me that a part of you is willing to try. So please let's just try again." With that, I have left all of my cards and my heart on the table.

It was now up to him.

Standing to witness my emotions unravel, he continues to stare at me without speaking. For a moment we both contemplate on what our lives will look like once he walks out of the door. Wanting so badly to profess to him how much I have fallen for him, I resist the urge and remain silent, waiting for him to decide our fate.

Grabbing my chin and tilting my head up, he softly whispers, "He was married. I've done my share of dirt, but I've *never* slept with a married woman. Goodbye Brooklyn."